NEW WORLD ORDER

(The Kyron Invasion, Book 2)
(1st Edition)

by Jasper T. Scott

JasperTscott.com
@JasperTscott

Copyright © 2021

THE AUTHOR RETAINS ALL RIGHTS
FOR THIS BOOK

Cover Art by Tom Edwards
TomEdwardsDesign.com

CONTENT RATING: PG-13

Swearing: Brief instances of strong language
Sexual Content: Mild
Violence: Moderate

Author's Guarantee: If you find anything you consider inappropriate for this rating, please e-mail me at JasperTscott@gmail.com and I will either remove the content or change the rating accordingly.

ACKNOWLEDGEMENTS

This book comes to you in its presently polished form thanks to my editor, Aaron Sikes and my proofreader, Dani J. Caile. Also, many thanks to my family. I never could have finished this book on time without your support.

I owe another big thank-you to my advance readers who helped track down any remaining typos. My heartfelt gratitude goes out to: Gaylon Overton, Davis Shellabarger, George Dixon, Bob Sirrine, Ray Burt, Paul Burch, Michael Madsen, Howard Cohen, Gwen Collins, William Dellaway, Jim Kolter, and Mary Kastle.

And finally, many thanks to the Muse.

PREVIOUSLY IN THE KYRON INVASION TRILOGY

WARNING the following synopsis contains spoilers from the first book in this series, *Arrival (Kyron Invasion, Book 1)* If you would prefer to read that book first, you can get it on Amazon here: https://geni.us/kyron1

SYNOPSIS OF ARRIVAL

2150 AD

The world is united under one government, the United Nations of Earth (UNE). Over the past century, the United Nations Space Force (UNSF) sent out four interstellar ships, each with the goal of exploring and colonizing nearby star systems. By now these four missions have all reached their destinations. The longest and most promising was that of *Forerunner One,* which went to Trappist-1, a star system with at least three potentially habitable planets.

Having traveled at half the speed of light to arrive, it will be a long time before the Forerunners can return to report back on what they found.

Earth

Christopher Randall is a bodyguard for a wealthy family in San Bernardino, California. His employer, Mrs. Pearson, informs him that she and her husband have decided to replace him with a pair of robots, known as civil defense units (CDUs).

Chris leaves the Pearsons' home with the promise of a severance package that he knows won't last in a world suffering high unemployment.

After an unsuccessful first day of searching for work, Chris is on his way to pick up his wife, Bree, from her job as a waitress at a local casino. Soon after picking her up, they see and hear a squadron of Union starfighters entering the upper atmosphere, followed by the sound of them exploding and raining flaming debris all over the valley. A hulking shadow is cruising through the clouds, headed straight for Los Angeles.

It can't be a Union ship, because they can't defy gravity like that, but then who, or *what* is it?

Fearing the worst, Chris speeds home in his truck, a much-loved relic from a simpler time. It still has an internal combustion engine and rides on the ground unlike the electric vehicles and air cars that everyone else uses. Along the way, Bree calls home to instruct Chris's mother, who lives with them and their two kids, to pack bags for them—along with warm winter clothes. Chris is planning to make a run for Big Bear in the mountains above the valley.

Upon arriving home, Chris hurries to put their bags into the back of his truck, along with plenty of guns. Bree gets their six-year-old daughter, Gaby, and their twelve-year-old son, Zach, into the truck along with her mother-in-law, and then they leave for the mountains.

The roads and intersections are clogged with traffic. After a few fender benders and run-ins with the desperate residents of the city, Chris and his family get clear.

Fleeing air cars light up the sky, also heading for the mountains.

Not long after that, a bright flash flares across the sky. All of the streetlights die, along with the lights inside the truck and those of other vehicles on the road. Chris realizes that they must have been hit by an electromagnetic pulse.

Moments later, he hears a sharp whistling noise, quickly rising in pitch. Explosions erupt on both sides of the highway. Air cars are crashing all around them.

When it's over, Chris gets out to take a look under the hood of his truck. He gets his truck working again by disconnecting and reconnecting the battery, while Bree stands guard with their shotgun.

Now his vehicle is the only one working for miles, and he's beginning to draw attention to himself and his family. Getting back in the vehicle, Chris roars off down the highway. Someone shoots at them as they're leaving, taking out two of the windows.

No one gets hurt, and they're on the way again, now the only vehicle on the road. The sounds of battle in the skies above LA fade into the distance.

When they reach the town of Big Bear, they find it mostly abandoned. The power is out here, too.

Chris takes his family straight to the Pearsons' cabin, thinking that his former employers probably didn't make it out of the city. The cabin is empty, and they make a futon bed in the master bedroom closet to stay out of sight of the windows.

The night passes uneventfully. In the morning Chris goes to get some supplies from his truck. Just as he's getting their guns out of the back, he sees a group of birds flying overhead, but they are far bigger than any birds he's ever seen.

He runs back inside just in time to see one of them land on the front deck. The 'bird' is short with skinny arms and legs. It's wearing a suit of black armor, with two iridescent wings on its back. It shoots a bright green laser at Chris, but misses. He fires back with his shotgun to no effect.

Rushing upstairs to protect his family, Chris arrives in the master suite just in time to see the alien creature sailing toward the master bedroom windows. They trade shots. Chris gets hit in the leg. The alien crashes inside and they wrestle physically. He manages to get the upper hand, killing the alien, but it injures him badly and he passes out from blood loss.

Chris wakes up almost a full day later with his injuries crudely bandaged. He's lying at the foot of the bed in one of the secondary bedrooms. Power is back on, but Chris's mother reveals that it's because she got the cabin's generator running. They watch a news report on a holoscreen broadcasting scenes of destruction around the world. All of Earth's biggest cities have been wiped out. The scene cuts to the president of the UNE standing beside one of the short, hunching aliens. The president is wearing a strange-looking helmet on her head, and the alien beside her is somehow speaking *through* her to issue the terms of the Union's surrender.

They will not be harmed, so long as they don't resist.

Welcome to the Kyron Federation.

Chris is reeling with these developments. The invasion is over, and humanity lost. But he has no intention of going back down to the valley where he expects the chaos to be much more pronounced as lingering pockets of resistance expend themselves against the invaders.

While Chris is still explaining to his family the importance of staying in Big Bear, the sound of an electric vehicle pulling up outside draws their attention to the windows. It's the Pearsons. They've arrived with their security bots and their two kids, Sean and Haley.

Limping downstairs, Chris goes to greet the actual owners of the cabin. Jessica Pearson is furious to find him there, and even more so when she learns that her safe haven has already been compromised with multiple broken windows and an alien corpse. Her husband, Niles Pearson, is the cooler head of the two, and both he and Chris agree that staying at the scene where Chris killed one of the invaders is a bad idea. They make a plan to leave for another home along the lake that also has a backup generator.

Both families leave the cabin, heading for their new refuge. They arrive to find footprints leading through the snow, past the fence to the front door of the home. No sign of cars, so it's probably not the owners. Chris goes to check it out and encounters a man inside who gets the drop on him with a hunting rifle. The man looks homeless, but seems harmless enough. His name is Bret. He agrees to share the home with them.

Everyone leaves their vehicles and they take up residence on the opposite side of the home from Bret, who has locked himself in the master suite.

Bree and her mother-in-law attend to Chris's injuries while everyone eats. About midway through the night, Niles Pearson comes to tell them that they have visitors. It's an army fire team; two bots and two soldiers. They go outside to greet the soldiers, learning in the process that the valley is overrun and fighting is ongoing despite the Union's surrender. The soldiers lost contact with their unit and fled for higher ground. They ask to stay on the property in the guest house above the garage. Chris and Niles agree to let them, thinking that having more eyes and guns couldn't hurt.

A few minutes later they hear a roar of gunfire coming from the direction of the guest house. Just then, the Pearsons' security bots both collapse. It's another electromagnetic pulse.

Chris and Niles hurry to provide support, telling the others to hide in one of the bathrooms. Chris arrives at the rear entrance of the home to see one of the soldiers running toward him with two monstrous four-legged creatures in pursuit. A brief firefight ensues, and Chris manages to kill the aliens, but not before one of them kills the soldier.

These monsters are not the small flying ones Chris faced before. Niles recounts a story of seeing the same type of aliens emerge from a lander in his neighborhood where they ran down two of his neighbors. The neighbors were eaten alive.

Chris realizes they're dealing with at least two different species of aliens. He goes to the guest house to see what happened to the other soldier, telling Niles to stand guard by the entrance.

Inside Chris sees one of the winged aliens gnawing on the other soldier's leg like it's a chicken drumstick. This one isn't wearing a helmet, and he is able to get a look at its face: it has sharp, bony features, and is hairless, with bright red eyes and four flexible stalks above its head, each ending in a cone-shaped orifice.

Chris runs away before he can be seen, but accidentally alerts the alien to his presence by dropping his sidearm on the stairs outside.

The flying alien comes out after him. Chris shoots it with his shotgun, once again to no apparent effect, but he does manage to chase it off.

Rushing back inside with Niles, they find their families unconscious inside the bathroom, and Chris's six-year-old daughter, Gaby, is missing.

Suspecting that Bret might have something to do with it, Chris and Niles go looking for him. The master bedroom is still locked, but they break down the door. Inside the closet they find two dead bodies—the owners of the home.

They find footprints on the back deck leading through the snow and down an external staircase to the yard. One set of footprints clearly belongs to the winged aliens, while the other might be Bret's. The prints end abruptly in a flat area of the yard, but other indentations suggest that something landed there.

Chris realizes that while he was fighting, another of the aliens was busy abducting his daughter.

In that moment Bree comes outside, asking where Gaby is. Chris goes back up to the deck to ask what she and the others saw. All she and the others remember is a knock at the door. They opened it, thinking it was him or Niles, and then a flash of light blinded them, and that is all any of them can remember.

Chris instructs them to get to one of the

neighboring houses. He and Niles are going after Gaby.

Back outside, Chris and Niles arm themselves with a combination of alien weapons and those of the dead soldiers. They take the soldiers' truck and follow the tracks of the four-legged aliens to a local resort.

After searching the area on foot, they find that the tracks vanish mysteriously in a flat snow-covered field. Chris discovers an invisible alien lander there and cuts a hole in the side of it with one of the alien weapons.

Inside the lander they encounter one of the flying aliens, also cloaked and perfectly invisible. Chris manages to see it with a smoke grenade and then kills it with a frag. They find Gaby and Bret on an upper level of the lander, both of them unconscious and hooked up to strange machines with wires and tubes trailing out of them.

Chris manages to extricate his daughter, but she's still not waking up. He leaves Bret, thinking that he's a killer and not worth saving.

Chris and Niles run back to their truck and drive to the nearest hospital to find some way to remove the tubes snaking out of Gaby's chest.

At the hospital they break in and meet the sole occupant of the building: Doctor Willow Turner. She decided to hide rather than flee when the invasion came. Dr. Turner performs a few tests and scans on Gaby before removing the catheter from her chest. Chris sends Niles back for their families.

Gaby wakes up. Not long after that, Niles returns with his family and Chris's. But Dr. Turner has bad news: Gaby appears to be infected with an alien virus. The doctor advises all of them to keep their distance until they know more about how it spreads.

Everyone spends the next day at the hospital, taking turns watching the entrance while Gaby battles a strange sickness that is turning her skin white and her blood black. She's throwing up almost constantly, and all of her hair is falling out.

Doctor Turner reveals that the virus can only spread through direct exposure to infected fluids, and it isn't airborne, but they should still be careful.

The following night, while everyone is asleep, Gaby becomes delirious and violent. Niles runs to help her, thinking that she's having a seizure. She bites him, and he becomes infected.

Soon after that, Gaby reaches a lucid phase. Her transformation appears to be complete. She is no longer fighting her restraints or throwing up, but she looks like some kind of strange combination between one of the flying aliens and a human. A hybrid.

She's craving raw meat. They get her some cooked diced beef from the cafeteria, and Gaby eats hungrily. By this point Niles is entering the violent, delirious stage of the infection.

They hear something outside, and Chris goes

out to look. He encounters another alien hybrid in the men's room of the ER. It turns out to be Bret. Chris gets the upper hand and has him subdued at gunpoint with a shotgun.

Bret is spouting an alien agenda that must have been implanted. He reveals that the invaders came to recruit Humans as soldiers for their war. The human-alien hybrids like him are called Chimeras and are charged with keeping the peace while the *Kyra* re-establish order. Bret makes a play for his weapon, and Chris kills him.

He returns to find both Gaby and Niles missing. A search of the hospital reveals nothing until Doctor Turner gets stunned by an invisible adversary. Chris suspects it's one of the flying ones with a cloaking shield engaged.

Searching further, they find Niles and Gaby in the pharmacy, behind the aisles of medication, both stunned and unconscious.

Bree, Chris, and his mother get trapped in the pharmacy as the invaders arrive. They stand guarding the door with their weapons. One of the aliens speaks to them through the door in a *human* voice—Bret's voice. But it's not him, it's one of the Kyra. The alien is asking them for a peaceful exchange. All it wants is Gaby.

Chris refuses. The Kyra sounds dismayed and says that he will try to convince the "Horvals" not to eat them.

The four-legged aliens break down the door and come bounding in. At the same time, Niles wakes up and begins grappling with Bree in the back. He's still violent and infectious. Chris and his mother barely manage to fight off the Horvals, and Chris takes multiple serious injuries in the process.

Then the same human voice returns, telling them to drop their weapons, or else.

Chris turns to see an invisible alien holding Bree hostage with an equally invisible knife at her throat, drawing a line of blood.

Bree tells him to shoot through her, to save their daughter. The alien releases her, apparently believing that he would. They shoot blindly at the alien, still unable to see it. Chris's mother and Bree both get stunned. Doctor Turner comes in, having now recovered. She has a fire extinguisher and she uses it to reveal the invisible alien. Chris kills the Kyra.

Everyone re-groups in the cafeteria, carrying the unconscious members of their group. Niles wakes up and flees the hospital. Chris tries to stop him, but fails. Soon after that, he succumbs to his injuries, losing consciousness, but Bree and Doctor Turner are able to get him to the treatment room where they patch him up and dose him with painkillers.

They all agree that they need to leave ASAP. Jessica Pearson wants to go out looking for her husband, but she is overruled. They leave the hospital in the Pearsons' Suburban.

Out on the main street they run into three

hovering troop transports. One of them backs up and a group of armored human-alien hybrids emerges. They insist that everyone exit the Suburban immediately.

These Chimeras used to be Union soldiers. They ask about Chris's injuries and Gaby's transformation. Chris manages to avoid giving any answers that might implicate them in crimes against the invaders. The Chimeras reveal that they found Niles, but they had to kill him, because he was a failed hybrid, a "Dreg." Dregs are contagious even after "ascending" and they are violent—he was too dangerous to let live.

Jessica and her children are distraught. The Chimeras take all of them into custody, saying that they need to return to the valley for their own safety. There are rumors of Kyron heretics operating in Big Bear. Chris asks what they mean by "heretics" but the Chimeras don't know anything else.

Inside the transport, on their way back down to San Bernardino, Gaby reveals that she might be able to read the thoughts of the other hybrids, but Gaby has four cranial stalks with cone-shaped ears, just like the Kyra, and Chris decides that she must be hearing the Chimeras' comms even *through* their helmets.

Chris isn't sure what to expect when they reach the valley, but he refuses to accept the new status quo. The invasion might be over, but the resistance has just begun.

PART 1: AFTERMATH

CHAPTER 1

The sun is cresting above rolling, snow-covered hills. A rosy light reflects off the snow and a low ceiling of scattered clouds. Pine trees cut dark shadows from the landscape. It feels like we're reversing down this winding mountain road as our seats are all facing in the opposite direction of our movement. I wonder if that's by design, to keep us from seeing where we're going until it's too late.

My gaze tracks to the metal guard rail at the edge of the road. Dirty snow is piled in drifts against the railing, growing patchier as we descend from Big Bear to the dry, dusty San Bernardino valley. Up here there are no signs of the devastation, no hint that just four days ago *they* came and changed the course of humanity forever.

But as the sun rises, I see that's not exactly true. A thin haze adds a graininess to the air and refracts the light. A hint of the fires that might still be raging in the valley. Before long, the smell of it begins filtering into the hovering alien transport where I sit with my battered, exhausted family, and that of my former employer, Jessica Pearson. Her husband, Niles is no longer with us; he was executed just a few hours ago by the human-alien hybrids manning this vehicle.

Silence hums as we follow the road almost soundlessly into the valley. The ride is impossibly smooth, hovering as we are on a cushion of air.

A weight shifts against my arm, and I turn from the view to regard the youngest of my two kids, Gabrielle Randall. I reach over to stroke her hair, but a fresh jolt of fear and revulsion slams into me as I realize that she doesn't have any. For a moment I'd forgotten what happened to her.

In place of my little girl's sleek black hair is a bony, chalk-white scalp whorled with black veins and interrupted by four six-inch cranial stalks. Those alien appendages are flattened in sleep, but as I watch, one of the cone-shaped ends twitches like a dog's ear.

This is what the invaders came to do: convert us into hybrids of their own physiology—*Chimeras*—and then to conscript them for their war.

But a war with who? And why not fight it themselves?

It paints a grim picture of the so-called *Kyra*, the small, hunching, winged creatures with demonic red eyes and chalk-white skin. They came and annihilated all of Earth's biggest cities to break our spirits and ensure the Union's surrender. Then they began rounding us up and turning us into Chimeras. And as far as I can tell, this isn't the first time they've done it. At least one other species appears to have fallen before we did: the giant, four-legged one we faced in Big Bear. Rhino-sized hybrids called *Horvals.*

A dull ache makes it through the morphine still flooding my system. My broken ribs making themselves known. The gash in my leg. We killed the ones that came for us, but I can't forget *why* they were there. The Kyra I spoke to wanted my little girl. After turning her into a Chimera, they wanted to study her further.

Heretics. That's what the human hybrids in this transport called the Kyra operating in Big Bear. I look up from my little girl's bald, alien head and glance around the interior of the troop transport. Sitting across from us are my wife, Bree, and our twelve-year-old son, Zach. Like Gaby, Zach is asleep, exhaustion having won out over adrenaline and fear.

Bree catches my eye and her hand twitches beside the outline of my Glock in her jacket pocket. I give my head a slight shake. Not yet. That gun is our lifeline, but it could just as easily get us killed.

Behind Bree, my mother and Doctor Willow Turner both stare out their window with glazed eyes. Twisting around further, I catch a glimpse of Jessica Pearson's tear-stained cheeks, and her kids, Sean and Haley. Jessica is holding them close, an arm wrapped around each of their shoulders as they sleep. Jessica's eyes are unfocused, staring straight ahead, her expression blank with shock. Maybe she's passing from anger to denial. A new stage of grief.

My gaze slides past Jessica to the armored soldiers sitting in the front (or back?) of the transport. Their black armor and faceless helmets gleam dully in the morning light. Four Chimeran soldiers who used to be ours, all of them freshly converted and brainwashed into switching sides. Three of them are facing us, with alien rifles balanced in their laps. The fourth, who introduced himself as Sergeant Diedrick, is sitting in the aisle at the far end of the vehicle. He's facing a broad holographic screen that looks out on the winding black ribbon of the road ahead. But rather than holding a wheel or joystick to actively drive us down, he appears to be simply watching the terrain. The vehicle must be self-driving like ours. Give it a destination and it automatically finds the best path to reach it.

I wonder how the Kyra managed that. Did they steal our maps, or take scans from orbit and generate their own?

Or maybe this technology doesn't even need maps, but rather real-time readings from the environment.

I shake my head, pushing aside those random

musings. I need to focus on more immediate concerns. These soldiers are taking us to a so-called *safe zone* in San Bernardino. If our home isn't located within it, then we'll go to a *communal facility* in the zone.

What does that mean? *Safe zone?* I wonder if it has something to do with the alien virus that changed Gaby into a Chimera. Niles Pearson got infected, too, but he turned into something called a *Dreg—a* violent hybrid that continues to be infectious even after the virus has run its course. That's why he was executed. No way to save him.

Or maybe the safe zone is *safe* because it's removed from on-going fighting between the invaders and scattered pockets of human resistance.

Whatever the new status quo looks like, it won't be long before we find out.

The transport rounds a bend, and I catch a glimpse of the city below. Dark columns of smoke rise above bright orange balls of fire. Blackened patches indicate where the city was hit the hardest, but I'm actually relieved. The fires look contained, and the devastation isn't as expansive as it might have been.

The road broadens out to four lanes, and I see a knot of frozen vehicles up ahead. That's as far as people got before the EMP hit.

Crashed air cars line both sides of the road. Patchy grass has been burned black; nearby trees were turned to naked skeletons.

And then we reach the clotted mess of frozen traffic.

Bree sucks in a sharp breath, and I grimace.

Char-blackened remains with flaking skin sit frozen behind steering wheels in burned-out cars. Others are hanging halfway out of broken windows or open doors. The ones who didn't die by fire look like they've been partially eaten. Others have holes burned through their torsos or their heads.

A battle was fought here, maybe not even that long after we left these people behind on the way to Big Bear.

It looks like we got out just in time.

The transport drives off onto the shoulder to get around the obstruction.

Bree slowly shakes her head. "Why kill them?" she asks. "Don't they need us alive?"

Why wipe out LA? I think but don't say. It's all part of the same doctrine. Phase one: shock and awe. Phase two: we surrender. Phase three: occupy and conscript.

I can't help but wonder what the next phase is. What happens when they've already conscripted as many of us as they can?

The transport takes the ramp onto Highland Avenue, hovering up and over the frozen traffic. We're retracing the path we took four nights ago, but this time in the light of day.

Back then, the city was chaos. Everyone fleeing at the same time. Now, it looks like a ghost town.

* * *

I untangle myself from Gaby's sleeping embrace to get a better look at where we're going. She murmurs something as I gently settle her against the seat. I twist around and lean into the aisle to watch the view from the holoscreen in front of Sergeant Diedrick.

My ribs ache sharply from my awkward posture. Pain is making a steady comeback. The morphine is definitely wearing off now.

I push the pain to the back of my mind to focus on the view. Roaring fires line the avenue, chugging dark smoke into the sky. We pass a Walmart on the right, but it's set too far back from the char-blackened trees for me to see much. The Burger King that used to share the same parking lot is right beside the road, and it's barely recognizable. It looks like an air car or a crashing starfighter might have hit it. Whatever was left burned to the ground.

Broken-down ground vehicles and crashed air cars line both sides of the avenue, shored up like snowdrifts. Two lanes have been cleared down the center, I'm assuming by the invaders.

Looks like they're using our own infrastructure against us.

As we whirr down the street, heading for

the center of the city, the signs of devastation multiply. Palm trees are blackened and stripped to their naked trunks. Downed power lines drape the road in a tangled mess.

I hear a stifled cry from my mother as she begins to notice the dead bodies. They're lying in the street in sticky puddles of dried blood. Some of them have been mauled beyond recognition.

The corpses get thicker the farther we go, rising like walls, mangled and bloody, pushed to the sides of the road just like everything else.

Buildings flash by, the windows all broken and gaping, roofs collapsing, nothing but shadows lurking within.

Popular family restaurants have been turned to ashes. Entire suburbs burned to the ground, others still ablaze.

This isn't the city I knew. It's an abandoned, post-apocalyptic caricature of it. We pass a ruined charging station for EVs, then come to a knot of burned-out military vehicles that crowds the four-lane avenue down to one. Three JLTVs and two tanks, even an assault mech. All of them are pushed to the sides of the road, surrounded by bodies in flak jackets and camo-patterned uniforms. We squeak through the gap and turn down a palm-lined street.

I recognize it as Victoria Avenue. A Frugal Foods supermarket appears on the left. The parking lot is littered with food and overturned shopping carts. It didn't burn to the ground or get hit by a bomb. This one was looted by desperate people.

We reach the overpass of the Foothill Freeway and the transport begins slowing down.

"What's happening? Are we there?" my mother asks, peering out her window.

Bree and Doctor Turner both twist around to look. Zach leans over the back of his seat like me.

Dead ahead, a chain link fence with spools of razor wire at the top has been erected across the avenue. It continues down both sides of the road, and a pair of armored Chimeras are guarding a broad gate in front of us. Black troop transports like the one we're riding in are parked to either side of that gate. As we approach, gun turrets on top of them swivel toward us.

It's only been four days since the invaders arrived, but they've apparently wasted no time. They already have a compound set up, and they've used our resources to do it. That chain-link fence looks like it was manufactured here on Earth, and it was probably erected by our own soldiers after they were turned into Chimeras.

This must be one of the *safe zones* that Sergeant Diedrick mentioned. It looks like a prison with those guards, the fence, and the razor wire.

I swallow thickly. I don't have a good feeling about this.

Our vehicle glides to a stop in front of the gate. One of the soldiers begins sliding the gate open, not even bothering to check who's inside first. Then again, I have no way of knowing what the soldiers in here are saying to the ones outside over the comms inside their helmets.

The soldier holding the gate waves us through, and the transport jerks forward, picking up speed as it races down Victoria Avenue—an ironic name if ever there was one. *Victoria.* Spanish for *victory.*

The destruction beyond the fence isn't quite as bad, and I can see actual humans working on both sides of the road while armored Chimeras supervise with rifles at the ready.

The people are pulling bodies out of ruined vehicles and gathering them into piles. Some of those piles are already burning.

We pass a trio of hovering black troop transports whirring down the other side of the road.

"Where are we going?" Bree asks.

I think I can already guess.

"The airport," the sergeant says in that deep, gritty voice that all the Chimeras seem to share.

"The airport?" my mother echoes. "W-why... are we flying somewhere?"

"No. It's our processing center," Diedrick explains.

Processing. An involuntary shiver works its way down my spine. I feel my broken ribs grinding around, and suddenly I'm sitting in the aisle, blinking in confusion as waves of nausea roll through me. Bree and my mother are both in the aisle with me, their eyes full of concern. Doctor

Turner joins them, and the three of them help me back into my seat. I'm breathing through clenched teeth as I ease down.

Gaby stirs awake beside me. She sits up, blinking the sleep from her bright red eyes and watching me with obvious confusion.

"What's wrong with him?" one of the Chimeras asks. I can't see their expressions through their helmets, but it occurs to me that they might suddenly be wondering if I could be infected with the virus.

"He has two broken ribs," Doctor Turner explains.

"They'll fix him up at the field hospital," the sergeant says.

"Where is that?" Doctor Turner asks.

"At the airport. We'll be there soon."

"Take it easy, Chris," Bree whispers through a shaky sigh as she returns to her seat.

I nod weakly and lean back with a gasp, seeing stars.

"Is Dad okay?" I hear Zach asking.

"He's fine, sweetheart," Bree replies. "He just needs to rest."

Poor kid. He and I have always had a special bond. Gaby is more affectionate, but Zach and I have more in common. We usually go cycling and play holo games on the weekends.

Those days are over now. Even if we get the power back, a return to normalcy isn't going to happen. We're a commodity, bought and paid for with blood—mostly our own.

I'm actually surprised that they've bothered to set up a field hospital. I'd just assumed from the way they annihilated LA, New York, Washington, and every other major city in the world that the Kyra would treat us as expendables.

The fact that they've gone from wholesale slaughter to trying to save as many of us as they can is a curious inconsistency. But I guess now that they've killed so many of us, they can't afford to lose what's left of their conscripts.

I wonder what that means for me. How long before they turn me into one of them? And what happens after that? Do I board one of their ships to go fight on some alien battlefield? Or do I get to stay on Earth to help them corral the survivors into these fenced-in safe zones?

"Does it hurt a lot?" Jessica Pearson asks suddenly from the seat behind mine.

"Like a mother—" I stop myself there, realizing I'm surrounded by kids.

"Good," Jessica says, her voice oozing with vindictive pleasure.

She probably blames me for what happened to Niles. But I wasn't even awake when Gaby infected him by biting his hand, and Gaby was delirious at the time, so it wouldn't be fair to blame her either.

Grief trumps reason every time. It's a raging bull, just looking for a target, and anyone will do. I have to respect that.

A few minutes later the transport stops again. I'm tempted to twist around for a look, but Bree dissuades me with a reproving look. "We've reached the airport," she says.

"Then why did we stop?" I ask.

"They have another gate."

Moments later, the transport rolls forward once more, and then it turns, wrenching my broken ribs. I bite back a scream as blinding pain wracks my body. Another sweaty surge of nausea rolls through me. Muffled voices are shouting outside, the familiar, commanding tones of soldiers barking orders at their subordinates.

Glancing out my window, I see more transports like this one flashing by, and dozens of armored Chimeran soldiers running in teams of four. A few of those four-legged monsters, the Horvals, are out there, too.

The San Bernardino International Airport has been converted into a military base. *Their* military base. It's unbelievable progress for just four days. We pull into an empty space between two matching transports.

"All right, everyone on your feet! It's time to get you processed," Sergeant Diedrick declares from the back of the vehicle.

Bree shares a worried look with me. Zach along with her.

I offer a reassuring smile and begin pushing up out of my seat. The smile turns to a wince as I stand shakily in the aisle.

A door slides open directly in front of my row of seats.

"Come on!" Diedrick says. "I don't have all fucking day."

"Mind your language!" my mother snaps. "There are children here."

"Get up, old lady," he growls, reaching for her arm to physically remove her from her seat.

"Get your hands off me!" she shrieks.

"Hey!" I add in a cracking voice. "We're leaving!"

"Didn't look like it," Sergeant Diedrick replies as he makes room for my mother and Doctor Turner to step into the aisle.

The sergeant is wearing his helmet now, but I still remember his bony white face, black lips, red eyes, and unnaturally sharp white teeth. A demon in all but name.

Gaby shimmies out after me and tucks herself against my uninjured side. As we begin shuffling together toward the exit, I realize that she's trying to carry some of my weight.

That puts a smile on my face. "It's okay honey, I can manage."

Bright red eyes flick up to mine, squinting as the rays of the morning sun hit us through the open door of the transport. "Why don't they like Granny?" she asks in a husky whisper.

"They're just impatient," I say as I start down a short flight of three steps to the gleaming asphalt outside.

"They said she's too old," Gaby adds. Her eyes are narrowed to slits, and she throws up a hand to shield them from the light.

I turn to regard my daughter with a frown while waiting for the others to emerge. The light seems to be bothering Gaby's eyes, but it's still early morning. Maybe her eyes are more sensitive now.

"I didn't hear them talking about her," I say.

"I did," Gaby replies, and two of her cranial stalks twitch, as if to remind me of her new superpower. Her hearing must be incredible. She could probably hear a cotton ball hitting the pavement a block away.

Maybe she heard the Chimeras talking inside their helmets.

My mother is too old? Too old for what? I wonder.

CHAPTER 2

Bree and Zach come out of the transport next, followed by my mother and Doctor Turner, then Jessica and her two kids. Finally, out come the Chimeran soldiers, all of them casually aiming their rifles at us.

What are they worried that we might do? I wonder. They're armored from head to toe. Even if we got our Glock out before they shot us, I don't think the bullets would do anything. And they don't even know we have it.

"All right," Sergeant Diedrick declares. "Eyes front. March."

"Where?" Bree asks.

He points. "See those tents?"

I do. Big white canvas tents with folding tables inside. Long, slouching lines of survivors cross the parking lot between us and those tables. Armed Chimeran guards watch from the tents as people shuffle forward. One of the lines is snaking away to another lot full of black troop transports like the one we just dismounted. Two of those transports glide away, headed for another chain-link gate on the far side of the parking area.

I lead the way across the lot, heading for the tent the sergeant pointed to. Three lines of survivors move with slow, sometimes staggering steps, bringing them closer to the tents. I aim for the nearest line, checking over my shoulder to make sure I haven't lost anyone along the way. They're all still there: my mom, Bree, Zach, Gaby, and Jessica and her kids.

"This is where we part company, Mr. Randall," Sergeant Diedrick says as I reach the end of the nearest line of survivors. "Good luck. Maybe I'll see you on our side of things once you get all fixed up."

I don't know what to say to that, so I just nod. The soldiers run with Sergeant Diedrick back to their vehicle. A moment later, they're whirring toward the chain-link gate where we came in.

"Now what?" Bree whispers, looking scared. A cool wind blows her hair in front of her face. Sunlight catches the strands, making them glow like amber.

Suddenly everyone is staring at me, waiting for me to reveal some brilliant escape plan. But I don't have any aces up my sleeve. I'm having enough trouble just staying conscious.

"We don't seem to be in any danger," I point out. "Let's see where this goes."

"What about the virus?" Bree asks. "You heard that sergeant. What if they decide to turn you into one of them? Or both of us?" She glances pointedly at Gaby, then looks away quickly.

I don't need Bree to tell me what could happen next. I've been thinking about it the whole way here. Unable to offer my wife any reassurance, I turn back to the fore and wait for the line to shuffle forward.

The man ahead of me is staring at us with glazed, haunted blue eyes. He might be around my age, but it's hard to tell through all the dirt and blood on his stubbled cheeks. More is matted in his hair. He might have lost someone close to him recently.

Then again, who hasn't?

Me. So far. My family is all still alive. But Niles counts as a loss. Hell yeah, he counts. He helped me rescue Gaby up in Big Bear without so much as a passing thought for his own safety.

The man in front of me is staring at Gaby now, his brow knitted and eyes tight.

"Line's moving," I point out, jerking my chin.

The man wordlessly turns and moves with it. After about ten minutes, we're only three places back from the front. A female Chimera sits behind the desk inside the tent. She's not wearing a helmet, and she's separated from the head of the line by about ten feet. People go in one by one, apparently. The Chimera is asking the woman at the front of the line questions that I can't quite hear from here.

Soon there's only one person ahead of us: the guy with the haunted eyes and the blood-spattered cheeks. This time I can hear the questions, but only just.

"Name?" the female Chimera asks. Her red eyes prick through the shadows inside the tent. Two more Chimeran guards in full body armor are flanking the entrance, their rifles at the ready.

The man in front of us shakes his head. "R-r..."

"R-r-what?"

"Royce Fields."

A shimmering hologram appears above a disc-shaped device beside the Chimera. The man's name appears on the screen.

"Age?"

"Forty-two."

"Almost at the cut-off."

"Cut off?" Royce asks in a cracking voice. His age appears beneath his name.

"Forty-five is the oldest that we'll take for the Guard."

I glance back at my mother. Her face is pale with dread. She's almost seventy. I remember what Gaby overheard the Chimeras saying about her—that she's too old. Maybe that's what they meant. She's too old for recruitment. Hope rises fleetingly in my chest. If so, it could turn out to be a good thing. Even if they conscript both me and Bree, at least my mother will be able to stay behind with the kids.

"Any kids?" the Chimera asks Royce.

"One. She's... she didn't..."

"No problem. Are you still fertile?"

"What?"

The Chimera fixes him with a bland look. "Can you have more kids?"

"Yes. I think so."

The holoscreen flashes green and a new line appears below his age.

Fertile.

"Okay Royce Fields, hold out your right hand and show me your wrist."

He does so, and I see that it's shaking. The woman picks up something that looks vaguely like a gun.

"Turn it over. Palm facing up."

Royce does as he's asked and the Chimera places the barrel of the device against the underside of his wrist.

She pulls the trigger, and it issues a click and hiss. Royce withdraws sharply, massaging the spot. I catch a glimpse of a blinking green light shining just beneath his skin.

"What was that?" Royce asks.

I am busy wondering the same thing.

"Your tracking ID."

"My..."

"If you get lost, we'll be able to use it to find you. Or, if you try to run away or do something else that you're not supposed to, we can use it to kill you. Instantly. So don't be stupid."

A cold weight settles in my gut. So that's what *processing* is for. They're tagging us like cattle.

"Move along," the Chimera says, and jerks a thumb over her shoulder to a second folding table with another Chimera sitting behind it, deeper inside the tent.

Royce shuffles by her, heading for the next desk.

In the line beside us, I notice an elderly woman being escorted away. "Come with me, ma'am," an armored Chimera says as he leads her away.

"Oh yes, of course. Where are you taking me, dear?" she asks in an overly bright tone that makes me suspect she's not entirely aware of what's going on around her.

The people from her line are all watching her go. Jessica Pearson takes advantage of their distraction to abandon her place behind us and jump to the front of the other queue. "We're next," she says to the Chimera at the desk. "We haven't slept all night. My kids are tired and hungry. You need to process us now."

"Name?" the hybrid replies in a weary voice.

"Hey!" the man who should have been next objects. "She jumped the line! She can't do that!"

"Shut it," another Chimera barks at him from the entrance of the tent.

"You! Step forward!" My attention snaps to

the guards at the entrance of my tent.

"Chris..." Bree trails off warningly.

I flash her a tight smile. "It'll be okay." With that, I turn and limp inside the tent.

"Name," the Chimeran woman says as I stop in front of her desk.

"Christopher Randall."

I see my name appear on the glowing screen beside the woman.

"Age?"

"Forty-three."

Again, my answer is automatically transcribed to the screen.

"Kids?"

"Two. A girl and a boy."

"Are they with you?"

I nod.

"Names and ages?"

"Gabrielle and Zachary, six and twelve respectively."

"Good. You're still fertile, I assume?"

"Yes, ma'am."

The screen flashes green as soon as I confirm that. I wonder if the technology can tell if I'm lying. Too late to find out now.

"Do you have any military or law enforcement training?" she asks, her red eyes squinting speculatively up at me.

"Former UNA corporal. About eighteen years ago."

"Excellent. With your training, you'll probably get assigned to the Guard. Good news for you."

"Why is that *good* news, ma'am?"

"Better to be the boot that stomps than the one getting stomped on."

I draw a deep breath, but it hitches in my chest as pain erupts from my broken ribs. My head starts spinning and I'm left gasping and clutching my side. "The soldiers who brought me here mentioned a field hospital?"

"You're injured?"

"Yes, ma'am," I manage to grit out.

"Not bitten?"

I shake my head. "Broken ribs."

"Tell Private Reese at the tasking and housing station." She jerks a thumb to the desk behind her. I see that Royce Fields has already moved on from there.

"I don't want to get separated from my family."

"Trust me, we don't want that either. Hold out your right hand, please."

I hesitate briefly before doing as I'm told. The Chimera places her implant gun to the underside of my wrist and pulls the trigger. The tracking ID goes in with a sharp prick and I see the blinking green light appear.

"You're all set. Move along."

"One more thing," I say.

The Chimera fixes me with a look of strained patience.

"I keep hearing about an age limit. The cut-off you mentioned. My mother is also with us. She's seventy. Is that going to be some kind of problem?"

The Chimera's eyes widen. "Seventy? How did she get here?"

"Some of your soldiers brought her in with us..."

The woman's lips flatten into a thin black line. Her cranial stalks twitch. She's trying to peer past me, to the rest of my family.

"Don't worry about it. We'll figure something out."

"What does that mean?"

"I told you, don't worry about it," the Chimera repeats, more slowly this time. "You're holding up the line."

"There is something else."

"Yessss?" the woman hisses through sharp white teeth.

"My daughter is already a Chimera."

"The six-year-old?"

"Yes, ma'am."

"She was bitten by a Dreg?"

I hesitate, remembering what the other Chimeras said about heretics in Big Bear. Could it be dangerous to reveal that Gaby is the result of an illegal experiment performed by the Kyra themselves? I decide to risk a lie, but not an overt one, so I simply nod my head.

The holoscreen with my particulars on it

flashes red and a negative tone sounds. So it *is* a lie detector. Worse, it isn't just listening to me, but watching me, too.

"Maybe you want to try that again," the Chimera says, nodding to indicate the screen and the flat black disk that is projecting it.

"She was taken by one of the flying ones. They did something to her, and then she turned into a hybrid like you."

"Gabrielle didn't infect anyone while she was turning?"

"One person. He's dead now. Your soldiers killed him."

"I see..." The woman looks like she's trying to work out a difficult math problem in her head. "Well, it doesn't matter. Your daughter is too young for the Guard to take her, so she'll stay with you until that changes. Now get your ass to the tasking station."

"Yes, ma'am..." I glance warily over my shoulder as I move past the desk, heading deeper into the tent.

Bree is holding Gaby protectively in front of her with Zach standing to one side and my mother behind him.

Bree starts forward, moving past the kids. Then stops as one of the guards holds up a palm.

"Dependent minors go with their parents," the man says in a deep voice.

Bree looks relieved and says something I can't hear to our kids. The three of them move into the tent together. A knot of tension releases inside of me. I flash a smile at Bree as the woman behind me asks her for her name.

Then I'm dealing with Private Reese. She asks me for my address and happily informs me that my home lies within the safe zone and that it has not been destroyed.

That's one piece of good news at least. I wonder wryly if I'll still have to pay the mortgage. Something tells me those types of obligations are a thing of the past. But I wonder what type of *task* I'm about to be assigned.

Private Reese says that Bree and I will have to be tested before they can assign *tasks* to us.

"Tested for what?"

"Compatibility. We need to know how you react to the proteins in the virus. If you react well, you'll join the Guard."

"And if we don't?"

"Then you'll help the others rebuild."

I nod woozily. That second option sounds a lot better than the possibility of joining an alien army. But it's entirely out of my control.

"They'll test you at the hospital."

I nod again. It's getting harder to think through the pain. "Is it a long walk?"

Private Reese turns and points through the tents to the end where lines of people are boarding more of those hovering transports. There are three rows of desks in here, one for each of the lines outside. "Can you make it?" Reese asks.

Before I have a chance to reply, I hear someone shouting—

"...your hands off me!"

I turn on the spot, swaying dizzily—

To see my mother wrestling with those two armored Chimeras outside.

It's her turn to go in. But they're not letting her.

"Hey!" I shout.

"Get her out of here," the first Chimera I spoke to snaps, rising behind her desk.

Bree and the kids are standing there. Zach looks shell-shocked, but Gaby is sobbing and straining to reach my mother. Bree is holding her back.

"Granny!" Gaby cries just as my mother takes the butt of a rifle to her gut and doubles over in pain.

"Hey! That's enough!" I shout, provoking a fresh wave of pain and nausea, but adrenaline is giving me new life. My heart is beating like a drum in my ears as I run out of the tent and its shadows.

My mother is still resisting, batting weakly at the soldiers' hands. I'm only a few feet away now. Almost in reach.

"Just get it over with!" the woman behind me says.

One of the two soldiers takes a step back, their rifle snapping up.

"Wait!" I scream.

A sharp, shrieking report sounds, accompanied by a bright green flash of light. And my mother collapses with a gasp, clutching the left side of her chest.

CHAPTER 3

"**M**om!" I fall on my knees at her side, heedless of the pain from my injuries. She's gasping soundlessly for air. Her eyes are roving sightlessly, searching for mine.

I take her hand and give it a hard squeeze. Her gaze finds mine. She tries to say something.

Doctor Turner is right there with me, her eyes wide, cheeks slack with horror. She takes a look at the entry wound. My mother's dirty pink ski jacket is burned black in a golf-ball-sized patch over the left side of her chest. Doctor Turner peels the jacket away to find the actual position of the wound.

It looks like the laser went straight through my mother's heart.

"Hang in there," I whisper past the growing knot in my throat.

But I can already feel her hand going slack in mine.

"Mom!"

Doctor Turner is checking her pulse. She looks to me and gives her head a slight shake.

The light leaves my mother's eyes, and an unintelligible roar bursts out of me.

Someone pulls me to my feet. It's one of the two soldiers. I round on him with a punch. It lands on the side of his helmet, staggering him back a step. My fist explodes with pain, but that doesn't stop me from taking another swing.

I hook a leg behind his to trip him as he backpedals away from me. As he's going down, my hands close on his rifle, and I wrench it away. No shoulder strap to keep it attached.

"Stun him!" the Chimera behind the desk orders.

I sweep the rifle around in her direction, hoping that Kyron weapons aren't all smart-locked like the Union's. The Chimera comes into view—

Along with my family. Seeing Bree's grief-stricken terror and the tear-streaked faces of my kids makes me hesitate.

A weapon goes off with a cracking report and a bright flash of light dazzles my eyes. A sharp jolt courses through my system. Crackling arcs of electricity race along my limbs, turning my entire body numb. I lose my grip on the rifle, and then I feel myself falling over backward.

The growing darkness inside my head catches me before the ground can, and it's a blessed release from my suffocating grief.

***

I wake up in a warm bed surrounded by beeping machinery for what feels like the umpteenth time in the past few days.

"Chris!" Bree jumps up from a folding chair at the foot of my bed.

"Daddy," Gaby snivels against my side.

Zach crowds in, looking uncertain and afraid.

"What..." I take a moment to work some moisture into my mouth. "What happened?"

"You don't remember?" Bree asks.

I shake my head.

But the brief spell of amnesia doesn't last long. It all comes rushing back, and I'm forced to relive my mother's death. Grief goes through my chest like a hot knife, leaving a burning ache where my heart should be.

"They killed her," I croak.

Bree nods wordlessly and bites her lip, her eyes brimming with tears. "I'm so sorry."

I push my own welling tears back down, and then wrap both of my kids in a hug. They're grieving, too, and they must be scared as hell. They don't need to see their father fall apart on top of losing their grandmother.

"What happened after I... after they stunned me?"

"They dragged you off to the hospital and we came with you."

"Where are we?" I ask, glancing around quickly. I see a window behind Bree. A door. An old desk pushed against the wall with a computer on it. This was an office, hastily converted to a recovery room. The machines around me don't look familiar. They look like the ones I saw blinking and beeping around Gaby when I found her aboard that alien lander with tubes snaking out of her chest.

Panic grips me and I release my children to track the lines of tubes and wires trailing from my bed. I lift the covers for a look...

And breathe a short sigh of relief. I'm naked, but I don't have any tubes protruding from my chest.

Taking a deep breath, I'm surprised to find it doesn't even hurt. My ribs...

I peek under the covers again.

They aren't even bruised.

"What the...?"

"They injected you with something," Bree explains, shaking her head.

I probe the area with my fingers, but there's no pain. "How long have I been out?"

"About two hours. I think they might have given you a sedative at some point."

"So in just two hours, my broken ribs have somehow been healed?"

Bree nods.

Amazing, I think to myself. Either my ribs weren't really broken, which I seriously doubt, or Kyron medical science is a lot more advanced than ours. I'm betting on the latter.

Bree glances at the door, then back at me. "Chris, they could come back here any minute. What are we going to do?"

I draw in another breath, then let it out slowly. "Nothing. We're going to toe the line."

"They killed your mother!" Bree hisses.

"I know! And they could kill us, too." Now that I have some distance from what happened, I'm thinking more clearly. Resistance is too dangerous. At least for now. We need to be patient. I turn my wrist over to show Bree the blinking light of my tracking implant. "They said they can use these to kill us at any time."

"We could cut them out," Bree suggests, her eyes darting around, as if looking for a scalpel.

"I'm sure they thought of that. You still have my gun?" I ask in a faint whisper.

"Yes."

"Good. Keep it hidden."

"Dad."

Zach's voice brings my head around. "Yeah?"

"What happens if they turn both of you?"

"What do you mean?"

"What if they change both you and Mom into one of them and then send you away to fight?"

I hadn't thought of that.

Gaby's red eyes widen and she straightens from awkwardly hugging my side. Her chalk-white skin turns paler still. "You're going away?"

"No, sweetheart. We're not going anywhere."
"You promise?"
"I promise."
"Pinky promise?"

I stick out my pinky and Gaby grabs it with hers. The long, sharp black claw at the end of her finger opens a hair-thin cut in my skin, but I keep the smile pasted on my face.

Gaby releases my hand with a smile, showing off sharp white teeth that don't look anything like they used to. How can she have changed this much in such a short time?

It's like my ribs: broken one minute, and then good as new the next. Remembering my injuries and where I am gets me to thinking about who's missing from our group. Doctor Turner was right next to me before I was stunned.

"Where is everyone else?"

Bree shakes her head. "I guess they were taken to their assigned living facilities."

The door to the room opens, and an actual human wearing Union Army fatigues comes in. He has short black hair and a baby-smooth face that belies the flecks of white in his hair.

"How are you feeling?" the man asks, stopping at the foot of my bed with a grim smile.

"Uhhh..."

"It's okay," Bree says. "Dr. Brown is the one who patched you up."

"Weren't expecting to see a human, huh?" he asks. "Don't worry, they haven't turned us all.

Not yet, at least. I'm what they call a *Dakka*. I think it means *unworthy* or *infidel*, but who the hell knows? The good news is they tested me and found that I'd react badly to their virus. And even the *chalkheads* don't want more Dregs running around. Which brings me to one of the reasons I'm here. I tested you both when you came in. No joy. You're Dakkas, too."

Bree's face lights up. "They can't infect us?"

"Well, they *could*, but they won't risk it."

Zachary's shoulders sag with relief. Gaby seems unaffected by the news, but I doubt she understands much of anything that's going on.

"Chalkheads?" I ask in a dark whisper and my gaze darts sideways to indicate Gaby.

"Sorry. I'm not used to seeing one that's so young. I keep forgetting she's there."

That didn't sound like an apology, but I'm too tired and heartsore to press the point.

I manage to work myself up to a sitting position.

"Easy," Bree warns.

"It's okay," I say, waving her off. My side doesn't hurt, neither does my leg. I peek under the covers for a look. The gash in my thigh is covered with a transparent patch or bandage of some kind. Beneath it looks like fresh pink skin. No stitches. Nothing. The laser burn in my other leg has fully healed, with nothing but a bald patch to indicate it was ever there. Even the gash in my side that Bree crudely stitched together with fishing line is gone.

"You'll probably want some clothes," Doctor Brown says.

"Yeah. That would be good," I reply.

"One minute." Doctor Brown turns and leaves by the door he came through. It swings shut behind him, closed by a pneumatic arm at the top.

A minute later he's back, and carrying a pile of army fatigues.

"Your ID says you used to be in the Army, so this should be appropriate," he explains as he hands the pile to me.

"Thank you," I manage.

There doesn't appear to be anywhere to get dressed, so I simply swing my legs over the side of the cot and step down lightly.

The sheets fall away, revealing my nakedness.

"Daaad!" Zach says, and spins away.

Gaby makes a face and follows suit.

But we're way past modesty, and my kids are accustomed to me not minding about such things. You get used to being naked around other people once you've served in the Army.

A catheter in my wrist tugs painfully as I reach for the pile of clothes.

"Let me help you with that," Doctor Brown says. He removes the device, which somehow looks both familiar and strange at the same time.

Bree steps into view as I get dressed.

"If we're incompatible with the virus, what happens if we get infected?" she asks.

"You'll still turn, but you'll lose your minds and turn into Dregs, so you best make sure that doesn't happen."

I'm nodding as I tug on my sand-colored t-shirt and move to button up the jacket. When I'm done, I find myself looking around for boots to go with the uniform, but don't see any.

"I didn't know your size," Doctor Brown explains. "Besides, I think a man should walk in his own shoes." He points to the floor beneath my cot. My old hiking boots peek out from beneath the bed frame.

They're looking a lot worse for the wear, but still serviceable. I tug them on.

"Now what, sir?" I ask.

"Now, you get out of here and go to your assigned housing. You know where that is?"

"Yeah, our home."

"That's a stroke of luck. God knows we could use more of those. Follow me, I'll show you out to the shuttles."

The doctor leads us out of the recovery room. Bree's hand slides into mine. Outside the door to my room is an armed Chimera. He glances sharply at us and steps back as I emerge, as if expecting me to try something. Maybe he's the one who shot my mother. A gut-wrenching wave of grief and rage tears through me at the memory, but I manage to push those emotions aside.

Doctor Brown sends the soldier an amused look. "Take it easy, Private."

"He's dangerous, sir."

"Not to me he isn't."

"I'll escort you," the private insists.

"Don't bother. I know the way."

The narrow corridor is lined with injured people on cots, but none of them are moaning or writhing; they all look to be sedated.

"Are they dead?" Gaby whispers.

That's actually a good question.

"Oh, no, they're fine," Doctor Brown says. "They're just sleeping while the nanites fix them up. Amazing little things."

Somewhere in the distance behind me, I hear someone screaming and snarling and banging on a door.

I glance over my shoulder.

"One of the infected," Dr. Brown explains.

"A Dreg?"

He shrugs. "We don't know yet."

I try to get my bearings, hoping to identify the field hospital's location. Based on the generic colors and bland décor, it was probably an administrative section of the airport. Everything is a different shade of beige in here. This corridor is lined with what probably used to be offices, now serving as treatment and recovery rooms. We pass by a small cafeteria and a couple of restrooms, then leave that area by another door and come to a familiar concourse lined with windows.

Yep, we're still at the airport.

Wind whistles in through broken glass. The sun glints off the metal railing of a staircase dead ahead. The escalators beside it are frozen—dead, like everything else on the grid. The hospital area seemed to have power, but I guess they isolated it from the grid and hooked it up to a generator. The sound of a crowd rises into range of hearing, countless voices mingling into a steady hum of background noise.

We reach the top of the stairs, and I see the source of that sound: hundreds of people sitting on chairs and the floor in the waiting areas around the departure gates below. For a second the scene almost looks normal, like all of these people could be waiting for their flights.

But the planes at the gates aren't going anywhere, and at least one of them is cracked into char-blackened pieces on the tarmac.

"Who are they?" I ask Doctor Brown as we start down the stairs.

"New arrivals waiting for their antibody tests. You jumped the line by picking a fight. You're lucky they didn't know you're a Dakka. Now you're worth a lot less to them, so they won't be as forgiving next time."

"Antibody tests?" Bree asks as we reach the bottom of the stairs.

Doctor Brown leads the way past the gates. Wary eyes follow us, most of them fixing upon

Gaby. She grabs my hand and tries to hide behind my legs.

Doctor Brown explains, "We expose a sample of blood to the virus. If antibodies develop, then we know they'll turn into Dregs. If they don't, then they'll become Chimeras. It's actually about a fifty-fifty chance either way, and the tests aren't a perfect predictor of success or failure."

"So half of us get to stay human, while the other half get conscripted," I say.

"That's right."

"What's the margin of error with those tests?"

"Ten percent, give or take, so if you get infected, don't slit your throat. Tell one of the Chimeras. They'll bring you here, and we'll keep you under observation to find out what you really are."

"Great," I mutter.

A scream erupts from the bedraggled masses at one of the departure gates. I whirl toward the sound to see some type of commotion developing.

A woman is attacking the people around her, almost at random.

"Infected!" someone screams.

Chimeran soldiers converge on the spot as people flee the waiting area. The infected woman is attacking two people at once, both of them bleeding profusely from their wounds. Her mouth is smeared with their blood, but otherwise she's as pale as death and nearly hairless.

Bright beams of light flash out of the Chimeras' rifles. The infected woman collapses, as do the two people she wounded. Just like that, the incident is over. Conversations gradually resume as if nothing happened, but everyone keeps their distance from the bodies as Chimeras come to collect them.

"Keep walking," Doctor Brown whispers.

"How did she get in here?" Bree asks.

"She was probably already here, hiding in some abandoned storage closet. But it's possible she snuck over the fence, or through it."

Doubt coils inside of me. "We're surrounded by soldiers, and the airport has been fenced off. Everyone here has supposedly already been processed, so how did they miss an infected woman? I thought this was a *safe* zone."

"Safe is probably an overstatement," Doctor Brown says. "All it takes is for us to miss one little scratch or a bite, and someone can be cleared when they shouldn't. Hell, we probably still have a few Dregs in here who turned before the fence went up. Either way it won't be long before they get past that flimsy little fence. Chalkheads are constantly sweeping inside the zone, especially at night when the Dregs come out, but it's a lot of ground to cover."

"So basically, sleep with one eye open?" I ask.

"You got it."

Bree shivers.

"Are we allowed to defend ourselves?" I ask.

"Sure, you are."

"With guns?"

Doctor Brown flashes a wry grin over his shoulder. "Wouldn't that be nice. Only the Chimeras are allowed to use guns. They catch you with one, and you're dead."

Bree's hand tightens on mine. I glance at her, and she swallows thickly.

"But they didn't search us or tell us that, so how can they expect us to know?"

"They probably think it goes without saying." Doctor Brown's voice drops to a whisper again. "Why, you have something to declare?"

Bree hesitates, then shakes her head.

"Keep it hidden somewhere safe," Doctor Brown says in a tone that tells me he can be trusted to keep our secret.

We leave the departure gates behind, then continue on through a security checkpoint guarded by a couple of Chimeras. Their faceless helmets track us as we walk by the dormant baggage claim area. We pass empty conveyor belts and luggage scanners and then down the tunnels of body scanners. Just as we're leaving the security checkpoint, a new group of survivors is shuffling toward us, accompanied by more Chimeran soldiers.

We step by them at the ticket counters, and then breeze out through sliding glass doors that are all either standing open or shattered. Outside, a few Chimeras with rifles wait beside a pair of hovering troop transports. A new one comes whirring in, stops behind them, and refugees begin spilling out.

"There," Doctor Brown stops before stepping off the sidewalk. He points to the transport at the head of the line. "Let them know where your assigned housing is. They'll take you, but be polite, and be careful. Besides the obvious physical changes, the virus turns people into bloodthirsty savages. Some are worse than others."

That might explain how the two in the processing area were able to cut down my mother in front of us. But that's no excuse. Even if the virus *does* make them more violent, they still have a choice.

"Thanks for the tip," I manage gruffly. They'd better not search us for weapons before we board that transport. Suddenly the Glock in Bree's jacket seems more like a liability than a lifeline. We should have ditched it when I woke up in the hospital.

"Good luck," Doctor Brown replies.

"Thanks." I step off the sidewalk, gripping Bree's and Gaby's hands tightly. Zach is holding his mother's hand on the other side. It's the four of us against the world—an occupied world overrun with infectious alien hybrids.

We don't need luck; we need a miracle.

CHAPTER 4

I sit quietly, staring out the window. Zach is sitting with me this time, and he's bawling in my lap like a little kid.

"Take it easy, buddy," I whisper, laying a hand on Zachary's back. "She's in a better place."

But he just cries harder. I don't blame him. This doesn't feel like the kind of world in which ideas like God and Heaven can survive.

The hovering transport flies low over the roofs of derelict sedans, trucks, and other types of debris clogging up the residential streets. The fact that these transports can fly over the blockages makes me wonder why the main roads have all been cleared to let traffic through. I guess the Kyra must have other types of land vehicles, or maybe they're starting to salvage some of ours.

A river of ruined and derelict vehicles blurs by beneath us. Two char-blackened Jilvees are surrounded by a group of dead soldiers, their smart-locked rifles lying around for anyone to take. That brings my mind back to the Glock concealed in Bree's jacket.

Thank God the Chimeras didn't search us when we came aboard this vehicle. I guess they don't get much resistance from refugees like us. Everyone's probably too worried about the Dregs and getting infected to think about opposing the Chimeras.

"Where's Granny?" Gaby asks suddenly.

"Not now, sweetheart," Bree replies.

"Where is she?" Gaby insists.

"Shhh."

"I want granny!" Gaby screams.

"She's not coming," Bree says.

"Why not?" Gaby sobs. Her voice pitches up in a stifled cry, and then she starts bawling like Zach. Her new voice is deeper and louder than it used to be. I can only imagine how loud it is to the Chimeras with their more sensitive hearing.

The realization that their granny isn't with us anymore seems to be hitting my kids in waves. It's hitting me in waves, too, but I'm pushing it down and putting it off with a healthy dose of reality. We could all be joining her soon if we don't keep our wits about us.

"Shut the fuck up!" one of the Chimeran soldiers finally snaps.

But that only makes my kids cry harder.

"Shhh," Bree tries. "It's okay. It's okay."

"Did you hear me?" the soldier intones. "Shut. Up!"

"They're just kids!" Bree screams back at him.

"I don't care if they're kittens. Make them be quiet or I will."

I twist around to see fingers resting inside the trigger guards of alien rifles. There's no way to be sure which soldier snapped at us, but both of them are sitting unnaturally still and straight, ready for action.

"We're almost there," I say in a level voice. "We'll be out of your hair soon."

"Was that supposed to be funny?" the one sitting beside the aisle growls.

"Just a figure of speech. Poor choice of words. Sorry."

Both Chimeras appear to relax somewhat, their fingers leaving the triggers of their rifles.

The apology sticks in my throat, but Doctor Brown's advice stayed with me. The Chimeras weren't just changed on the outside. They're all ruthless killers now, and we need to walk on eggshells around them.

As if finally realizing how much danger we're all in, Gaby and Zach manage to muffle their sobs, and a relative silence falls inside the vehicle.

After about five more minutes of winding along chaotic suburban streets, we arrive on our block.

"This is your destination," the driver says as the transport glides to a stop in front of our driveway.

I take a second to peer out the window on my side, checking our house for signs of damage. The sycamore in our front yard is charred black, splintered down the middle and fallen over in two pieces, like it got hit by a fork of lightning. But I'm betting that 'lightning' was an alien laser.

Bree leans across the aisle to see for herself. She breathes a sigh beside my ear. "Oh, thank God. It's still there."

I know just how she feels. In the middle of so much destruction, seeing our home still standing makes it feel like we've just won the lottery.

And maybe we have. We're alive. We're not infected—at least, not turned into Dregs, I think, as I remember Gaby—and our home is still our home.

A vivid flashback echoes through my mind's eye of my mother crumpling to the tarmac at the airport. We're not lucky; we're just waiting for our turn. The cows in a slaughter house aren't lucky just because they're standing at the back of the line.

"Did you hear me?" the driver calls. "Get the fuck out!"

"We heard you!" Bree retreats to her seat, and I nudge Zachary's shoulder with mine. "Let's go." I slide out with him, and Bree follows behind us with Gaby.

We emerge from the transport, stepping down onto our old street. As soon as we've left the vehicle, it hovers up and goes whirring off in the opposite direction, not even bothering to turn around first. That reinforces my speculation that the vehicles can fly forward and backward with equal ease.

Bree heaves a sigh, and Gaby hugs her mother's legs.

Our cul-de-sac is strewn with all types of garbage. A suitcase is lying in the middle of the road with clothes scattered around it; a scarf flutters in the breeze. A fallen tree blocks the road two doors down. Looks like a car crashed into it.

But plenty of cars still line our street in orderly positions, all of them covered in ash and dust now, parked just as they were when we left four nights ago. Some of our neighbors obviously stayed, but others had multiple vehicles and they simply left the less useful ones here. None of the homes on our street appear seriously damaged. Some show signs of superficial damage. Broken windows, most of which are now boarded up. Probably from looters or shockwaves.

Wordlessly, I lead the way up our driveway with Zach shadowing my steps. My truck isn't here, of course, and we don't own any other vehicles. Not that I suspect they'll be of much use. The EMP knocked out all the EVs, maybe permanently, since they use a lot more sensitive electronics than my old F150.

We reach the slouching front steps. They creak and sag as we walk up. I've been meaning to replace them. Maybe now I'll finally have the time, but where will I get the wood? The supply chain must have been decimated. I'll have to salvage it somewhere.

My thoughts trail off suddenly as I notice that our front door is cracked open. The frame is splintered around the lock.

"Chris," Bree says in a sharp whisper. She's reaching for the gun in her jacket, but I stop her by grabbing her wrist.

"Give it to me," I whisper back.

She withdraws the Glock slowly. I quietly pull back the slide to check the chamber. It's loaded. I eject the clip and check that, too. Still full.

"Stay here," I whisper to my family. Zach nods with huge eyes. Gaby's alien ears twitch, the cone-shaped openings dilating and then contracting to listen for sounds that only she can hear.

I push the door open with the barrel of the pistol. The door creaks, sounding impossibly loud in the aching silence. Gone is the distant hum of traffic and the sounds of kids playing in the street.

The darkened interior of our house sweeps under the sights of my sidearm. A hallway entrance with a coat closet to my left and the door to the garage to my right. Next comes an office on the left, and a TV room on the right. Snatches of the main living room are visible at the end of the hall. A shut door to the basement sits between the TV room and the kitchen.

I step smoothly into the foyer, my aim alternating between the openings that I can see. No signs of anyone yet. I check the light switches beside the door. They don't work. It was worth a shot.

Stopping beside the garage door, I spare my left hand from the gun to open it. A quick scan of the empty garage reveals that it's probably clear —unless something is hiding behind the boxes in the corner. So far, we're good. I shut the door and turn the deadbolt to close off that access.

Heading down the hall, I check the office on my left and the TV room to the right. Both are clear. On to the kitchen and living room. I pause briefly to lock the basement door. A rotten stench fills my nostrils and my guts clench up with dread.

A dead body? I wonder.

No signs of movement ahead in the living room. I step smoothly out of the hallway. The living and dining room are both empty. To my right is the source of the smell: the fridge is standing open with brown slime pooled around it. A broken pickle jar is on the floor. Open containers of rotten leftovers and discarded bottles of condiments lie stewing in the juices. That mess is the cause of the smell. Of course it is. The power has been out for four days.

A knot of tension releases inside my chest. My gaze pans across the living area once more, conducting a more thorough examination.

The sliding glass door at the back of the house is broken. Jagged shards of glass lie gleaming in slanted bars of sunlight coming through the panel blinds. The dining room beyond the kitchen island is clear, but the chairs are overturned. Garbage and clutter are strewn across the table. Looks like the looters were sorting through their haul over there, figuring out what to keep and what to discard.

So far the main level looks clear, but with those panel blinds drawn and the curtains across the dining room window, I can't see the back deck or yard. Moving quickly through the kitchen, past the cluttered dining room, I pick my steps carefully between the broken glass to part the vertical slats of the blinds for a look outside.

The lawn is empty except for a dusting of ash and fluttering bits of garbage. The garden shed at the back is busted open, with both doors ajar, but it doesn't look like anyone is hiding in there. It would be a dumb place to hide, anyway. Letting the blinds fall back into place, I hurry back the way I came.

Time to check the basement. I stop in the kitchen on the way there and rummage around in the cabinets to find our flashlight.

Looters must have taken it. Great.

But there's a candle. Taking it and a box of matches, I set my gun down and hurriedly light the candle.

"Chris?" I hear Bree calling from the front

door. Her face peeks around the splintered frame just as I lean out of the kitchen.

"Shhh. Stay there," I warn.

She nods and ducks back behind the front door.

Pocketing the matches, I pick up my gun and the candle, and head for the basement door. At the door I'm confronted with the twist knob that I locked a moment ago. I manage to grip the candle with my palm and manipulate the lock with my fingers to avoid pocketing my gun. Hot wax drips onto my hand as I awkwardly turn the door handle. I grit my teeth and quickly release the door to shift my grip on the candle.

Using the barrel of the Glock, I nudge the door open and aim into the flickering shadows of the landing on the other side. So far so good, but this candle isn't doing much to light the way. Steeling myself, I start creeping down the carpeted stairs. Halfway to the bottom, one of the steps creaks loudly, and I freeze, my ears straining for a reaction from someone—or *something*—in my basement.

Nothing happens.

I continue down. Reaching the landing, I wave the candle around while bracing my right arm on top of my left in a shooter's stance. The basement is completely below grade, and barely lit by a pair of window wells with curtains drawn across them.

The family room is clear, but it was obviously

hit by looters, too. The couch cushions and pillows are lying all over, a few of them bleeding stuffing—cut open to see if we'd stashed credit chits or other valuables inside. *Really? It's the end of the world, and you think money and diamond earrings are going to save you?*

I head for the door to the combined laundry and machine room. It's already open, so I nudge it the rest of the way with my gun.

More chaos in here. Powdered detergent is all over the floor. Another window lights the space, making it easy to see.

All clear.

Next comes the bathroom. Shadows part under the flickering light of the candle. I step over to the shower and reach for the curtain. Curtain rings screech on a rusty rod as I point my gun into the tub.

Empty.

On to the guest room. Another door. It creaks as I ease it open. Again, it's better lit than the family room. This window is partially above grade, and I can see a slice of sky. No sign of anyone in here, either, but the bedsheets are rumbled, as if someone might have slept down here.

I'm more concerned about the contents of the closet. The folding, louvered doors are bent in the middle. I push them the rest of the way open. The door snags on something. Adrenaline kicks my pulse up a notch.

But it's just a discarded protein bar wrapper.

Muttering a curse under my breath, I yank the wrapper out and push the closet door open the rest of the way, revealing my gun safe. It's big enough to hold plenty of firepower, but I took most of my guns with us to Big Bear, and we ended up leaving them all behind.

I set my gun down on top of the safe and use the candle light to work the combination lock. I spin the dial to the right a few times to clear any attempts the looters may have made to open the safe. Then I enter my combination: 1217. December 17th. The day that Bree and I met. It was fourteen years ago, but I still remember it like yesterday. Walking through the door of her parents' place at a Christmas party, seeing her standing there with that smile and those brown eyes, sparkling and so full of life. Her mom knew my mom. They conspired to set us up, and it worked. Love at first sight is real. I'm a witness to that.

The locking mechanism thunks as I turn the handle. The safe pops open, revealing a mostly empty interior. We took the two shotguns, the hunting rifle, and my two Glocks, one of which I still have. We also took most of the spare ammo.

But there is one other shotgun in here, and a box of shells. There's also a box of bullets for the Glock, peeking out behind a compact Ruger revolver. I bought it for Bree after she was nearly assaulted in the parking lot outside the casino where she worked. I reach for the gun, remembering that incident with a scowl.

Bree was on her way to an automated taxi after a late shift of waiting tables at the restaurant where she worked. Some drunk she'd been waiting on at the bar followed her out and started to grope her; he seemed to think she'd been flirting. Dumbass didn't realize that it's part of her job to flirt. How else do you get bigger tips?

She kneed him in the groin and got away before things got out of hand. She didn't want to file a report, because he was a regular at The Pines, and she didn't want to lose her job. So I bought her a gun. And she refused to take it with her to work.

I check the cylinder. Empty. I take a minute to load the weapon, then pocket it. Next comes the shotgun. I load that, too, and then stuff a handful of spare shells into my other pocket. Finding a tac light, I clip it to the barrel and flick it on.

Much better than the candle. I blow it out and leave it atop the safe beside the Glock.

A muffled scream comes from upstairs, followed by the crash of a breaking window.

Bree!

Grabbing the shotgun in both hands, I pump the action and dash out of the guest room, running for the stairs.

CHAPTER 5

Before I even reach the top of the stairs I hear the snarling and scrabbling of sharp claws on wooden floors—

Dregs.

I hear Zach shout, "Leave her alone!"

Followed by another set of snarls.

Bursting through the door at the top of the stairs, I turn my shotgun toward the commotion. Bree is pinned beneath a raggedy creature with stringy hair and pale skin, its jaws snapping for her throat.

Zach and Gaby are standing behind it. Zach is pounding on its back with his fists while Gaby claws at its legs.

"Hey!" I shout.

The monster looks up with a snarl and flashing red eyes.

Bree kicks it between the legs, and it shrieks in pain.

I switch the shotgun to my left hand and

draw the revolver. Taking careful aim, I shoot it in the back.

The Dreg shrieks again, and this time it jumps off Bree and comes running toward me. I pocket the revolver, backpedaling fast, and bring the shotgun into line.

Boom.

The monster's head explodes in a grisly rain of pulp and bone, some of which spatters my face. The Dreg falls at my feet. One leg kicks spasmodically and then it lies still. I carefully wipe my face on my sleeve. Doctor Turner said the infection spreads through infected fluids. I hope to God that I haven't just ingested some of that Dreg's blood.

I run past the body to check on Bree. She's picking herself off the floor, looking shaken. My eyes are darting, scanning for injuries.

"Are you hurt?" I ask.

She checks herself over, then shakes her head. "I don't think so."

There is a fresh set of parallel gashes torn in her dirty red ski jacket, but those claws didn't make it all the way through. Saved again by her layers. This isn't the first time she's grappled with a Dreg and come out unscathed. The last one was Niles.

I pull Bree into a quick, one-armed hug. "Thank God," I breathe beside her ear.

Then I notice the front door standing wide open to the street. Zach is just inside the entrance, looking terrified. Gaby is on all fours beside him, her hands black with the Dreg's blood.

Infected blood.

I withdraw sharply from Bree and hand her the shotgun. "Keep watch. I'll get Gaby cleaned up."

Bree nods mutely.

I shrug out of my blood-smeared jacket and drop it over the body of the Dreg. I'll drag it out and burn it later.

"Come on, Gabs," I say, beckoning to her with one hand. "Let's get you cleaned up."

She climbs to her feet and hurries over, her eyes on the bloody remains of the Dreg as we walk around it.

"Is it dead?" Gaby asks.

"Yes."

"Stay away from the body," I call to the others as we reach the kitchen.

Maybe that goes without saying, but I don't want to take any risks.

I grab a dish sponge and pump soap all over Gaby's hands before opening the tap. *What kills this virus?* I wonder as I scrub away the infected blood, paying special attention to Gaby's long black nails. Not nails—claws. I suppress a grimace and go on scrubbing. *Is soap good enough or do I need to use bleach?*

"You're hurting me," Gaby says.

"Sorry." I stop scrubbing and rinse her hands off. They look clean, but just to be sure I wash them again, more gently this time.

"All right. My turn." I wash my face at the sink, keeping my eyes and lips clamped shut.

At least we still have water, I think to distract myself from the possibility that I'm already infected.

I wonder how long the water will last. Where does it come from? For all I know this is residual water in the pipes and they're about to run dry.

I finish up at the sink and dry my face with a kitchen towel from one of the drawers. Heading back to the hall, I find Gaby standing there, staring at the dead Dreg.

"Don't look at it, sweetheart," I say, and gently turn her away from the carnage.

"We should find some way to collect water before we run out," I call to Bree.

"We can do that," Bree says. "Zach?"

He doesn't immediately respond.

"Zach!" Bree hisses.

He snaps out of it and walks over to his mother.

"What are you going to do with it?" Bree asks as she creeps past the dead creature with Zach.

"I'm going to take it out and burn it, then use bleach to wash the floors."

Bree nods. "Good."

"Where did it come from?" I ask, peering out the open door.

"The Jacksons' place."

My brow furrows. I use the barrel of the shotgun to lift the jacket I threw over the body. It's wearing blue jeans and a tattered black t-shirt. The figure is masculine. Trim and fit. What's left of the man's hair is long and stringy, but it looks light enough that it might have once been blond like mine. Greg Jackson had long blond hair, and he usually wore blue jeans. The body is about the right height and weight, but beyond that, I don't see how we could possibly identify him one way or the other. I suppose I could scan his ID implant if I could find a portable scanner, but those scanners all need the Internet to function, and the databases they rely on probably went up in smoke with LA and San Francisco.

"It doesn't matter," I decide, then move to grab the body by the legs. "Keep that shotgun handy. There could be more of them out there."

"What about you?" Bree asks as I start dragging.

"I've got your Ruger. I'll be okay."

"Be careful," Bree says, and then turns and heads for the kitchen.

I reach the front steps and the body gets stuck in the doorway as one of the arms hooks behind the door. I yank it free with a grunt and the door smacks me in the face. I stifle a curse and wait for the pain to subside.

Dragging the dead Dreg out the rest of the way, I take a break on the porch to catch my breath. The air is sharp and acrid with smoke, burning my eyes and throat. Ash still flutters from the sky and swirls on the street.

My warning to Bree echoes through my thoughts. There could be more Dregs out here. I study the broken front door, and recall the shattered one at the back. I'll have to secure this place somehow.

I regard the body at my feet. "You have any buddies out there, Greg?"

Looking up, I scan the street, checking between the parked cars and sycamore trees. No signs of anyone else around here, infected or otherwise.

Maybe the neighbors are all out working to clear the streets like the people I saw on the way into the safe zone. That makes me wonder about us. When are we going to be assigned to work details? We didn't get that far at the tasking and housing station before they shot my mother.

A sharp pang of grief leaves me suddenly gasping for air. I stumble to the porch railing and lean hard on it, squinting against the glare of the rising sun. The smoke makes my eyes burn, bringing them to tears.

Then again, maybe it's not just the smoke.

CHAPTER 6

I'm out on the back deck, using a hammer to knock old two-by-sixes loose, then prying the nails out and banging them straight to save as many as I can. Rather than risk going anywhere to salvage the wood I need to secure our house, I'm using what I have at hand. And stripping the deck has the added advantage of making it harder to enter the house from the back.

"Chris," Bree says suddenly.

I look up to see her standing in the broken sliding glass door. "The kids are hungry."

My stomach growls and rumbles with the mention of food.

"Yeah..." I say, nodding.

"The looters took all of our food."

"All of it?"

"The only thing we have left is a couple cans of peas."

"Great." My nose wrinkles. I hate peas. *Especially* canned peas.

Beads of sweat are prickling my forehead. I wipe them on my sleeve. "I can't go anywhere yet. The house isn't secure."

"I can watch the kids."

"What if another Dreg comes in?"

Bree crosses her arms over her chest and arches an eyebrow at me. "You think you're the only one who knows how to shoot a gun?"

"No, but—"

"You can't secure the house on an empty stomach. This is going to take you all day. Besides, it's been more than an hour with you banging away out here. If there were more Dregs around, by now they should have heard you and come running."

She makes a good point. A sigh deflates me, and I set the hammer aside. Getting up, I wipe dirty hands on my jeans and meet Bree's gaze at eye level. "I need you to stay in one of the bedrooms with the door locked and shut."

"Fine."

Noticing that Bree is empty-handed, I fix her with a dark look. "Where is the shotgun?"

She reaches around, just inside the broken door and pulls it out. "Right here." She pumps the action to chamber a shell.

"The kids?"

"Locked in the basement. Are you going to go look for food, or should I?"

"I'll go."

"Then you need this." She starts handing me

the shotgun, but I shake my head.

"Remember what Doctor Brown said about guns? If the Chimeras catch us with one, they'll kill us. I can't risk it. The Ruger is small enough to conceal in my jacket." After dragging the Dreg outside, I picked a slick black windbreaker from the coat closet (now tied at my waist). It seemed like a better idea than putting on the blood-spattered Army jacket I threw over the Dreg. "I'll stick with the revolver."

Bree frowns at me. "You shot that Dreg with it. The Ruger didn't stop it."

"So next time I'll aim for the head."

"Chris."

"Bree."

We spend a moment squaring off with each other.

"Don't be long," Bree says, giving in with a sigh.

"I won't." I lean in and drop a kiss on her cheek. Pulling away, I start back across the deck, being careful to mind the gaping holes where I pried up the boards.

"Where are you going?" she asks.

"The Jacksons' place," I reply as I step down from the deck and cross the lawn to the fence that separates our yards. If that Dreg was Mr. Jackson, then there's a chance that his place is empty. Of course, Mrs. Jackson could still be there, but something tells me if her husband turned into a Dreg, she didn't last very long.

A shiver rocks my shoulders as I reach the fence. Standing on tip toes, I peek over.

The outdoor furniture has been thrown around. The back door is broken like ours, and so are both of the windows. One of them is streaked with blood and the wooden side door to the Jacksons' back yard is splintered. Based on the angles of the splinters and remaining planks, it looks like something broke *out,* not in.

So far my theory about the Dreg being Greg Jackson seems to be holding. No signs of movement in the yard or the house.

I reach up and grab the top of the fence. Rough wood digs into my palms as I pull myself up and over. I land hard, and a sharp pain erupts in the arch of my left foot. I'm not as young as I used to be.

Reaching into my jacket pocket, I pull out the Ruger and head for the broken door and the gaping darkness of the Jacksons' living room.

Here's hoping Greg the Dreg didn't eat everything in their pantry.

Another thought grips me as I reach the stairs. What if Mrs. Jackson turned into a Dreg, too?

Maybe Greg left his house for the same reason I did—to scrounge up a meal at his wife's behest.

My heart rate spikes, and I hesitate with one foot on the back steps. Bree was right. I should have brought the shotgun.

***

As I reach the gaping threshold between the Jacksons' home and their yard, the same rotten smell that pervades our home fills my nostrils. This time the smell is worse, and I have a bad feeling that something really did die in here.

I pause in the entrance, waiting for my eyes to adjust to the dimmer light inside the home. The layout is similar to ours, but the Jacksons' place is two floors plus the basement whereas ours is a bungalow.

As soon as my eyes have adjusted, I head through the living room to the kitchen. A soft spot in the floor creaks.

The fridge stands open like ours was. Rotting food and broken bottles lie on the floor. I cover my nose with my left sleeve, keeping my right hand free for the Ruger.

Was this the work of looters or Dregs? I wonder.

Some of the upper cupboards are open. Broken dishes and glassware lie on the floor below and on the granite countertops. Hunting around in the lower drawers and cabinets, I find a pair of rechargeable flashlights and a barbecue lighter. Those are items the looters took from our house, so this mess was probably the work of a mindless Dreg hunting for food. I flick on the flashlight and pocket the lighter.

What do Dregs eat? I wonder. Gaby developed

a craving for raw meat when she finished turning. Does that mean they're carnivores? If so, they will have left most of the dry food alone.

Finding the kitchen bare, I straighten up and sweep the beam of the flashlight around, bracing it under my gun hand. I spot a door off to my right that looks like it might lead to a pantry. The door is cracked open. It could also lead to the basement for all I know. We were on decent terms with the Jacksons, but we only came over to their place once for a dinner party, and even then we only saw the dining room and the living area at the front of the house.

Flexing my hand on the grip of the Ruger, I edge forward, keeping my eyes and ears open. Reaching the door, I toe it open and take a quick step back.

It's not just a pantry, it's a mudroom, and it's lined with shelves full of cans and boxes of food. There's also a chest freezer that's probably full of rotten meat.

Some of the cans are scattered on the floor. They're dented and the labels are flaking off. A few of the dents look like teeth marks, but I don't have time to waste being picky.

Spying a matched set of floral-print luggage on an upper shelf, I pocket the flashlight and the Ruger, then reach up and pull the luggage down. I zip it open on the freezer and pull out the smaller piece of luggage inside. Starting with the cans on the upper shelves, I take only a second to scan the labels as I put them in: corn, corned beef, peach halves, green beans, mixed vegetables, more corn, tomato sauce, diced tomatoes, a can of tomato sauce. I force myself to slow down and be more selective. Calories. We need food that is high in calories. A can of condensed milk catches my eye. Perfect. There's another one hiding behind it. Two boxes of sugary cereal. Some crackers. A bag of rice. Boxes of pasta. Mac and Cheese. A packet of lentils. All good stuff.

I finish off the luggage with a few rolls of toilet paper. I'm used to dealing with less than ideal bathroom solutions from my time in the army, but I'm pretty sure Bree will send me out scavenging again if it comes to wiping our asses with leaves.

Once the bag is packed to overflowing, I zip it up and heave it off the counter. Halfway through the kitchen, I hear a familiar whirring sound—followed by the sound of boots on pavement and debris crunching.

The coordinated sound of those movements brings to mind soldiers, not Dregs, but that doesn't exactly warm my heart. How do Chimeras deal with looters?

I freeze on the spot, my heart racing. I should just run for it.

But the side door to the yard was open. If it were me in command, I'd send part of my team through there, and the other part through the front door.

Running out the back would be a good way to get myself shot. I set the luggage down on the floor and nudge it around the back of the kitchen island. Keeping my hand close to the Ruger in my jacket pocket, I step over the mess in front of the open fridge, then ease around the corner for a glimpse down the hall to the front door. The front door is standing wide open. Two Chimeras in shadowy black armor are creeping toward the front steps with their rifles raised.

I duck back out of sight and drop to my haunches behind the kitchen island. The ones coming around the side will be in sight of the kitchen soon.

There has to be another way out of here. I cast my mind back desperately to that one time we came over for dinner, trying to remember the layout of the Jacksons' place.

It was years ago...

I went looking for the guest bathroom and accidentally opened the door to the basement. It's around the side of the kitchen, at the end of the hall past the office and the formal dining room.

Creeping along behind the kitchen island, I reach the spot where I left the luggage full of food. I can't afford to take that with me now. It's too big and too heavy.

Hopefully I'll be able to come back for it later.

Still down on my haunches, I sneak past the mudroom and out through the side entrance of the kitchen. I'm in a hallway now. The office is right in front of me. A dormant holoscreen sits on the desk. Decorations, glowing holo frames, and antique books line the built-in shelves. A guitar and a piano are on one side of the desk. The room looks untouched, an island of normalcy.

The creaky floorboard at the back entrance signals that the soldiers have arrived. I reach for the door beside the office, turn the knob and slip through to the basement stairs. Easing it shut behind me, I turn and draw the Ruger from my pocket before starting down the stairs.

It's almost too dark to see the bottom of the stairs, but a pale glow coming from the window wells guides me down to the landing. I hear footsteps upstairs and more creaking from the floors.

A foul smell wafts to my nose. Hopefully it's from another fridge or a chest freezer. No way to know, and I can't risk using the flashlight. If someone opens the door to the basement, they'll see it instantly.

Heading for the nearest window, I hurry through the carpeted family room. As I walk past the couch, my foot hooks on something and I almost fall on my face.

Spinning around, I see an outstretched hand. My gaze follows it to a body, and my stomach heaves. Blood and gore glisten darkly in the dim light. There's another corpse behind it. I can just make out familiar features through the dim light: Greg Jackson's long hair and lanky frame.

Mrs. Jackson's pear-shaped figure and short black hair. It's enough to identify them. They didn't turn into Dregs. They turned into food for one.

A blinking green light draws my eye to the hand that almost tripped me—Greg Jackson's hand. I turn over my own wrist and see a matching light wink on and off, on and off.

I forgot about the tracking implants. Is that why the soldiers came here? They can probably tell when someone with an implant dies. If so, they'll be coming down here to investigate what happened to the Jacksons. For all I know, they've already seen that I'm down here with them, which makes me the prime suspect.

The door at the top of the stairs clicks open, drawing my attention back the way I came.

Shit. I'm out of time. I whirl around, searching for the nearest exit. A door lies open to what looks like a bedroom. The pale light spilling out implies a window. I step over the dead bodies of my neighbors, moving fast. Reaching the door, I dart behind it. A window is right beside me. A wardrobe beneath it. I get my knees up on the wardrobe, coming to eye level with the window.

The sound of boots clomping down the basement stairs carries to my ears through the open door. I should have closed it. Too late now.

Flicking the latch up, I open the window. A metal hinge snaps straight leaving the window propped open at about 30 degrees. Nothing bigger than a cat is getting through that.

I grab the metal arm and wrench with all of my strength. It bends and twists—then pops free. My arm flies back and I smack my hand on the other side of the window frame.

My heart rate spikes and I freeze, my ears straining for a reaction from the soldiers. The sound wasn't loud, but...

It doesn't matter. I need to move. Pushing the window up with one arm, I reach through and pull myself into the window well. The space is cramped, and I only manage to get my head and shoulders out before I have to reach for the gravel-covered ground above. I drag myself free and the window bangs shut behind me.

If they didn't know I was here, they do now. Have to run for it. I'm on the side of the house, right beside the splintered gate to the back. I spot the hedge between my front yard and the Jacksons. Running for it, I vault straight over the bushes. The troop transport that brought the Chimeras here is hovering on the street in clear sight. If there's anyone inside, they must have spotted me already.

No time to worry about it. I'm committed to this plan. Sprinting across my driveway, I race up my front steps and fly through the broken front door. The floor is still wet in the hallway, but the pool of infected black blood has been reduced to a faded smudge.

Stopping in front of the basement door, I knock twice, then twice more before turning the lock and opening the door to let myself in. Shutting the door behind me, I call out, "Bree? Kids?"

No answer.

I hurry down the stairs.

Pounding footsteps reach my ears from below, approaching fast. I hit the landing and come face to face with Bree. She has the shotgun, but it's not aimed at me.

"What's wrong?" she asks in a sharp whisper, already having heard the alarm in my tone.

"Chimeras at the Jacksons'," I say between gasps for air. My heart is still pounding.

"Did they see you?"

"No, but..."

She waits for me to recover. I'm leaning on the post at the bottom of the basement stairs. "The Jacksons are dead. Looks like the Dreg was eating them. Either they called for help somehow, or their implants did it for them when they died."

"Did you find food?"

"Plenty, but I had to leave it there."

Bree winces and shakes her head. "We need to eat."

"I know. I'll go back for it after the Chimeras leave. Let's just wait it out down here. The kids...?" I trail off, looking around. Then I see Gaby and Zach both peeking around the door to the guest room.

"Let's go in there."

Bree nods and turns to lead the way.

I take a step to follow her—

And then hear the door at the top of the stairs click open.

"Freeze!" a deep voice booms down to me.

CHAPTER 7

I stare hard at Bree and mouth to her: *go.* My eyes flick to the shotgun in her hand. She appears to notice it, and quickly retreats to the guest bedroom.

I raise my hands above my head and slowly turn toward the soldier who told me to freeze. There is a Chimera in matte black armor standing silhouetted at the top of the stairs, aiming an alien rifle at me.

"Is something wrong?" I ask in a mild tone.

"We detected you fleeing the property adjacent to this one."

So I was right about the tracking implants. I incline my head. "Yes, sir."

"What were you doing there?"

"Looking for food."

"You need to wait for your rations to be delivered. Deliveries are bi-weekly. Mondays and Fridays. Looting is a capital crime."

"No one told us that, but I didn't steal anything."

"Is this your residence?"

"It is."

"Assigned?"

"It was ours before the invasion."

"Lucky you. My records say three others live here with you. Your wife and two kids. Where are they?"

"Here in the basement with me."

"I'll need to see them."

"Sure." Half turning to look for Bree, I see her in the guest room, already stepping out with the kids to comply. I call out to her anyway, for the Chimera's benefit: "Bree, kids, come over here, please. The officer would like to speak with you."

"Coming," Bree says as she leads the kids over. I'm glad to see that the shotgun is nowhere in sight, but there's a suspicious bulge in Bree's jacket that looks like the Glock I left on top of the gun safe.

Damn it, Bree! It's bad enough that I still have the Ruger. If they decide to search us, we'll both be dead.

"Hello," Bree says brightly as she leans into view of the soldier.

Zach peeks between us, while Gaby hides behind her mother's legs.

A long stretch of silence is the only answer from the soldier. Eventually, his posture shifts, and his head tilts to one side. "Your daughter is a Chimera?"

"Yes, sir," I say. "Is that a problem?"

"What are you four doing here?"

"What do you mean?" Bree asks.

"You should be on the work details."

"We're new arrivals," I explain. "We just got here this morning."

"I see... who are your task leaders?"

"We don't know yet."

The Chimera hefts his rifle higher and adjusts his aim to my chest. "Work details are assigned during processing," the Chimera says darkly, as if we might have somehow snuck into the safe zone and skipped that step.

Gaby hisses at him.

"Our processing was interrupted," Bree explains, stepping in front of me. I try to push her aside, but she won't budge.

"I'm going to have to call this in," the Chimera says.

"And then what?" I ask, stepping around Bree to make sure I'm in the line of fire again.

"You'll be given your assignments."

"What about our children?" Bree asks.

"They'll go to school with the other children."

"School?" Zach asks, his voice rising incredulously. "What for?"

"Be quiet," Bree warns.

"One moment. Stay where you are," the Chimera says. He backs out of the basement stairwell and partly closes the door behind him.

The gun, I mouth to Bree, making a gimme gesture.

She frowns and shakes her head, not getting it.

I reach for the weapon, and she withdraws sharply.

"Damn it, Bree!" I hiss at her.

"What?"

The basement door swings wide and the Chimera is back.

"Chris Randall, your detail is on street clean-up and construction. Your task leader is Corporal Ward, and your team is based in Fire Station 224. Bree Randall, you will be teaching elementary school at George Brown."

I recognize both of those buildings. They're about a block away from each other, maybe only ten blocks from here. We could walk to our jobs if we had to.

"When do we start?" I ask.

"The transports come by at six am sharp. Make sure you're standing outside and ready to go."

"The kids, too?" Bree asks.

"Yes. Your daughter will go with you to your class, and your son will go to Arrowview next door."

"It's still there?" I ask. That's where Zach went before all the shit hit the fan.

"Mostly intact, yes," the Chimera replies.

"Thanks for your help," Bree says.

"There is one other matter we need to discuss. Did either of you see a Dreg around here?"

Bree starts to say something, and I step casually to one side—onto her foot. She cuts herself off with a yelp.

"Sorry, darling," I say, then quickly nod to the Chimera. "We did see it, but we don't know where it went."

My mind flashes back to the body. I burned it in the fire pit in our backyard, then shoveled dirt over the bones to put the fire out. So long as they don't go digging around in there, it shouldn't be a problem.

"I see. It didn't try to attack you?"

"No," I say.

"But you saw what it did to your neighbors."

"I saw the bodies, but I was in a hurry to get out of there."

"Why? You said you didn't steal anything. Did you take something and forget to mention it?"

"No," I answer quickly. "I just didn't want you to find me there and think that I had something to do with their deaths. Is that what killed them? A Dreg?"

"Yes. You'd better secure your home. They come out in force at night and our patrols are stretched thin as it is."

"There are more of them around here?" Bree asks.

"Secure the entrances. If you spot anything,

hold a thumb to the skin above your implant for five seconds. That will send an alert for us to come investigate."

"Good to know," I say.

Silence falls once more, and the Chimera lingers, staring fixedly down at us.

My heart starts hammering in my chest again. "Is something wrong, officer?" I ask as casually as I can.

"They didn't say anything about her at the processing center?"

"About who?" Bree asks. "Me?"

"Your daughter, ma'am."

"No. Why? She's one of you, right? Isn't that a good thing?"

Another long stretch of silence.

"Stay safe," the Chimera finally says, and then backs out of the stairwell.

I listen to his footsteps retreating down the hall.

Bree turns to look at me, her eyes fierce in the dim light of the basement. "What do they want with her?"

Gaby is watching me, waiting for my answer with her cranial stalks flattened to her bony, chalk-white head.

I hesitate, not wanting to give voice to the fears swirling through my thoughts.

"Maybe they want to take her with them," Zach answers.

We both send him a sharp look.

"What?" he asks innocently.

"Take me where?" Gaby asks in a shrinking voice.

"Let's not jump to any conclusions. If they wanted to take her away, they would have done it already."

Bree seems to relax, and Gaby, too. But I can't entirely put to rest my own concerns. What if Gaby was actually meant to go somewhere else, and she slipped through the cracks with all the commotion at the processing center?

"We still don't have anything to eat," Bree points out.

She's right. "The soldier said rations are delivered bi-weekly. Mondays and Fridays."

"What's today?" Bree asks.

I cast my mind back, counting forward from the day the invasion began—it was a Thursday night... "Today is Tuesday," I answer after a few seconds.

"We can't last three days without food," Bree says.

"They already warned us about looting."

"Then what are we supposed to do until Friday?"

"That's a good damn question."

CHAPTER 8

"I'm hungry..." Gaby whines for the umpteenth time.

"Me, too," Zach says.

"Shhh," Bree soothes. "Daddy's working on it."

Am I? I frown at that while studying my hands and the blinking green light of my tracking implant.

Bree and the kids are huddled on the basement couch with their backs to me. The three of them are staring at a dormant holoscreen while I sit on the landing, waiting an appropriate amount of time for the Chimeras to leave. I can't get that suitcase full of food from the Jacksons' place until they're gone.

But what happens if I jump the fence and whoever is watching their tracking system sees the signal from my implant wandering back over there? Will they dispatch the Chimeras again? Will they automatically assume that I'm looting?

Maybe they won't even notice. The one we spoke to said their patrols are spread pretty thin, so unless they have some kind of AI monitoring the locations of everyone's tracking implants, I can't imagine anyone noticing that a particular blip has moved over by a few dozen feet.

"Chris." Bree's voice pulls me from my thoughts. She's looking over the back of the couch at me. "What if they found the body?"

It takes me a second to remember what she's talking about. The Dreg in the fire pit. "They won't," I say.

"But if they did?"

I shrug. "Then they'll know I lied. I don't think lying is a capital offense."

"You don't know that. We should have told them the truth."

"And then showed them the body? Don't you think they would have asked how we killed it without getting bitten? They would have investigated further and maybe even found our guns. Then what?"

"We hand them over and say we didn't know that owning guns is illegal."

"And then we'll be defenseless tonight when more Dregs come crawling out of whatever holes they're hiding in."

"More of them are coming?" Gaby asks in a shrinking voice.

Bree's gaze sharpens accusingly on mine. "No, sweetheart. It's just in case," she whispers, and kisses our daughter on her bony head.

"But if—"

"Daddy will make sure that none of them can get in."

It's ironic to hear that Gaby is scared of them when she has the same nightmarish features that they do, but I have to remember that she's only six years old, and her brain is probably still catching up to her new appearance.

I push off the landing to join Bree on the couch and help her reassure our kids. Zach hasn't said anything, but he's hugging a throw pillow to his chest, looking shell-shocked.

"Give me a second, kids," Bree says and begins extricating herself from Zach and Gaby. Zach reaches for her suddenly, but she gently removes his hand.

"I'm not going anywhere. I just want to talk to your father for a moment."

She grabs my hand and pulls me aside, back toward the stairs.

"One of the neighbors must have heard you shooting," Bree whispers to me.

"So?"

"So, what if they report us?"

I hadn't thought of that. "I think it's too soon to worry about collaborators. What would they have to gain by turning us in?"

"I don't know," Bree says, rubbing her arms. "But I don't like it. You need to hide those guns really well."

"I will."

Bree holds my gaze for a few more seconds and starts biting her lower lip.

"What's wrong?" I ask. That's her go-to nervous tick.

"Everything."

"I meant—"

"What if they see Gaby at school tomorrow and they decide to take her away from us, or worse, they—"

"I won't let them," I say quickly.

"You won't even be there!"

I grab both of Bree's arms and squeeze. "She's one of them. They want soldiers, right? They're not going to hurt her."

"But she's just a child, not a soldier."

"Exactly, so we have time before we need to worry about this."

"Then what do they want with her? The ones in Big Bear died trying to get her back!"

I wince as the memories trickle back. Those events feel fuzzy and distant now, even though it was only last night. But it feels like a nightmare, not something that actually happened.

One of the actual aliens—those short, hunching winged creatures that call themselves Kyra—wanted Gaby back badly enough to die fighting us for her. That means she's important to them, but so far the Chimeras we've met don't seem to know why. The ones who found us in Big Bear mentioned *heretics* operating in the area, but what does that mean?

Was Gaby a part of some kind of illegal experiment? That drifter, Bret had something to say about it. He was taken by the Kyra along with Gaby, and they turned him, too. I asked him the same question that Bree just asked me: why all the interest in Gaby if the Kyra want soldiers? She's too young to fight.

Bret said that the Chimeras are all sterile. Gaby was taken because the Kyra thought that if they turn girls before they reach puberty, they might still be able to have kids.

So they turned my little girl into a hybrid because they want her to breed more soldiers one day. An involuntary shiver rocks through me with that recollection.

"Chris," Bree says, pulling me out of my thoughts.

"Yeah?"

"What is it? You went quiet."

"Nothing." I look away from her.

"I know when you're not telling me something."

I hesitate, wondering if I should tell her.

"I *can hear* you," Gaby says, sounding suddenly far older than her six years. Her chin is propped on the back of the couch. Red eyes gleaming in the gloomy basement. All four cranial stalks are turned our way, listening. *Super-ears. Right.* That gives me an idea.

"We'll talk about it later," I say to Bree. Turning from her, I nod to our daughter. "Gabs," I say.

One ear twitches.

"Can you hear the soldiers?"

She shakes her head. "No."

"Did you hear it when their transport came?"

"The black bus?"

"Yes, the black bus."

"I heard it."

"And did you hear when it left?"

Gaby appears to think about it.

"It would have been recently. It makes a whirring, whooshing sound. Maybe whistles like a flute. Is it gone yet?"

Gaby nods. "I think so."

"Thanks, kiddo."

Bree looks skeptical. "She could be wrong."

"I'll check the street first."

Bree nods slowly.

I start moving toward the stairs, then stop myself. Reaching into my jacket, I withdraw the Ruger and hand it to her.

"You need it," she objects.

I shake my head. "The Chimeras already swept the area for Dregs, and it's not worth the risk of me being caught with it."

Bree gives in with a sigh and takes the weapon. "Where are we supposed to hide the guns?"

"For now, in the guest room closet. I'll come up with something better later." Leaning in quickly, I drop a quick kiss on Bree's cheek. "See

you soon."
    "Be careful."
    "I will. Love you."
    "I love you, too..." Bree says.

CHAPTER 9

A quick look from the front porch reveals that the troop transport is gone. From there I run back through the house, vault over the gaps I left in the back deck, and fly across the yard. I pull myself over the fence, dash through the Jacksons' yard, and into their kitchen. The suitcase is right where I left it.

Finally, some good luck.

Heaving the heavy luggage off the floor, I hug it to my chest and run back the way I came. When I get to the fence I have to throw the bag over. It lands with a crash, but I didn't pack any glass bottles in there, so the contents should be fine.

I jump over the fence next, and then run back inside my house. Putting the suitcase up on the island counter, I zip it open and then rummage through the kitchen drawer to look for the can-opener.

It's missing.

The looters took that, too. Of course, they did. Unbelievable! What else can I use?

A good strong knife would do. I have a hunting knife in the safe downstairs.

Leaving my haul where it is, I run down into the basement.

Bree points the Ruger in my face, then quickly lowers it.

"You need to warn us when you're coming!"

"Sorry," I say.

"Did you get the food?"

I nod and step by her on my way to the guest room.

"Where is it?"

"In the kitchen. We need a way to open the cans."

The gun safe is still standing open. Bree put the shotgun and the Glock back inside.

Seeing the hunting knife, I pull it out. It's still safely tucked into the leather sheath.

"Let's go," I say, breathless as I hurry back the way I came. Bree and the kids follow me up, and within minutes we're each spooning cold food out of the cans of our choosing. I've got two: canned corn and another of pork and beans. Gaby is eating a can of processed meat—it was the only thing she felt like; yet another sign that maybe the hybrids are carnivores—Zach chose dry cereal, and Bree is eating a can of mixed veggies.

Silence is our only conversation while we eat.

No time to waste with words. Our mouths are too busy chewing.

As I eat standing beside the kitchen sink, I notice all the pots and Tupperware standing around filled with water. I wonder if Bree only filled them partly because she ran out of time before I told her to go hide in the basement with the kids—or because we ran out of water.

Reaching for the kitchen faucet, I open the tap, and water trickles out. The pressure is definitely down. Will the toilets still flush? Water pressure might not even be the problem there. The sewers could be backed up with debris. How long will it take to get our infrastructure back up and running? What about electricity and refrigeration? Heating? It's warm enough at the moment, but it's going to get pretty cold at night.

Soon I'm scraping sauce from both of my cans and my stomach feels reasonably full.

"I'm going to get back to work on the deck."

Bree looks up from stabbing my knife into another can. "Do you want me to help?"

I consider the offer briefly. Bree is capable enough, but she's not very handy with tools. Besides, I only have the one hammer. "No, I need you to keep watch. Maybe finish filling whatever you can with water."

Bree nods. "Okay."

I start toward the back door.

"I can help," Zach says.

"Me, too," Gaby adds.

I don't really want them getting in the way, falling through the holes in the deck or stepping on nails... but they want to do something, and keeping them busy will be a good distraction. "Okay, Zach, come out and join me when you're done eating."

He nods, crunching another handful of dry cereal. "I'm done," he says, spraying crumbs.

"Gaby, you stay and help your mother."

"But—"

"No buts."

Her cranial stalks flatten, but she doesn't object again. I feel bad, but I don't want Bree to be alone in here. Besides, after the way the Chimeras were looking at Gaby, I definitely don't want her standing around outside where the neighbors can see her. If she's drawing attention from her own kind, how much more so from regular humans?

"It's okay, Gabs," Bree says. "Let the boys go out and get sweaty and dirty. We'll get things organized in here. Maybe we can make a pillow fort when we're done."

Gaby perks up.

"Really?"

Bree nods.

I flash her a smile and head outside. Soon I'm straddling a beam and hammering out more two-by-sixes and nails with the sun beating down on my neck.

Zach comes out to join me, and I put him to

work dragging the boards inside so we can use them to fortify the house.

By the time the deck is half missing, I have both my jacket and my shirt off. It must be about midday now. Bree comes out with a glass of water and I gulp it down greedily. What I wouldn't give for ice!

"Thanks, honey," I say, handing the glass back.

"You're welcome. Give me a shout when you want more."

"Sure."

Bree takes the glass back inside with a smile. Zach replaces her in the broken doorway, waiting for orders. He wipes his brow. Blond hair is pasted to his forehead with sweat.

"Now what?" he asks.

I nod to another pair of boards that he missed.

He groans and then bends to the task of dragging them inside.

I watch him go with a smile of my own. This abrupt return to normalcy is a beguiling illusion. If it weren't for the fact that I'm busy salvaging wood from my back deck to board up my home, I could almost be fooled into thinking that this is just a normal afternoon in my neighborhood.

But our situation is about as far from normal as the invaders are from home—wherever *that* is.

I pick up my hammer and shimmy down the beam I'm sitting on to hammer out the next set of planks. If what those Chimeras said about the Dregs coming out at night was true, then I'd better do a damned good job of securing this place.

CHAPTER 10

It's almost dusk. I can barely see the shadows of fallen trees and parked cars lining the street.

We're in the master bedroom with the door shut and locked. I'm sitting on the cushions in a box bay window with my shotgun balanced in my lap. The kids are tucked into bed with Bree, one on either side of her. She's telling them a story that she's making up as she goes. Something about fairies and elves. They don't like each other, and then two of them fall in love. That only leads to more conflict, but eventually the fairies and elves learn to put aside their differences.

It sounds a bit like Romeo and Juliet. The story is probably meant to take the kids' minds off our situation, but I can't help drawing parallels. Isn't that always how it goes? Two divergent groups meet, divided by ideology and race, and they hate each other's guts. Then over time, they find common ground and learn to get along. I wonder how long it will take us to find common ground with the Chimeras. Hell, that's not even the most important issue. We need to find common ground with the Kyra, and that's going to be a lot harder. Somehow, we need to get them to see us as sentient beings with rights—as equals, not as cannon fodder for their war.

And I'd still like to know who they're fighting. Why are they so desperate for soldiers? Is their enemy even more advanced than them? Maybe we could make an alliance...

I stare absently through the window. The light is fading fast. Trees shiver with the wind. A distant rattling sound connects to memories of my time in the army.

Bree abruptly stops telling her story as another rattling roar erupts.

"What was that?" Bree asks.

"Gunfire," I whisper back.

"Ours?"

"I think so."

"But we're not allowed to use guns."

"Someone obviously didn't get the memo."

We wait, listening in the dark, but the sound doesn't return.

"Whatever that was, it's over," I say.

"No, they're still shooting," Gaby says.

"You can hear them?" I ask, raising my eyebrows at her.

"Yeah. And someone else is shooting back."

"How can you tell?" I ask, focusing on the

gleaming pinpricks of Gaby's eyes.

The covers shift around her in what might be a shrug. "There's two different sounds. One is kind of high and screechy, and the other is like a gun."

"Lasers and bullets," I decide, looking back to the window.

"What does that mean?" Bree asks.

"It means there's a human resistance out there somewhere."

After a long pause, Bree goes back to telling her story.

My view through the window is unobstructed. I didn't manage to salvage enough wood and nails from the back deck to board up all of the windows, so I just secured the ones at the front of the house and all of the broken doors. Hopefully any Dregs that are out there don't find and break one of the exposed windows. On the bright side, the sound of breaking glass will wake me up if I fall asleep.

I'm on first watch, until 1:00 AM. Bree will take the next one until five. A quick look at the glowing green digits of the clock at my feet reveals the time:

18:05.

We found an old travel alarm clock with the camping supplies in the garage. It's solar powered, so we left it out in the sun, and I was able to estimate the time from the angle of the sun.

At least it gives us a way to comply with the Chimeras' demand that we be ready and waiting outside at 6:00 tomorrow morning. We'll have to leave a margin for error, but I figure so long as we're ready and waiting by about 5:30, we should be on time.

A flicker of movement catches my eye. I sit up straighter and squint out into the night. There. Moving between two cars.

My grip tightens on the stock and action of the shotgun.

"What is it?" Bree whispers.

I slowly shake my head. "I don't know."

Long seconds pass with my heart pounding and my whole body wound up like a spring.

"A Dreg?" Bree asks.

"I don't think so..." I say, replaying the memory in my head. "Too small. Maybe a stray dog or cat." With that realization some of the tension eases inside my chest, and I lean back against the side of my perch.

Silence falls in the wake of our conversation. It's so quiet that I can hear my own pulse. I glance over at the bed. The kids look like they're asleep. This is probably the earliest they've gone to bed since they were babies. It's been a long day, and without any kind of light to disturb our internal clocks, I guess this will be the new norm. Asleep at dusk, up at dawn. We're back to the stone age.

Only Bree's eyes are still open—twin stars winking at me with each sweep of her eyelids. After a moment, I hear the rustle of covers swishing over her as she crawls out of bed to join me in the window.

"You should get some sleep, too," I suggest, even as I move the shotgun and shimmy over to make room for her to sit beside me.

Bree curls up against my side. Her head tucks into the curve of my shoulder and chest; she works one hand under my jacket and t-shirt and splays it out on my chest. It's as cold as ice.

We both lie staring out the window, gazing above the trees to the stars.

"What do you think is going to happen to us?" Bree whispers.

"I guess we'll clear the streets and rebuild. We'll get the power back, hunt down the Dregs... get the water running. As long as we toe the line, we should be okay."

Bree nods against my shoulder.

Then she stiffens and sits up.

I'm about to ask what's wrong, but then I see it, too. Flickering shadows on the street. The combination of the stars and moon are just enough to see vague, human outlines.

"Are those..." Bree trails off.

"Could be Chimeras. They mentioned patrols."

One of the shadows darts quickly to one side.

And then comes a screeching yowl—the cat we saw earlier. The sound cuts off sharply.

"Did they *kill* it?"

"Shhh."

The shadowy figures vanish between the gleaming outlines of parked cars. There's no way to know if they're Chimeras or Dregs, but both are equally dangerous in their own ways.

Silence gathers around us, and Bree tucks herself harder against my side while I scan for more signs of movement.

Nothing yet.

A sigh builds inside my chest and whistles out softly. It's going to be a long night of jumping at shadows.

CHAPTER 11

Something sharp is jabbing me in the ribs, my body rolling with each jab. A Dreg's blood-smeared face looks up from my side. I see a gaping, bloody wound. It's eating me!

Panicked and nauseated, I try to react, but my body feels thick and heavy, my limbs paralyzed.

The Dreg licks my blood from its lips with a black tongue and goes back to feasting on my ribs.

"Chris!"

I wake up, blinking furiously.

Bree is sitting right where the Dreg was, looking up at me with concern and confusion.

I recoil from her, banging my elbow on the window with a resounding *boom* before my sleep-addled brain catches up.

"Are you okay?" Bree whispers.

"Yeah. Sorry." I let out a breath to steady myself, then rub the sleep from my eyes and turn to look out the window. Still pitch black out there.

I check the glowing green numbers on the clock at my feet.

05:05

We'd better get up and get ready. Bree retreats from the window, holding the shotgun one-handed with the barrel pointed at the ceiling.

Behind her, the kids are still fast asleep in our bed. They must have had eleven hours of sleep by now.

I head over to Zach's side and shake him by his shoulder to wake him. He startles awake with an abbreviated shout before I clamp a hand over his mouth.

A muffled scream makes it past my hand.

"Quiet," I whisper sharply. "It's me. Dad."

He subsides and I remove my hand. The last thing we need is to attract Dregs to our position when we're just about to go outside and wait for one of those transports.

Gaby sits up, blinking sleepily at us.

"We need to get some food in your bellies," Bree whispers. "Come on."

I leave Zach to crawl out of bed by himself and then walk around to Gaby's side and scoop her up. She wraps arms and legs around me and her head drops to my shoulder.

We reach the kitchen and Bree serves us a cold breakfast from our supply of rations. Another can of processed meat for Gaby, more cereal for Zach, and a can of pork and beans for me and Bree.

We eat quickly and quietly around the kitchen island. As soon as I'm done with my can of beans, I wash them down with a glass of water from the tap. The pressure is back up. Maybe we'll get lucky and the water supply will hold. I hope it's safe to drink the water, but I guess we'd know by now if it wasn't. I run back to the bedroom to grab the clock and the flashlight. It's still dark out. The clock reads: 05:51.

We need to hurry. Rushing back to the kitchen, I set the clock on the island so everyone can see the time. "Hustle up. We've got to go."

I take the shotgun from Bree, flick on the tac light beneath the barrel, and hand her the flashlight instead. Her eyebrows lift in question as she stares at the gun.

"We can't let them see us with that," she says.

"It's still dark out," I explain. "We'll hide it before we leave."

Gaby drains her glass of water and jumps down from one of the bar stools. Zach goes next. Both of them are moving for the front door. Bree steps in front of them with her arms crossed.

"Not so fast." She's looking them over with a critical eye. They're still wearing the clothes they slept in, but she managed to get them showered and changed before bed, so they're clean enough.

Maybe she's wondering if they should brush their teeth.

The sheer absurdity of that thought lifts one corner of my mouth in a grim smile.

"Cavities are the least of our worries right now," I say as I breeze by.

"How did you know I was thinking about that?" Bree whispers back as she follows me down the hall.

"We've been married thirteen years."

"How are we going to get out?" Bree whispers, changing the topic as we approach the front entrance that I boarded up yesterday.

I stop at the door to the garage and spare a hand from the shotgun to turn the deadbolt. "Through here," I whisper.

Cracking the door open, I stick the barrel of the shotgun through. A quick sweep with the beam of the tac light reveals the garage is empty and the doors are both still shut.

I lead the way down a short flight of stairs. Heading straight to the nearest of the two garage doors, I set the shotgun aside. Grabbing whatever handholds I can find on the steel frame inside the door, I heave with my back and arms. The door grinds and screeches, riding up a few inches before I have to take a break.

Giving myself a few seconds to recover, I try again and buy myself a few more inches.

Once I have it up to about a foot and a half, I make a gimme gesture to Bree. She hands over the flashlight, and I drop down to my belly to check the driveway.

It looks clear. No sign of Dregs. But that doesn't mean they aren't out there.

Grabbing the door again, I heave once more. The gap is almost two feet now. More than enough for us to crawl out.

"There," I say.

"What if something crawls in while we're gone?" Bree asks.

I glance back at the open door from the garage to the house. She's right. "I'll go get the keys."

Running back inside, I check the rack beside the front door. The right key is on a bear-shaped key ring that I got in Big Bear a few years ago. Taking that one and a matching set on a penlight key ring, I race back into the garage, then shut and lock the door behind me before going over to Bree and handing her the penlight key ring.

"What about you?" she asks.

"I have the other set."

Bree nods, and I lead the way to the garage door. A pale bar of light is pooling beneath it. The sun must be coming up.

"They're here," Gaby whispers.

Everyone turns to look at her. I'm about to ask how she knows that when I hear the whistling *whirr* of a troop transport pulling up outside.

"I guess that's our cue. Is everybody ready?" Heads bob affirmatively. "I'll go first." Just before I drop down to crawl out, I spare a rueful glance at the shotgun I left beside the door. I grab it and hide it behind my skis. Hopefully that'll be enough to keep it hidden. Then again, with the Chimeras' laws against looting, I don't think anyone is going to risk poking around in here.

Dropping down to my stomach, I take a second to scan the street again before crawling out. The transport is right at the end of the cul-de-sac. A group of people are walking down the driveway from the mansion at the end. An armed Chimera is waiting for them outside the vehicle.

Our old neighbors were a snooty pair of yuppies who made their fortune by investing in robotics and AI companies like the ones that put me out of a job.

But none of the people in this group look like them. Two different couples and one kid are now living in their place.

I watch as they board the transport, wondering what happens if we don't go out and join them.

"Chris?" Bree prompts me.

"Let's go." I say, and crawl out under the garage door.

If the penalty for looting is death and the penalty for owning a weapon is death, then I probably don't need to ask what the penalty is for shirking work detail.

The Chimera outside the transport turns to look at me as I emerge. A booming voice says, "You're late!"

"Sorry! We're coming." I wait for the rest of my family to emerge, then lead the way at a brisk pace. We reach the entrance of the transport and I start up the short flight of steps. All eyes are on us as we climb aboard.

The only ones inside are the ones I saw emerge from the big house at the end of the street: two women and two men, all about middle aged, and a boy who looks to be around Zach's age, sitting beside one of the two women. That must be his mother.

She gasps as I slide into the seats across from her. But her eyes aren't on me; she's looking at Gaby. She shrinks away from the aisle, pulling her son toward her as Gaby slides into the seat beside me.

"Is there something wrong?" I ask.

The woman looks away quickly, shaking her head.

"Chalkhead," the boy mutters.

"What did you say?" I ask.

His mother's head comes back around, no longer afraid, but sneering with disgust. "Don't look at her, Alex. She's a demon child."

Gaby hisses softly at that.

Bree and Zach take the seats in front of ours, and Bree turns to give the woman a deadly look. "That's my daughter you're talking about. Aside from her appearance, she's no different from any other child."

Our new neighbor sets her jaw and looks away, deliberately ignoring us.

Two more people come aboard, a young woman of maybe eighteen, and a boy around Zach's age. Their eyes widen as they spot Gaby, and they freeze up for a moment. The Chimera who was standing outside climbs aboard. "What's the hold up?" he demands. "Move!"

The butt of his rifle slams into the young woman's back. She cries out in pain and staggers forward.

"Leave her alone!" her brother cries.

"It's okay, Matty," the young woman manages.

They shuffle past us with the boy glaring at Gaby and me glaring back. His big sister looks more horrified than hostile. Gaby shrinks away from them both, practically crawling into my lap to get away. I pick her up and shimmy over to give her the window seat.

"Better?" I ask as I wrap an arm around Gaby's shoulders and pull her tight against my side to shield her from view. Gaby nods and sinks into her seat with her cranial stalks flattening like a dog's ears.

Bree catches my eye. Her gaze is full of dread. It doesn't take a genius to figure out why. If this is the reception that Gaby is getting on a bus with armed guards and *us* around to defend her, what will the kids at school do when there isn't as much supervision?

"That's everyone," the Chimera says to another one sitting in the driver's seat at the far end of the vehicle.

The door slides shut, and we jerk forward in our seats as the transport flies away, whirring and whistling as it picks up speed.

CHAPTER 12

The transport stops to pick up another six people along the way, four kids of various ages and ethnicities, and two more adults who definitely don't look like they are their parents.

Everyone seems to have found a seat, and there's even an empty row. I do a quick head count to pass the time. *The four of us, plus the seven from our neighborhood. Six more at this stop, and the two Chimeras. Nineteen in all.* With six rows of four seats, plus an extra one for the driver, these vehicles can carry twenty-five soldiers. I file that detail away for future reference and turn my attention to the view outside.

The streets are cluttered with vehicles and random debris from all the looting and general chaos that must have ensued during the first few days of the invasion. Most of the buildings in the safe zone seem to be intact, but I still don't see any signs of electricity. Every couple of intersections we cross a tangled mess of felled power lines and stoplights. I have a feeling getting our infrastructure up and running is going to be a lot harder than we'd like.

The transport veers off the main road and flies over a chain link fence. I turn to look over my shoulder, out the driver's viewscreen, and see a knot of matching transports waiting outside of a familiar brown and blue edifice.

"Arrowview!" one of the Chimeras announces.

"It'll be okay, Zach," Bree urges, nudging him toward the aisle. "Gabs and I will be right next door, okay?"

The elementary school is conveniently located right beside the middle school. I'm glad that they'll be close together.

As far as I can tell from here, both schools were untouched by the invasion. The street-facing side of the middle school is a blank, windowless cinder block wall. I'd be surprised if no one thought to take shelter in there during the invasion.

Zach reluctantly steps into the aisle. The young woman's brother gets up, too, as does the boy who called Gaby a "chalkhead," and two of the four kids who came aboard at the last stop. The five of them shuffle down the aisle to the exit.

"See you later, buddy!" I say, waving and adding a smile. Zach nods stoically, saying nothing as he walks down the steps and disappears outside with the others.

Gaby and I watch him go through our window. He joins a trickling stream of other kids from matching black transports parked around us. Together they make a line to the painted blue metal doors of the school and begin filing into the featureless brown cinder block building. A pair of armed Chimeran guards stand by the entrance of the school with a regular human inside waving the kids in. It gives me a chill to see the guards.

They have soldiers guarding a school?

Maybe that's because the safe zone hasn't been cleared of Dregs yet. But then a darker possibility enters my mind. What if they're here to keep the kids in line? Would they shoot children the way they shot my mother?

A scowl furrows my brow. Zach looks back at us. I wave to him through the window. Bree appears suddenly leaning over my shoulder and blows him a kiss.

But Zach doesn't seem to see either of us. The windows must be tinted. My heart is in my throat as the door of our vehicle slides shut. I want to get up and go after Zach. What if something happens to him? I'd never forgive myself.

The transport jerks into motion once more, and Bree grabs my shoulder to steady herself. A whirring sound fills the air as we fly up and straight over the fence to the elementary school next door. Our vehicle sets down a moment later in front of the school and behind three other transports that are already offloading young kids.

"Okay, Gabs," Bree says, straightening in the aisle and holding out a hand to our daughter. "Our turn."

This building has a much more inviting entrance. I read the name off the top: George R. Brown Elementary, and below that, a sign that says Welcome.

The Chimera in the driver's seat repeats the name, announcing the stop.

"Come on, Gaby," Bree says again, wiggling her fingers to indicate her outstretched hand.

Gaby tucks harder against my side and shakes her head.

"Your mother will be with you the whole time," I whisper to her. "You're going to be in Mommy's class."

"I don't want to," Gaby says.

"We don't have a choice, sweetheart," Bree adds.

She shakes her head again.

The others are piling up behind Bree, looking impatient.

One of the two Chimeras at the back (or front?) of the vehicle gets up and shoves his way down the aisle to reach us. A woman cries out as he steps on her toes. He stops behind us with one hand resting casually on the grip of his rifle. "Is there a problem over here?" he asks in that deep, husky voice that all the Chimeras seem to share.

"No problem," I say through a tight smile. Coming to my feet, I pick Gaby up and physically set her down in the aisle in front of her mother.

"No..." Gaby pouts, looking and sounding like she's about to burst into tears.

"Come on, baby," Bree says. "We can do this." She starts nudging Gaby down the aisle, pushing her gently as she walks.

"Daddy!" Gaby cries, reaching back for me.

"I'll see you soon. Go with your mother!"

Gaby's forehead wrinkles up. Tears slip down her cheeks. "Go!" I say again. "You'll be fine!" She slowly turns around and shuffles down the aisle. I catch Bree's eye for a moment. "Love you."

"Me, too."

There are so many other things embedded in those few words, things we need to say, but don't. After thirteen years of marriage, sometimes words just get in the way of what needs to be said.

I watch Bree and Gaby slip away, down the steps, then turn to stare through the window as they walk together to the double doors of the elementary school. Another two Chimeras are guarding that entrance, just like they were at Arrowview.

I swallow thickly past the aching knot in my throat, and take a deep breath. *They're going to be okay. They have to be.*

The door slides shut again, and the transport jerks into motion, yanking my family out of sight. I twist around for one last glimpse—

And see the darkness inside the school swallow them whole.

"Next stop, Station 224," the driver says.

I glance around the inside of the transport, taking in the people around me: the mother of the boy who bullied Gaby. She has short blonde hair, ice-blue eyes, and a leathery face that suggests she's pushing fifty. That, or she really likes the sun.

The man sitting alone behind her has a scraggly brown and gray beard. He's wearing a black 66ers baseball cap, and a denim vest over a blood-stained t-shirt.

Sitting opposite him, one row back from me, is a married couple. Or, at least, some type of couple. The woman is leaning on the man's shoulder, looking apprehensive. She's relatively pretty, and maybe only thirty-something. She has long dark hair like Bree's. A big black man sits beside her. He has a thick crop of stubble on his face and looks like he probably spends a lot of time working out, but I don't recognize him from my gym.

Behind them is the young woman whose brother got off with Zach. She has long wavy brown hair and eyes to match.

Across the aisle from her are the two adults who came aboard with the four kids from the street behind mine. A young, small-bodied Asian man, and an equally young Latina woman with long black hair and a face that would be pretty if she hadn't injected her lips with so many fillers.

Their kids are all at school, but there's no way that these two are their parents. They're too young, and those kids looked nothing like them.

Some kind of foster situation? I wonder.

That makes sense, considering that a lot of parents will be either missing or dead. But who assigns orphans to homes? Do the Chimeras pick couples without children, or just assign orphans to households at random?

It only takes a few minutes before the transport begins slowing and dropping back down for a landing. We jerk to a stop and the vehicle touches asphalt with a *thunk.* I see the fire station outside. Both of the engines are missing from the open garage. Groups of people stand at attention in orderly rows, assembled for inspection like they're in the army. Chimeras are walking along the length of each group, looking them over. Another type of alien hybrid is there with them: the massive four-legged ones.

Horvals.

"Everybody out! This is the last stop," the driver barks at us.

I'm the first one to my feet. Stepping into the aisle, I glance back at the others, and say, "Let's get this over with."

A mixture of shaky smiles and apprehensive looks meet mine.

I lead the way to the open door of the vehicle, wondering absently if they're all new arrivals like me, or if some of them have worked with the clean-up crews before. Those apprehensive looks make me think the latter. Their experience has taught them to be less eager than me. And that raises the question: what do they know that I don't?

CHAPTER 13

My feet touch the ground, and I hear Chimeras shouting instructions as they walk up and down the length of the assembled groups of humans.

Not knowing what I'm supposed to do, I aim for the nearest Chimera to report for duty.

He's busy pacing in front of a line of ten men and women. A Horval is padding along behind him, snorting and snarling like a bear.

Like all of the hybrids, the Horvals have ghostly white skin whorled with black veins, but they wear only a token set of armor, leaving their heads and arms exposed. They have four thick, trunk-like legs and two powerful arms curled against their chests. Broad, high jaws and stubby snouts full of jutting, interlocking white teeth. Bony spikes line their massive, hairless heads. Two dark red eyes the size of golf balls sit to either side of their snouts, and their wrinkled necks slowly inflate and deflate as they breathe.

Bulky rifles rest in chest harnesses, but from what I remember of fighting the Horvals up in Big Bear, they prefer their claws and teeth to guns.

That actually made them surprisingly easy to kill. I suppose that might mean the Horvals are less intelligent than us, which would explain the way they're shadowing the armored human Chimeras.

I stop my approach at a cautious distance from the human hybrid and its four-legged *pet*. Someone sucks in a sharp breath behind me.

"What is that?"

I turn to see that it's the young woman from the transport. Her brown eyes are wide as she stares at the Horval. I wonder where she's been if she hasn't seen one of those creatures yet.

"Dreg-killers," the big black man says. The woman clinging to his side cringes at the mention of Dregs, and he jerks his chin to indicate the Horval. "Our hybrids send them into nests to clear them."

"They don't get infected?" the young woman asks.

The black man arches an eyebrow at her. "Where you been?" he asks. "The Chimeras are all immune. It's *us* who have to worry. We're *Dakkas,* as they like to say. *Sewer rats.* Useless chaff. If we get infected, we turn into Dregs, not Chimeras."

"They tested you, too?" I ask.

"They test everyone they bring in," the black

man replies.

"What are we supposed to do now?" asks the woman with short blonde hair, the one who sneered at Gaby.

Behind us, the transport whirrs to life. Armored boots touch pavement, and I see one of the two Chimeras that were on board stalking toward us. Our vehicle flies away, and the Chimera stops a few paces away. "Make a line!" he shouts at us.

I stay right where I am, but everyone else hurries to line up on either side of me. The Chimera appears to focus on me. He crosses the gap between us.

"Am I going to have trouble from you, Dakka?"

"My name's Chris."

"Dakka."

"Chalkhead," I reply.

An armored fist slams into the side of my head, staggering me into the black man, and leaving my ear ringing on that side.

"The Kyron Federation has a zero-tolerance policy for defiance," the Chimera says, raising his voice. "That means no back talk, and you do what I say, when I say it, and without hesitation!"

The Chimera turns and starts walking down our line.

The black guy beside me whispers, "Either you've got nothing to lose, or you're dumber than you look. Watch yourself, man."

I recover slowly, straightening with a grimace and gently probing the injured side of my head. It feels soft and spongy, as if it's already swollen. That, or the Chimera busted my skull open and I'm touching brains.

The Chimera reaches the end of our line, then turns, heading back the other way. To my right is the young woman. She shrinks back a step as the Chimera approaches. He stops in front of her, and my whole body tenses up, getting ready for a fight.

"Get back in line," the Chimera intones.

"O-okay." She takes a hesitant step forward.

The Chimera continues on. "Since some of you are new here, I'm going to explain what we do. Listen up, because I won't repeat myself. This is Gamma Crew, and I am its leader. One of our jobs is to find dead bodies and burn them before the stench attracts Dregs. Number two, we look for nests of Dregs, and we send in the Horvals to clear them. Number three, we scavenge for rations, weapons, clean clothing, blankets—anything and everything that could be useful. We deposit those items in collection crates, and we do *not* attempt to withhold any of those items for ourselves. Stealing is strictly prohibited and punishable by summary execution, do I make myself clear?"

My group mumbles affirmatively. "Good. Any questions? Now is the time to ask."

I nod and take half a step forward. "What

happens when there isn't any food left to scavenge?"

"Scouring the Wastes for rations is only a temporary mandate, until the Krya get all of their factories up and running."

Factories? I think to myself. That's a new piece of information. I wonder what they're going to be producing besides food. That broadcast we saw in Big Bear, the one where the Kyra were using our president like a hand puppet to dictate the terms of our surrender, mentioned rebuilding our cities, so construction materials is another possibility. But we're going to need a whole lot more than that: clothes, food, toilet paper—diapers!

"What about weapons?" the young woman asks.

The Chimera looks to her. "Weapons?"

"You said one of our jobs is to look for Dregs. How do we defend ourselves if we find them?"

"By running away and leaving them to us," the Chimera says darkly.

The girl swallows thickly and nods.

"Are we all clear on our mission?" the Chimera asks, looking up and down our line.

Heads bob and scattered mutterings of agreement fill the air.

"What do we call you?" I ask.

The Chimera's helmet finds me and he holds my gaze for a protracted second, as if remembering that I called him a *chalkhead* a moment ago.

"Corporal Ward," he says. "Hold your positions. I'll be back in a minute." Ward turns and strides away, heading for the fire station. I see big, hulking shadows in there.

"Where's he going?" the young woman asks.

"To get our Horval," the black man replies. "We call him Hank."

"Hank the Horval?" I ask, smiling grimly.

"That's right. Hey, you're Chris, right?"

I nod, and he sticks out a hand.

"Sam. Welcome to Gamma Crew."

"Thanks," I say, shaking his hand.

Looking back to the fire station, I see a group of humans in flak jackets and urban gray fatigues running past the entrance with two Chimeras in the lead. The humans are carrying Union Army rifles, with matching sidearms holstered at their hips.

"I thought we weren't allowed to carry weapons?" I ask.

"We're not. *They* are," Sam says.

"And who are they?"

"We call them Gladiators. People like us who can't become Chimeras, but with combat training—former military, mostly. They go out into the Wastes with the Chimeras to conduct search and rescue and bring in more survivors."

"Collaborators."

"We're all collaborators at this point, man."

My heart sinks. Maybe that was what we heard last night. It wasn't a human resistance, just these Gladiators fighting off Dregs.

"Are they brainwashed like the Chimeras?"

Sam shakes his head. "Not as far as I know."

"Then why risk it? Giving our soldiers guns seems like inviting trouble."

"There's a selection process of some kind. But the Chimeras don't really have a choice. They're stretched too thin as it is, and they can't do everything by themselves."

"Hmmm."

"What?" Sam asks.

"Just thinking. I wonder what it takes to get on one of those teams."

Sam drops his voice to a whisper. "If you're thinking what I think you're thinking, you'd better scrap that thought. There's nothing to gain. We lost."

"Yeah, maybe," I whisper back.

Switching mental tracks, I look away from the Gladiators to glance up and down the line of people around me. "You want to make the introductions?" I ask Sam. "I get the feeling we're going to be spending a lot of time together."

Sam winces. "Maybe, maybe not. There were ten of us in this crew yesterday. Now there's only nine, and that's with two new arrivals. You and..." Sam looks at the girl beside me.

"Ellie," she supplies.

"Ellie," Sam confirms.

"You lost three people in one day?" I ask.

Sam nods slowly. "And that was *inside* the

safe zone. Nowhere is safe anymore, saf*er* maybe, but not safe."

My mind flashes back to the Dreg that greeted us after we returned to our home. "Yeah, I guess so."

Sam points to the dark-haired woman beside him. "This is my wife, Naomi."

"Hi," she says.

"Nice to meet you," I reply.

Beside her is the guy with the scraggly beard and the 66ers cap. "I'm Grant," he says in a gruff voice.

"Those two are fairly new as well," Sam adds, pointing down to the couple on the other side of Ellie.

"Haruto," the Asian man says in a perfect American accent.

"We just call him Harry," Sam adds. "Then there's his girlfriend—"

"Ana Lucia," she says in a Spanish accent, before Sam can introduce her.

"And finally, we have Helen."

That's the woman whose son insulted Gaby. She doesn't even look at me when she's introduced. She's too busy watching the fire house where Corporal Ward went.

"Hey, Helen! We're talking to you!" Sam calls.

Her head comes around. "Be quiet," she says through her teeth. "You want to get us into trouble?"

Sam shrugs. "Maybe just you."

Helen scowls.

I think I'm starting to like Sam.

Helen's ice-blue eyes find me and narrow to slits. Her attitude and demeanor remind me somewhat of Jessica Pearson. I wonder what happened to her and the kids and Doctor Turner.

"You're the one with the demon girl," Helen says.

It takes me a second to realize that she's talking about Gaby.

"Watch it," I growl.

Helen huffs and looks back to the fire house.

"How did that happen?" Sam asks me in a whisper. "Did your girl get bitten out in the Wastes?"

I'm about to tell him the real story of how Gaby got infected, but then I catch myself. Telling people that my daughter is the result of possibly experiments conducted by 'heretics' is probably a bad idea. "Yeah," I say instead. "We didn't know what was happening to her."

"You're lucky she didn't infect you while she was turning. That happens a lot. Strange, though... I haven't seen any Chimeran kids around. You'd think there'd be at least a few of them in the zone by now."

That catches my attention. Suddenly I'm staring at Sam. He's at eye level with me, standing head and shoulders above the others. "What do you mean?"

Sam shrugs. "Harry and Ana were assigned

to look after four little rascals, all of them orphans, right? But not one of them is a Chimera. Your girl is the first hybrid we've seen who isn't a soldier with the Kyron Guard. So where are all the kids who got infected?"

"Maybe kids are immune?" I suggest.

"They're not. They go to the academy," Helen interrupts.

We all look to her. "The academy?" I ask.

"How do you know?" Sam adds.

"Because my stepson was taken there after he turned."

That's a surprise. She was sneering at my daughter when her own son is a Chimera?

"How old was he?" I ask, my mind racing for an explanation that might make Gaby exempt from going to the academy.

"Fourteen," Helen replies. "It's some kind of military school. I'm surprised they didn't take your girl there during processing."

I'm feeling cold all over. Is that why Gaby has been getting so much attention from the Chimeras? Because she's not supposed to be here?

Helen looks smug. "You didn't know?"

"I have to get back to the school…" I mutter, glancing around quickly to get my bearings.

"Too late now," Sam whispers, jabbing me in the ribs with his elbow.

Corporal Ward is back with Hank the Horval. That monster is busy licking bright red blood from its bony black lips and jutting white teeth.

What was it eating? I'm not sure I want to know.

Both Corporal Ward and Hank stop in front of me. The Horval snarls, its nostrils flaring and cranial stalks twitching, as if it can tell that I'm thinking about making a run for it.

Maybe Gaby was some kind of an exception because she's so young. That must be it. *We've got time,* I tell myself, willing it to be true.

"Let's move out," Ward says. He turns and leads the way toward an empty parking lot beside the fire station. Our Horval follows him and we trail cautiously behind.

Five more groups fall in around us as we go, each of them led by a Chimera and another Horval. The air shimmers ahead of us, and a large black vehicle appears with six cylindrical engines arrayed around a central hull.

It's one of the Kyra's landers, like the one we encountered in Big Bear.

* * *

The lander is just as I remember it, about five stories high, square at the base, and as wide as a tennis court. A landing ramp leads up to a set of doors in the side of the central hull. Corporal Ward leads us to those doors, and they open in advance of his approach, revealing a large, dimly-lit airlock. Fuzzy blue light strips frame the inner set of doors. They spring open, and we proceed into an octagonal room.

I've seen all of this before, but I'm looking around with Ellie as if it's the first time. Revealing my previous encounters with the so-called *Kyron heretics* might not end well for me.

The ceiling in this chamber is at least twelve feet high, and six sets of extra-wide doors lead to each of the cylindrical engine segments. The floor is covered in thick metal grates concealing crawl spaces full of machinery. Curving, illuminated tubes rise up from the floor at the far end of the space. To one side of them is the open entrance of a winding access ramp.

"All the way to the back," Corporal Ward says, waving us on. "Hustle up! Make room for the others!"

We paste ourselves to the far wall. Our Horval pads over to one of the engine segments. Stacks of big black rectangular crates flank some of those doors.

Hank reaches for the control panel with one massive three-fingered hand. He makes a swiping gesture, and the doors slide open to reveal a large, dimly lit compartment. I don't get more than a glimpse of it before the doors slam shut behind Hank.

The other crews crowd in with us, and each of their Horvals goes through the doors to one of the other engine segments. Six segments, six Horvals, six crews.

I glance around, trying to figure out who's in charge. The Chimeras all look the same in their armor. No distinguishing features to indicate their ranks. The Chimeran team leaders stay in the main chamber with us, none of them making a move to ascend to one of the lander's higher levels. Both sets of airlock doors slam shut, and a moment later, there comes a meaty *roar* from the engines.

The ship shudders and shakes, and I feel a subtle tug as we lift off. I look around for some way to brace myself, but the sensation of movement abruptly vanishes.

"Is something wrong?" I whisper to Sam. "We stopped."

He shakes his head. "They have some kind of tech to cancel out the sensation of movement."

"That's... impressive." *And that's an understatement,* I think to myself as I glance around the interior of the ship. The deck is crowded with more than fifty people counting the Chimeras. Everyone is standing around, shuffling their feet, talking in low tones. I don't see any of those armed human collaborators in here with us. The Gladiators must have taken another lander.

I have to hand it to the Kyra, it's only been five days since they arrived, and they've already managed to organize us to the point that this operation is not only running smoothly, but it's actually become routine.

"Where are we going?" Ellie asks quietly.

"Maybe to the Wastes," Sam replies. "We were working in the zone yesterday, and they seem to like rotating details in and out of the zones."

A jolt of dread shoots through me. "Corporal Ward said one of our jobs is to burn the dead bodies because they attract Dregs. I thought he was talking about the safe zone."

"He was, but we're constantly expanding to make more room for survivors. That means clearing out the Dregs, then moving the fence. After that, we find and burn the bodies, and then salvage whatever we can from the area. Rinse and repeat. How do you think we've established such a big perimeter in such a short time?"

I'm not sure what I thought, but the idea of going into a hostile environment without even so much as a knife to defend myself has my heart pounding.

"I'm starting to see how you lost three people yesterday."

Sam nods grimly. "Stay close to the Chimeras and the Horvals and you'll make it home to see your kids tonight."

I nod back, thinking to myself, at least I've got combat experience. That'll give me an edge, but what about the rest of these people? All regular civilians by the look of them, and some of them are still just kids, like Ellie.

"They should be giving us guns," Ellie says in a shaky voice.

"You're preaching to the choir, girl," Sam says. "But not many of us would know how to use them if they did. We'd be just as likely to shoot each other as the Dregs."

Sam actually makes a good point, but if that's the reason we don't have any weapons, then maybe I should reveal my background to Corporal Ward. I'll be a lot more useful with a weapon than I'll be without.

CHAPTER 14

I don't even notice that we've landed until the airlock doors spring open, followed by the doors to the Horvals' compartments. Our Chimeran commanders bark orders at us, and we march out into the parking lot of a Frugal Foods supermarket. The Horvals follow us out, each of them somehow knowing how to find their particular units. I'm glad they can tell us apart, because they all look the same to me.

It takes me a second to recognize where we are. It's the same plaza we passed outside the gates when we were brought to the safe zone yesterday.

Overturned shopping carts and mounds of spoiled food litter the parking lot. A scattering of parked cars are still here, along with the shattered debris of what might have been air cars caught flying overhead when the EMP hit.

A fine dusting of ash covers everything like dirty snow, but the air isn't as smoky as it was yesterday. The wind must have changed directions, or else the fires burned out. Probably too soon for that. The Kyra turned LA into a crater, after all. I hope we don't need to worry about radioactive fallout.

"What are we waiting for?" Ellie asks as the other crews fan out around the parking lot, heading for their target buildings in the plaza.

"That," Sam says, pointing back up the ramp to the inside of our lander.

The black crates I saw stacked inside the vessel are now floating out, defying gravity by unseen means. Four of the crates stop beside our crew. The rest fly after the other teams, two crates per team, following them to their destinations.

"Fall-in," Corporal Ward says. "We're going to clear the supermarket and collect rations." He and Hank turn and start across the parking lot to the entrance of the Frugal Foods.

We follow them at a cautious distance, none of us speaking. Ellie is sticking close to me, Sam, and Naomi.

Helen brings up the rear, followed by Grant, then Harry and Ana. A pecking order has been established.

A dark cloud catches my eye as it drifts in front of the rising sun. Staring at it for a moment, I realize that it's not a cloud. It's one of the Kyra's cruisers. Fuzzy streams of black specks trail from it like tentacles. They're writhing and changing shapes, splitting into groups of four specks and then taking up positions around the cruiser.

It's a fighter escort, I realize.

The cruiser comes about, and the sun emerges, dazzling my eyes. I blink to clear them and throw a hand up to shield my gaze.

"It looks like that cruiser is headed this way," I say.

"Maybe they're coming to drop off another factory," Sam says.

"*Another* factory?" I ask.

Sam nods. "They landed the first one at the airport. It's already churning out building materials. How do you think we built the fence for the perimeter?"

"I thought maybe we salvaged the material. It looked like a plain-old chain-link to me."

"It is. The Kyra aren't here to redecorate. Everything they produce for us is copied and usually recycled from something that we're already familiar with. Maybe they think we'll be more comfortable that way, or they just don't want to share more advanced designs. Either way..." Sam trails off as Corporal Ward stops and holds up a closed fist indicating that we should stop as well.

We're about twenty feet from the broken glass doors of the Frugal Foods.

Everyone stops talking, and we watch as the corporal slowly turns his head back and forth. I realize he's looking for something, and wonder if the Chimeras have some type of sensors integrated in their suits.

"I'm reading at least ten Dregs inside," the corporal says after a moment, confirming my suspicions.

Ten Dregs, and I had trouble yesterday just dealing with *one.*

Ward growls something unintelligible to our Horval. It snorts like a bull and advances slowly on the supermarket.

The nine of us watch breathlessly. I glance around, checking for other entrances to the supermarket. There's one down to our left.

I point to it and whisper to Sam, "Shouldn't someone be covering that exit before we send in Hank to flush out the Dregs? We could get outflanked."

"Good point," he whispers back. "Be ready to run if that happens."

I wonder if Ward isn't bothering to cover those doors because he's sloppy, or because he knows something that I don't. Maybe Dregs flock mindlessly to targets like moths to a flame.

The seconds pass slowly with my heart hammering in my chest. I check the others behind us. Helen looks terrified. Harry and Ana are both fidgeting restlessly.

A loud crash sounds from the supermarket, and all three of them flinch.

Then comes a cacophony of shrieking and

snarling, followed by pitiful screams. It goes on for a while, punctuated by more crashes...

And then silence.

After a few seconds of that, Corporal Ward shuffles his feet and starts looking around.

"What's going on?" Ellie whispers.

Corporal Ward shakes his head. "I've lost contact with the Horval."

"You're kidding, right?" Sam asks.

As if by some unspoken agreement, everyone starts backing away from the doors. I keep pace with Sam, watching his reaction. He looks scared.

"Hold your position, Dakkas," Ward growls. "I'm going in to finish the job."

Corporal Ward raises his rifle and begins stalking toward the broken entrance of the supermarket.

Of course, he's not scared. He's covered from head to toe in armor. Dregs can't possibly get through that with only claws and teeth, and he can't get infected even if they could.

But a niggling thread of doubt worms its way into my head. If the Dregs are so defenseless, then what happened to Hank?

"I don't like this," Sam says quietly. His eyes dart to the other entrance and back.

"What is it?" Helen whispers, pulling alongside us.

"We send in the Horvals to clear out nests for a reason. Their hide is too thick for Dregs to bite through. So how did they kill Hank?"

Before anyone can venture a guess, the screeching reports of laser fire echo out of the supermarket, accompanied by flickering flashes of emerald light.

A moment later, Corporal Ward comes running back out. "It's a swarm! Run!"

Then comes the ground-shaking thunder of a stampede. Pale-faced, hairless dregs in stained and soiled clothing emerge from the supermarket en masse, shrieking and scrambling after the Corporal.

It takes a second for us to recover from our shock and come unglued from the pavement. "Move, move, move!" I shout, all but physically shoving the others ahead of me.

We sprint across the parking lot, heading for the lander.

Cracking reports fill the air and blinding green lasers flash out from the top of the vessel, drawing shrieks of pain from the Dregs. I twist around to look. There must be hundreds of them, and they're gaining fast. As I watch, they overtake Corporal Ward and he gets sucked under and trampled. Flickering green lasers flash out in all directions, and then abruptly stop.

Did they somehow manage to kill him, even with his amor? I pull ahead of Grant, Helen, and Ana, catching up with Sam, Naomi, and Ellie at the front. "Run faster!" I cry, hoping to spur them on.

"I *can't* run any faster!" Helen screams. Glancing over my shoulder, I see that she's clutching her side from what's probably just a cramp. But Grant is bringing up the rear and limping from a more genuine impediment.

"Come on!" I scream at them.

"Go!" Grant shouts back through a grimace. "I'll slow them down!"

"Are you crazy?" I sputter.

But he's already stopped running. He holds out both arms in surrender. "Come and get me motherf—"

The swarm of Dregs knock him down before he can finish.

I whirl back to the fore and push myself to run faster. The lander is at least two hundred feet away.

"We're never going to make it," Sam gasps.

My eyes alight on a bright yellow school bus parked off to one side. It's maybe only forty feet away.

"Over there!" I point to it as I pull ahead of Sam and Ellie. A touch of survivors' guilt nags in the back of my mind as I realize that being the faster runner here gives me the best chance of survival.

Flashes of laser fire from the lander are strobing all around us. The glare of it is too much and brings tears to my eyes. The lander's barrage is better than nothing, but the Dregs aren't falling back, and their numbers aren't thinning fast enough. It's like they've lost all sense of self-preservation.

Helen screams desperately behind us. With Grant gone, she's next. "Help me, please! Someone help!"

Throwing another glance over my shoulder, I can tell she's just seconds from going out the way that Grant and Corporal Ward did. Harry has fallen back a few steps to drag Ana along, but after the swarm gets Helen, the two of them will be next.

I'm not even sure if getting to that school bus can save us. There's just too many of them. They'll break the door and the windows and then drag us out. But what other chance do we have?

I could just keep running. I might be able to make it to the lander on my own. I have a family to think about. I don't know these people.

But I could also try to lead the swarm away, to be the distraction while the rest of my crew gets to safety.

Just then, I spot a familiar object amongst the overturned shopping carts and scattered items in the parking lot: a gleaming aluminum baseball bat. And right beside it is the galvanized metal lid of a trash can, as if someone was wielding those items like a sword and shield.

Veering off from my beeline for the bus, I grab the bat and the garbage lid, and then turn and run *toward* the swarm. It's a seething sea of feral red eyes, gnashing teeth and churning limbs.

Lasers are flashing into their ranks from the lander, incinerating Dregs two and three at a time, but there are still a hundred more where they came from.

Harry and Ana flash by me, followed by Helen. She's gasping raggedly for air, the spittle flying from her lips.

And then it's just me standing between the Dregs and their next meal. "You want me?" I scream at them while smacking the bat into the trash can lid to get their attention. "Come and get me!"

Spinning away, I run at a forty-five-degree angle from the bus, screaming at the top of my lungs and banging my bat and shield together to make sure the swarm stays focused on me.

After a few seconds of that, I look back to check on the swarm. They've veered away from the others, and now they're chasing me.

I almost don't believe it. My plan is working.

Now I just have to make sure I don't stop running. But I can't run forever, so where am I running to?

CHAPTER 15

Countless feet slapping asphalt and the shrieking roars of the Dregs spur me to run faster. I'm still banging my bat and shield together to keep their attention.

It's working. The rest of my crew made it to the bus, and all but a handful of the Dregs are chasing me.

I'm aiming for a pair of buildings on the other end of the plaza with several more school buses parked out front. At least one of those buildings must be a school. I'll either take shelter in there or in one of the buses.

A bright green laser flashes over my shoulder, missing the horde, or maybe passing straight through it. The pavement explodes beside me in a searing rain of debris.

Up ahead, the doors of the school burst open, and the Horvals come bounding out, followed closely by the rest of the Chimeran team leaders.

Reinforcements. Perfect. My legs and lungs

are burning, and I'm reaching the limits of my endurance. *Not much farther,* I tell myself.

Dregs are snorting and snarling behind me. A frantic look back reveals that the faster ones have pulled ahead, and they're actually gaining on me.

I pour on a burst of speed and widen the gap once more. By now I'm seeing spots. I can't draw air into my lungs fast enough to supply my screaming muscles. My head is spinning. Stinging rivers of sweat drip into my eyes, and they blur with tears.

Come on, Chris! I scream to myself, squinting to see through the film of tears and sweat.

The Horvals tear past me, and suddenly their snarls and roars mix with the shrieking of the Dregs. The Chimeran team leaders make a line and start shooting. Lasers are flashing by me on both sides now, blinding me even more thoroughly.

I reach the Chimeras and careen to a stop behind their line. Dropping my bat and shield from nerveless fingers, I fall on my hands and knees.

Pins and needles are shooting up and down my limbs as my circulation gradually catches up. My ears are ringing and they feel stuffy. I glance back the way I came, hardly able to believe that I made it. The Chimeras pour streams of laser fire into the swarm while the Horvals tear it apart from within.

Despite their efforts, at least fifty Dregs are still going to reach us. I watch as two of the Chimeras begin backing up steadily.

"We'll be overrun!" one of them screams.

"Hold the line!" another says.

One of the four turns and runs for the safety of the school. The other three stay where they are for a few more seconds. And then a second one breaks ranks and runs to join the first.

I grab my bat and shield and push off the ground. The Dregs are close enough now that I can begin to see their individual features. They're all in various stages of turning. Some still have scraps of hair clinging to their heads. Others are fully turned and looking as alien as can be.

Taking a few steps forward, I join the two Chimeras who are still holding their ground.

One of them notices me standing there. "Are you crazy?" he asks. "Get into cover!"

Maybe two dozen Dregs are still running toward us. The others are engaged with the Horvals and getting literally ripped to shreds.

"Give me a gun!" I shout, eying the sidearm on the belt of the Chimera beside me.

But he makes no move to offer the weapon.

Glancing back at the school, I see that the two who ran for cover are still firing into the swarm from the open doors of the building. They might have had the right idea. I'm not sure what this blaze of glory is about, but I like our odds much better with those doors as a barrier to keep the Dregs out.

Running back to the school, I approach the doors from the side to avoid getting hit by a laser beam from one of the Chimeras' rifles.

Suddenly the shrieking roars of the Dregs intensifies. Both of the remaining Chimeras have been knocked down, and they're thrashing under the assault as Dregs tear at their armor and weapons. The two by the doors have stopped firing.

"I can't get a clear shot!" one of them says.

Then the horde splits and a group of them comes running toward us.

"Shit!" one of the Chimeras says.

"Close the doors!"

"Hey, wait!" I say, stepping into view just as the entrance begins swinging shut.

The Chimeras shut the doors in my face, leaving me alone with the other two to face the horde.

Cursing under my breath, I spin around and find myself facing a group of six Dregs, approaching fast. The first one is already within reach: a man with sallow white cheeks, black lips, and bloodshot eyes. His slavering jaws are full of yellow teeth, several of which are already missing.

I swing my bat as hard as I can. It whistles and hits his skull with a ringing *crunch.* The Dreg goes down, and I raise my shield to ward off the next one in line.

Shoving back, I manage to deflect its momentum, and it crashes into the doors of the school. Backpedaling fast, I swing my bat again at a third Dreg. This time I hit it in the ribs. Something gives way, and it shrieks and staggers sideways.

Swinging my bat like a madman, I hit another Dreg in the head, and it goes down like the first.

Still four left. The three uninjured ones charge me at the same time. I push back against two of them with the shield, spinning away to avoid their swiping claws and flashing teeth.

I manage to get behind them and put some distance between us. I drop my shield in a risky move to get more force behind the bat. The injured Dreg darts in on my left flank. I elbow it in the throat and it stumbles away, making gagging sounds and sinking to its knees.

Three left. They're pacing cautiously around me, trying to outflank and corner me against the school. Maybe they're not so brainless, after all. Their eyes are all narrowed to slits and streaming with tears. I remember how Gaby reacted to sunlight when we arrived. Maybe those red eyes can't see very well in daylight.

I feint to one side, as if to make a run for it. All three of them surge blindly in the same direction. I make a two-handed swing and crack another skull.

The remaining two hiss and snarl in frustration before turning and running back to the supermarket. A bright green laser flashes out from the lander and cuts them both down in one shot.

Breathing hard, I spin in a quick arc to check for more targets. There are five Dregs mobbing the two Chimeras who held their ground, and no lasers are shooting in or out of that group. The two Chimeras on the ground are grappling physically with their assailants. Their armor is keeping the Dregs at bay, but for how long?

Whoever is manning the guns in the lander must realize they can't shoot the Dregs without hitting the Chimeras that they're trying to save.

The Horvals could help them, but they're far off, busy chasing stragglers around the parking lot.

Batter up, I think to myself as I raise my dented, bloody bat in a two-handed grip and start toward the Dregs.

And then I'm cracking skulls again while dodging furious swipes of claws and snapping teeth.

It's all over in less than a minute, and I'm the last one standing. Silence falls, broken only by the ringing echoes of my bat and the drumbeat of my own pulse in my ears.

One of the two Chimeras lies motionless in a pool of his own black blood. His helmet is off, and his throat is slashed open, his bright red eyes wide and staring. The other one also has his helmet off. The Chimeras' armor obviously has a serious design flaw, and the Dregs know it.

I walk over to the survivor and hold out a blood-spattered hand to help him up.

"Thank you," the survivor says in a deep, husky voice. But that voice is actually slightly higher than usual. As the Chimera stands up, I'm startled to see softer, more feminine features. I'm not sure why I've been assuming that all of the Chimeras are male, but this one clearly isn't.

Her red eyes are narrowed to slits, clearly bothered by the light without her helmet on. Her right cheek is bleeding from a nasty-looking gash, but otherwise she seems to be fine.

"You saved my life," she breathes, while reaching experimentally for the gash in her cheek. She probes it gently and then examines the oily smear of blood on her clawed fingertips. She hisses through sharp white teeth, and her eyes flick up to mine. "Thank you. I owe you."

I nod quietly back, not sure what to say to that.

She turns and bends down to collect her helmet. Moving on, she recovers her rifle a few feet away, and then her sidearm, about five feet farther still. It looks like the Dregs ripped their weapons away and then flung them as far as they could.

Walking back over to me, she now has both weapons holstered: the rifle dangling from her chest plate by means of an unseen clip, and the pistol at her side. She has her helmet tucked under one arm.

"I told you to get into cover," she says.

"I tried," I reply, gesturing vaguely to the sealed blue doors of the school.

"Yesss..." the Chimera trails off with a hiss. "Are you bitten or scratched?"

I check myself over briefly, then shake my head.

"You're either an amazing fighter, or an amazing idiot."

"I'll take option one. What's your name?" I ask.

"Commander Hill. I'm in charge of this operation."

"Nice to meet you. I'm Chris. By *this operation*, you mean...?"

"New San Bernardino."

My eyes widen at that. "So, you're like the mayor of the city?"

"Something like that."

A pair of blood-covered Horvals come padding over to us, interrupting the conversation.

Commander Hill slips her helmet back on, and inclines her head to me. "Let's go see who else survived," she says.

I hesitate and glance back to the school. "What about the others?"

"They know better than to come out. They are *slekess*. Exiles. Their lives are now forfeit thanks to their cowardice."

That's interesting. I thought the Chimeras were only ruthless with humans, but apparently

Chimeran life is just as cheap. "Actually, I was asking about the other human crews."

Commander Hill shrugs. "I imagine they are still hiding in the school. Few of your kind possess the courage to fight as you did, much less to save the life of a Chimera. Fall in. We need to finish clearing the area. We'll come back for them after that."

I stare after the commander for a heartbeat, wondering what it means that the leader of *New* San Bernardino now owes me her life. The two Horvals take up flanking positions on either side of her as she begins picking her way across the parking lot.

One of the remaining two Horvals is limping toward us from farther off, but there's no sign of the fourth. Maybe it died like Hank.

This was a massacre on both sides.

Remembering my crew and the school bus that I sent them to, I break into a jog to catch up with Commander Hill. Sam's and Ellie's faces flash through my mind's eye. I hope they managed to keep the Dregs out of that bus.

CHAPTER 16

"It's about time you got here!" Helen says as she steps down from the bus. Right behind her is Sam, his wife Naomi, and Ellie, followed by Harry and Ana.

They're all still alive and none of them appear to be injured.

"No one got bitten?" Commander Hill asks.

"Nope," Sam says, his eyes on the blood-covered Horvals standing to either side of the commander. He looks up and nods to me. "Thanks to him."

Commander Hill's helmet turns my way. "Yes, Christopher Randall is quite the hero it seems."

I frown slightly at that. I didn't tell her my last name. Maybe she scanned my tracking implant. If so, she might know other things about me, too, like where I live, who the members of my family are, and the fact that I'm a former Union Army corporal.

Commander Hill looks back to my crew. "All right, Gammas, let's get back on task. The supermarket is clear, and I need you to collect those rations. Corporal Ward is KIA, as is your Horval, so I'm assigning Mr. Randall as acting corporal. He will supervise ration collection and you will answer directly to him."

My eyebrows shoot up with that.

Commander Hill turns to me and draws her sidearm. "Here."

I hesitate for a second before tucking my trash can lid under one arm and reaching for the weapon.

"Is there a safety?" I ask, leaning my bat against my legs and turning the long-barreled black pistol over in my hands.

"It's already on," the commander replies. "The dial above the trigger has five settings. The symbol that looks like a curvy X locks the trigger. The next one, that looks like two wavy lines, is the kill setting. Then comes stun."

"And the other two?" I ask.

"You won't need them," Commander Hill says. "Stinger pistols get six shots to a charge pack, and I've already fired one, so you have five left. It shouldn't take more than one hit to take down a Dreg as long as you aim for the chest or the head."

I look up from the weapon, nodding slowly. "You trust me with this?"

"You saved my life, and you stayed to fight

when my own men ran away, so yes, I trust you. Don't make me regret it." Commander Hill's helmet turns back to the rest of my crew. They look even more surprised than I am. "Now if you'll excuse me, I have to go rally the other crews."

Commander Hill turns and strides away, heading back to the school. One of the two Horvals lingers, seeming to be in some type of distress. Its guts are heaving and its massive head is bowed low.

A moment later, it hacks up a severed hand, then snorts and licks its jutting teeth with a fat black tongue before turning to follow the Commander.

"Disgusting," Ellie mutters.

Helen looks like she's about to pass out.

I tuck the Stinger pistol into my belt, and pass the baseball bat and shield to Sam.

He accepts them both with a grimace, probably because they're covered in infected Dreg blood. So am I. Hopefully, it's not that easy to catch the virus.

"Let's get to work," I say, starting toward the Frugal Foods. "Maybe we'll find a sink and some soap to wash up with inside."

Sam pulls alongside me. "It didn't take you long to become a Gladiator."

"What?" I ask, not getting it.

"That Chimera gave you her gun. The only humans who get to carry guns are Gladiators."

"She made me acting corporal. It might just

be for today."

"Maybe," Sam agrees with a shrug. "Did you really save her life?"

"Yeah."

"Nice work," Sam says.

"You're not mad?"

"Why would I be mad?" he asks.

"Because they're working with the enemy, and I saved one of them."

"Corporal Ward was an asshole. Lots of Chimeras are because of their indoctrination and whatever else the Kyra do to them, but Commander Hill is one of the good ones. She doesn't just see us as Dakkas."

"You're saying she's on our side?" I ask, slowing down to meander between the bodies of dead Dregs. The parking lot is growing thick with them as we get closer to the supermarket.

"There is only one side, man—the Kyra's. Anyone who thinks otherwise is just fooling themselves."

"Right," I say, while keeping my actual thoughts to myself. There has to be a human resistance out there somewhere. Maybe not this close to one of the safe zones. But somewhere.

"You don't sound convinced," Sam says.

I shake my head and offer him a grim smile. "I'm just processing what you said. And anyway, what would be the point to resisting? It's not like we actually have a chance against the Kyra." I nod to their starship on the horizon. It looks a lot closer to us now.

Registering movement in the foreground, I stop and squint into the distance to figure out what it is. Five black specks growing swiftly in size. A whirring roar is rising with their approach.

"What are those?" I ask, pointing to them.

Sam raises a hand to his forehead to shield his eyes from the glare of the sun. "Hoverbikes. The lander pilot must have called for backup."

"They're late," I say, watching as the bikes roar overhead, circle the parking lot, and then streak down for a landing beside Commander Hill and the Horvals. The riders of those bikes look like human hybrids, rather than Kyra.

"We'd better get to work before Commander Hill catches us slacking," Sam says.

"Yeah," I agree, nodding absently, and putting one foot in front of the other once more. The shattered entrance of the Frugal Foods looms dark and ominous before us.

As we approach, the whirring roar of a hoverbike racing into view catches our attention. It stops by the entrance of the supermarket, and the rider gets off. The Chimera bends down beside one of the dead bodies.

"What's he doing?" I ask.

"Retrieving Corporal Ward's weapons before we can get any bright ideas about using them," Sam replies.

The rider packs both Corporal Ward's rifle

and his sidearm into the back of his bike and then races up and away, looping back toward the perimeter of the safe zone.

From the back of our group I hear Helen suck in a sharp breath. That gets me searching for the source of her alarm.

"Damn," Sam mutters, stopping suddenly.

Dead ahead are Grant's remains: his body was completely shredded, his clothes are drenched in blood to the point that there's no white left on his t-shirt, or any sign of his denim vest. It looks like he went through a wood chipper. The only way I can tell that it's him is by the 66ers cap lying about four feet away.

"How did they do that?"

"Claws and teeth. You've seen your daughter's claws, right?" Sam asks.

I nod uncertainly.

"They're as sharp as knives," Sam goes on. "Same as the Kyra's."

"Let's keep moving," I whisper, averting my gaze from Grant's body.

We find Corporal Ward lying just outside the entrance of the supermarket, right where that hoverbike rider stopped to recover his weapons. Ward's helmet has been ripped off just like the other Chimeras. I notice the black crates that followed us from the lander are still here, hovering mysteriously to either side of the corporal.

"Stay here," I say, drawing the 'Stinger' pistol from my belt. Turning it over, I flick the dial above the trigger from the curvy X to the two wavy lines of the *kill* setting. "Wait for my signal before coming in," I add.

"Take your time," Sam says.

Raising my borrowed weapon in a two-handed grip, I advance slowly on the supermarket. With the power out, it's impossible to see more than vague shadows inside. There could be any number of Dregs still hiding in there, and I don't even have a flashlight to see them coming. Corporal Ward had an automatic rifle, a full suite of sensors, and probably some type of infrared optics, but none of that was enough to save him. Of course, he said there were only *ten* Dregs inside when the swarm actually numbered over a hundred.

Five shots left, and it takes one shot to kill, I think, remembering what Commander Hill said about the weapon I'm holding. *As long there aren't more than five Dregs in here, I should be okay.*

Assuming I see them before they see me…

CHAPTER 17

The inside of the Frugal Foods is a mess. Flies buzz around in swarms and settle all over me no matter how many times I bat them away. Food is scattered everywhere, and the smell is horrific. I have a feeling the Dregs that were hiding in here forgot the cardinal rule of *don't shit where you eat.*

It doesn't take long for me to find Hank. He's not far from the entrance, surrounded by dead Dregs, and crushed under the weight of two overturned aisles of canned foods. Given how big the Horvals are, I'm actually surprised that was enough to kill him, but as I move in for a closer look, I notice the gleaming silver handle of a butcher's knife, sunk all the way to the hilt in the monster's wrinkled gray throat. Maybe that's a weak spot in the Horvals' anatomy. But what's even more interesting is that some of the Dregs clearly still know how to use tools.

Moving on, I stalk quietly down the aisles,

dodging sludge and scattered products on the floor. I'm checking for signs of living Dregs. Nothing yet, thank God. But while I'm at it, I'm also looking for something I can use to help me see better. Squinting up at the signs above the aisles, it's nearly impossible to read them in the gloomy light. One of the signs reads:

Automotive
Hardware
Pet

That seems promising. I start down that aisle, stepping carefully over discarded tools, car cleaning products, and broken light bulbs.

Something soft squishes under my foot and a fetid stench assaults my nose. "Shit," I mutter to myself and try unsuccessfully to shake it off the sole of my boot.

Soon I'm dodging matching piles like land mines. I make it halfway down the aisle before my eyes alight on the gleaming metal shell of a heavy-duty flashlight still hanging on a rack. Several more are lying on the floor beneath it, but they're covered in that nightmare sludge.

Lucky me, this is also the aisle for batteries. It takes a moment for me to figure out which way to load them into the flashlight before flicking it on produces the desired result.

A bright cone of light peels back the shadows in the supermarket. It's not the blessing that I thought it would be.

My surroundings are all the more horrific

now that I can see what's what. Besides the piles of raw sewage, there are half-eaten human corpses all over the place. I can't help burying my nose in my sleeve. Feeling dried blood rasp against my mouth brings my arm back down, but it's a struggle to choose between possibly infecting myself and being forced to breathe unfiltered lungfuls of this nightmare.

Keep moving, I tell myself. *Just keep moving.*

I'm almost done sweeping the aisles. After that, I can get back outside. But then comes the even more grueling task of scavenging this place for food and supplies. There seems to be plenty that the Dregs and looters haven't already ruined, but I'd far rather light a match and burn this place to the ground than try to salvage any of it.

I reach the last aisle and shine my flashlight down to the end. Something catches the light and reflects it back at me. Two bright specks, peeking around the edge of a door.

The door bangs shut, and I hear the sound of hurried footsteps receding on the other side.

My heart starts to pound, and I stand there frozen for several seconds, trying to decide what I just saw. The eyes were low to the ground, which makes me think it was a child. The fact that it didn't burst out of its hiding place and come shrieking and scrambling toward me means it wasn't a Dreg.

But how? How could a human child have survived in here with that swarm?

Snapping out of it, I run toward the door, shouting, "Hey! It's okay! You can come out now!"

It only occurs to me after I've already opened my big mouth that maybe shouting isn't a good idea.

But it probably *is* the fastest way to finish clearing this place. I wait a beat, listening for a response...

No shrieking voices or scrambling feet echo back to my ears. I guess the Dregs really did all die. Running toward the door, I spare a few fingers from my flashlight to turn the handle. It's locked. Of course, it is; how else would that kid still be alive?

Seeing the sign on the door that reads Authorized Personnel Only I realize that it must lead to the administrative section of the supermarket. There is a keyhole to open the door, but I don't have any keys. I try knocking. "Hey, kid!"

No answer.

Then I remember the alien gun in my hand. There doesn't appear to be a deadbolt, just a regular twist lock on the other side of the handle. Taking aim, I point the gun at the metal bit that goes into the jamb.

I pull the trigger. The gun goes off with a sharp report and a bright green flash of light that dazzles my eyes.

The metal door is glowing orange around the impact. I try the handle again. It's hot to the touch.

It still doesn't turn, but the door pops open with a gentle tug. Checking the other side with my flashlight, I see a brief hallway, lined with doors to offices and storage areas. At the end of that, the space opens into a break room. The floor is littered with garbage, but at least there aren't any piles of sewage.

At first, I don't see any sign of the kid, but then the beam of my flashlight bounces off the top of his head. He's hiding behind a big silver garbage bin next to an empty water cooler.

"Hey, it's okay," I say. "You can come out."

A whimper is the only reply.

I lower my gun and slowly approach. As I draw near, I get a better look and realize that it's a girl. She has long, dark brown hair and bright blue eyes. Just like Gaby used to have. She looks about the same age, too.

A lump forms in my throat as I realize how terrified she must have been, hiding in here all by herself.

I stop a few feet away from the garbage bin. "What's your name?"

Another whimper, followed by a sniffle. I realize she's crying, but she still doesn't say anything. "I'm Chris," I say. "I have a girl about your age. Can you come out? I'm not going to hurt you."

The girl stops sniffling and slowly stands up. She's filthy—her face is covered in... is that chocolate? I guess she had to survive in here somehow. Her jeans and t-shirt are stained and smeared with all kinds of residues. Hopefully just more food.

She looks up at me with trembling lips and big, terrified eyes. I must look pretty scary—six-foot-three inches tall and covered in blood from those Dregs. I drop down to my haunches to make myself less threatening.

"Where are your parents?" I ask.

She just shakes her head, and I wince.

If they were alive, they'd be in here with her. They probably turned into Dregs or got eaten by them. Either way, it was a dumb question.

"It's okay. I have people outside. We'll take care of you. Can you come out with me?"

The girl shakes her head vigorously.

"Don't worry, there aren't any more of them. We got them all."

The girl sniffles once more. "You died them?"

I smile at the odd turn of phrase. Kids. She must be a bit younger than Gaby. "Yes."

She steps out from behind the garbage can. I reach for her hand, then notice that mine is covered in crusty black blood, and think better of it. I lower my hand and gesture for her to walk with me.

"Follow me, okay?"

She nods, and I lead the way back through the admin area. Once we're back in the supermarket, the stench hits me anew. The girl whimpers and wraps her arms around my leg.

"Don't look," I say quietly, struggling on a few steps with her clinging to my leg like a crab. It doesn't really work. "Hang on." I use the flashlight to check the setting of my pistol. Setting it back to the *safety-on* position, I tuck it into my belt and then scoop the girl up into my arms.

"Better?"

She nods again.

I manage to maneuver the flashlight so I can still see where I'm going. Less than a minute later, we're stepping into the blinding light of day, and my crew comes running to greet us.

"You found a survivor," Sam says as I set her down in front of them. She shrinks back behind my legs, looking scared again.

"Oh my, you poor thing," his wife, Naomi says. "Were you in there all alone?"

"How did she survive?" Ana marvels.

"What's your name?" Ellie asks, stepping forward and then dropping to her haunches like I did.

"M-Megan," the girl says.

"Nice to meet you, Megan. I'm Ellie."

"We'd better take her back to the lander while we work," Sam says, glancing around quickly. "Just in case."

"And leave her there by herself?" Helen asks.

"I'll stay with her," Ellie says. She straightens up and holds out a hand. "Would you like that, Megan? We can be friends."

The girl hesitates, then steps out from behind my legs and takes Ellie's hand. The rest of us watch them leave.

"Someone should go with them," Naomi says after a moment.

The parking lot looks clear, but she's right. They're unarmed.

"I'll go," Sam says. He goes loping after them with the baseball bat and trash-can-lid shield.

"I guess that means we'd better get to work," Harry says, squinting in the direction of the supermarket. "You find anything useful in there?" he asks, looking back to me.

"Yeah plenty, but recovering it is not going to be fun. It's really bad in there."

Harry laughs, and his girlfriend Ana makes a face. "Let me guess, Dregs shat all over the place?"

"Shat?" I ask.

"Past tense of you know what."

"Aha." That's a new one for me. "Yes, they did."

"Animals," Ana mutters.

"That's exactly what they are," Harry says.

Helen looks like she's about to be sick.

Harry gestures with an open palm to the supermarket. "Lead the way, Corporal Chris."

CHAPTER 18

We've set up half a dozen flashlights from the hardware aisle, leaving them on shelves around us to provide basic illumination while we work. And that work is grueling. I find myself wishing for a mask, or gloves, or maybe a full-on hazmat suit, but apparently our safety isn't a priority for the Kyra.

Helen throws up for the second time and goes to stand by the door to get some air. I'm starting to wonder if that isn't actually a strategy to avoid work.

"It's almost lunch time. I'm going to wash up," Harry says from beside me.

"Lunch?" I ask, glancing around. "I'm surprised they even bother to feed us."

"They know we'll work better on a full stomach," Sam explains.

I nod absently as I reach for another can of food. We're both filling the same shopping cart with items that seem to be intact and not covered in too much filth. Naomi and Ana are filling a cart of their own one aisle down.

Ellie was given a free pass to stay in the lander and watch Megan. Lucky her.

"We'll need to wash all of this before it gets to people," I say as I drop a crusty can of who-knows-what on top of the others. "The virus is probably all over this stuff."

"The Chimeras take care of that. We just have to collect everything into the crates, then they clean it and scan for infected items."

I grab a box of cake mix off a shelf and drop it into a second cart that we've reserved for items that aren't waterproof. I assume the waterproof ones will get washed in some kind of cleaning solution. The rest, who knows.

"This one's done," Sam says, slapping the side of the cart that's full of cans. "Let's see if we can get it unloaded before we eat."

I take one of the flashlights from a shelf, drop it in the dry foods cart, and then wrangle it around to face the entrance. Sam leads the way out with the canned foods. The path is reasonably clear since we cleared it earlier with brooms and rakes from the garden aisle.

A loud, blaring horn sounds just as we're about to cross the sunlit threshold to the hovering crates outside.

"I guess we're out of time," Sam says, abandoning his cart in the entrance. He heads back in, aiming for the restrooms, and I follow him there.

Naomi and Ana pull alongside us—along with Helen. She's too affected by the sights and smells to work, but apparently getting washed up for lunch isn't a problem. That's convenient.

Sam nods to his wife. Naomi smiles faintly back as she and the other two women peel off to the women's restroom.

Harry is on his way out of the men's room as we go in, his arms and face are scrubbed clean. Even his hair is slick with water.

"What'd you do, take a shower?" I ask.

He snorts. "I wish."

Sam and I pick adjacent sinks and squeeze out liberal amounts of a green dish soap that we found in one of the aisles. Then we open the faucets and use a combination of dish sponges and bristly grout brushes to scrub ourselves clean.

The water is still running here, which seems like a miracle, but Sam explained it when I went to wash up a few hours ago. The pumping stations and water treatment plants were among the first things the Kyra repaired, even before the fences went up.

After we're done in the restroom and walking out into clean air and blinding sunlight, I notice something interesting: two more landers have appeared in the parking lot since we went in. Each of them is at a different end of the plaza, and I can see some activity in the distance. More crews are bustling around them, looking like ants from this distance.

"Are they going to help us?" I ask.

Sam frowns and shakes his head. "No. They're working on the fences."

"Oh, that was fast."

Sam nods. "It has to be. Search and Rescue is bringing in hundreds of people per day. We need supplies to keep them clothed and fed, and places for them to stay."

"Makes sense."

"There'll be dozens of sites like this one, all around the perimeter. Tomorrow we'll focus on clean-up inside those areas."

Up ahead, Harry is leading the way across a field of dead Dregs to our lander. I glance back the way we came to see Ana and Naomi about twenty feet away, just emerging from the supermarket now.

Right before we reach our lander, I spot Commander Hill and our three remaining Horvals leading the other crews across the parking lot from the school. The two Chimeras who hid inside of it are trailing meekly behind the group, keeping as much distance from the commander as possible. Maybe she decided to spare them. The ones we saw fly in on hoverbikes are nowhere to be seen. They must have left after they realized the action was already over. My focus switches to the forty-odd humans marching behind the commander.

I wonder what they've been doing that requires four times the manpower we've had to help us in the supermarket. Maybe they've been helping put up those fences. Gleaming rolls of chain link fencing and big bundles of metal posts are scattered around the other landers. Two separate lines of fence have already gone up, partially closing off access to the parking lot.

As we reach our lander, Ellie comes out and stands at the top of the ramp with Megan. She waves to us. Sam and I wave back.

Commander Hill beats us to the lander, and one of those floating black crates comes out and drops to the ground in front of her. Commander Hill keys something into the side of the crate. The top pops open and slides away.

"Make a line!" Commander Hill says. "One meal and one canteen per person!"

Harry is the first in line, followed by Sam and me. Ellie and Megan walk down the ramp to join us. We get our food, each of us grabbing a glossy gray box and a black bottle that holds about a liter of water.

We take our meals and canteens and go sit in the shade beneath one of the connecting "spokes" between the main fuselage of the lander and the cylindrical engines.

The meal box is made from a glossy gray material that reminds me of plastic or polycarbonate. Searching for a catch or release, my finger touches a button near the seam, and the top pops open up with a hiss of steam boiling out.

Inside, the box is divided into three sections,

each with a different type of food: rice, some cubed pink meat in a red sauce that probably came from a can, and lentils. A fork and a spoon are clipped to a compartment beneath the box.

I use the spoon to eat and sit contemplating the line of people shuffling across the parking lot to the meal crate. I can't help but notice that no one has moved the Dregs' corpses yet. All those bodies, warming in the sun. It's an invitation for diseases other than the alien one they're already infected with. What happens if it starts to rain and their infected blood and guts get washed into the water supply? Maybe that's why the Kyra made water filtration their first stop on the road to repairing our infrastructure.

"How are there so many of them?" Ellie asks, breaking the weary silence around us.

"So many of who?" Sam asks.

"Dregs," Ellie says, gesturing vaguely to the corpses that I've been eying.

That's something I've been wondering for a while now.

"Where were you when they invaded?" Sam asks.

"A farm about sixty klicks from here," Ellie says.

"That explains it. If you were in the city, you'd know why there are so many." Sam's gaze drifts out of focus as he stares over the parking lot. Naomi looks like she's fighting back tears.

Harry and Ana nod along grimly and shake

their heads.

I look around, from one person to the next. "Is someone going to elaborate?"

Sam tears his gaze away from the horizon with a visible effort. "After the first night, we surrendered. On the second night, they came and infiltrated our homes and shelters. Invisible soldiers. We didn't see or hear anything, but people woke up in the night, complaining that they'd felt something prick them in the neck or the leg or the arm."

"They were infecting us with the virus," I realize.

"Exactly. They didn't do it with everyone. I don't know if they were picking people at random, or if they were using some type of selection criteria. But after that, those people started to turn, and when they did, they got all violent and crazy. Each of them would wind up infecting one or two others, sometimes more.

"A few turned into Chimeras, others to Dregs. It was total chaos until the safe zones were established. People were fighting their families and their friends, getting infected, and then the cycle would repeat as the newly infected lost their minds, too.

"The Kyra and Horvals landed en masse on night three. They went around rounding up the Chimeras, killing the Dregs, and consolidating the humans into safe zones. They were the ones who set up the original perimeter for New San

Bernardino, and it went up in just one night. I've never seen anything like it. There was this massive, coordinated effort. They had their cruisers landed at the airport, surrounded by these big, automated factories. They put the wreckage of our cars and planes in one end, and churned out fences on the other."

"How do you know all this?" I ask, washing down a mouthful of rice and lentils with a swig of water from my canteen.

"Because we were at the airport. We were headed out for a fami—for a vacation, when the Kyra arrived. We got stuck there."

Sam tripped over his words. He was about to say *family* before he caught himself. I wonder who he lost that he's trying not to think about. Naomi has averted her eyes and she's suddenly very interested in the contents of her meal box. They definitely lost someone. So did I, so I can appreciate how avoidance is easier than grief.

"Were the soldiers they landed actual Kyra?" I ask.

"Yeah," Sam nods. "Short, hunching things with wings? Half of them were Kyra, the other half Horvals, I'd say."

"I haven't seen many Kyra. Where did they all go after that?"

"Back to their ships just as soon as they could. By night four they were already on their way out and putting our hybrids in charge."

"Why infect all of us systematically like that

if they knew a ton of us would turn into Dregs?" Ellie asks.

"Maybe they didn't know," Sam replies. "They were in a hurry and they made a mistake."

"Seems like kind of a big mistake," I point out.

"Maybe it was part of their invasion plan," Sam counters. "By the end of night one we officially surrendered, but that doesn't mean we would have all suddenly given up. They had to give us something else to think about. Having our ranks divided and being forced to fight against ourselves did the rest of the work for them. Then when they came along to herd us into the safe zones, we didn't resist because we were too terrified of the Dregs and the virus to argue."

"Yeah, I guess that makes sense," I say.

Sam shrugs. "Either that, or they fucked up and had to make the best of it."

Silence falls over our group once more. The other crews are scattered around us. They took our example and came to sit beneath the lander in whatever shade they could find.

The Horvals aren't eating with us. One of them is sitting on its haunches and using its arms to gnaw on the body of a Dreg about fifteen feet away. Maybe that's why the bodies haven't been cleaned up yet. Food for the Horvals.

Looking around once more, I realize that the Chimeras are nowhere to be seen. Maybe they went inside the lander to eat. With those sensitive eyes and chalk-white skin, they probably can't stand it out here with their helmets off, and there's no real need to supervise us. We've already seen that the landers have some powerful guns. If anyone tries to make a run for it, they'll be cut down in seconds.

Something like a fog horn blares with deafening force from the lander, making several of us flinch.

"Time to get back to work," Sam says. He stands up and hurriedly scrapes the last of the food from his meal box.

Helen makes a face and holds a hand to her stomach, looking like she's about to be sick again. Just the thought of going back in the supermarket has her acting up. At this rate, she should go help the others with the fence.

Sam and Naomi lead the way to a second crate beside the one that our meals came in. It must have hovered out while we ate. A pile of empty meal boxes is already inside. People from the other crews shuffle over to add theirs. We drop ours on top. I'm about to add my canteen when Sam puts out a hand to stop me.

"You'll want to hold onto that."

He's right. It's still about a third full, and I could probably refill at the sink in the men's room of the Frugal Foods. I look for a way to affix it to my belt.

"It has a clip near the top," Sam explains, then turns sideways to show me where he's clipped his to the waistband of his jeans.

"Clever," I say as I slip the clip over my belt. The canteen hangs comfortably there, banging lightly against my hip as I walk back to the others.

A flicker of movement at the top of the lander's ramp catches my eye. It's Commander Hill. As she walks down, she slips her helmet on, and then her voice booms across the plaza: "Everyone get back to work! Break's over!"

Scattered groans and mutterings fill the air as people clamber to their feet and gather around the dirty-dishes crate to deposit their meal boxes.

The other two Chimeras follow Commander Hill down the ramp. She glances at me. I nod, and she looks away. I guess our rapport has reached its end. Or maybe she just doesn't want anyone to see her being too friendly with a Dakka. She is the leader of this entire safe zone, after all. *New San Bernardino.* A smirk lifts one corner of my mouth. What a creative name they came up with.

Whatever the reason she's keeping her distance, it *is* remarkable that Commander Hill is out here with us, risking her life, when she could probably be lounging in a cushy office in the heart of the safe zone. Sam must be right about her: she's not like the other Chimeras.

All three Horvals come bounding over to Commander Hill. Two from behind the lander, the other one from where I saw it eating that

Dreg. They fall in on either side of her, licking blood from their lips and hands.

Commander Hill stops and turns impatiently to regard the other crews as the other two Chimeras reach the bottom of the ramp.

"Get them on their feet! We need that fence up by nightfall."

Looks like I was right about what the others have been working on. The Chimeras begin shoving and shouting to get their crews into a loose formation. I'm glad Corporal Ward isn't here to do that with us.

Everyone in my crew is gathered around, ready to go. Ellie walks by with Megan, heading back up the landing ramp.

"Everybody ready?" I ask.

"No," Helen says.

"Let's get it over with," Sam replies.

Ana is staring longingly after the other crews. "How come they get the easy job?"

"Embrace the suck," I say, and begin trudging back to the Frugal Foods.

"You served?" Sam whispers to me.

I cock an eyebrow at him. He must have recognized the expression. "Yeah. A long time ago. Former Army Corporal, why?"

"So you're not just an *acting* corporal."

"I guess not."

"I was with Space Force," Sam puts in.

"Me, too. I transferred at the end, but I only served for two years before they replaced me with a bot."

Sam snorts at that. "And where are all of those bots now? They trade us for machines, and then those machines all stopped working the minute the invaders arrived. A few well-placed EMPs and suddenly half of our forces were out of commission."

"I saw a few working ones," I say, remembering the soldiers who found us up at Big Bear and their Mechanized Assault Units (MAUs).

Sam nods. "And for every working unit there's a hundred piles of scrap sitting undeployed in a warehouse. The Kyra hit too hard and too fast for us to recover. There wasn't time to go around reactivating them all manually."

Sam makes a good point. I wonder how much military hardware is still out there, just waiting for someone to find and reactivate it. If there is a human resistance, I'm sure they're busy working the problem. Fighting the occupation is probably suicide, but it's nice to know that we at least still have the means to do it.

CHAPTER 19

With the light fading fast, I'm walking toward a blazing bonfire full of dead Dregs. Sam and I are carrying yet another corpse to the fire. I've got the feet, and he's got the head. The bodies stink like hell, and not just because they've been sitting out in the sun all day. They were living in that supermarket, stewing in their own filth.

We managed to load six crates to the brim with supplies that we salvaged. Now we're out here collecting and burning bodies. The rest of our crew is really struggling to do the work, dragging rather than carrying the dead Dregs, but the three Horvals are here helping us, and they're a lot stronger than we are.

It would be nice if the other four crews would help, too, but they're still working on the fences.

"On three," Sam says as we get to within about four feet of the bonfire. The heat and the noxious fumes pouring off it make my eyes burn and my throat itch. "One, two... three!"

Sam and I swing our Dreg into the fire and then turn around to find the next one. The others are working to drag the bodies closer to the blaze, leaving us to throw them into the fire. It's a team effort.

A Horval walks by us, grunting and snorting as it carries a stack of three Dregs to the fire in its thick arms.

Just as Sam and I are bending down to pick up the next one, a loud horn blasts out from our lander.

"What does that mean?" I ask.

"End of the day," Sam says.

I glance around the parking lot. "We're still not done."

"We'll finish up tomorrow," Sam says with a shrug. "Or some other crew will. Why, you want to stay here all night?"

"Hell no."

Sam waves to the others, but they've already got the idea. Even the Horvals. Two of them go bounding past us, followed by the third. Their heavy footfalls shake the ground as they go. Within minutes, all five crews are lined up outside the lander. Two of them beat us there, and they're in front of us. The surviving Horvals have already gone in. Now it's our turn, but there's obviously some kind of hold up, because the line isn't moving.

I glance around while I wait. It looks like the fence is done. Lamps have been erected on every fourth post, making it easy to see the barrier, but not much else. Each of them radiates a dim, fuzzy blue cone of light that doesn't look very bright to my eyes. Kyron lights remind me of UV blacklights, which makes me think that maybe Chimeras or the Kyra can see UV light.

Ellie and Megan come strolling down the line to wait with us.

"What are you doing out here?" I ask. They've been hiding out in the lander all day. Lucky them. I guess someone had to look after Megan.

Ellie shrugs. "The commander sent us out to line up, but she didn't say why."

"They have to scan us before we go back into the zone to make sure that none of us are infected," Sam explains.

My guts clench up with that, and I step out of the line to get a look at what the Chimeras are doing up ahead. Two of them are standing at the bottom of the lander's ramp, holding familiar wand-like scanners. A bright blue light blazes from the tip of each of the wands, and then a glowing display appears projected in the air at the back.

I've seen those scanners before. They look just like the ones the Chimeras up at Big Bear used on us before they cleared us to accompany them to the safe zone.

"How can they tell if we're infected?" I ask. My heart is racing. I'm worried about the fact that I've been in close contact with infected bodies and fluids all day. My clothes are still crusted with blood.

"The initial stage of the infection produces a fever," Sam explains. "You'd notice that first."

"How long does it take?" I ask, struggling to remember how long it was for Gaby. When we found her, she already had a fever, but it couldn't have been long between her rescue and when she was taken.

"About an hour," Sam confirms.

The line shuffles forward.

"What if we're just hot?" Helen asks from the back of our group.

"Or sunburned," Harry suggests.

Sam shakes his head. "Maybe the scanners look for something else, like pupil dilation or iris color—who knows?"

Helen mutters something that I can't make out.

"Am *I* infected?" Megan asks in a small voice.

"No," Ellie says. "You're immune."

"Really?" Megan sounds hopeful.

"You bet."

I wonder if that's true. Ellie's tone makes it sound like she's offering one of those empty reassurances that adults like to give to kids. I twist around to regard Ellie with eyebrows raised. She sends me a scolding look. I get the message, but I'm not sure that giving a five-year-old misinformation is a good idea in this situation. It might make her less careful than she should be.

"No one is immune, Megan," I say with a rueful shake of my head. "But you're not infected. We'd know by now if you were."

"I *am* immune," Megan argues.

"How do you know?"

"Cause Ellie said so."

"She doesn't know if you're immune or not."

Uncertainty creeps into Megan's eyes. She looks back to Ellie for support, and Ellie smiles sheepishly. "Well, how else could you have been hiding out in that supermarket all this time and not gotten infected?"

Megan smiles triumphantly. "Cause I'm immune."

"Or just lucky," I suggest.

"Special," Ellie counters.

Megan nods along with that. "Yeah, I'm special."

Ellie steps toward me and whispers in my ear, "You're an idiot."

"Fear isn't the enemy; it keeps people alive," I whisper back.

"Are you going to be there to tell her that in the middle of the night?"

"Are you?" I challenge.

Ellie steps back with a frown. "If they let me, I will."

"Great. Kids raising kids. That's exactly what we need."

"Better than adults without a clue."

I clamp my mouth shut before I can say anything else. We're all tired. Arguing for the sake of arguing is a waste of our remaining energy.

I hear Megan and Ellie whispering conspiratorially behind me. This time I don't butt in, and soon even that conversation dries up. Silence falls, and our exhaustion feeds it until the only sounds are of the wind blowing an empty soda can around, and the crunch and scrape of our shuffling feet.

The line jerks forward, then stops, then forward again. We're chugging along like cars in heavy traffic. That's something I'll probably never have to deal with again. For some reason, the realization makes my heart ache. A disconnected feeling washes over me. Like this is all just a dream, and I'm going to wake up soon.

My brain is stuck in denial. A stage of grief. I'm not just grieving my mother's death, but also the death of our world.

The line chugs ahead of me again, and I take another two steps forward. My whole body feels heavy and sore, and I'm starving. Maybe they'll give us our dinner in the lander. If not, I guess I still have plenty of food from the Jacksons' place.

It's fully dark now, and a bright dome of stars is out and shining overhead. The lamps along the fence and matching blue glow of the ones from the landers isn't nearly enough to diminish their splendor.

I wonder what Bree and the kids got up to on their first day at school. Hopefully their day was less eventful than mine. They've probably been home for hours already...

A bright blue light dazzles me, and I realize that I've reached the front of the line. There's a scanner in my face. Sam and Naomi are already walking up the ramp ahead of me, cleared for their return home. A fan of blue light flickers over me. My whole body tenses as I wait for the result of the scan.

There comes a beep, and a glowing screen full of alien symbols appears projected from the back of the wand-shaped scanner.

"You're clean," the Chimera says after a second.

Relief washes over me, and I glance back at Megan and Ellie as I start up the ramp.

The two Chimeras scan them both simultaneously, study the screens, and then wave them on. They walk on, hand-in-hand.

Thank God.

I'm walking backwards, slowly, watching as Harry and Ana go next. Another wash of blue light and a confirmation beep. Also clean.

Finally, it's Helen's turn. She's so scared that she's actually shaking.

"I'm fine," she snaps at the Chimeras, and then tries to push by them so she can follow Harry and Ana up the ramp.

They move to stop her, and one of them physically shoves her back.

"Let me by! I told you, I'm fine!" Helen shouts

at them.

Harry and Ana both stop and turn to watch the commotion.

"Scans are mandatory," one of the Chimeras says as he raises his wand.

Instead of a beep, his scanner makes a harsher buzzing sound, and both the blue light at the tip of the device and the screen projected from the back turn red.

"W-hat does that mean?" Helen asks.

"Step out of the line, ma'am." The second one says, drawing his sidearm and aiming it at her.

My blood runs cold, and I find myself reaching reflexively for the weapon Commander Hill gave me. I stop myself halfway. It would be suicide to make a stand here, and what would be the point? If Helen's infected, she's as good as dead anyway.

"Run it again! I'm fine!" Helen screams.

Her forehead is shining with sweat under the crimson lights of the scanners, and she's still shaking with fear—or maybe that's a fever...

I think back to the way she was avoiding work all day, looking pale and sick and throwing up. I thought it was just the unsavory conditions, but maybe it was more than that.

"Step *out* of the line, ma'am; I won't ask again."

The people behind her are stepping out of line, even if she isn't. They're obviously afraid to get hit if the Chimeras start shooting.

My breath is caught in my chest. I'm frozen on the ramp with Harry and Ana, helpless to intervene, and yet unable to look away.

"Run the scan again," I suggest, going to Helen's defense.

Helen sends me a grateful look. One of the two Chimeras glances back at me—

"What's going on out here?" Commander Hill asks, appearing at the top of the ramp.

"She's infected," the Chimera says.

"And?"

"She's not cooperating."

"Well, why would she?"

Commander Hill draws a sidearm that she shouldn't even have, levels it at Helen—

Her eyes widen. "Wai—"

A flash of green light drops Helen to the ground with a meaty *thud.*

"Keep the line moving!" Commander Hill orders as she holsters her smoking weapon.

"Yes, ma'am," the Chimera replies.

His partner grabs Helen's feet and drags her to one side.

I watch with a sick weight in my gut. My whole body is singing with adrenaline and impotent fury. Maybe Sam was wrong about the commander being sympathetic to us. She's just as bad as the rest of them.

I turn and stalk up the ramp, my hand hovering close to the weapon tucked into my belt. I could kill her.

And then the other two Chimeras would kill me.

My hand drifts away.

"What about her son?" Ana whispers as she and Harry follow me into the lander.

"I don't know," Harry replies.

"We could offer to take him."

"We already have four kids to look after."

"Then maybe Sam and Naomi could volunteer?" Ana suggests.

"After what happened to their kids? They won't do that. It's too hard."

So I was right about them having lost someone. I didn't realize they'd lost their kids.

"Don't worry," Harry whispers. "We'll take him for tonight. He'll get assigned to someone else after that."

We press in to the back of the lander where we find Sam and Naomi, and Ellie and Megan. Both of the girls are crying.

Sam looks about as grim as I feel. "It happened last night, too," he whispers to me.

He makes it sound trivial, like we should just accept this as normal. We get sent out, some of us get infected, they cull the infected ones. Rinse and repeat.

"How many times have they sent you out here?" I ask through gritted teeth.

"This is the second night. Before that, the Kyra were the ones working on the perimeter. Now that they've pulled out it's *our* job."

My anger boils over. "But they're sending us out empty-handed! What do they expect? We don't have armor like they do!"

"You want to lodge a complaint?"

"You're damn right I do!"

Sam gestures vaguely to an armored Chimera standing by the access ramp at the back of the troop bay where we're standing.

"Maybe she'll listen to you," he says. "She gave you a gun, right? That might mean something."

"Yeah, maybe," I agree with my hand twitching restlessly beside the grip of the weapon. I start pushing through the crowd to reach the Commander.

"Don't get yourself killed!" Sam calls after me.

My brain is buzzing and my pulse is hammering in my ears. Only the thought of my family waiting for me back home is holding my temper in check.

"Commander Hill," I say as I step in front of her.

"Ah, Corporal Randall," she says. "I've been meaning to find you." She makes a gimme gesture. "My weapon, please."

I hesitate.

"You can have it back tomorrow," she says. "But I'm afraid you cannot take it home with you. I wouldn't want you to get yourself killed over a misunderstanding if it were to be found in your possession."

This mundane exchange is making it even harder to hold my temper in check. "Why did you shoot her?" I ask.

"The infected woman? I would think that's obvious."

"You could have handled it differently."

"How?"

I throw up my hands. "I don't know. A lethal injection? A pill that would put her to sleep? Something! Anything! Or better yet, you could give her some kind of treatment to get rid of the infection. You can't honestly tell me that the Kyra don't have a way to counter their own virus!"

Commander Hill's helmet cocks to one side. "You really think they would risk inoculating people with a vaccine when their whole modus operandi here is to infect people against their will? Soon we would have rebel scientists inoculating everyone with the very same vaccine that they used. Losing a few people here and there is better than losing them all."

"Then at least give us suits of armor like yours."

"We need all of our armor for actual soldiers. We can't spare any suits for low-priority operations like this one."

I'm really struggling to contain myself now.

"Corporal Randall, my weapon, please."

It takes every ounce of my will to draw the weapon from my belt and not use it on the commander.

"Thank you," she says as she takes it from me. "Now go back and take your place with the others."

"Yes, ma'am," I manage to say through gritted teeth.

CHAPTER 20

The lights inside the lander flash alternately between red and blue as we lift off.

"They're sterilizing us and our clothes," Sam explains, pointing to the lights. "An extra measure to prevent an outbreak in the safe zone."

I nod absently. I'm still going back over the conversation I had with Commander Hill. Our working conditions are extremely dangerous. Helen underscored that for all of us. How did she even get infected? Did she get too close to one of the Dregs that followed them to that school bus? Or maybe she consumed some infected rations for breakfast. After seeing where our rations come from, it's not hard to imagine that happening.

The safe zone is a huge misnomer. I'd rather take my chances out in the Wastes than be stuck in here with the illusion of safety, waiting for the Dregs or the virus to get me and my family.

But how do we get out of here? We'd have to

leave in the middle of the night, get to the fence, and climb over, all the while avoiding Chimeran patrols and any Dregs still lurking inside the zone.

And that's not even the biggest problem.

I turn my wrist over and stare at the blinking green light of my tracking implant. The Chimeras can tell where all of us are at any given moment, and if they are to be believed, our implants can also execute us remotely. That means escaping from the safe zone isn't even an option.

I grit my teeth in frustration. There has to be a way to disable the implants without triggering the kill switch. Looking to Sam, I study him curiously in the flashing blue and red lights of the lander. Maybe he knows of a way to defeat the implants, or maybe he knows of someone who successfully escaped.

It's too late to ask now. I need to wait for a more private moment. We're surrounded by people who could report our conversation to the Chimeras.

Patience, I tell myself. It's still early days. That might mean that no one has found a way around the implants yet, but sooner or later someone is going to try to escape. When they do, maybe I'll have a chance to join them with my family.

* * *

It takes all of five minutes to reach the fire

station. The lander sets down with an almost imperceptible bump. We file to the open doorway, emerge into the growing dark, and head for the hover transports that will ferry us home. I'm in a daze, moving like a robot and barely conscious of the world around me.

In a span of seconds, the night has fully fallen. The streets and buildings around us are cloaked in shadows, but the fire station is lit with those fuzzy blue lamps I saw along the fence.

The two surviving Chimeras march out with us, directing each of the crews to their transports by name.

"Gamma Crew!" one of them calls to us, pointing to a space between two painted white guide lines in the parking lot. Alien symbols have been added between those lines. Ours is a circle with a dot in the center.

"My feet are tired. Pick me up," Megan whines.

"I can't pick you up," Ellie says. "You're too heavy."

"Pick me up!" Megan screams, drawing a look from the Chimera who called to us.

"Shhh," Ellie mutters. "We're almost there."

I switch my attention from Ellie to the Chimeras. They're the same cowards who hid in the school. Commander Hill must have chosen to remain aboard the lander with the Horvals. I wonder if it serves as some type of mobile command center.

Glancing back the way we came, I'm just in time to see the landing ramp slowly rising back into place. A moment later, the lander shimmers and then vanishes as its cloaking shield re-activates.

I reach the transport and slowly climb the stairs behind Sam and Naomi. I don't blame Megan. I wish someone would pick *me* up, too.

Sam and his wife are sitting one row back from the entrance. I slide into the seats across the aisle from them and lean against the small, circular window, using my arm for a pillow.

Ellie and Megan shuffle by, followed by Harry and Ana. The door slides shut, and our vehicle jerks into motion with a rising whirr.

"Where is she going to stay?" I hear Ana asking.

"With me," Ellie replies.

"You already have your brother to take care of."

"I'll manage."

"We could take her," Ana suggests.

"No," Harry says. "We already have four to look after, and now Helen's son. We can't look after a sixth."

"Well, what about Sam and Naomi?"

"No, it's too soon for them to be dealing with kids."

I glance across the aisle. Naomi is leaning on Sam's shoulder with her eyes closed while he stares straight ahead with glazed eyes.

I wonder again about who they've lost. They lost their kids, but was it during the invasion or after? Did they have to watch their children turn into Dregs?

"What if a Dreg comes in the night?" Ana presses Ellie. "How are you going to defend them all by yourself? Is your house secure?"

"The bedrooms are. We'll lock ourselves in one of them. We'll be okay."

A weary sigh builds inside my chest, but I manage to hold it in. "We could take her," I say, twisting around in my seat. "I secured our house yesterday. No Dregs will be getting in there."

Ellie greets my suggestion with an indignant frown. "We'll manage."

Ana is leaning across the aisle, glancing uncertainly between the two of us.

"Look, don't be stubborn," I insist. "We're only using one bedroom, and we have three. You can come, too, and bring your brother. Safety in numbers."

Ellie looks more interested now. Maybe she thought I was only inviting Megan to stay with us. I guess she and Megan have developed some kind of bond after spending the whole day together.

I should probably be running this plan by Bree first, but the thought of three kids spending the night alone in a home with broken windows or doors doesn't sit well with me, and I'm sure it wouldn't sit well with her either.

Ana glances back at the Chimera in the driver's seat. "It's not really up to us to be making changes to our housing assignments."

"I can approve it," the driver says, revealing that he's been listening in the whole time.

I'm surprised that he cares enough to get involved.

"Well, what do you say, Ellie?" Ana asks.

"Okay," she says quietly. "But I have to go pick up my brother first."

"No problem," I reply. "I'll get off with you and we can walk down to my place. You're staying on our street, right?" I ask, remembering that she and her brother came aboard right after I did.

Ellie nods. "Yeah, I think so."

Thank you, Ana mouths to me before leaning back into her seat.

A look of relief crosses Harry's face. I get it. He and Ana are in their mid to early twenties. I doubt they're even married. For all I know their relationship started out as some kind of end of the world hook-up, and now here they are, assigned to play house with four kids. So, of course Harry doesn't want to take on yet another one.

But now I'm the one who's going to have extra kids to look after. That's what I get for opening my big mouth.

CHAPTER 21

I'm standing on Ellie's front porch, keeping watch by the splintered door and the broken windows. The same looters that hit our place must have hit hers, too. Probably looking for guns.

It's a dark night, and unnervingly quiet. The transport that dropped us off is long gone; I can't even hear its engines whirring anymore.

We've only been here for about five minutes, but it was enough for the transport to finish dropping off the others. Harry and Ana are one street down from us, but they got off at our stop to go pick up Helen's son from the mansion where Sam and Naomi are staying.

Glancing up and down the street, I trace the shadows and remember how it looked in the morning. Only a few of these homes were damaged to the point of being uninhabitable. That means there are a lot of empty houses here. I wonder why Commander Hill is getting us to expand the perimeter when we can't even fill the spaces we have. Are we expecting a big influx of refugees from somewhere?

"Stay close, Matty," I hear Ellie whispering to her brother.

The beams of multiple flashlights sweep over me, and I turn into the glare, squinting to shield my eyes.

"Here," Ellie says, handing one of the flashlights to me.

"Good thinking," I say.

Ellie nods and hands me a gleaming butcher knife next.

"Just in case," she explains.

"Better than nothing."

Ellie has kept a cast iron skillet for herself, and her brother, Matty, has a wooden baseball bat and a second flashlight.

Megan is empty-handed, unless you count the stuffed panda bear she's clutching to her chest.

Switching to a reverse grip on the butcher knife, I lead the way across Ellie's front yard to the sidewalk and step over the picket fence at the end.

Ellie, Matty, and Megan are forced to go around the fence. The beams of our lights bob among the shadows as we hurry down the sidewalk. I'm sweeping mine back and forth, checking for signs of movement.

Nothing yet, thank God.

We pass four houses, and then the fifth is the Jacksons' place, next to ours.

"Almost there," I whisper. Getting anxious to see my wife and kids, I pick up the pace.

"Slow down," Ellie hisses at me. "Megan can't walk that fast."

I turn and wait for them to catch up, taking the moment to check if anything is creeping up behind us.

No sign of Dregs.

Continuing on, I veer off the sidewalk to go around the split halves of the sycamore tree in our front yard. As soon as I reach the garage door, I tuck the flashlight under my arm and pat my jeans pocket to make sure my keys are still there. Feeling the bear-shaped keyring through crusty blood-stained denim, I breathe a shaky sigh of relief and duck down to shine my flashlight into the garage.

It's empty. The door to the house is shut. I wonder if Bree remembered to retrieve the shotgun from behind my skis.

"We're clear," I say. "You three go first."

Ellie nudges Megan forward. She crawls under, followed by Matty, then Ellie. I slide my knife through before army-crawling under the door. Scrambling to my feet, I slide the knife into my belt, and then cross to the side door. My heart is pounding with anticipation.

I'm not sure why I'm so nervous: they were at school today; there were armed guards at the school. My wife and kids have probably been here for hours already, bored and anxious, waiting for *my* safe return, and here I am worried about theirs.

Drawing the keys from my pocket, I use my flashlight to find the right one, stick it in, and then turn the deadbolt. The knob has also been locked, so I'm forced to reach for the second key on the ring and unlock that, too.

I pull the door open—

And then freeze as the muffled sound of a woman crying trickles out.

"Is that..." Ellie trails off.

I jump across the threshold and go tearing down the hall, screaming, "Bree! Where are you?"

CHAPTER 22

"Bree!" My flashlight washes over her. She's sitting on the living room couch with her knees drawn up to her chest in a fetal position. Zach and Gaby are nowhere to be seen.

"They took her!" Bree cries as her head comes up.

Horror stabs through me, and the room spins, making me stumble forward and grab the back of the couch. My heart is beating painfully in my chest, and my ears are ringing.

"What do you mean they took her?" I ask quietly.

Bree jumps up with flashing eyes and balled fists. "I mean they took Gaby!" she screams.

My unspoken fears coalesce around the bits and pieces of warnings I'd been collecting throughout the day. My instinct on arriving at the fire station this morning was right. I should have gone back to the school to get Gaby.

I step around the couch until Bree and I are

standing face to face. My flashlight is making Bree squint, but she's looking past me, her gaze wild and feral like a Dreg's. Yet there's no sign of her eyes turning red.

I flick the light away from her face and set it on the coffee table before grabbing Bree gently by her arms.

"We will get her back. Do you hear me?" My whole body is shaking with adrenaline and impotent rage, making me feel like I could take on a whole army by myself.

It takes a moment for Bree's eyes to swim back into focus. She blinks and stares hard at me across the gulf of shadows between us.

"How?" she asks in a cracking voice.

"I saved a Chimera today. She's in charge of the entire safe zone. She'll help us."

Bree blinks a few times more, rapidly. "You..."

"It's going to be okay."

"Dad?"

Zach's voice comes from the hallway to the bedrooms. I can't make out more than his shadow.

"I'm here," I say.

The shadow comes running and slams into me. I wrap an arm around his shoulders, and another around Bree's, pulling both of them in close. I kiss the top of Bree's head.

"I couldn't stop them," Bree says, her voice muffled against my jacket. "The kids went outside for recess. I was there, watching them, and the next thing I knew Gaby was missing. I spotted her back by the doors, talking to one of the guards. And then they just grabbed her and dragged her away!"

I lean back to regard my wife.

"Did you hear what they were saying?"

"No. It all happened so fast. I ran after them and tried to pull Gaby away. Then one of them drew his gun and shot me. I woke up in the infirmary half an hour later to find out that they'd stunned me, and Gaby had been taken somewhere, but no one could tell me where!"

"Why would you let her talk to them?" I ask, feeling suddenly frustrated that I wasn't there.

"I didn't *let* her! She was only out of my sight for a second! I was watching the rest of the kids and one of the other teachers was talking to me..." Bree trails off, her whole body is shaking.

I pull her back in, but she's rigid and stiff. "It's okay, I'm not blaming you."

Zach's face crumples and tears well up in his eyes, making them shimmer. "The other kids on the bus said that Gaby's never coming back."

A creaky floorboard makes Bree flinch and spin around.

"It's okay," I say before she or Zach can overreact to the three shadows standing beside the kitchen. "They're with me."

CHAPTER 23

The alarm clock's chiming wakes me from a deep, groggy sleep. I sit up quickly, reaching for the clock—and trigger a painful spasm in my back. The muscles are still tired from clearing out all those dead Dregs last night.

Zach and Bree are both curled up around the window seat in the master bedroom where I fell asleep keeping watch. Bree murmurs something in her sleep, and falls back down into the cushions where I was sitting. I manage to turn off the alarm at my feet. It's 05:01. Twisting around, I shake Bree by her arm.

"Wake up, honey. It's time to get ready."

Bree sits up, rubbing her eyes, looking confused and disoriented. A moment later, the memories come rushing back; she winces and her eyes fill with tears.

"We'll get Gaby back," I whisper, taking one of her hands and squeezing it.

Bree bites her lip and nods once, grabbing the

lifeline I just gave her.

I ease out of the window seat, taking the alarm clock with me and tucking it under my arm. Stepping over Zach, who made a ramshackle bed beside the window from couch cushions and sheets, I gently shake his shoulder to wake him, too.

He mumbles and groans, then his eyes snap open.

"I'm awake," he croaks.

"Good," I whisper back.

It's still dark, so I use the shotgun's light to find the way to the kitchen. Bree follows me with the flashlight I brought from Ellie's last night. We shuffle to the kitchen, and I begin opening a few cans of food for our breakfast.

A door clicks open down the hall we just came from. Zach grabs the flashlight off the island counter and sweeps the beam in that direction. Ellie throws up a hand to shield her eyes.

"Ouch."

"Sorry," Zach says, angling the light away.

I watch Ellie stepping into the kitchen with her brother, Matty, and Megan. All three of them look like they haven't slept. I go about opening a few extra cans of food for them, then rummage around in the drawer for spoons and forks.

"Come, help yourselves," I say, nodding to Ellie.

Yesterday's dirty dishes are still piled in the sink. I guess Bree didn't have the energy to deal with them. Can't say I blame her.

We eat quietly around the kitchen island, each of us locked in our own private head space. Scraping the last of the corn from my can, I move to the kitchen garbage bin and wave a hand to open it.

Nothing happens.

Right. No power. I must be groggier than I thought. What I wouldn't give for a hot cup of coffee...

Reaching for the garbage can, I manually open the lid. The bin is already full to the brim with empty cans. I drop mine in, and stare fixedly at the garbage for a second. My hands flex restlessly. I should take the garbage out. But where do I take it? What are the Chimeras doing about garbage collection? The streets aren't even clear yet.

Zach passes into my peripheral vision and drops his empty can in the bin, snapping me out of it. A quick look at the glowing green digits of the alarm clock tells me we don't have time to deal with clean-up. It's already 05:37. At least we all showered and changed last night. A smart move in hindsight. We slept in our clothes for added warmth, so we don't need to get dressed.

"We'd better get outside and wait for the transport," I say.

Ellie nods, and Zach mumbles an acknowledgment. I take a few anxious steps, pacing as I wait for everyone to finish their breakfast. Once they're all done, I lead the way down the hall to the garage. From there we lock up, hide the shotgun, and crawl out under the door.

It's been only one day since we got here, and we're already sinking into a new routine. But there's a vile, creeping sense of wrongness to everything, and Gaby's absence makes it all so much worse.

Now, we're waiting on the curb and glancing about nervously. It's still dark out, and we're mostly unarmed. I kept the flashlight, which I'm sweeping around constantly, and Ellie has the butcher knife she gave me last night, but if even one or two Dregs were to sneak up on us, it wouldn't end well.

Hurried footsteps send me spinning around—

To see Sam and Naomi.

I avert the flashlight. Sam nods to me as he joins us on the curb. "Chris," he says.

I nod wordlessly back.

Sam's gaze lingers, and a frown touches his lips. "Where is your..." he trails off suddenly.

"They took her," I whisper back.

He raises eyebrows at me. "Just like that?"

I nod again.

"Shit. Any idea where? Did they say why?"

I shake my head.

Bree is staring straight ahead, her eyes glazed.

A swiftly rising *whirr* signals the approach of

our hover transport. Soon it's dropping down in front of us, and the door slides open. A Chimera appears standing in the entrance. "Hustle up! We have a long day ahead of us!"

I lead the way aboard the transport, and find a row for my family. Bree almost shuffles right past me, looking dazed.

"Over here," I say, waving a hand to catch her attention.

She blinks and turns, falling into the seat beside me and curling up against my side like a little girl. She's hugging herself, her arms crossed over her chest, like she's afraid she'll fall apart if she doesn't physically hold herself together.

Zach catches my eye as he slides into the window seat across from us. His gaze is full of apprehension. He's never seen his mother like this: an empty husk, hollowed out and shattered like a discarded egg shell. Maybe he's afraid that I'm next. I wonder if he's right.

But I can't afford to fall apart. Someone has to stay strong. "It's going to be okay," I say to him, even though my throat is aching like it's been cut.

He nods, then looks away, out his window.

The door slides shut and the transport jerks into motion.

I slide an arm around Bree's shoulders and study her quietly. She's not even blinking.

"Hey."

She doesn't respond.

"Bree."

Nothing.

I nudge her shoulder with mine. She blinks and looks up at me. "Yes?" she asks in an odd, lilting tone that makes her sound like a little girl answering to her father.

"I'm going to talk to Commander Hill. She'll help us."

Bree just stares at me, saying nothing. After about five seconds, she blinks again, and asks, "And what if she won't?"

That knot in my throat is getting tighter, making it hard to breathe. "Then I'll work something else out. You just hang in there, baby. Trust me. I'm going to fix this."

She nods and cracks a smile, her eyes drifting out of focus once more.

* * *

We reach the fire station, and line up outside like we did the day before. I don't see any new arrivals, so today it's just the six of us: me, Sam, Naomi, Harry, Ana, and Ellie.

Another faceless Chimera paces in front of us, along with a monstrous Horval to replace Hank. Our new team leader is Corporal Solis. The surname sounds Latin, but his accent, if he had one, is no longer recognizable.

"Any questions?" Solis asks, stopping beside the Horval with his hands clasped behind his back in a parade rest position. Definitely former military.

No one raises their voice to ask a question.

"All right then. Today, our work detail is street clean-up inside the zone. We will be working these." The corporal reaches over to his Horval counterpart and opens some type of saddle bag to withdraw a set of flat, palm-sized black discs

"These are grav discs. Slap a few of them on a wreck or a piece of debris, and myself or one of the other team leaders can use them to remove the obstruction. Would someone like to volunteer for a demonstration?"

Sam steps out of line. "I'll go."

Corporal Solis gestures for him to approach.

Sam walks up to him, and the Corporal sets the discs on the ground. "Put your feet on the discs."

Sam does as he's asked.

Solis takes a step back. "Ready?"

Sam shrugs. "Go for it."

The corporal gestures to Sam with his palm facing up and his hand slowly rising. A humming sound fills the air and Sam goes floating off the ground. He wobbles a bit, then throws out his hands and bends his knees, like someone learning to surf for the first time.

"Damn, that's some fine tech," Sam mutters. Once he gets to about three feet off the ground, he begins to look worried. "All right, man, you can bring me down."

But he keeps rising.

"Hey!" Sam shouts. He gets to about shoulder height before Solis reverses his rising-palm gesture, and Sam comes floating back down. He hurriedly tries to shake the discs off the soles of his boots. "They won't come off!"

Corporal Solis makes another gesture, and the discs detach with a *thunk*. Sam stumbles away and hurries back to our line.

"The discs will self-adhere to any flat surface," Solis explains. "They do not need to be facing down, since the fields are self-stabilizing, but try to space them out. Each disc produces a field of about eighteen feet in diameter, and the field strength diminishes the farther out you get. Ideal placement is six feet from each other. Two discs will be enough to lift the average car. A bus will need four. Six for a tank or a mech. Am I making myself clear?"

Heads bob and we murmur acknowledgments.

"Good. Rexi has forty grav discs packed into her hip packs, but we have thousands more in the lander. Today's goal is to completely clear the streets inside the zone. Any questions?"

I nod and step forward.

"Where is the debris going?"

"To the factories for recycling."

"And where is that?"

The Chimera stares long and hard at me before replying. "That's need to know, Mr. Randall."

Corporal Solis bends down to recover the two discs he used to demonstrate. Dropping them back in the pack on our Horval's right hip, he turns to indicate the lander in the empty lot beside the fire station.

"Follow me."

The corporal leads us across the parking lot with Rexi trailing behind him. The rest of us keep a wary distance from her.

Sam leans over my shoulder as we go and whispers, "With tech like that, it's no wonder they kicked our asses."

I nod absently. My thoughts are fixed on the lander and on finding Commander Hill. I'm already framing my thoughts, picking and arranging the words in my head, as if there's some secret combination that will unlock the commander's sympathy and support.

Bree's doubts worm their way into my thoughts. What if she won't help us?

I shake my head to clear it. I saved her life. That has to count for something.

Soon we're tromping up the boarding ramp with the other four work crews. We line up three abreast, and the lander fills up quickly. I glance around, counting Chimeras. One for each team. Five teams. If Commander Hill is here, there should be six...

But my count stops at five.

She's not here.

I look to the gleaming lift tubes and the

winding access ramp beside them. No sign of her standing there, either.

The nearest Chimera is the one who led us aboard, our new leader, Solis. I push past Harry and Sam to reach him.

"Corporal," I say.

His helmet turns. The dim blue lights inside the lander gleam dully on the matte black finish of his armor.

"Yes?" he asks in a tone of strained patience.

"Where is Commander Hill?"

"What business is that of yours?"

"I saved her life yesterday. She was impressed with my performance, so she promised that today we'd discuss the possibility of making me a Gladiator." The last bit is a lie, but it's close enough to be true.

Corporal Solis doesn't reply immediately.

"She had other business to attend to today."

My heart plunges. "So she's not coming?"

"What did I *just* say? Am I speaking Kyro?"

"Is there some way I can contact her?"

"You could try her comms."

"Okay, how do I—"

"I was being sarcastic. Now fuck off."

My fists clench up, and suddenly my whole body is singing with adrenaline, ready for a fight. I'm scanning the corporal's armor, hunting for weak spots. The Dregs seem to get their helmets off easily enough. I could yank the helmet off and then break the corporal's jaw. Or maybe steal his sidearm and shoot him in the face.

"Did you hear me?" Solis intones. His hand lands on the grip of the rifle clipped to his chest, and I feel someone pulling me back by my shoulders. The rest of Gamma Team folds in around me, cutting me off from danger.

"That's not the way to help your daughter, man," Sam whispers as he pulls me back. "Keep it together. We'll figure this out."

My whole body is shaking with rage. I have to force my fists to open. I'm nodding slowly, staring at my palms, my eyes drifting out of focus. Now I know how Bree felt this morning.

Gaby is gone, taken to God-knows-where, and I can't do a damned thing about it. My one and only plan has just fallen flat. And to be fair, it was probably a fool's hope to begin with.

Now what?

I've never felt so helpless.

"It's going to be okay," Naomi says just as the lander's doors slam shut and it lifts off with a subtle jolt.

"Is that what you said to Helen when she arrived? Or maybe to her son last night when you and Ana told him that his mother was dead? Hell, was that what you told your own kids before..." I stop myself there.

Naomi's expression cracks, her eyes suddenly agleam with tears. She looks away quickly, shaking her head. Sam sweeps in and wraps an arm around her shoulders, muttering reassurances in his wife's ear. He shoots me an angry look.

"You and me, we're done, man. Next time you start to boil over, I'm gonna let them put your ass down."

I wince. "Look, Sam—"

"Save it."

CHAPTER 24

I slap another grav engine on the side of a tank, then step back to watch. Corporal Solis uses a combination of gestures and unseen commands issued through his suit to raise the old burned-out war machine impossibly into the air. He sends it floating west with a trickling stream of cars and other debris. My best guess is all of that junk is headed for the airport in the center of the safe zone, since Sam mentioned there's a factory somewhere over there.

"Pretty crazy, huh?" Ellie says.

She helped me prep the tank, since Sam and I are not on good terms at the moment. I still have to find some way to apologize to him and Naomi.

"Hey, get back to work!" Corporal Solis snaps at us.

"Come on," I whisper, nodding sideways to indicate the next obstruction—a fallen palm tree. I'm wearing a backpack full of grav discs that was probably a kid's school bag a week ago.

Rexi isn't the only one who has to carry spares. I stop by the tree, and Ellie comes over to zip open my pack and pull out a few more grav discs. She hands me two, and keeps another two for herself.

"How do we attach them?" she asks.

I stare at the trunk of the tree, frowning.

"The corporal said to attach them to flat surfaces, but there aren't any flat surfaces on a tree!" Ellie says.

"Hey! Not that, you *se'leps!*" Heavy footfalls interrupt us and we turn to see Solis running over.

He points past the fallen tree to a knot of disabled EVs on the other side. "Focus on the cars. Trees have to be moved with grav sleds. We'll get to that later."

"Okay." I begin turning away with Ellie. She's already throwing a leg over the tree to get to the other side. It landed on a pair of cars, so it's sitting at about waist height.

Just as she's swinging her other leg over, a dark shadow passes over us. Ellie and I both look up to see what it is.

It's another lander.

"Reinforcements?" I ask.

It looks like it's headed for the parking lot of the plaza where our ship set down earlier. Corporal Solis and a few of the other Chimeras are running to greet it, leaving their teams unsupervised.

"I wonder what that's about..." I mutter.

Ellie and I watch the second lander drop down beside ours. The parking lot is about a hundred feet away, so it's hard to see what's going on over there.

Our Horval, Rexi, saunters over to us and growls something.

Ellie flinches and almost falls off the tree that she's straddling.

The Horval growls at me next, then points imperiously with an arm as thick as one of my thighs to the cars that Corporal Solis told us to clear.

"All right, all right, we're getting back to work."

Rexi snarls as she turns to leave, heading for Harry and Ana. They're working on a X1R assault mech that's fallen over on its side.

Ellie finishes clambering over the tree. I jump over next, casting a backward glance to the commotion by the landers.

The Chimeras have multiplied. It even looks like there's a few hoverbikes out there. As I'm watching, two of the bikes come racing across the lot, headed straight toward me.

"Ellie, hang on," I say.

"What is it?" The sound of the bikes approaching catches her attention. "Are we in trouble?" she asks.

"I don't know." Climbing back over the tree, I stand my ground before the approaching soldiers.

Maybe they found the guns stashed in my house and they're here to make an example of me. But that seems like a lot of trouble to go to. Especially since I haven't actually used those guns on anyone—well, except for that Dreg I killed.

Another thought occurs to me. Maybe, this is something to do with Gaby.

My guts clench up. I cross my arms over my chest. One of the bikes slows to a whirring stop and the rider hops off. The second one stops farther back, and I see the rider prop his rifle on the control bars, aiming it at us.

"Can I help you with something?" I ask.

"I hope so," the Chimera standing in front of me says.

I recognize the voice. "Commander?"

The Chimera reaches up and removes its helmet, revealing her face. She inclines her head to me. "I need your help."

My head is buzzing with questions, but my heart is already soaring with tenuous hope. If the commander needs my help, then maybe she'll be willing to help me in return. "What do you need?"

"Volunteers. We located a group of survivors out in Beaumont. They're armed. We sent in Gladiators to talk them down, but it didn't work, and one of them almost died. We're looking for peaceful solutions."

Ellie steps into view beside me. "So, what can

we do about it?"

"You can go in and tell them what life is like in the safe zones. Convince them to come in peacefully and lay down their arms."

"What if they don't listen to us?" Ellie asks.

"They have to listen. We need them here."

"What for?"

Commander Hill's eyes narrow, and her black lips flatten into a thin gray line. "Because the Kyra need more soldiers. Some of this group might be eligible for ascension. Besides, even Dakkas are good for something."

"Yeah, like what?" I ask, jerking my chin to her. "Seems like all we're good for is slave labor, but the work you have us doing is all about making the safe zone more habitable for us. We're serving ourselves, not the Kyra."

"I'm glad you realize that, but this isn't just about you. It's about your children and your children's children."

A cold weight settles in my gut with the mention of children. "You mean like my daughter?" I ask in a low voice. My fists ball up, and my blood is suddenly boiling.

Ellie glances nervously at me.

"What about your daughter?" Commander Hill asks.

"Chimeras took her from school yesterday while I was busy saving your life."

"Why would they take her?"

"You tell me! If they've hurt her..." My voice

trails off in a strangled growl.

"No. That doesn't make any sense. Children are extremely valuable to the Kyra. The entire purpose of the safe zones is to raise and educate children."

Ellie takes a quick step back. "What do you mean by that?"

Commander Hill frowns at her. "You haven't figured it out yet? The Kyra need soldiers, not slaves. Dakkas like you serve the Federation by breeding. The more children you have, the more soldiers they can conscript. Your incompatibility isn't a genetic defect. Some people are worthy of ascension and some are not, and one of the prime factors is their *acceptance* of the process. We're educating children to make them more eligible. Impressing upon them the importance of this war and of defeating our enemy."

Ellie is gaping in shock at the commander, but I'm taking these revelations in my stride. My brain is laser focused. The Commander needs me, and I need her to get Gaby back. The question is, how badly does she need me? What's my bargaining position?

"Why us?" I ask as a roundabout way of getting to the answer. "Anyone could talk to those people in Beaumont for you. You said you needed volunteers, but you came straight here, like you knew you needed *me* for this."

"You aren't the average Dakka. No one in the safe zone would have done what you did yesterday. So, who better to talk to a group that is highly suspicious of us? I need someone I can trust not to paint us or the Federation in a bad light. I gave you a gun yesterday as a test. You didn't use it on us, even when I provoked you by executing one of your team in front of you. All of that makes you my first choice, but if you won't do it, there are others I could choose."

"No, I'll do it."

"Excellent. Get on the bike. We need to leave before things in Beaumont escalate any further." Commander Hill's gaze darts to Ellie. "Bring the girl. She has an honest face."

Ellie shuts her gaping mouth. "Me?"

"Hang on," I interrupt. "I wasn't finished."

The commander cocks her head in question.

"My daughter was taken. I need you to promise you'll get her back."

"First, I'll need to find out *why* she was taken, but if you get these refugees to surrender, I promise to look into it for you. If it's possible to get your daughter back, I will."

"That's not good enough."

"It'll have to be."

I set my jaw. "How do I know I can trust you to keep your end of the deal?"

"I don't have to prove myself to you, Mr. Randall, but any good leader knows you can get more done with loyalty than with fear. I'll leave it to you to decide what kind of leader I am. Now let's go."

CHAPTER 25

I glance around the inside of the lander. Apart from a squad of eight armored Chimeras and six Horvals, who are waiting in their individual compartments, the lander is empty. Ellie and I are the only humans in here. Commander Hill's explanation for why she chose *me* made some sense, but I still don't feel like the man for this job.

What am I going to tell a group of militant survivors? That they should lay down their weapons and march peacefully into the safe zone so that they can have the Kyra take away their kids, too? Commander Hill even admitted it: kids are their target now. The future generation. Indoctrinate them, make them *want* to become Chimeras, and then conscript them to fight in the Kyra's war. I wonder what kind of syllabus Bree has been given to teach her class.

Ellie glances at me, but her expression is hard to read in the murky blue light inside the lander.

"What is it?" I whisper.

"You didn't ask what happens to us if we fail."

I frown at that, considering the matter. "Probably nothing."

"They kill people for talking back, for being too old, for stealing food, so why not also for failure?"

She makes a good point. "They won't kill us, because they need people. The Commander said it herself, we're valuable because we can breed more soldiers. Without breed stock, what's the point of the safe zones?"

"You make it sound like we're cattle."

"We are. So long as we don't deliberately sabotage the negotiations, we'll be fine. They're not going to make an example out of voluntary collaborators."

"Maybe. But what do we tell those people when we get there?"

I stare hard at Ellie. I've been wondering the same thing. "We tell them the truth."

Ellie's eyebrows shoot up.

"But only the good parts."

* * *

Commander Hill leads Ellie and I down the boarding ramp. At the bottom she stops and points across a cluttered parking lot that gleams like a field of diamonds in the sun. At the end of that expanse is a familiar warehouse-style building with a brown and gray facade and blue trim around the name—

Walmart.

It's a supercenter.

"The refugees are hiding out in there," Commander Hill says.

"They picked a good spot," I reply. "Plenty of supplies to keep them going."

"Maybe, but not for long with their numbers. Estimates from the lander's scanners suggest there are more than two thousand people inside."

That figure rocks me back on my heels. "All military?"

"Mixed. Army and civilian."

"The approach is too exposed," I point out. "If there are military in there, then they already have us in their sights. How do we get in to negotiate?"

"They won't shoot two unarmed humans," Hill says.

"Easy for you to say."

"Approach slowly, with your hands up. And remove any excess clothing so they can see that you're unarmed."

Dread coils up in my guts. "This sounds like a good way to die."

"They need to negotiate just as badly as we want them to. They can't stay in there forever, and they know it."

I suck in a shaky breath and trade an anxious look with Ellie. "You ready for this?"

"No," she says.

I let out my breath in a sigh. "Yeah, me neither." But remembering Gaby gives me strength. I need to do this to buy some good will. "Let's get this over with." I shrug out of my jacket and remove my belt. Beside me, Ellie does the same. She hugs her shoulders and shivers at the sudden loss of warmth.

"After you," she says, nodding to me.

"Hold up," the commander interrupts. "Here." She opens a compartment on her belt and passes a small black capsule to me."

"What is it?" I ask.

"A comms piece. Kyra tech. Put it in your ear. It's already set to my personal frequency. We'll be in communication with each other the whole time."

I nod and fit the unit to my right ear. A moment later, a smaller tinnier version of the commander's husky voice ripples through the unit. "It's touch activated, so you'll need to reach up to your ear to open the comms for a reply. Try it now."

I touch my index finger to the device. "Comms check."

"Loud and clear," Commander Hill replies. Somehow her voice is no longer making it past her helmet. Those suits must be sound proof when the external speakers are disabled.

I nod and drop my arm back to my side. Looking to Ellie, I say, "I'll lead. Stay behind me in case they start shooting."

"Actually, that might be unwise," Commander Hill says. "I instructed you to bring her, because it makes you seem less threatening. Family man, versus suicide bomber."

I grimace at that analysis, but give in with a nod. "Okay."

"As far as the refugees are concerned, you are her father. Copy?"

I nod again.

"Good luck, Corporal."

"Yeah, thanks..."

I raise my hands above my head and start across the parking lot to the main entrance of the Walmart. Ellie keeps her hands raised, too.

We haven't made it more than fifty steps before an electronic squeal erupts from the Walmart and an amplified voice booms out.

"Stop and return to your vehicle or we will open fire."

"It's a bluff," Commander Hill growls in my ear. "They know they can't afford to compromise these negotiations."

"We're just here to talk!" I shout at the top of my lungs, hoping my voice will carry across the parking lot. "We're unarmed!"

A tepid silence follows.

Wind sends garbage and dead leaves fluttering. An empty water bottle jumps and skips along until it hits a dead body, lying face down in a pool of blood. A human woman with long blonde hair.

"You are to approach to within fifty feet. We will send someone out to search you."

"Understood!" I shout back, and slowly resume my approach.

Ellie is hanging back a step, but still approaching with me. We make it to within approximately fifty feet of the main entrance, and I stop once more. By this point my shoulders are aching from keeping my arms raised for so long, but I wait patiently, my eyes locked on the shattered glass doors of the supercenter.

Shadows are darting around inside.

One of them comes stepping through the doors. It's a soldier with a flak jacket and urban gray fatigues. He looks to be unarmed, like us, and the single chevron on his shoulder patch tells me he's a private.

The man stops in front of me. "Keep your hands raised," he orders, and then starts patting me down, checking for weapons. He reaches my boots and steps back.

"Take them off."

"Seriously?"

He gives me a sullen look.

"Okay." I drop slowly to one knee, and then gradually lower my arms to reach for my right boot. "We're here to negotiate a peaceful resolution," I say as I remove the first boot.

"That's between you and the general," the Private says.

"General, huh? Army?"

"Yes, sir."

"What division?"

"Cut the chatter and remove your other boot."

I do as I'm told.

"Take two steps back."

The soldier picks up my boots and shakes them both out to make sure there are no blades hidden inside.

"Put them back on."

He steps sideways and repeats the process with Ellie. When he's done checking her shoes, he turns and says, "Follow me."

We march across the parking lot to the darkened interior of the Walmart. As we cross the threshold of the shattered entrance, the shadows inside begin resolving into the familiar shapes of automatic checkout scanners and aisles of products. The smell is horrendous, but mostly of unwashed bodies and rotten food rather than raw sewage and corpses like the Frugal Foods from yesterday.

People are everywhere, sitting on the floor with sleeping bags, pillows, backpacks, futons, and whatever else they could find to make the floors more comfortable. The steady hum of conversation floods into hearing.

"This way," says the soldier walking ahead of us. He removes a flashlight from his belt and flicks it on. Moving past the entrance, I see the snipers flanking the doors, one to either side. More soldiers stand with them, out of sight of the doors, keeping watch with regular rifles.

Our guide makes a left past the checkout counters, then down an aisle that's fully stocked with dry foods. The opening of the aisle is guarded by two soldiers with rifles, probably to enforce a system of rations. At the end of the aisle are another two soldiers.

We walk down an aisle stocked with toilet paper and bottled water and emerge at a pair of swinging doors, also guarded. The soldiers guarding the entrance raise their rifles. Their weapons are equipped with tac lights, and they blind us with the beams. I notice that they also have night vision goggles attached to their helmets, but at the moment those optics are flipped up above their foreheads.

"State your business," one of the two says to our escort.

"I'm taking these negotiators to see General Gold," the private answers.

"We'll need to check them for weapons."

"Already done, sir."

"All the same. Raise your arms above your heads," he says to me and Ellie.

We do as we're told, and the guard lowers his rifle to pat us down again. After about a minute of that, he steps back, satisfied.

"Proceed," he says, and the other one pushes the doors open for us.

The private leads us through into a storage area with racks full of non-perishables. Forklifts stand idle in front of garage doors and concrete ramps leading down.

The smell of rotten meat invades my nostrils, making my stomach churn.

"I think I'm going to be sick," Ellie says.

No sign yet of what might be causing the smell.

We come to the end of the aisle, turn the corner, and come to another door. It's also guarded, but only by one soldier this time.

"State your business," the guard says.

"Private Gibbons delivering negotiators to the general."

The guard nods, and turns to knock on the door in a particular pattern. Three knocks. A pause. Then two more.

"Identify yourself," a muffled voice says.

"Corporal Harvik, Sir." He repeats what the private just told him.

"Proceed."

The guard pulls the door open, revealing a medium-sized office with a window. A man of average height and build is sitting behind a desk. He's wearing army fatigues. He stands up as we come in. His face is deeply-lined and tanned beneath a pronounced widow's peak. He has razor short white hair that practically glows in the pale wash of daylight flooding through the window beside him. The three stars on his fatigues indicate that he's a Lieutenant General.

"General Gold, sir," Private Gibbons says, saluting smartly.

"At ease, Private." The general's gaze flicks to us. "What are your names?"

"Former Army Corporal Christopher Randall, sir, and this is my daughter, Ellie."

The General nods. "Sit down," he says, gesturing to the chairs in front of his desk.

We take our seats and he sits with us. "Tell me, how did the demons convince you to risk life and limb coming in here, Corporal? Are they holding the rest of your family hostage?"

"No, sir," I reply.

"Really?" his eyebrows drift up.

"We are here of our own volition, sir. We were hoping to convince you to surrender peacefully and join the safe zone in San Bernardino."

The general leans back in his chair and folds his hands over a modest belly. "And why would we do that, Corporal? So that they can turn us into monsters and brainwash us to fight in their war?"

"Only about half of us are eligible to become Chimeras, sir," I point out. "They do screening tests on arrival. The rest of us get to live peacefully in assigned housing in the zone. Rations and supplies are distributed twice weekly, and we are assigned to work details designed to make the zone safer and more comfortable. The zone is fenced and guarded by Chimeran patrols. It's not ideal, but it's a hell of a lot safer than anything out here in the Wastes."

The general spends a moment glancing between me and Ellie. "What if we refuse to surrender? What do you think they'll do to us, Corporal?"

"I don't know, sir... but I have to believe the fact that they're going to this much trouble to negotiate with you is a good sign."

The general shrugs. "Maybe it is, but if we keep stalling, eventually their patience will run out, and they'll make an example out of us."

I frown, and Ellie speaks up, "If you already know that, then why haven't you surrendered?"

General Gold nods to Private Gibbons, taps his ear and then points to mine—the one with the comms in it.

Shit. I should have known that walking in here with an ear piece would get me into trouble. For all I know, it's also a bug. The private mimes to me the action of removing the comms. I do as instructed and he reaches for it.

As soon as I've handed it over, the private pockets the device.

"Dismissed, Gibbons," General Gold says.

"But, sir—"

"I can look after myself, Private."

"Understood, sir." Gibbons salutes again and then exits the room.

"Now we can speak freely," the General says as the door clicks shut. "You want to see why we haven't surrendered yet?"

I nod hesitantly.

"Follow me." The general stands up and walks around his desk, crossing behind our chairs. He grabs a camping lantern off a standing safe, turns it on, and then heads for the door. I stand up with Ellie and we follow the general out. He leads us back through the storage area, down aisles stacked high with boxes and pallets of large, non-perishable items.

After a while we come to a sealed room with no windows. The general opens a steel door with suspicious rust-brown stains around the handle. The rotten smell I detected earlier slams into me with dizzying force. My arm flies up, and I gag into my sleeve.

"Packs a punch, doesn't it?" the general says.

I look up from my sleeve to see what looks like it used to be a walk-in freezer. In the center of the space, dangling from the ceiling by chains and hooks is a dead human. Ellie curses and stumbles away from the entrance, coughing and gasping for air.

My stomach does a queasy flip, and my mind jumps in a dozen different directions at once: are these people cannibals? Is this what happened to the last negotiator the commander sent in here? He's already missing an arm. There is a puddle of blood beneath the body, congealed around a drain in the floor.

"Are you *eating* people?" Ellie blurts out.

"That's a negative, ma'am," General Gold replies. "And don't worry, the boy was already dead when we found him. But we had to feed the prisoner somehow, and they only eat meat."

That's when I notice what else is in the freezer. Sitting at the back is a small, hunching black shadow.

A low hiss rolls out of the gloom as it stands up and turns to face the light, revealing a ghostly-white face, four cranial stalks, and two bright red eyes. Skinny arms uncurl from its chest, and the chains that bind them rattle as it reaches half-heartedly for us with a three-fingered hand.

I gape at the general and slowly shake my head. "It's a Kyra."

"Any ideas about what we should do with him, Mr. Negotiator?"

CHAPTER 26

We're standing inside the freezer now, right at the edge of the Kyra's reach.

"You have to let him go," Ellie says, her voice muffled by the respirator she's wearing.

One of the General's men gave them to us before we went in, but it's not good enough. The rotten smell of death is still making my eyes water and my guts churn.

The Kyra is standing defiantly in front of us, his red eyes unblinking and blazing with feral hate. A black mask with a grille covers his mouth and nose—an alien version of the respirators we're wearing.

"I'm not sure it's that simple," the General replies. "If we let him go, there will be reprisals. It's not like we've had the bastard locked up in a five-star hotel. And there have been... incidents."

I grimace, noting the darkened patches of what might be bruises on the Kyra's face and head. A few dark lines criss-cross his cheeks and scalp, wounds that might have been made by a whip or even a blade. Rather than their usual armor, this Kyra is wearing baggy human clothes stained black and shredded in long vertical lines, lending credence to my whip theory. "He's been tortured," I say.

"Yes."

I glare at the general. "You authorized that?"

"We needed intel."

"And torture was the way to get him talking?"

General Gold shrugs.

"Did it work?" I ask.

"No. He doesn't speak our language. Or if he does, he's not talking."

"If you kill him, and they find the body, this will be even worse for you and your people."

"They won't find the body," General Gold says.

"It sounds like you already have this all figured out," I say. "So what are we here for?"

"To see your reaction. You were genuinely shocked, so I take it that you didn't know about the prisoner. And I doubt the demons would send in negotiators who didn't know the score."

"You can't be sure of that," I point out.

"No, I can't," the General admits. "But it's all I have to go on."

The Kyra looks to me and hisses something.

"There has to be another way," Ellie says.

"Even if there was, why would we spare its

life? These are the monsters that butchered billions of us just a few days ago. I'd put a bullet in its head myself if I could."

That statement gives me pause. Suspicion and icy dread trickle into the pit of my stomach, making me shiver despite the stuffy heat inside this freezer.

"You want us to do it," I realize.

"Of course. I can't let a couple of collaborators like you leave here knowing about our little house guest. You'd probably sell us out for a hot meal."

The General draws his sidearm and hands it to me. "Do your duty, soldier. Make the Union proud."

***

I stare grimly at the weapon in my hands. It's a smart-locked M99. "I can't fire this," I point out, stalling.

"I've unlocked it," the General says. "The safety is already off. Just point and shoot."

"I can't watch," Ellie whimpers before turning and running out of the freezer.

I look the general straight in the eye and shake my head.

"And if I say no? You can't kill a negotiator without reprisals, either."

The general's gaze narrows swiftly. He crosses his arms over his chest and jerks his chin to the alien. "You'd defend this demon butcher over your own kind?"

"He's defenseless. It's one thing to kill in combat or in self-defense, it's another to do it in cold blood."

"Well, I've got news for you, Corporal. This *is* self-defense. You have any idea how many of us they would kill if they knew what we did here?"

"There has to be another way."

"There isn't."

"I'm not shooting him."

"Then you're a gutless traitor. To hell with it! Give me the gun. I'll do it myself!"

The general snatches his weapon back and aims it at the Kyra.

The alien hisses and takes a swipe at him with its claws, but the chains binding its wrist snap taut, keeping the general out of reach.

"Wait," I say.

"What?" General Gold glares at me.

"Where did you put the Kyra's guns and armor?"

"In our armory, why?"

"Get the sidearm. It has a stun setting."

The general snorts and shakes his head. "I think you've missed the point of this exercise, Corporal."

"Stun the Kyra, then put its armor back on, except for the helmet. Remove its respirator after that. He'll suffocate without it. Hide the body outside if you can. Then, even if it's found, at least it will look like its death was an accident."

"So he was just wandering around like an idiot and he magically lost his helmet and his respirator?"

I shrug. "Break them and leave them nearby."

General Gold holds my gaze for several seconds, as if trying to decide whether or not I'm trying to trick him.

"What if he wakes up before he suffocates?"

"Stun it a few times. The effects are cumulative, and I saw one of them suffocate without its mask. It doesn't take long." That last part is a lie, but it seems like a reasonable assumption.

"You're asking me to take a big risk."

"A bigger risk than the Kyra finding one of their own with a bullet in its head in the same place where you and your people were hiding? With its armor on at least most of the signs of torture will be gone. And besides, you don't know if that lander or the Chimeras outside have acoustic sensors that could detect a gunshot. Their weapons are much quieter than ours, especially on the stun setting, so it will be a more discreet way to deal with this problem. Not to mention more humane," I add.

General Gold appears to be grinding his teeth as he considers the idea. "Well, aren't you the humanitarian. It's just a pity that these fuckers aren't human." He pulls the trigger. The gun goes off with a deafening report that leaves my ears ringing so badly I barely hear the subsequent *thump* and rattle of chains clattering as the body hits the floor.

"Let's go," General Gold says.

Blinking in shock, I stand there staring at the spreading pool of black blood for several seconds before following the general out.

Ellie catches my eye. "Did you..."

"Not me," I manage.

General Gold whistles between his teeth and waves to a group of soldiers, who come running over. "Lieutenant, get these two escorted outside and clean up that mess." He points to the inside of the freezer. "It's time to end this charade."

"Yes, sir." The lieutenant snaps orders at two others who take up flanking positions around us. "Let's go," one of them says, gesturing with the barrel of his rifle.

I'm feeling defeated and miserable as they escort us back through the storage area to the inside of the Walmart. On the one hand, I agree with the general. The Kyra deserve every bit of violence and fury that we can mete out. The Chimeras killed my mother in front of me. The Kyra experimented on Gaby and now they've taken her away to parts unknown. To say nothing of the billions of people that they killed or conscripted as soldiers for their war.

But I was hoping to save that particular Kyra and that would give me some kind of extra leverage to get Gaby back. I feel like a disgusting human being for even thinking it—a gutless traitor, just like the general said.

CHAPTER 27

My comms piece is returned to me at the exit. I fit it to my ear and touch a finger to the device.

"The general has agreed to a surrender," I say.

"Get back here ASAP," Commander Hill replies in a clipped tone.

Not exactly the congratulations I was expecting. I wonder if I was right about them detecting a gunshot. Commander Hill is probably waiting to debrief me. I swallow thickly. The question is, what will I tell her?

"Let's pick up the pace," I whisper to Ellie.

She nods, and I break into a jog, weaving a path between abandoned shopping carts, crashed air cars, and paralyzed ground vehicles sticking halfway out of their parking spots.

As soon as we reach the lander, a pair of armored Chimeras grab us and physically drag us up the ramp.

"Hey! We're volunteers, not prisoners," I object. Part of me is surprised that they can drag me at all. I'm not exactly a lightweight.

Ellie looks terrified, but she's not struggling. Maybe she doesn't want to make things worse. My heart is pounding in my chest. A false sense of guilt makes me want to crawl out of my own skin. Somehow, they know about the Kyra prisoner, and now we're in trouble for letting the general kill it.

At the top of the ramp, we find Commander Hill standing just inside the airlock with her hands on her hips. I've learned to recognize her by her slightly shorter, slimmer frame.

"What's going on?" I ask, even as the lander takes off with a sudden roar. I glance out the door as the ground goes spinning away in a dizzying blur.

"We're performing an emergency extraction," the commander replies.

I was right. "You knew about the prisoner?"

"Your tracking implant has limited sensors. We were able to detect the Kyra with them. Is he still alive?"

Sensors? A microphone? I wonder. No, if they'd been listening to my conversation with General Gold, the commander wouldn't be asking me what happened.

"I don't know if he survived. He took a bullet to the torso at point-blank range. He wasn't moving when I left."

"*Ka'ra!*" Commander Hill growls.

The lander is already dropping back down for a landing. I hear multiple sets of hurried footfalls and turn to look just in time to see armored Chimeras streaming down from the access ramp at the back of the troop bay. As I'm watching them, the soldiers vanish into thin air, one after another. Cloaking armor. I stare blankly after the invisible wraiths.

Ellie leans out of cover, and a bullet plinks off the lander's armor.

"Stay away from the entrance," Commander Hill snaps, and yanks Ellie back into cover. "Who shot the prisoner?" the commander asks, looking back to me.

I plaster myself to the bulkhead beside Ellie. At this point, lying is only going to make things worse, so I don't even bother trying to come up with an explanation.

"The general shot him. He wanted me to do it, but I refused. I did my best to talk him out of it, but he was convinced that covering up what they did would be better than letting the Kyra go."

Commander Hill goes suddenly very still. "And what exactly did they do?"

I grimace. "They tortured him."

Commander Hill mutters another alien curse word. "Thank you for your cooperation, Corporal Randall."

I hear the muffled reports of gunfire and men shouting rumbling out of the storage area of the supercenter. I wonder how the general's soldiers can even see the Chimeras to shoot at them.

After a few short minutes, I hear a *boom,* and a blinding flash of light dazzles us. A wash of heat roars in, along with the sound of pulverized bits of concrete *thunking* against the lander's hull.

The steady thunder of hurried footfalls returns, chased up the landing ramp by a plinking, hissing hail of bullets. I see bobbing scraps and snatches of a small, bony creature with chalk-white skin. It's being carried and shielded by a tight formation of cloaked Chimeran soldiers.

The lander roars and jerks suddenly into the air. The soldiers de-cloak. They're huddled around the Kyra. One of them administers aid from a bulky black pack. Commander Hill strides over. Ellie and I follow curiously.

"Is it alive?" Ellie whispers.

"Yes," Commander Hill replies. "Barely."

The soldier attending the Kyra injects multiple silver cannisters around the hole in the Kyra's torso, then sprays both the entry and exit wounds and applies a translucent patch of a jelly-like material.

The medic delivers a fourth injection, then sits back on his haunches.

"Well?" Commander Hill demands.

"Any second now..." the medic replies.

The Kyra's eyes blink open. It sits up, and hisses something. Its gaze fixes on me, and it utters a series of growls.

An uneasy feeling makes my stomach churn.

Commander Hill turns to me.

"He says you tried to save him."

So he does know English.

"It didn't work," I point out.

"No, but he appreciates the effort."

I incline my head to the alien in a shallow nod and paste a tight smile on my face. A Kyra saying thank you? Maybe there's hope for our species to find some common ground, after all.

"What are you going to do with the refugees?" Ellie asks.

"We'll make an example of the ones who did this," Commander Hill says. "The rest will be taken to the safe zone as promised."

I'm just about to ask how they're going to get that many people to the safe zone, but then I glance behind me, out the open airlock and see a stream of landers roaring by, followed by a glimpse of an even larger, cigar-shaped vessel.

"Take him to the med deck," Commander Hill orders.

"Yes, ma'am," one of the others replies.

The Chimeran soldiers carry the wounded Kyra between them, aiming for the access ramp they came down earlier.

"Where are we going now?" Ellie asks.

"Back to join your work detail," Commander Hill replies, moving to follow the soldiers to the ramp.

"Wait! What about my daughter? Have you learned anything yet?"

The commander stops and looks back at me. "Come. We'll talk about it in my cabin."

Ellie and I start after her, but the commander holds up a hand to stop us.

"Not the girl. Just you."

Ellie fixed me with a worried look, and I shrug helplessly. "It's okay," I say to reassure her.

And then I'm climbing the ramp behind Commander Hill, using the guide rail to steady myself. My veins are singing with a heady rush of adrenaline. My head is spinning with anticipation and the urgent need to know what the commander learned. I can't climb fast enough.

The ramp flattens out beside a set of extra-wide doors. Commander Hill gestures to them, and they part to reveal a utilitarian space with dim, glowing blue lights, gray walls and glossy black floors. The room holds some generic, but vaguely recognizable furniture: a glossy black desk and a chair facing the door, a bed built into an alcove around a dim viewport, a sitting area with gray couches, a chair, and a low table between them. Along one bulkhead is some type of bar or workspace with drawers and appliances that I don't recognize. To my right as we come in stands a glossy black table with no chairs around it.

The commander leads me to the sitting area and gestures to one of the couches before taking a seat in the chair.

The doors to the living area swish shut just as

I sit down. The couch is more comfortable than it looks, adapting to my shape like some type of memory foam.

"Where is Gaby. Did you find her?" I ask.

Commander Hill nods once, and reaches up to remove her helmet. Her red eyes look purple in the blue light. "I did..."

Hearing the hesitation in the commander's voice, my heart starts hammering so hard that it feels like it's going to explode. "Is she okay? What aren't you telling me?"

"Actually, it's what you didn't tell me that's of more importance. You didn't mention that Gabrielle is a Chimera."

"I thought you knew. Can't you look up everything about us just by scanning our implants?"

"I didn't bother looking up your daughter until you asked me to find out what happened to her."

"Well, so what? Isn't it a good thing? She's not a Dakka. Chimeras have more rights than us, don't they?"

"It's not that simple. Your daughter is a K'sari."

I blink and shake my head. "A what?"

"It's what the Kyra call their leaders. A K'sari has royal blood. They're chosen by the gods to rule."

"Again, that sounds like a good thing."

"It is. Among the Kyra. How did your daughter become a Chimera, Mr. Randall?"

My cheeks bulge with a reply, but I hesitate just a second before blurting it out. "She was bitten by a Dreg."

"No, she wasn't. Try again."

Apprehension swirls around me like a dark cloud. I feel like I'm standing on a cliff, peering over the edge. If I tell her what really happened, will that help or hurt my chances of getting Gaby back?

CHAPTER 28

"Let me save you the trouble of coming up with another lie, Mr. Randall. The virus doesn't result in Chimeran K'sari. Your daughter is special, and it's because she was the result of illegal experiments conducted by Kyron heretics."

"Why her?" I ask.

"Who knows? Maybe she was easier to reach, or maybe she was a good candidate for other reasons. Whatever the case, the heretics want to create royal blood lines for all the different species of Chimeras in the Federation so that they can lobby for equal rights and independence. Your daughter is part of a rebellion, Mr. Randall, and that makes her a threat."

"But she's just a child!"

"Her very existence is an abomination to the Kyra."

"So, she's in danger."

"Along with all of the other K'sari, yes. But she's still alive. I was able to trace her implant's tracking ID to a staging area in Santa Monica."

"Wasn't LA bombed during the invasion?"

"That's why Santa Monica is a staging area. It's relatively free of Dregs and human refugees who might interfere with the Kyra's operation."

"I have to get Gaby out of there."

"It's over a hundred and twenty kilometers to Santa Monica. Not to mention the staging area is swarming with soldiers and Kyra."

"I saved one of them," I point out. "That has to count for something."

"You *tried to* save one of them," Commander Hill corrects.

"Well, I *did* save you."

We hold each other's gazes for a long moment.

"Help me get her out. Please. You want me to beg?"

"And where will you go after that? The Wastes? How long before Dregs get you, or before Chimeras pick you up and discover that you're wanted in connection with your daughter's escape? Even if I could find a way to help you get Gabrielle out, you'll be exiles for the rest of your lives."

I clasp my hands in front of my lips in a pleading posture. "What if it were your daughter? What would you do to get her back?"

Commander Hill winces and looks away, out the window by her bed. She stares at the horizon for several seconds, watching several landers zipping by.

"I'd do anything," she says quietly. The commander drags her gaze away from the window. "We'll talk more about this later. Go back down and wait with Elenore."

"Who?" I ask.

"Ellie."

"What if later is too late?"

"Pray it isn't. I cannot plan such an intricate rescue and escape without any advance preparations."

My spirits soar with the commander's words. "So, you *will* help me."

"I'll do what I can."

"Thank you," I breathe through a sigh as I stand up. "Sam was right. You're not like the other Chimeras."

Commander Hill smiles thinly at that. "Maybe I am, maybe I'm not, but you can save your thanks. You have to be alive to be grateful, and what you've asked me to do is likely to get both of us killed. Go back down to the troop bay. We're about to land. Not a word of this to anyone, understood?"

"Yes. How will I know when it's time to..." *Escape?* I finish quietly in my head.

"Tonight. I'll be in touch. Don't do anything until I tell you to."

I nod my agreement, and the commander waves to open the doors of her quarters. As I hurry down the ramp to join Ellie, I can't help but feel like an unbearable weight has been lifted from my shoulders. I know where Gaby is, and the commander is working out a plan to rescue her. But that feeling of elation and relief is tempered by what else the commander told me. The Kyra consider Gaby an abomination. That means she could be in serious danger.

Hang on, Gabs, I think to myself. *Just hang on.*

Commander Hill said we're moving tonight. She probably means for us to escape under the cover of darkness, when the patrols are thinner and the clean-up crews are off the streets.

I just hope tonight is soon enough, and that the commander's idea of helping isn't just to get us outside the fence and then leave the rest to us.

Crossing a hundred and twenty kilometers to reach Santa Monica on foot would take us a week or more, and by then Gaby might not even be alive to rescue. Assuming we survive the journey ourselves.

I wince at the thought and shake my head to clear it. *We're going to get her back,* I insist to myself.

CHAPTER 29

Ellie regards me with eyebrows raised. "Well? What did she say about your daughter?"

"She's going to look into it some more."

"That's it? You were up there a long time for such a short conversation," Ellie says.

Unable to come up with a more detailed excuse, I just shake my head.

Ellie looks away with a frown.

The lander sets down with an audible *thump,* and both sets of airlock doors spring open, letting in a bright wash of sunlight.

Approaching footsteps draw my attention to the access ramp. A Chimera hands me the pack full of grav discs that I was wearing this morning.

"Here," he says. "Get back to work."

I shrug into the pack and start toward the airlock with Ellie. We walk down the ramp together to find that we're in the same parking lot as before. Both the lot and the street we were clearing are much emptier now. Only a few fallen streetlights and power poles remain. Horvals are busy strapping those down onto hovering sleds for removal.

"I don't see our team," Ellie says, scanning the horizon with a hand pressed to her forehead to shield her eyes from the sun.

"Over there." I point to another parking lot on the other side of the street where a stream of debris is floating up and away to join a broad river in the sky. Farther off, more lines of derelict cars and debris are snaking together like the tentacles of some giant, mechanical squid.

"At this rate the zone will be clear by nightfall," Ellie says.

"Maybe," I agree.

A horn blast sounds from the lander beside ours.

"Looks like we made it back in time for lunch," I say.

"Good timing," Ellie says as she hurries toward the other lander.

I hesitate before following her.

A groaning *whoosh* sounds from the vehicle we just left. I turn and peer into the shadowy bowels of the Commander's ship in time to see the airlock doors slamming shut. The landing ramp telescopes into place beneath the hull, and the lander rockets into the sky with a *roar* and a blast of wind that's no warmer than our surroundings. The ship's glowing blue thrusters ignite and angle away from the ground, and then it speeds up, rapidly dwindling to a tiny black speck.

Will the commander honor her word?
I guess I'll find out tonight.

* * *

After lunch, the day passes with agonizing slowness. Sam and Naomi still aren't talking to me, and Harry and Ana are also keeping to themselves. I keep looking up at the sun, willing it to sink faster.

The work itself is easy: slap grav discs on debris and watch them fly away. But the mindless tedium of it leaves a lot of space for worries to crowd my thoughts.

What if Commander Hill can't find a way to help us rescue Gaby? What if she changes her mind? Or worse, what if it's already too late?

Looking up again, I'm relieved to see the clouds ablaze with the fiery reds and oranges of sunset.

I place another grav disc in the rear wheel well of an army JLTV. Ellie is about to place the last one when I spot the dead soldier curled up in the back between two big metal cases of ammo.

"Ellie, hang on, there's a body in here!" I call.

Just as I'm reaching in to drag it out by the feet, a galloping sounds interrupts me, approaching fast.

A Horval leaps up and grabs the soldier in its massive jaws. I watch in shock as it runs off with its prize. A second Horval streaks toward the first and soon they're fighting over it like two dogs with a bone.

I look away with a grimace, but Ellie is still staring fixedly at the gruesome spectacle. I head over her way and slap a final disc on the JLTV. Moments later it starts floating up to join the other debris in the sky.

Whatever technology is behind the grav discs, it's completely soundless, but the more powerful main thrusters of the Kyra's ships are not. A rising roar draws my attention to another object in the sky—one with six glowing blue thrusters facing down. It's a lander, and it's headed straight for us.

My heart rate soars with anticipation. That's the commander. It has to be. I break into a sprint, tracking the vessel's approach to a probable landing site.

"Hey, where are you going?" Ellie calls after me. "Our shift hasn't ended yet!"

But I'm not listening. My mind is laser-focused on finding and rescuing Gaby.

Corporal Solis's voice booms across the parking lot next. "Hey, Randall! Get back to work!"

I pretend not to hear him.

"Stop, or I'll shoot!" Corporal Solis intones.

I stop, reluctantly, and turn to face the corporal with my lungs heaving for air. Corporal

Solis is striding purposefully toward me with his sidearm raised and aimed at my chest.

I glance longingly to the lander. It's busy setting down less than a hundred feet away.

"Eyes on me, Randall," the Corporal adds.

My fists ball up in frustration. I look back to him just as he stops in front of me.

"Explain yourself. Where did you think you were you going? Did you see a Dreg or something?"

"Yeah. I thought I saw a Dreg."

Corporal Solis holds my gaze for several seconds. "With a mouth like yours it's a wonder you're still alive. The sensors in my suit will warn me if any Dregs are nearby. I'll let you know if that happens. Otherwise, just assume you're hallucinating from exhaustion, and keep working until your shift is over, understood?"

"Yes, sir."

I hesitate, my gaze tracking back to the lander that just arrived. The ramp is down, but no one has come out yet.

"What are you waiting for, get back to—"

Just then, a pair of hoverbikes go roaring out, headed straight for us.

Ellie catches up to me, gasping for air. She plants her hands on her knees and bows her head to get the blood flowing. "What got into you?" she asks.

The hoverbikes arrive, interrupting us, and one of the riders jumps off.

Corporal Solis snaps to attention and salutes. "Commander."

"At ease," she says. "It looks like I'm in need of volunteers again."

"You need Mr. Randall *again?*" Corporal Solis asks. He sounds suspicious this time, as if he's beginning to suspect some type of collusion between us. "His shift is almost over. We were about to head back to the station."

"I don't need Randall specifically," the commander replies. "I need a team. Yours will do."

"May I ask what for, ma'am?"

"Bait. Aerial scans discovered another nest of Dregs just outside the perimeter. We need to flush them out before they catch the scent of all the fresh meat living inside the zone."

"I see. Of course, we are at your service, Commander," Solis says.

"Good. Get the rest of your team and meet me at my lander. We're skids up in five."

"Copy that."

Commander Hill jumps back on her bike, guns the engine, and roars away with the other soldier.

"You heard the Commander!" Solis snaps. "Get over there."

"Yes, sir," I reply. He leaves us alone, running off to find the others.

It's getting too dark to see clearly, but it's easy to tell that Ellie is scared. "They want us to be *bait?*" she asks in a shrinking voice.

I send her a reassuring smile. The mission is probably just an excuse to help me escape and find Gaby, but I can't tell her that. "Don't worry. I'm sure they have a plan to keep us safe."

"You mean like they kept Grant and Helen safe?" Ellie counters.

"That was different. They surprised us. This time we're surprising them."

The sound of approaching footsteps interrupts whatever Ellie might have said next. Our team is running toward Commander Hill's lander in a loose formation behind Corporal Solis and Rexi, our Horval.

"We'll be okay," I say, waving to Ellie over my shoulder. And then I go sprinting across the parking lot to reach the lander.

CHAPTER 30

I'm beginning to doubt that flushing out the Dreg nest is a ruse, after all.

"Just so you know, I blame you for this," Sam whispers to me.

"I blame me, too," I whisper back as we creep along behind Commander Hill and Corporal Solis.

We're approaching a meat packing plant that's supposedly teeming with Dregs, and we're armed with nothing but Kyron lanterns. They radiate a pathetically dim blue light that is just enough to see where we're going. Supposedly it's also of a wavelength that won't wake the Dregs once we get inside.

Of course, there's a nest of Dregs in a meat packing plant. Dregs are carnivores, so this is a logical place to find them congregating. And that's yet another detail which makes me doubt this mission is a ruse. Still, I'm clinging to hope that Commander Hill will keep her word.

But then why is my whole team here? The others don't have anything to do with the plan to rescue Gaby.

My spirits fall precipitously. Everything is adding up to this mission being exactly what Commander Hill said it is. I glance back the way we came. Besides the Commander and Corporal Solis, our lander is the only backup we have. Not even Rexi, our Horval, is with us. She was ordered to stay on board.

We're the warm bodies, the soft, unarmored bait that the Dregs will smell as soon as we open the doors of the meat packing plant. Once they catch our scent, we're supposed to run back to the lander as fast as we can with them on our heels. It's a terrible plan.

Behind me, I catch peripheral glimpses of Ellie and Sam sweeping their lanterns around. Harry and Ana are keeping to the back of the group with Naomi. The three of them are the slowest runners among us, so it's better that they keep their distance.

There has to be a better way to do this, I think.

The steel doors we're approaching are dead ahead and growing swiftly with our approach. Hardly any windows break the solid expanse of the building. It's just a sprawling rectangular structure, all on one level. The better way to deal with this nest would be to drop a bomb on the packing plant.

That gives me hope. Maybe this *is* a ruse. Just

a very dangerous one.

Commander Hill stops in front of the entrance and tests the handle. It turns freely. She opens the door a crack and aims her rifle through the gap. A moment later, she opens it further and waves for us to follow her in. Corporal Solis turns and holds a finger up to the faceless visor of his helmet. As if we needed to be told to be quiet.

The corporal follows Commander Hill inside, and Sam gestures ahead of us, as if to say, *after you.*

Fair enough. I take point and walk through—

The smell knocks the wind out of me and staggers me back a step, but I force myself to keep going. Dead ahead, the two Chimeras are moving smoothly forward. Easy for them. They're wearing helmets that probably have air filters to block out the smell.

The inside of the plant is a maze of conveyor belts, gleaming robotic arms, and meat processing equipment. Bloody plastic bins are overturned everywhere I look. Animal bones picked clean litter the floor, glowing brightly in the dim blue light radiating from my lantern. I weave a path around the overturned bins, trying to avoid the bones and the black patches on the floor that are probably pools of blood.

I can't see any sign of the Dregs that are supposed to be hiding in here, but both Commander Hill and Corporal Solis seem to know exactly where they're going. They're checking corners and cover positions with their rifles, but their unhesitating, purposeful progress through the facility tells me they already know where the Dregs are hiding.

Or else Hill has been lying to me all along and this is a trap. Maybe she sees me as a loose cannon now that my daughter is missing, and the easiest way to neutralize that threat is to kill me and make it look like an accident.

Get it together, Chris.

There's enough immediate danger to worry about without me adding conspiracy theories to the pile.

As I move through the facility, I try to keep my eyes everywhere at once. Footsteps echo quietly behind me, along with the steady rhythm of shallow, panicky breathing. We're all doing our best to keep quiet, especially knowing how good the Dregs' hearing is.

The loudest sound is my own heartbeat, thumping like a war drum in my ears.

We come to a door made of plastic flaps. Commander Hill stops and holds up a closed fist, then removes a black cylinder from her belt. It looks like some type of grenade. Corporal Solis removes a matching one, and then moves to another door of plastic flaps, located about twenty feet farther down.

Once he's in position, the commander gestures emphatically to the entryway in front of her.

I get the message. The Dregs are in there. She's going to use that grenade to flush them out. I can't help wondering: doesn't that make our presence here unnecessary?

Too late to argue about it now. My whole body tenses up, getting ready to run for my life. Maybe the grenades will take out most of them and we just have to lead the stragglers out.

Commander Hill holds up a hand like a stop sign for us to wait, then raises that hand, palm up, and glowing words appear in the air between us.

When this goes off, follow me. Do not *go back the way we came.*

That puts a knot of tension between my eyes. Is there another exit that's closer? I glance over my shoulder at the others. Sam looks equally confused.

I try to picture the position of the lander in relation to the facility and our current location inside of it. I don't think the vessel has a clear line of fire to any side of the building except for the one we came in on. That means if we take a different exit, closer or not, we'll be cut off from our fire support.

That's yet another inconsistency to this mission. They're piling up now. I watch breathlessly as a blinking red light appears on the side of Commander Hill's grenade. By some unspoken agreement, both she and Corporal Solis push through their respective doors of plastic strips. I watch the flaps waving restlessly in the wake of the commander's passing...

A split second later she comes running back out. "This way!" she shouts, breaking the silence. She's headed in the opposite direction of Corporal Solis, down the back of the rows of conveyor belts and the meat packing machinery.

A rising tumult of shrieks and growls fills the air, seeming to come from everywhere at once. Ellie streaks by me.

"Naomi! Let's go!" Sam cries, waiting for his wife to go ahead of him. I race after Ellie and pull alongside her. She sends me a terrified look.

"Eyes front!" I say.

We pour on an extra burst of speed just as a dazzling flash tears out behind us, followed by a muffled boom. An echo of that explosion follows as the second grenade goes off.

I glance back to see the others right on my heels, but the corporal is trailing at least fifteen feet back, struggling to catch up. His door was farther away from the commander's chosen escape route.

While I'm looking, a shrieking wall of flames boils out just behind Corporal Solis. It's the Dregs. They're on fire, and mad as hell.

The corporal takes hasty aim over his shoulder with his rifle and a stuttering stream of emerald light strobes out.

I'm perversely satisfied that he's bringing up the rear. Maybe *we're* not the bait after all. Up ahead, I spot a dormant red exit sign and the blank gray rectangle of a door beneath it.

Commander Hill is still leading the charge, barely a dozen feet away. The door is about another fifteen, maybe twenty.

We're going to make it, I realize.

But even as that thought enters my head, another door bursts open right in front of us. It slams into Commander Hill and sends her sprawling.

A tangle of bodies emerges, shrieking and snorting furiously. Four sets of gleaming eyes turn on us, and the Dregs shriek again, their cranial stalks twitching and heads tilting curiously from side to side, as if sizing us up before they make their move.

My knees lock up as I struggle to arrest my momentum. I stumble and nearly fall on my face. Ellie screams and grabs my arm for support, using me to propel herself away from the Dregs.

They shriek again, and their knees bend as if they're about to leap through the air to reach us. Everything happens in seconds, but it feels like minutes. I whirl around, searching for another way out.

"This way!" Sam cries, and dashes down between two rows of conveyor belts. Naomi is right beside him, with Harry and Ana on their heels, followed by Ellie.

"Wait!" Commander Hill shouts to us.

Screeching reports from her rifle and flickering flashes of green light illuminate the rising walls of machinery around us. The Dregs snarl and growl like a pack of wild animals as they round on her. I'm scanning my surroundings desperately for something I can use for a weapon to help her. If the commander dies, there goes my hopes of escaping and finding Gaby.

But there's nothing. This time, all I can do is run away with the others.

My hectic retreat has me leaping over empty plastic bins and skidding through puddles of congealed blood. Between two bins, my foot rolls on something metal and I almost smack my head on one of the conveyor belts. I drop my lantern and manage to catch myself by grabbing a metal guide rail. Seeing that there's a gap in the railing, I whirl around and spot the object I tripped over. A sturdy metal pole about nine feet long.

Perfect.

I snatch the pole off the ground and test the weight. It's heavy, maybe ten or fifteen pounds, and it's far too long for me to wield it like a club, but it should work well as a spear. It's just a pity there's nothing sharp at the end.

Up ahead, Sam cries out in alarm as a Dreg leaps down from a conveyor belt and lands in front of him, blocking the way. "Get back, get back!" he cries to the others, and they come surging toward me.

The way behind us is clear, and those screeching flashes of emerald light are approaching the end of the aisle. Commander Hill must have survived. Relief pours through me. There's no sign of a second stream of fire to indicate that Corporal Solis is still alive. Dancing shadows and flickering orange light pinpoint where those flaming Dregs must have fallen as they succumbed to their injuries.

The sinister sounds of scrabbling feet and of plastic bins being kicked around echo on all sides of us, indicating just how many of those monsters are still alive in here.

I'm tempted to make a run for the Commander's position, but Sam is halfway down to the other side of the building, warding off a Dreg with nothing but a plastic meat bin to protect himself. Grabbing my Kyron lantern where I dropped it, I clip it to my belt and dash down the aisle with my spear raised.

Ellie, Harry, and Ana go flashing by me, headed back the way we came. Naomi is with her husband, looking for something she can use to help him.

"Go!" I shout to her. "I've got this."

She looks up from hunting around blindly on the floor, and I see she has a jagged white bone that might have come from the thigh of a cow—or maybe a human. She blinks once.

"Go!" I scream again while jumping over another plastic bin, this one full of foul-smelling juices.

"I'm not going anywhere," she hisses and

rounds on the Dregs with her bone-knife.

Crowding in beside Sam, I stab my metal pole straight into the abdomen of the Dreg in front of him. It cries out in pain and staggers back a few steps, clutching its stomach with both hands. Flashing demon eyes flare wide as they find me, looking purple in the light of my lantern.

I raise the pole and slam it into the creature's forehead with a ringing report. The Dreg goes limp and drops to the floor with a *thud*.

Sam lets out a shuddering sigh. "Thanks, man, I—"

A hollow *boom* sounds behind us, followed by Naomi yelping with fright. Another Dreg is standing behind us on an overturned bin.

"Get back!" Sam cries even as Naomi squeezes between us. Sam and I close ranks like a poor man's Phalanx. He's got the shield; I have the spear.

Slap.

Naomi screams, and we both flinch. The sound came from behind us.

Two more Dregs are standing over the motionless body of the one I knocked down.

"We're surrounded," Sam breathes. He glances about frantically for an escape, but the conveyor belts beside us are too high to reach, and the ones below are too cluttered with machinery for us to slip through.

Making matters worse, the rest of our team is nowhere to be seen, and the reassuring flashes of emerald fire coming from the commander's rifle have stopped.

CHAPTER 31

"**W**here is everyone?" Naomi whimpers.

"We're on our own," I whisper. "Stay close to me. I'll try to keep them at a distance."

Sam steps in front of us with his plastic bin raised. "I'll hold this one off. You take the two behind us."

I nod and turn around, re-arranging my grip on my makeshift spear as I do so. The two Dregs behind us look furious. One of them has a long bundle of stringy hair trailing down like a topknot from its otherwise bald head. That, plus its smaller frame makes me realize it used to be a young woman. The male Dreg beside it pushes her back, as if trying to protect her from me.

She shrieks and slashes his cheek open with her claws.

Maybe not.

The male dreg turns on her with a braying howl and then lunges. The two of them fall over in a shrieking heap.

"Back the other way," I whisper to Naomi. We surge toward Sam and the other Dreg. I stab at it with my pole, but it darts sideways to avoid the blow and then grabs the other end and wrenches it out of my hands with shocking force.

My weapon lands on the floor and bounces around with metallic thunder. The Dreg hisses and springs toward us.

"Shit!" Sam cries as it slams into his plastic bin and knocks him over. Its arms blur as it flails and scrapes its claws against the barrier, tearing the bottom of the bin open.

Naomi and I stand frozen in horror, struggling to find a way to help him that won't expose us to the Dreg's claws. Snapping out of it, I grab the creature by the crusty scraps of its shirt and try to throw it off. It rounds on me with a snarl and a swipe of its claws. I shove it away and jump back just before it can tear my throat open.

A blinding flash of green light slams into the creature from behind, staggering it. The stench of burned flesh joins the fetid horror of rotten meat in my nostrils.

Another screech and a flash sends the creature to the ground.

A dark figure waves to us from the far end of the aisle.

Naomi and Sam fly past me.

One of the two Dregs behind us is busy picking itself off the floor, and it's not alone. Dozens more are busy crawling down from the conveyor belts like spiders.

I spin away and scramble to pick up my spear.

"Leave it! Just run!" Commander Hill cries.

And so I do.

The Dregs answer the commander's voice with cries of their own, and I hear the steady slapping of their bare feet on the polished concrete floors behind me.

I reach Commander Hill's side, and she grabs my arm, physically dragging me toward the exit we were headed for mere minutes ago.

The ragged panting and gasping of the horde reaches my ears, becoming louder and more frenzied the closer it gets.

Up ahead, Sam and Naomi crash into the exit and push through, stumbling into a world of starlight and shadows. We reach it and Commander Hill slams through with a thunderous boom.

She spins around, holding the handle and using it to pivot with her momentum. "Help me get it shut!" she cries.

My boots skid on the pavement as I struggle to stop and turn the other way. Commander Hill shuts the door.

The sound of bodies slamming into the other side is like a cannonade.

"The handle!" the commander screams, just as I plant my shoulder against the exit.

It's then that I see she's still holding the gleaming silver handle of the door. Despite her efforts, it's turning steadily. I reach over and add my hands around hers, forcing the lever back up.

"I'll have to fuse the lock. Brace yourself."

"Brace my—"

Commander Hill lets go, and I'm left to hold the handle on my own. My cheeks bulge with the sudden exertion, and I feel the handle cutting into my hands.

Either I'm dealing with what used to be the world's strongest man on the other side of this door, or the Dregs are unbelievably strong. My feet start slipping as I struggle to brace myself.

"Hurry the fuck up!" I grit out, wondering what's taking the commander so long.

"Quiet!" she hisses back at me.

I risk a look to see the cause of the alarm in her voice.

A group of maybe fifty Dregs is running across the back lot of the building where we're standing, and they're in hot pursuit of my team.

A flash of light and a scalding wave of heat makes me recoil from the door with a curse. The handle is glowing white-hot.

"That won't hold long," Commander Hill says. "Run!"

"Where to?"

Before she can reply, I see one of my team run straight into an invisible wall and bounce off. The others dig in their heels to avoid the same thing happening to them.

And then the air shimmers and a familiar

sight appears. A lander. They just found it.

"Head for the ramp!" Commander Hill shouts back to me.

A torrent of laser fire erupts from the top of the ship, strafing over the horde below. The Dregs scatter, shrieking and screaming as they go.

My team recovers quickly. Harry and Sam stoop down to carry Ellie up the ramp as Naomi and Ana go bounding up to the airlock. She was the one who ran into the cloaked lander.

Commander Hill strafes the horde with her rifle as we go, giving them something else to think about as we make our retreat. Naomi and Ana are already banging on the doors of the airlock, begging to be let in.

The doors begin parting in the middle just as my feet touch the bottom of the ramp. I fly up past Sam and Harry, then turn back to pull them inside.

Commander Hill is the last one in, backpedaling and firing steadily as she goes. The Dregs reach the ramp and come surging up it.

The airlock doors slam shut, but several arms and legs are sticking through, reaching blindly for us.

The snarling and shrieking on the other side pitches up sharply into wails of agony as the doors crush the intervening limbs and cut them off. The severed appendages fall and hit the grated floor with meaty slaps. The lander's main thrusters start up with a roar, and the floor kicks up beneath us, sending me stumbling into the nearest wall.

I hear the fading screams of Dregs as they fall off the ramp or get incinerated by the ship's thrusters.

After that initial burst of acceleration, the g-forces fall away suddenly, and we're left gasping and staring at one another in shock. Pulsing red and blue lights start up, sterilizing us with different wavelengths of light.

Ellie looks to be unconscious. Sam and Harry lay her out gently on the deck. I walk over and drop to my haunches beside her.

"Ellie?"

She doesn't respond. I check her pulse and feel it skipping weakly beneath my fingertips.

"She's still breathing," Sam says, leaning his ear close beside her lips.

"Is anyone injured?" Commander Hill asks suddenly, and I turn to see her twisting off her helmet.

"Yes!" Ana snaps. "Can't you see? She knocked herself out on your stupid ship!"

"I meant are any of you bitten or scratched? And this 'stupid ship' saved your lives."

"Lives that you made us risk," Sam growls.

Commander Hill's gaze tracks around the airlock, looking at each of us in turn. Her cranial stalks are twitching, possibly with annoyance. "I thought you'd all be eager for this opportunity.

Maybe I was wrong."

"Opportunity?" Harry shrieks a full octave higher than his usual voice. "*What* opportunity? The opportunity to get infected or eaten alive?"

"No," Commander Hill answers with a dark look. "The opportunity to escape."

Sam's eyebrows knit together in confusion. "Escape?" he asks.

A muffled *boom* roars beneath us, drawing all of our eyes down.

"What was that?" Naomi breathes into the silence that follows.

"An incendiary missile hitting the meat packing plant. No one is going to find anything but charred skeletons in the rubble. We'll be counted among them and given up for dead."

CHAPTER 32

"We?" I ask. "You're escaping, too? From what?"

The inner airlock doors rumble open before Commander Hill can reply. Standing behind them is a short, hunching alien in a form-fitting black suit of armor with a faint fishscale pattern to it. I recognize it immediately as the one we rescued from General Gold. Darkened patches and faded black lines of bruises and cuts mar the creature's otherwise pale white skin.

Sam jumps to his feet with his fists balled. "It's a trap!"

Ana, who was standing closest to the doors, jumps back with fright.

"Reiniar is on our side," Commander Hill explains. "And I'm here for the same reason he is: to escape persecution. He's a heretic, and I'm an abomination—a Chimera with royal blood, just like your daughter, Mr. Randall."

I blink in shock at that revelation and watch

as Commander Hill steps by me, crossing into the troop bay to stand beside Reiniar.

Commander Hill regards us mildly. "Are you planning to stay in the airlock?"

Without speaking, Sam and Harry move to carry Ellie through. Naomi and Ana trail behind them. I'm the last one out.

"What about the missing lander?" I ask. "They'll know that you're still alive."

"What missing lander?" she asks. "It's right where we left it, on the other side of the facility." Commander Hill nods to the Kyra beside her. "This is Reiniar's vessel, not mine. And before you ask, Rexi is already on board in one of the Horval pens. She is also a K'sari."

"Won't someone detect us?" I ask, remembering the roar of thrusters firing as we took off, and the missile that took out the meat packing plant.

"They'd have to be very close to see through our cloaking shield," Commander Hill replies.

Reiniar growls something at her.

She replies with a chattering hiss.

"What is it?" I ask.

"He's reminding me we need to remove your tracking implants before we forget and blow our cover."

I turn over my wrist to look for the blinking green light of the implant, but it's no longer blinking, nor is it green. The status light is glowing a steady purple beneath my skin, but in this lighting, that probably means that it's actually red.

"Isn't it already too late for that?" I ask. "They should be able to see that we survived."

"I've been jamming the tracking signals since we entered the packing plant," Commander Hill explains. She reaches into a compartment on her belt and produces a small black box. "With this," she adds.

Reiniar gestures to the airlock with a skinny three-fingered hand, and the doors beside me slam shut. He turns and starts toward the illuminated tubes at the back of the troop bay.

"This way," Commander Hill says, heading for the ramp.

Ellie is laid out on the deck again with the others gathered around her.

"Where are we going?" I ask, hurrying after the commander.

"To Reiniar's lab. The med deck."

One of those glowing tubes opens up, and Reiniar steps inside. With a loud *whoosh,* it spirits him away to one of the upper decks.

"I meant, where is this ship going?"

The commander glances at me. "To Santa Monica, to rescue your daughter and the other K'sari."

Anticipation, hope, and fear swirl together, warring inside of me. "Is she okay?"

"For now," the commander whispers darkly.

"What about Ellie? She's still unconscious," Naomi says.

"Not for long. Bring her," Commander Hill replies.

I stop and go back to help Sam carry Ellie. Harry steps aside and thanks me with a grim smile as he goes to Ana's side. She loops an arm through his, clinging to him for support.

Seeing them together reminds me of Bree. What will she think when she hears that I've died? She won't know that it's part of a plan to rescue Gaby. If she thinks that she's lost both me and Gaby, she might fall apart completely. And then what will happen to Zach?

Those concerns run in circles inside my head as Sam and I carry Ellie toward the access ramp.

Commander Hill waits for us at the bottom. As soon as we arrive, she leads us up. We stop at the first landing, and she takes us through into a gleaming compartment full of alien equipment. It's brighter in here, and the light is white rather than blue. My eyes ache and water with the sudden change. Commander Hill has her helmet on again, probably to shield her sensitive eyes.

"Put Elenore on one of the beds," the commander instructs us.

Something about this room is familiar. It holds three cubicles with transparent walls, each with a big, gleaming metal bed inside.

It's exactly like the place where Gaby was taken and experimented on by Kyron heretics. Commander Hill wasn't lying about Reiniar being one of them.

The commander opens a door in the nearest cubicle. We carry Ellie inside and lay her on the bed.

"Now what?"

"Now we wait for Reiniar."

"That's a mouthful," Sam says. "Can we just call him Ray?"

Commander Hill stares silently at him.

"What, are nicknames offensive to the Kyra?"

"Know your place, Dakka."

"Hey, you're the one who chose to abduct us. We didn't ask for this."

"Then perhaps you would like to return to the zone. That can be arranged."

Sam shuts up.

I'm actually surprised by Commander Hill's attitude. It's the first hint I've seen that she shares the Chimeras' bigoted view of regular Humans.

"What's *your* name?" I ask the commander, hoping to defuse the situation.

"Christina," she replies, surprising me with an answer.

"Her head is swelling up," Naomi says, brushing the hair away from Ellie's forehead. "And I think her pulse is getting weaker. Where is Ranier?" Naomi asks.

"Ray-nyar," Christina corrects her.

A swishing sound draws our attention to a pair of gleaming tubes to either side of the doors we came through. One of them opens up, and

Reiniar steps out, now wearing a glossy, triangular black helmet that comes to a beak-like point beneath his chin.

"Speak of the devil," Sam mutters.

He moves wordlessly into our cubicle, opens a compartment in the wall beside the bed, and pulls out another type of helmet, this one with a bundle of cables trailing from it. Reiniar places it over Ellie's head.

"Hey, what's he doing to her?!" I ask, remembering that I found Gaby with one of those helmets on her head.

"Relax, he's just waking her up," the commander says.

We watch anxiously while Reiniar stares fixedly at Ellie. I get the impression that he's interfacing with the technology through his own helmet.

Ellie's eyelids flutter.

Naomi sucks in a sharp breath.

Then Ellie sits up with an abbreviated shout, her eyes wide and darting. Naomi grabs her shoulders, but Ellie starts screaming and thrashing to get away.

"It's okay!" Naomi says. "You're safe!"

Ellie's gaze finds the Kyra at the same time as she reaches up to check what's on her head.

And then she starts screaming again.

"He's on our side!" Naomi cries.

Ellie throws the helmet off, and Reiniar catches it deftly before it can hit the floor.

Sam hurries over to help restrain her, but she seems to have calmed down already. We gather around. Ellie sits staring sightlessly ahead with her lungs heaving and her body rigid. She blinks a few times, and her eyes come into focus, finding me first. I crack a tight smile.

"Where am I?" Ellie asks.

Naomi brings her up to speed while Ana looks on worriedly. Even after they've finished explaining, Ellie doesn't look reassured.

"What about my brother—and Megan? They're still inside the zone."

"And our fosters," Ana adds.

Their questions remind me of my concerns about my own family. Commander Hill had to fake our deaths to get us out of the safe zone. Does that mean we're going to be permanently separated from everyone who is still inside? I round on the commander with narrowed eyes. "My wife and son are in there, too."

"Ouch! What the hell?" Sam cries. He's rubbing his wrist, and Reiniar is moving from him to Harry with a gun-like device that I recognize from the airport. "Fucking leprechaun," Sam mutters.

"He's removing your implants," Commander Hill explains.

Harry holds out his wrist hesitantly, and the Kyra places the barrel of the device against his skin. He winces as Reiniar pulls the trigger.

I step forward to go next. The implant gun

clicks and hisses softly as it removes my tracking chip with a sharp prick. As Reiniar moves on, I examine my wrist. The glowing purple light is gone.

Between that device and the signal jammer that Commander Hill showed us, I'm feeling more hopeful about this escape plan.

"We can go back for your families later," Commander Hill belatedly replies.

Ellie grimaces as her implant is removed. "Why not now?"

"Because the Kyra have my daughter, and they're going to kill her," I say.

"Not just his daughter," Commander Hill adds. "They have captured nearly a hundred other K'sari just like her, and we need them for our rebellion."

"A rebellion?" Sam asks.

"K'sari?" Harry adds, looking equally confused.

This must be what my face looked like when Commander Hill explained it to me.

"The K'sari—royal Chimeras—are ordained to lead other Chimeras, just as the Kyron K'sari are ordained to lead their respective castes. Having royal blood lines among each sub-species gives them the legitimacy they lack, and a path to become officially recognized as equal citizens by the Kyra. Not only that, but K'sari can read other Chimeras' thoughts, and that will help us to choose future recruits without bringing possible traitors into our midst."

"Who the fuck cares?" Sam asks.

"*You* should. Until we are recognized as equals, we are at war with the Federation, and the enemy of your enemy is your friend."

Sam frowns. "Yeah, but we're not Chimeras, so where do we fit into your rebellion?"

"We need soldiers. The Kyra only take Chimeras for their war, but we can't afford to be so picky."

"Should I feel flattered?" Sam asks, his gaze sweeping around to address everyone. "We were passed over as cannon fodder for one war, but now we've been signed up for another!"

"Would you rather take your chances in the safe zone?" Commander Hill asks mildly. "It won't be long before you are being forced to have children to bolster the next generation of recruits. There will be quotas to be met, and consequences for those who don't comply. Single adults and teens will be given a month to find someone to breed with, or else someone will be assigned for them. The Kyra are keeping you Dakkas around to raise a crop of children for harvest."

Naomi, Ellie, and Ana all look horrified, and Sam and Harry are trading apprehensive looks.

"What do you need us to do?" Sam asks.

"Help us rescue the K'sari. Then you'll have earned your place on our side. You'll become honorary *Rek'd'va*—*s*ons of Kyroth."

"Do you have a plan to rescue them?" I ask.

"We do. Would you like to see it?"

PART 2: RESCUE

CHAPTER 33

Commander Hill and Reiniar lead us up to the level directly above the lab. The setting of this deck is exactly the same as the commander's quarters were aboard her lander. The heretics must re-arrange things on their landers to put the lab closer to ground-level access. Probably makes it easier to move test subjects in and out.

Commander Hill has us gather around that glossy black table I saw aboard her ship, the one with a suspicious lack of chairs around it.

Reiniar gestures to the table, and it glows to life with a series of floating displays full of alien symbols, three-dimensional images, and what looks like a satellite map.

The commander points to the map, and it enlarges to fill the entire surface of the table. The map isn't strictly 2D like the ones I'm used to seeing from our own satellites, but rather populated with 3D projections of trees, hills, mountains, buildings, ruins, and everything else. The map is centered on us with a 3D model to represent our lander. The terrain scrolls steadily below the model as it flies above the ruins below.

"Here we are, headed west to Santa Monica," Commander Hill says, pointing to the lander. She makes a sweeping motion with her hand, and the map scrolls rapidly sideways. Her hand stops as we reach the coast. Ruins are everywhere along the beach, while the beach itself is filled with boxy black structures. Two Kyron cruisers hover over the water, and one more is landed parallel to the shore, right beside the water.

"This is the staging area," the commander explains. "We're going to land here." She gestures to a clearer section of the street running between the beach and the ruins of commercial buildings and restaurants that used to face the water. A floating purple diamond appears above the spot, marking it on the map.

"The prisoners are being held in this building," Commander Hill adds, pointing to a large rectangular structure in the center of the compound. A red diamond appears above that spot. "A sympathizer from the staging area will deliver both me and Rexi to the facility where the other K'sari are being held. Reiniar will follow us in with his cloaking shield engaged, and then he will help us escape from the inside."

"What are we supposed to do?" Sam asks.

"You're going to lead a horde of Dregs to the beach to create a distraction. Once they arrive and draw away the guards, Reiniar will lead us out."

"So, we're the bait. *Again*," Sam says.

"Dregs are attracted by the scent of other humans much more than they are by Chimeras or Kyra, so you six are the ideal choice for such a mission."

"That sounds like a convenient excuse," Ana says.

"Convenient, yes, but it's not an excuse. Dregs being attracted to uninfected hosts was part of the initial design to ensure that the virus would spread on its own. The Dregs are spreaders. Chimeras are the desired outcome. And the chaos and fear inspired by the virus helps the Kyra to maintain control of occupied worlds."

A vein pops out on Sam's forehead. His fists ball up and his eyes look like they're about to jump out of his head. "Dregs were an *intentional* side effect?"

The air grows suddenly thick with tension. Commander Hill answers in a low voice, "No, but the Kyra found ways of incorporating the failures into their occupation plans."

Sam is still glaring at her, but the Commander's answer seems to have talked him down from a violent outburst. Naomi is rubbing his arm and whispering something in his ear.

Putting bits and pieces together, I wonder if their kids, assuming they actually had any, might have turned into Dregs.

Commander Hill breaks the staring match first, her attention back on the holographic map. "Long before the Dregs arrive, we will have our cruiser attack the factories in New San Bernardino to draw away the Kyra's air support."

"You have a *cruiser?*" I ask.

Commander Hill glances at Reiniar. "*He* does."

Sam crosses his arms over his chest. "Are we at least getting armor and weapons this time?"

"Reiniar managed to acquire three ACE units. That stands for Advanced Combat Exosuits." Commander Hill gestures to the table, and another image appears floating above the map. It's a suit of matte black armor that looks just like a bulkier version of the one she's wearing. "Exosuits are reserved for Chimeran Elites—combat veterans who survive at least their first two drops. They're equipped with grav engines, so you can even fly, which should help you to avoid the Dregs on the ground."

"But there's only three suits and six of us."

"And we don't know how to use them," Naomi adds.

Sam is nodding along with that. "We don't all have combat experience, either."

"Only the ones who do will be wearing ACE suits," Commander Hill says.

"So me and Randall," Sam concludes. "Who's the third? My wife has never fired a gun in her life."

"Neither have we," Harry says, and Ana nods hesitantly.

"I have," Ellie says quietly. "My grandfather used to take me and my sisters skeet shooting."

"That's not exactly combat," Sam replies.

"It's marksmanship," Ellie counters.

"It'll do," Commander Hill adds.

Sam jerks a thumb to the hologram of the armor. "We still don't know how to use that tech."

"You won't need to. Chimeran technology is designed to be extremely intuitive. The helmets will read your thoughts directly and translate intention into action. Think about using your weapons, and they'll deploy. Think about flying, and the suits will make you fly. If you want to hide, the cloaking shield will engage. It's as simple as that."

Sam doesn't look convinced, and his wife is watching him with wide eyes, as if terrified at the prospect of him piloting one of the alien suits.

"What are the rest of us going to do?" Ana asks.

"You will be the bait, and you'll work together with the ones wearing armor to lead as many Dregs to the staging area as you can."

"This could work," I say slowly.

"It could also get us all killed, or infected," Sam points out. "Three of us wearing armor, three of us without?" He shakes his head. "That's a damn fine way to get the unarmored ones killed, and probably the armored ones too when we try to save them."

"The ACE suits have augmented strength and speed that will enable you to carry or fly the others out of danger."

Ana, Harry, and Naomi don't look encouraged by that.

"Where do we find the Dregs?" Harry asks.

"Where have you found them so far?" Commander Hill counters.

"Supermarkets," I say.

She nods. "Dregs congregate wherever the food is. They prefer meat, but they'll eat almost anything they can find."

I gesture vaguely to the ruins of Santa Monica. "It doesn't look like any supermarkets survived the invasion. How far will we have to go?"

A floating blue diamond appears on the map, about twenty blocks from the beach and the staging area.

"Luckily for us, not very far," Commander Hill replies. "Almost five hundred Dregs are hiding out in this Frugal Foods."

"Five *hundred?*" Ellie asks. "That's a bigger nest than the one that surprised us outside the zone."

"It will make a good distraction if you can lead all of them to the beach," Commander Hill says.

"Looks like rough terrain," Sam points out,

gesturing to the vague grid lines of streets, now littered with debris from collapsed buildings.

"It is, but the way is still clear enough to navigate on foot," Commander Hill replies.

"What happens after you get the prisoners out?" I ask.

"We extract them with Reiniar's lander." The commander points again to the purple diamond and a relatively clearer part of the debris-lined street along the beach. "From there, we'll rendezvous with the cruiser at San Bernardino and make our escape."

"You make it sound easy," Sam says.

"It won't be. As you know, no plan survives contact with the enemy, and the timing of this operation will be crucial. You need to make sure that once you've led the Dregs to the staging area, you get to the lander before we arrive with the prisoners, or else we'll be forced to take off without you."

"So, we're not just bait, we're also expendable," Sam says. "Fucking inspirational."

"We can't afford to lose the K'sari," Commander Hill replies. "They are the heart of our rebellion. Everything depends on rescuing them."

I'm starting to realize what a small part we have to play in this mission. It definitely isn't for my benefit, or Gaby's. The operation must have been planned long before I went to the commander for help. The fact that we've been included at all is probably her idea of repaying me for saving her life. Or maybe it was Reiniar's decision after I tried to save him from General Gold. Whatever the case, it's a dubious honor. We've been given a very dangerous job, and Gaby's actual rescue will be conducted without me.

"How do we coordinate on the ground?" I ask.

"Reiniar will be in comms contact with you the entire time, but you're to observe strict comms silence unless he or I contact you first. We don't want to draw any extra attention to ourselves."

"But the demon can't even speak English!" Sam points out.

Reiniar hisses in response, then speaks in a chattering growl.

"His translator is damaged, but your suits will translate Kyro to English text inside your helmets. Does anyone have any questions before we reach the drop zone?"

"Yeah, about a million," Sam says.

"We have time for one."

"How do we get our families out of the zone after the mission ends?" I ask.

"We can drop you off, but the rest will be up to you," the commander says.

"You'll drop us with the suits?" Ellie asks.

Commander Hill hesitates. "The armor is extremely valuable."

"We're risking our lives for you," Sam points out. "You can afford to risk some hardware for us."

Reiniar growls and hisses something.

"He agrees. You can use the armor, but on the condition that you rendezvous with him after you have escaped."

"Just tell us where to go," I say.

Reiniar gestures to the map and it scrolls back over to San Bernardino. He points to a large building at the north end, and I recognize it immediately. The old San Manuel Casino where Bree used to work.

"Perfect. We'll meet you there."

Commander Hill inclines her head to me. "Let's get you suited up."

CHAPTER 34

The level directly above Reiniar's cabin is some type of armory. Racks of alien weapons line the outer walls. The guns are both familiar and new to me. I notice the Horvals' bulky plasma rifles, the Kyra's laser rifles and stinger pistols, and even some swords that look vaguely like katanas.

Commander Hill and Reiniar guide us to a pair of standing racks in the center of the room with five suits of armor lining each side. Three of those suits stand out as bigger and bulkier than the rest. I assume they must be the *ACE* suits that Commander Hill mentioned. To either side of them are slimmer versions like the one she is wearing.

"Put them on," Commander Hill instructs, nodding to the exosuits.

"How?" Sam asks, standing with his arms crossed over his chest and studying one of the suits with a critical eye.

I take a step toward the suit in the middle of the three, hoping to figure it out intuitively.

I jump back a step as a flurry of *whirring* and *clicking* sounds erupts from the rack of armor. All three suits splay open at the same time. The helmets don't open up so much as they extend upward from poles in the neck of each suit.

"Remove any bulky items from your pockets and your belts, and then step inside the armor," Commander Hill orders.

We do as we're told, ditching our Kyron lanterns and canteens before stepping forward and lining ourselves up inside the suits. I glance over at Ellie, wondering how the armor will accommodate her smaller frame. Sam and I are both about the same size, but she's a full foot shorter than either of us, and maybe a hundred pounds lighter.

Commander Hill walks over to me. "Line up your feet with the soles of the boots," she says, pointing to my right foot. I see that it's half-in and half-out of the armored boot of the exosuit. "Make sure your hands are inside of the gloves, and your heads are tucked at least partially into the helmets. You can pull them down if need be," the commander adds, and I notice that Ellie is craning her neck to find her helmet. It's about a foot above her head. My helmet is just barely brushing the top of mine. I reach up and tug it down until I feel it slide over the top three inches of my forehead. That done, I look around for the gloves. They didn't open up like the arms of the suit did. I slide my hands into the gloves and try flexing them experimentally. The movement feels remarkably natural.

"Good," Commander Hill says, pacing by us like a sergeant inspecting her platoon. "Flatten your bodies against the padded backing, hold still, and imagine the suits closing up with you inside of them."

I frown, wondering at those imprecise instructions. Can Kyron tech actually read and understand our thoughts? If so, it's remarkable that they managed to calibrate the technology to us in just one short week since they arrived. Moreover, how did they create and tailor suits of armor to fit our anatomy?

I think about my suit sealing up with me inside, and it responds to my thoughts by doing exactly that. Soon I'm staring at a glowing screen within the helmet. It's populated with strange icons and alien symbols that I don't recognize, but even as I'm trying to decipher them, those symbols shimmer and transform into familiar letters and words. The entire interface just translated itself into English.

"Wow," Ellie mutters, her voice amplified through external speakers. She steps away from the rack beside me and begins waving her arms around.

Wow is right, I think. Somehow her suit shrank itself down to fit her frame. And the interface translating itself...

I shake my head, and hear a soft whirring from mechanisms inside the armor. A circular display in the top right of my HUD catches my eye. It appears to be some type of sensor display, with colored dots arrayed around a bright purple one in the center. I count three yellow dots and five purple ones. The number of blips corresponds to the number of beings in the room, but I'm not sure yet what the different colors might mean.

All of this tech was designed with humans, or at least *human hybrids,* in mind. That means that the Kyra must have come here already knowing exactly who and what they would find. The only way that's possible is if their arrival a week ago wasn't actually their first encounter with us.

I wonder if one of the Forerunners ran into them. Over the past century, Earth sent out four colony ships. It was part of the Union's bold initiative to expand beyond our solar system and become an interstellar empire.

The only problem is, we haven't heard back from any of those four missions, and by now we should have at least heard from *Forerunner Two*. They left almost eighty years ago, and they were headed for Wolf 1061. At just over fourteen light-years away, cruising at half the speed of light, it would have taken about thirty years to arrive, and then another thirty to return to

Earth.

That means they're about twenty years late. Did they run into the Kyra, and that's why they never returned?

Sam is stomping around in circles in front of me, pulling me from my thoughts. "I can't figure out how to fly," he says.

Commander Hill explains, "There are intelligent safeties to prevent actions that might harm the suit or its wearer, such as activating grav engines in a confined space."

"And what if I *need* to activate them in a confined space?"

"You'd have to override the safeties." Commander Hill's gaze tracks away from Sam to me and Ellie. "We don't have long before this operation commences. I'm afraid you'll have to figure out the rest on the ground. It's time to go."

"What about weapons?" Sam asks.

I think about deploying whatever weapons my suit has, and feel a flurry of movement in my shoulders and armored gauntlets. Three five-inch darts or maybe rockets slide up out of each gauntlet. Glancing from side to side, I see weapon barrels riding high above my shoulders. Each of them looks like a miniature auto turret.

"Hey, how did you do that?" Sam asks.

Ellie's weapons deploy next. And then Sam figures it out and his deploy, too.

A bright yellow *X* has appeared in the center of my HUD with a spinning circle around it. The crosshairs follow my head, always dead center of my field of vision. The turret guns rotate with my head to keep their aim fixed on whatever I'm looking at.

Commander Hill passes under my crosshairs; they turn purple and the spinning circle around them stops and flashes purple while making an annoying beeping sound. I turn away from her, and look to Reiniar with the same result. Then I look at Harry. The crosshairs turn back to yellow, but this time there's no annoying beeping noise, just a pleasant chime, as if the suit is encouraging me to pull the trigger.

"You can mark friendly targets so that you won't accidentally shoot them," Commander Hill explains, nodding to me. "Just think *friend* when you're looking at someone who's on your side."

I do that with Harry, and watch as the targeting circle and X in the center turn purple. The suit starts beeping insistently again, the way it did when I was targeting Commander Hill. Looking at Naomi and Ana next, I repeat the process with each of them. Ellie and Sam are glancing around to do the same. Now the sensor display is showing eight purple blips.

The commander continues with her explanation, "The suits will automatically recognize each other as friendlies, as well as other Chimeras and the Kyra, so at the staging area, you'll have to deliberately think about re-classifying the Chimeras before you can open fire on them.

But anyone who shoots at you will automatically be classified as an enemy."

I nod along with that explanation. Like the commander said, it's all pretty intuitive.

"And how do we shoot?" Sam asks while taking aim at doors to the access ramp where we came in. Before anyone can answer, a screeching report erupts and two bright emerald lasers leap out of his shoulders, converging on the doors. A smoking, molten orange circle appears where they hit.

"Never mind, I figured it out."

Reiniar hisses something.

"What did the demon say?" Sam asks.

"He said including Dakkas in this mission was a mistake." She sends me a pointed look. "Don't make me regret it, Corporal."

"Speaking of weapons, shouldn't we at least have something to defend ourselves?" Harry asks.

Commander Hill and Reiniar both look at him.

"He's right," Sam adds.

"You'll want to travel light so you can run faster," Commander Hill replies. "But stinger pistols would be a good choice." She heads for a rack of weapons on one of the sides of the compartment. We follow her there and watch as she passes out long-barreled pistols and utility belts with holsters attached.

Commander Hill draws her own sidearm and

explains the different settings on the fire-mode selector dial.

"Safety and Kill settings are the only ones you really need," she adds. "But this button here, right above the trigger, will engage the weapon's cloaking shield for concealed carry."

That's new, I think to myself, and file that bit of information away for future use.

"What about flashlights?" Ellie asks. "It's dark out."

"The suits have lanterns and various types of optics built into your helmets."

"Oh. Okay."

The unarmored members of our group still have their lanterns.

Reiniar chatters something to the commander.

Her helmet dips in acknowledgment, and she says, "It's time to leave." She goes striding past us, heading for the exit.

Sam and I hurry after her with the others right behind us. Commander Hill waves to open the doors that Sam tried to kill a moment ago. As we follow her down the winding access ramp, she says, "Corporal Randall is in charge of your group, and you will all follow his orders without question. Anyone who doesn't will be subject to disciplinary measures."

"You're in the Army now," Sam mutters. "I didn't sign up for any of this shit."

"Actually, you did," Commander Hill replies.

"I offered to return you to the safe zone, and you declined."

"I didn't say a damn thing," Sam says.

"Exactly. Your silence was your consent. When the mission is over, you will have another chance to return to your civilian life, should you want it. Until then, you will be treated the same as any other soldier in our army. Now, cut the chatter and get your head in the game, Private Jones."

Ellie bumps shoulders with me as we reach the landing on the second level. "I'm glad you got us into this," she whispers.

I glance at her. My crosshairs turn purple and start beeping insistently again.

"What makes you think it was me?" I ask.

"Because you saved the commander's life, and she put you in charge of us. She trusts you. Also, because you went to speak with her alone after we rescued Reiniar. You were talking about this mission, right?"

I hesitate to confirm her guesswork. Sam glances pointedly back at me, and Harry speaks up from behind: "So this is *your* fault?"

I wince at the accusation. I guess it's too late to deny my involvement. "Gaby is one of the ones we're going to save," I explain. "The commander agreed to help me rescue her, but she didn't tell me that all of you would be involved."

"I'm not sure if we should be *blaming* Chris," Naomi says slowly. "Didn't you hear what the commander said about the Kyra forcing us to have as many children as possible? We'll be better off outside the zone."

"Maybe," Harry concedes.

"We're only better off if we survive this," Sam adds darkly.

And with that, I know exactly where I stand with him. He's going to blame me for any deaths that occur on this mission.

CHAPTER 35

"That's a big drop," I say, peering out the open airlock to the ground below. The lander is hovering about nine feet above the ground, but jumping from that height is like jumping from the second-floor of a building.

"Unfortunately, the debris on the street prevents us from getting any closer to the ground," Commander Hill explains. "The suits will protect you from injury even without engaging grav engines."

"What about the others?" Sam asks, glancing back at his wife.

"Pick them up," the commander suggests.

"I'll take Harry," I say, stepping toward him. He eyes me dubiously.

"You better not drop me."

"I won't," I reply, and scoop him into my arms with surprising ease. The augmented strength of the exosuit makes him feel no heavier than a bag of potatoes.

Sam picks up Naomi, and Ellie sweeps Ana off the deck.

Turning to the open airlock, I walk through to the edge. Ellie and Sam both join me. The three of us paint a comical picture, like newlyweds about to carry their spouses over the threshold.

"Ready?" I ask.

"Hooah," Sam replies.

"Good luck," Commander Hill adds.

I step over the edge, dropping swiftly. The broken street rushes up to greet me. I bend my legs, and absorb the impact with ease. Echoing *thunks* of armored boots on shattered asphalt sound to either side as Ellie and Sam touch down.

I set Harry on his feet and turn in a quick circle, scanning for signs of trouble. Shadowy piles of rubble, fallen street lights and traffic lights litter the street. The scanner in the top right of my HUD is only showing six purple blips now.

Glancing up, I can't see the lander. With its cloaking shield engaged, it's perfectly invisible, along with everyone inside of it. For all I know, it's already moved on.

"Where's the supermarket?" Ellie asks.

I shake my head. It's too dark to see very far, and all of the buildings look the same—crumbling ruins that paint jagged shadows around us.

Focusing on the scanner, I wonder if I can zoom out to see life signs that are farther away. Maybe that will show me where the nest of Dregs is.

Even as I'm thinking about it, the scanner zooms out and the blips around me grow closer together as the scale of the display increases. A solid mass of blue appears near the top of the circle. I focus on that area and the display stops zooming out. Turning my head one way, then the other, I see the display rotating around my blip in the center. It takes a second for me to get oriented. The top half of the display seems to correspond to what's in front of me, while the bottom half is everything behind.

I look to the fore and the mass of blue signatures sweeps back around to the top of the circle. I'm staring across the street at a rubble-covered parking lot. Beyond that is a large building with all the windows blown out and one corner blasted into a pile of rubble. Otherwise, the structure seems to be intact.

"The Dregs are in there," I whisper, pointing to the building.

"How can you tell?" Ellie asks.

I explain how to use the scanners, and soon both Sam and Ellie confirm my discovery.

"So purple is for friendlies and blue is for Dregs?" Sam asks, referring to the colors of the blips.

I nod my agreement with that.

The three unarmored members of our group flick on their lanterns, and dark blue pools of light spill out around them. I think about turning on whatever lights I have in my suit, and twin cones of azure light leap out from my helmet.

"How are we going to do this?" Ellie asks quietly as she turns on her own helmet lamps.

I notice that Sam has left his off. Maybe he's afraid that using the lanterns will draw too much attention to himself.

"I'll go flush them out," Harry suggests.

"Are you crazy?" Ana objects.

"We're the bait, right?" Harry shrugs. "There's no point in all three of us risking our lives."

"I won't let you," Ana says.

"Someone has to do it," Harry replies, "and I'm a faster runner than either of you."

"Like hell you are," Ana counters.

"He's right," I say. "Harry, you'll take point, but I'm going in right behind you for backup."

Harry sets his jaw and nods wordlessly.

"We should figure out how the grav engines work before we go anywhere," Sam says. "We might need them to get out of a bind."

"Agreed," I say and imagine myself slowly lifting off the ground. Immediately, a soft whirring sound starts up, and I begin drifting into the air, just like the debris we helped Corporal Solis remove from the streets.

Sam and Ellie fly up at varying rates—with Ellie going the fastest. She lets out an abbreviated shout of alarm, then comes crashing back down with a thunderous impact. She lands poorly and collapses on the ground.

"Are you okay?" I ask, taking a quick step toward her.

She bounces back to her feet.

"That was stellar!" she crows.

"Be more careful," I reply. "If you damage that suit, you'll be defenseless out here."

"Uh, guys..." Harry trails off quietly.

The note of alarm in his voice catches my attention, and I notice that the mass of blue at the top of my scanner is rapidly changing shapes and flowing toward us. Spinning around, I stare across the parking lot to the grocery store, but it's too far away to see anything. I find myself wishing my headlamps were more powerful so that I could get a visual of the Dregs.

My armor provides another solution instead. It superimposes blue shading on my helmet display, highlighting the Dregs so that I can see them clearly.

A seething wall of blue is creeping steadily toward us, flowing out of broken windows and doors. Commander Hill was right about their numbers. There are hundreds of them.

"Here they come," Sam whispers, stepping in front of his wife.

Harry, Ana, and Naomi each draw their Stinger pistols in quick succession.

A prickle of warning raises the hairs on the back of my neck. "Hold your fire," I grit out as quietly as I can, but I'm too late.

Two bright green lasers snap out of Sam's shoulder turrets, converging on the approaching horde.

The Dregs respond with shrieks and snarls of outrage, and like ants stirred up with a stick, they scatter and start running in all directions—but mostly toward us.

"Run!" I shout, no longer worried about keeping my voice down.

CHAPTER 36

I wait for the others to race by me, putting myself between them and the Dregs. Sam hangs back, too, but I'm guessing that's because he wants to keep Naomi ahead of him.

The Dregs are scrambling along behind us, still reasonably far off, but close enough that I can hear the thunder of their approach.

Ellie takes point, leading the way down the debris-lined street. We're forced to weave awkwardly around the debris, sometimes jumping over chunks and piles of concrete with exposed rebar that could impale us if we're not careful.

It's slow going in places, and I can see the blue mass of Dregs inching toward us on my sensors.

"Where are we going, *sir?*" Sam asks.

Ignoring his sarcasm, I begin wondering about the same thing. I'm all turned around down here. For all I know the beach and the staging area are behind us, and we're leading the Dregs in the wrong direction.

Thinking about a map brings one into view, but that makes it hard to see where I'm running, and I almost trip over a tangled pile of wood and roofing.

Recovering quickly, I imagine the map shrinking into the top left corner of my HUD, and it does exactly that. A bundle of purple blips lies in the center of the map. That must be us. Our movement is causing the terrain to scroll slowly to the right, bringing us closer to the beach. A blue splotch that corresponds to the Dregs is close beside us on our right.

Given the location of the water with respect to the map, I realize that it's oriented with North at the top and South at the bottom, like any good map should be.

All we have to do is stay on this street to the end, and we'll eventually reach the red diamond that Commander Hill used to mark the holding facility. The purple one that marks our extraction point is just behind the staging area and a few blocks farther south toward the old Santa Monica pier.

"We're on the right track," I tell Sam before shrinking the map down even further.

"Better tell Ellie that," he says, and points up ahead. She's turning left down a side street at an intersection to get around a thick knot of debris from a multi-story building that fell over.

"Damn it," I mutter and pour on a burst of speed to catch up with her.

The suit makes running almost effortless, but I can only go so fast without tripping over something and falling.

I imagine myself flying above it all, and the suit complies. Soon I'm soaring above the debris, headed straight for Ellie. I experience a brief thrill at the sensation of flying before forcing myself to focus on the mission.

I land beside Ellie and stumble with my momentum.

"Wrong way," I tell her.

"I know," she says. "But there's no way through. We have to lead the Dregs around the debris."

She must have figured out how to use the map already. "Lead on," I reply.

We're forced to slow to a crawl as another mountain of debris soars in front of us. This one looks like we can climb over it, which is exactly what Ellie starts to do, hopping from one flat surface to the next.

I stop and wait for the others to catch up. Ana and Harry reach me first, both of them are breathing hard, their lanterns bobbing on their belts, and eyes flashing darkly in the gloomy light of my own headlamps.

"Up and over," I tell them.

Naomi is next, followed by Sam. He stops beside me to look back the way we came.

The thunder of the approaching horde is actually shaking the ground.

"They're almost on top of us," Sam breathes. "Come on!"

But I hesitate, staring at the intersection where Ellie took a left. "We have to make sure they follow us," I say.

A distant *boom* shatters the night, drawing our attention eastward.

"Sounds like the attack on San Bernardino just started," Sam says.

Before I can reply to that, the horde bursts into the intersection. They slow before the wall of debris, then a few of them spot us. They go streaking ahead of the others, some of them dropping to all fours to run faster. Sam takes aim on the leader, and opens fire, sending the creature tumbling in a tangle of limbs.

"Stop it. We need them alive!"

"We want them to follow us, right?" he counters, and opens fire on the next closest Dreg with the same result.

But there's twenty more where they came from, and hundreds of others running behind them.

I grab Sam's arm. "I think you have their attention. Let's go!"

We both turn and start scrambling up the mountain of debris. Ellie has already reached the top, and she's waving us on.

Naomi is the closest to us, picking her way carefully over boulders and chunks of concrete. The gaps between the debris and unstable sections make for a slow and treacherous ascent. One wrong step could send us tumbling down, or worse, bury us in an avalanche.

And the Dregs are almost upon us. When they reach the debris, I doubt they're going to climb as slowly as us.

"There's no way we're going to beat them to the top. We should fly over this," I say.

"Yeah," Sam agrees. He surges past me to catch up with his wife.

She grabs a boulder to pull herself up, and it comes rolling down toward her. She cries out in alarm and throws herself out of the way. But she's too slow. The boulder catches her leg and pins it against a piece of a wall.

Naomi screams.

And the Dregs answer with shrieking wails of their own.

"Naomi!" Sam cries, struggling up the mountain.

I cut a quick look behind me. The first Dregs are already bounding up, no more than thirty feet away.

Taking aim at the closest one with my guns, the crosshairs turn blue and chime pleasantly.

Fire, I think—and a pair of green lasers snap out to either side of my head, converging on my target. The Dreg tumbles back down with a smoking hole in its chest.

The other Dregs pause in their ascent to stare at it, as if thinking twice about pressing on.

"Chris!" Sam cries. "I need your help! Her leg is stuck! I can't move this rock on my own."

Then the rest of the horde arrives, and dozens of Dregs begin surging up to reach me. I only have a few seconds before they reach me. That's not enough time for me to get to Naomi and help move the boulder that has her leg pinned—not even if I fly up the slope.

"Ellie! Help him!" I shout.

And then I open up on the horde, spraying the Dregs with a continuous stream of fire.

CHAPTER 37

I'm half-blinded by the lasers I'm raining down on the Dregs. They're shrieking and screaming as they fall, and it's only making the others angrier.

Behind me, Naomi is screaming almost as loud as the Dregs.

"We can't move it!" Ellie says. "It's too heavy!"

"Try harder!" Sam barks at her. "We almost had it!"

This is a disaster. The Dregs we needed for a distraction are dying by the dozen, and Naomi is about to get eaten alive if I don't find a way to kill them even faster.

Remembering the five-inch rockets that deployed from my suit gauntlets, I take aim with my left arm and imagine firing one of them into the thickest concentration of Dregs.

Sure enough, one of the rockets flares to life and streaks down. It explodes with a *boom* and a fiery burst of light.

At least twenty Dregs go flying, while others burst into flames and run around shrieking piteously. The rest scatter, leaving only five or six still climbing up to reach me.

I mow them down with my lasers and then whirl around to see Sam and Ellie still grunting and heaving to get Naomi free. Harry and Ana are there, too, adding what they can to the effort.

"Just roll it off!" Sam says.

I clamber up to reach them and add my hands to the task. Naomi screams again as the boulder comes tipping toward me, probably crushing her leg even more. I have to jump out of the way as it goes rolling down into the milling horde below. It knocks more debris loose, starting a mini avalanche. The Dregs still climbing look up just in time to get flattened by the landslide.

There go another dozen distractions.

Ellie and Sam are helping Naomi up, but I can see from the amount of blood glistening under my headlamps that her injury is bad. A jagged white bone is sticking out of her calf, and her foot is hanging at an odd angle. Naomi moans softly at the sight of it, looking and sounding like she's about to pass out.

"We'll fly her out of here," Sam says. "She needs medical attention."

"We could get her to the lander," Ellie suggests. "If we can get it open, we could take her to Reiniar's lab."

"What about the Dregs?" I gesture to the

horde below. "We still have to get them to the beach."

Only the most determined ones are picking their way up the slope again, while the others mill around restlessly. The nearest ones are lifting their heads, tilting their noses up and snorting at the air.

More rumbling explosions roll in the distance, reminding me of the battle raging over the safe zone.

"This is *your* mission," Sam says. "You're going to have to finish it without me. I'm taking Naomi to the lander."

"I'll stay with Chris," Ellie says.

Sam's helmet turns sharply to her. "Good luck," he snarls. "I hope you're not the next casualty."

And then he goes floating into the air with Naomi draped limply across his arms.

More snorting reminds me of the imminent danger we're still in.

"We need to move," Harry whispers urgently.

"They can smell the blood," I say, peering down into a sea of feral, gleaming eyes and flaring nostrils.

A large Dreg in the front throws its head back with a piercing shriek, and then the rest of the horde does the same, as if it was a rallying cry.

"Here they come!" Ellie says.

"Run!" Ana adds.

CHAPTER 38

"**W**ait!" I lunge to grab Harry's arm and stop him from climbing higher. "Let's fly to higher ground. Ellie, take Ana."

Ana stops, and Ellie scoops her up. I do the same with Harry. He stares wide-eyed over my shoulder. "Move!"

I activate my grav engines and leap into the air, jetting straight up just as a trio of Dregs reach the spot where I was standing. They waste a few minutes swiping the air and jumping comically in an attempt to reach me.

I hover over their heads, my mind racing for options.

"I've got an idea," I tell Harry.

"You'd better not be thinking what I think you're thinking."

Dropping a few feet closer to the Dregs, they snarl and hiss excitedly. A few of them clamber higher on the pile of debris, thinking to reach us like that.

Floating slowly above their heads, I manage to lead them on up the slope. Dead ahead, Ellie is standing on the crumbling rooftop of a six-story building. Two floors are blasted open and exposed above the highest point of the debris we're climbing, so she's safely out of reach.

Stay up there, I think at her.

A line of text appears at the bottom of my display, surprising me with a reply: *Oh, I will!*

My suit just interpreted my thoughts to send Ellie a text message, and then interpreted *her* thoughts for a reply.

More text appears at the bottom of my screen: *Did we just...*

I think we did. Let's stick to text-based comms from here on out. We don't want Chimeras to hear us.

Yeah.

I drift up to the top of the debris and wait for the scrambling Dregs below to catch up.

"When the commander said we were the bait, I didn't think you were going to take it so literally," Harry says. "You're dangling me like a carrot!"

"Just be glad we're out of reach," I whisper back.

"I'll be glad as long as you don't drop me."

The Dregs reach the spot beneath us, and I begin floating down the other side. Checking my map, I see that we need to take a right at the bottom of this debris pile.

The street looks relatively clear, but I won't know for sure until I can see around the corner. Drifting down with the horde in hot pursuit, I reach the bottom and turn right, sailing over chunks of concrete and fire-ravaged vehicles.

My heart sinks as the cross street comes into full view. Another skyscraper toppled over, blocking our way with a five-story wall of shattered columns and floors. Some of the piles of debris form natural ramps up to gaping windows on the far side of the building, but the Dregs would have to find a safe way down, and with their minimal intelligence, they're just as likely to jump like lemmings.

"Where to now?" Harry asks.

I glance down at him, having forgotten for a moment that I'm still carrying him.

"We'll find another way around."

I lead the shrieking, scrambling Dregs to the collapsed building, then make a left in front of it to go around. The next intersection is clear, so I make a right there. This time the way is clear all the way to the end, and I can see moonlit water gleaming darkly along the horizon. A rumbling roar catches my ear. Two massive black clouds are scudding toward us from the direction of the beach.

But they're not clouds.

We've got company, Ellie says over comms.

I noticed.

"Chris..." Harry whispers.

I flick off my headlamps and peer down at the horde. They've stopped below us, and they're back to jumping and swiping at the air.

The sound of the approaching cruisers is swiftly rising above the din of the horde's snarls and shuffling feet. Those ships are burning hard in our direction.

"They're coming this way!" Harry says.

Hide, I think at Ellie.

Way ahead of you, she replies.

I streak up into the nearest building, flying through a third story window, and set Harry down. The floor has crumbled away along with most of the side of the building, giving us a clear view of the approaching cruisers. If we can see them, then they can probably see us. Spying a chunk of upended floor, I run over to it and crouch behind it for cover. Harry joins me, breathing hard.

"You think they're coming for us?" he asks.

It takes a second for my stress-addled brain to come up with the answer. "No, you don't use a hammer to kill a flea. Those ships are headed for San Bernardino."

The rumbling roar of the approaching vessels reaches a crescendo. A hot gust of wind whistles through the ruins, and then a dark shadow passes over the moonlit rubble. A few seconds later, the shadow falls away, and the air grows gradually still and cool once more.

Harry begins peeking out of cover, but I pull

him back down with a shake of my head. I'm watching the blips on my scanner. There are dozens of purple blips flying around us. The two biggest ones are the cruisers, now disappearing off the bottom edge of the scanner, but what are the others? I'm tracking two trailing blips in particular, willing them to vanish, too.

But they don't.

A familiar whirring sound catches my ear, mingling with the confused babbling of the Dregs below.

Those two blips have stopped right beside us.

Chris, Ellie says over comms. *You have two ships right above you. They look like shuttles.*

I manage to spot one of them, hovering up ahead at about eye level with us, directly above the street I was going to lead the Dregs down. It's a boxy black vessel about twice the size of the hovering troop transports that ferried us around inside the zone.

Harry sends me an urgent look. "Are they here for us?" he whispers.

Before I can reply to either him or Ellie, thick green lasers begin spitting out of the shuttle with a *thumping* roar.

"Get down!" I cry.

CHAPTER 39

I'm half expecting to be vaporized on the spot.

But it doesn't happen, and that flashing roar of laser fire isn't hammering into the debris we're using for cover.

Hundreds of Dregs all start screaming and wailing at the same time. The transport is shooting at them. Peeking above the ragged edge of the debris in front of me, I confirm it visually.

"We have to do something or they're all going to die before they reach the staging area," Harry says. Then another thought appears to occur to him, and he sits up sharply. "Where is Ana? Is she okay?"

"She's with Ellie. They're fine for now."

Harry nods uncertainly and appears to relax.

He's right about the Dregs. I find myself staring at the remaining five rockets in my forearm gauntlets. Would that be enough to take the transport down? Maybe. Maybe not.

As I'm wondering about it, the transport turns on the spot, presenting its side to us and the horde. Fat green lasers continue thumping out from turrets on the top and bottom of the vessel.

Then a door opens, and an armored figure appears. Another stream of lasers pours out from there, needle-thin by comparison. A laser rifle.

Chris? What do we do? Ellie asks.

An idea occurs to me. Commander Hill mentioned these suits have cloaking shields. It's risky, but maybe we could hijack one or both of the shuttles. If so, *that* distraction would put whatever the Dregs can muster to shame.

Wait, I think at Ellie.

Okay...

Holding my arms up, I think about them shimmering and vanishing as my cloaking shield engages. Sure enough, the suit responds by doing exactly that. A moment later, my suit reappears, marked on my helmet display with translucent purple shading. That's a relief. I need to be able to see what my hands and feet are doing. And hopefully the Chimeras on that shuttle can't see me.

Harry gasps in response to my sudden disappearance and starts feeling around blindly to check if I'm still there. "Chris?"

"Stay here. I'm going in," I whisper back. With that, I creep out of cover and walk around to the nearest edge of the crumbling floor, getting as close to the open door of the transport as I can.

It's only about thirty feet away now. *Here goes...* I think, and then jump off the edge.

I fall for half a second before the grav engines catch me, and then I'm zipping toward the shuttle, aiming for the open doorway. I raise my arms, getting ready to grapple with the soldier in the open doorway.

He hasn't noticed me yet, but he's still firing steadily into the horde, and those lasers are going to slice through me if I don't do something to interrupt the stream.

Fire, I think.

A sharp beep erupts from speakers beside my ears. Chimeras are still classified as friendlies.

Mark all Chimeras as enemies, I think, hoping the suit will understand what I mean.

My targeting reticle turns red and chimes pleasantly.

Fire.

Twin laser beams tear out of my shoulder cannons and catch the soldier full in the chest. He drops the rifle out the door, and staggers backward, clutching a smoking hole in his armor.

I sail through the open doorway and knock him over with my momentum. Springing to my feet inside, I see three more soldiers just like the first jumping to their feet and bringing their rifles into line with me.

"Who's there!" one of them cries. "Identify your—"

I strafe the inside of the shuttle, filling it with blinding streams of light.

The soldiers go down in a clattering heap, and acrid smoke fills the compartment. Someone cries out in alarm behind me, and I feel a searing heat shoot through my side, stealing the breath from my lungs.

Gritting my teeth through the pain, I stumble into the nearest bulkhead and spin around and take aim on my attacker. It's another Chimera, sitting in the co-pilot's seat, aiming a Stinger pistol at me. He shoots again. Misses.

Fire, I think. And lasers slam into the back of his seat. He drops his pistol and slumps over into the aisle between him and the pilot. The pilot leans into view with his own sidearm.

I fire at him with the same result.

Shit. Now who's going to pilot the ship? I wonder.

Speakers buzz to life from the cockpit.

"Three-one, report status." A brief pause follows. "Three-one, come in!"

My mind races to come up with a plan, but my side is throbbing and pulsing with the fiery heat of a laser burn, making it hard to think.

I brace myself on the bulkhead and prop one knee on a bench seat, trying to decide what to do next.

"Three-one, respond."

Chris, are you okay? Ellie asks.

The sound of laser fire thumping into the horde below abruptly stops, and I have a bad feeling I know why.

The other shuttle is redirecting its guns.

CHAPTER 40

Hairs prickle on the back of my neck in anticipation of the flash of searing heat from the other shuttle's guns.

Steeling myself and gritting through the pain in my side, I push off the wall, and rush to the open door of the shuttle, leaping out like a skydiver.

The flash of heat I was expecting comes just a split second later, and the shuttle explodes with a *whoosh* of superheated air and debris that pelt my armor and throw me to the ground. I try using the suit's grav engines to reverse my momentum before impact, but it doesn't work, and I slam hard into the ground.

Lying there, stunned and motionless, I wonder if I've just broken every bone in my body.

Chris! Chris! Are you okay? Ellie is filling the bottom of my display with text.

Before I can reply, my sensor display flashes. Blue blips are converging to all sides. I push partway off the ground to see Dregs shuffling toward me, their eyes and teeth gleaming in the dark and their cranial stalks twitching.

A spurt of adrenaline sends me flying off the ground, and I'm surprised to find that my limbs are still working.

But my cloaking shield is not. My arms are no longer shaded purple; they're pitch black and perfectly visible.

The shuttle can probably see me too.

Leaping into the air, I'm grateful my grav engines still work.

Fat green lasers shatter the ground where I was standing a moment ago, and I twist around to see the second shuttle facing me, presenting a thinner profile and keeping its vulnerable side door out of view.

They're not going to make the same mistake twice.

I imagine flying in a zagging line toward the shuttle, and the suit complies. Lasers flash by me on all sides, missing by mere inches.

I fire back, aiming for the cockpit, but my shots flare brightly, absorbed by some type of shield. A second stream of fire joins mine, stitching out from the rooftop where I last saw Ellie. And then more shots open up from Harry's position as he opens fire with his pistol.

None of it is doing anything, but it proves to be just the distraction I need. The shuttle's bottom turret turns away from me to fire back at

Ellie.

I drop down below the top turret's range of motion, approaching the shuttle from underneath. And then I let loose with two of my gauntlet rockets, aiming straight for the turret that's firing on Ellie.

Fireballs bloom, and shields flare brightly, absorbing the impacts. Then I fire again. This time the turret explodes and bursts into flames.

Feeling the heat of the shock waves, I reverse course and fly up to the side door of the ship. This one is sealed. I grab a rail beside it, and cling to the ship, trying to figure out how I can get inside.

The shuttle turns sharply, trying to shake me off. That prompts me to loop my other arm through the grab rail.

Then comes a *roar* and a flash of light from the ship's thrusters. It leaps suddenly forward, almost throwing me off.

The pilot executes a barrel roll. My legs and body fly out with my inertia, leaving me to flap in the wind like a flag; I slap into the side of the ship, then fly out again...

But I'm still latched on like a parasite. Those maneuvers are nothing against the augmented strength of my armor.

Finally, the shuttle rights itself, and the door beside me springs open. A flashing blade appears, and I catch the wrist of the soldier holding it before he can slice my arm off. The sword is humming and glowing with a blurry energy field.

The Chimera brings his offhand up to free his weapon, but he's made a critical mistake.

Fire. I think. Lasers punch through his armor, and a gout of flames bursts out of his chest from the air in his lungs igniting.

He drops the sword and tumbles out the open door. I jump through and strafe the inside of the shuttle once more. Lasers converge on me, but only one of them hits, glancing harmlessly off my thigh.

This time I'm ready for the ones in the cockpit to join the fight. I dive to the deck and twist around to face the other way—

But the cockpit is sealed.

The pilot executes another barrel roll, and I go flying toward the open door.

CHAPTER 41

Just as I'm about to sail out, I manage to catch a hand rail inside the door and arrest my momentum. One of the dead soldiers sails out past me. I'm dangling out the side of the shuttle and hanging on for dear life for the second time.

I wait for the shuttle to roll back the other way, but rather than complete the maneuver, the pilot holds that position and flies low over the ruins and the horde below. The Dregs shriek and snarl, reaching eagerly for me and waving their hands like groupies in some apocalyptic concert.

Straining my arm and the mechanisms inside the suit, I manage to yank myself up one-handed and grab the rail with my other hand.

Feeling Dregs snatching at my feet, I pull my legs up and drag myself inside before they can get a good grip. Back in the shuttle, I lie breathless against the bulkhead beside the door. The pilot finally rights the vessel.

Chris, are you on board that ship? Ellie asks.

Yeah.

See if you can take control.

What do you think I'm doing?

Pushing off the side wall, I take aim on the door to the cockpit, and open fire.

But a sullen click is the only response. Two empty green bars are flashing at the top of my display. I wonder if they represent the charge level of my lasers. Moreover, my suit feels sluggish. I notice a third flashing bar, up in the top right corner, above the sensor display. This one is blue. It's also hollow, but there is a sliver of solid shading with a notation beside it: 3%.

Apparently all that flying around had a cost. My suit's power levels are nearly depleted. But there are still two Chimeras in here with me, and I'm practically defenseless. All I have left is one rocket, but firing it in these close confines would probably kill me, too.

My attention snaps over to the three dead Chimeras in the back of the shuttle. Their rifles are lying with them in a tangled heap. At my feet is that strange, katana-like sword.

The door to the cockpit springs open, and I duck just as a laser beam flashes overhead. Grabbing the sword, it thrums to life in my hand, the blade glowing dimly. I spring off the deck and lunge for the Chimera. He adjusts his aim—

And my sword plunges up to the hilt into his stomach, sizzling and hissing. The pistol drops from nerveless fingers and he goes stumbling backward, batting feebly at the hilt of the blade.

I grab the Stinger pistol and shoot the pilot just as he's lining up his own sidearm. My shot burns a hole straight through his visor, and he slumps against his seat restraints.

Dead ahead, I see that we're flying directly toward another building. Ellie's building. She's on the roof, firing steadily at us.

I scramble to reach the control yoke in front of the dead pilot and yank it toward me, hoping that the Kyra's human-friendly tech extends to flight control interfaces, too.

The shuttle skips up, but too slowly. We graze a jagged brick wall behind Ellie's position. It explodes, and the shuttle veers sharply toward the ground and the pile of debris we climbed earlier.

Even pulling back as far as the controls will allow, it's still not enough to arrest the shuttle's momentum. It goes skidding along the slope of rubble with the shrieking thunder of concrete and metal scraping against the hull.

Then the nose hits a jutting boulder and digs in, sending the ship spinning around. I lose my grip on the controls and slam hard into the cockpit canopy.

I lie there dazed and listening to a sudden ringing silence.

Text is streaming across the lower portion of my HUD as Ellie frantically tries to contact me.

I'm okay, I manage to think back at her. *I got them.*

Then my eyes focus on what she's saying.

Dregs! Get out of there! They're coming for you!

Moments later, I hear the shrieking snarls of the horde. Then comes the sound of rocks clacking together as hundreds of hands and feet send loose debris rolling down after me. A few pieces *thunk* into the side of the shuttle. I pick myself off the controls, stepping on and over the dead pilot and co-pilot. Finding my footing on the sloping deck, I stumble woodenly forward to grab whatever handholds I can find.

As soon as I reach the open side of the shuttle, I see them: a seething wall of moonlit shadows flowing down the shattered slope of concrete boulders to reach me and the mechanical beast that they probably think they've slain.

My suit's power level is down to two percent now. I can't fly out of here or engage my cloaking shield to disappear. How long will it take a hundred sets of clawing hands to tear my helmet off and then rip out my throat?

CHAPTER 42

I spot a control panel beside the door and frantically slap it, trying to find the button to close the door. Almost immediately, the door grinds shut—but only part way. A chunk of concrete has it jammed open.

I'm coming! Ellie says.

But the Dregs beat her to it. I jump back from the door as six different arms come reaching in and begin swiping around blindly for me.

One of the Dregs manages to get his body wedged into the opening. He snorts and drools between gritted teeth, trying to squeeze his chest through. The door groans and begins inching open.

I cast about for a weapon. One of the rifles is a few feet away, sandwiched between two dead Chimeras. I scramble over and yank it free. Bringing it into line with the doorway, I pull the trigger and hold it down. A steady stream of green fire stutters out. The Dreg in the doorway shrieks briefly as he dies, causing the others to shy away.

"You like that?" I scream.

Then the rifle clicks and hisses with steam as it runs out of charge.

The Dregs come swarming back in. Hands curl around the edge of the door and it starts groaning again as they force it open. A female Dreg jumps through the widening gap, and hisses sharply at me. I throw the expended rifle in her face, and dive for another one.

The Dreg scrambles after me, grabbing my foot and pulling me back. I kick her in the face. Another one jumps in behind her and lands on my back, its claws screeching against my armor like nails on a chalkboard.

Twisting around to fight back, I come face to face with flashing red eyes and slavering jaws. The Dreg grabs my helmet in dirty hands and begins twisting and tugging.

My displays go inching up, and I feel cool air brushing my sweaty neck. This is it. That damned flaw in the Chimeras' armor is going to be the end of me.

A blinding torrent of lasers comes streaming through the door. The two Dregs on top of me turn to look just as a familiar armored figure stomps in and guns them down.

"Ellie! The door!" I scream, grunting to roll the bodies off of me.

Ellie twists around, sees the chunk of concrete jamming the door, and gives it a sharp kick.

Dregs swipe at her, their claws sliding harmlessly off her armor.

The door goes grinding shut and catches two dirty, ghostly white arms. Bones snap and the Dregs scream.

Pushing off the deck, I stumble forward into Ellie, almost knocking her over.

"Careful!" she says.

"Sorry. I forgot we're not on level ground." I'm staring at the door as Dregs begin banging and scraping mindlessly on the other side. I can't see any gap this time, so I doubt they'll be able to get it open.

Tearing my eyes away, I nod to Ellie. "Where's Ana?"

"Safe. Up on the roof. Does this ship still fly?"

I frown at the question and peer down into the cockpit. "I don't know. It crashed... so maybe not."

"You'd better hope it works," Ellie says as the commotion from the Dregs outside intensifies. "Because if it doesn't, then we're trapped in here, and who knows how long it will be before they give up."

If time weren't so short, we could probably wait them out, but we're supposed to lead the Dregs to the staging area. Without that distraction, what will happen to the escaping prisoners? More to the point, what will happen to Gaby?

I begin edging down the sloping deck to the cockpit, silently cursing Commander Hill and

Reiniar for coming up with a plan that hinges on our involvement. Surely she has contingencies. They have an entire cruiser at their disposal. Couldn't they spare a few squads of soldiers to cover their escape?

Those thoughts chase me to the cockpit. The flashing power bar of my suit catches my eye again. Down to one percent.

An audible alert sounds inside my helmet: "Warning, power levels critical. Shutdown imminent."

Just what I needed. Another reason to believe this mission was doomed from the start.

CHAPTER 43

Bracing my back against the bulkhead behind the cockpit, I imagine my exosuit splaying open to let me out. With a whirring flurry of movement, it does just that, and I step out carefully. My body feels strangely heavy and clumsy now that my movements aren't being augmented by the armor.

Ellie is standing back a few steps, watching me.

"How are your power levels?" I ask.

"Fifty percent," she replies.

"Good. At least we still have one suit."

She nods, but says nothing.

I turn and clamber into the cockpit, using whatever handholds I can find to negotiate the sloping deck. Reaching the front, I tug at the bodies of the pilot and co-pilot to get them out of their respective seats. Ellie bends down to help and we manage to wedge them behind the seats.

Sitting at the controls on the pilot's side, I

spend a moment surveying a dizzying array of hundreds of glowing dials, levers, and buttons, as well as half a dozen displays with three dimensional holograms jumping out of them. One of the displays is shattered and dark, but everything else seems to be in working order.

The only problem is, I have no idea how to pilot the shuttle.

"Can you fly it?" Ellie asks, leaning over my shoulder.

"I don't know. I've never flown anything in my life, let alone an alien shuttle."

"So that's a *no,*" Ellie decides.

"Hang on..." I trail off, reaching tentatively for the control yoke. I do have a faint hope. The Kyra designed all of their technology to be as intuitive and user-friendly as possible. Our ability to use the exosuits is a good example of that. So maybe flying one of their ships won't be any different?

"The commander must have a backup plan," Ellie adds.

"She might, but even if she does, as soon as they reach the lander, they'll leave without us. She already warned us about that."

Ellie regards me silently.

She reaches up to twist and lift off her helmet, then shakes out her sweaty hair.

I spare a glance at her from examining the flight controls. "You should take the suit off for now. Save the charge."

"First let's see if you can get us off the ground."

"Right." I let out a breath and tentatively grab the flight yoke in both hands. Pulling back on the yoke like I did before results in a noisy shifting of debris around the shuttle. The Dregs outside momentarily stop banging and scraping on the door.

"That did something," Ellie says.

"Yeah, but I think we're wedged in." I try again, pulling up and jerking the yoke from side to side. Rubble scrapes and roars against the hull. This time the nose skips up, and we begin sliding forward. A groaning, creaking sound indicates that we're still stuck, but slowly breaking free.

"Almost..." I say.

Ellie is gripping the armrests of her seat, looking nervous.

Something snaps with a *ping!* and the shuttle leaps forward, heading straight for the next jutting mound of debris.

"Look out!" Ellie cries.

I pull up hard, and the shuttle responds by nosing above the ruins. Now we're headed straight for the sky. If I get too far away from the Dregs, they'll lose interest, and there goes our distraction. I need to figure out how to fly, and fast.

Checking the control panels around me, I spot a likely looking set of three sliders that might control the throttle. Reaching over, I slowly drag the biggest of the three down toward me. A corresponding sensation of our momentum slowing confirms my guess. The slider reaches a notch in the middle, and the shuttle stops on the spot and hovers.

Noting that one of the other two sliders is already set to the notch in the middle, I peg that one as the throttle for the grav engines that are keeping us aloft.

"Maybe we should land again?" Ellie whispers.

Sliding the yoke to the right, I bring the nose around to face back the way we came. It feels like we're hovering on a cushion of air.

Nosing down slightly, I see the horde sweep back into view. Despite the fact that we're now pointed at the ground, the shuttle remains hovering.

"I think I've almost got this."

"You *think?*" Ellie echoes anxiously.

I try nudging up the second of the three sliders—

And the shuttle rises steadily. The rooftop of the building where Ellie went with Ana comes into view. Some type of visual overlay immediately highlights her on the roof, shading her yellow.

I bring the throttle of the grav lifts back down to the notch in the middle and we stop rising.

A grin springs to my lips. A child could fly

this thing.

That might be an overstatement considering the vast array of switches, dials, and displays that I still don't know how to operate, but I have enough to work with for basic flight. The proof of that will be what I'm going to attempt next.

Nudging the main throttle up a hair, the shuttle drifts toward the rooftop where Ana is hiding. She's crouched behind a crumbling stairwell entrance and a pile of char-blackened air conditioners that were tossed into a pile by the blast waves that ravaged the city. As soon as the roof is under the shuttle, I stop our forward progress and nudge the throttle of the grav lifts down.

One of the displays has switched to what looks like the feed from a camera beneath the hull. Bits of pebble-sized rubble and fluttering ash skittering away from the landing zone. The cracked and buckling rooftop rushes up to greet the camera—too fast for the soft landing I had in mind. I quickly nudge the grav lifts up another notch, and the shuttle hits the roof with a muffled thump and a sharp jolt to my spine.

I'm half expecting the damaged rooftop to cave in with the added weight of the shuttle, but then I realize why it doesn't: the grav lifts aren't disengaged. They're just running below the level that they need to in order to keep the shuttle aloft. It's almost like this is a submarine and I have a slider to control the ballast tanks. The shuttle is only resting on the roof with a minor fraction of its overall weight.

Turning to look at Ellie, I find her staring sightlessly ahead, her expression taut with a grimace, as if she's also waiting for the roof to collapse.

"Go get Ana. Quick."

She jerks back to life, blinking rapidly and standing up from her seat. Ellie puts her helmet back on and leaves the cockpit, heading for the side door.

"How do I open it?" she calls back to me.

Before I can answer, the door swishes open.

"Never mind!" she replies.

And then I hear her armored boots touching pavement. Moments after that, she goes running out in front of the shuttle, waving to Ana.

But Ana isn't budging from her hiding spot.

Then I hear a muffled voice: "It's me—Ellie! Let's go!"

Ana steps out from behind the stairwell and the two of them meet halfway across the roof. I watch them run back to the shuttle together.

My confidence in this mission is rising steadily.

The sound of hurried footsteps ringing on the deck signals that Ellie and Ana are aboard.

"Where's Harry?" Ana asks.

"We're getting him next," I reply.

Hearing the side door slide shut, I nudge the grav lifts back up, and then apply some forward throttle. Checking the buildings ahead, I spot the one where I left Harry and fly us over there.

A chime and a blinking red light draws my attention to another control panel, but I have no idea what that could be about.

Ellie and Ana come into the cockpit just as I'm dropping down again. Another yellow-shaded overlay indicates where Harry is hiding behind a wall of char-blackened office furniture.

Unlike the rooftop, there's no place for me to land, so I have to get as close as I can to Harry's building and then turn the shuttle to present the side door to the crumbling edifice.

"Someone go open the door for him."

"I'll go," Ellie says, but Ana is already on her way back.

The side door opens again, and the shuttle rocks like a boat as someone jumps out. The shuttle is facing the beach, not the inside of the building, so I can't see who left.

Another chime sounds, and I spot a glowing number 2 on the panel with the blinking red light I saw a moment ago. I don't know what those chimes are about, but I can guess.

Whoever sent these shuttles to deal with the Dregs saw one of them blow up, and now they're contacting the remaining one for a status report.

Having this ship at our disposal might turn out to be more of a liability than a boon. The shuttle rocks again as several sets of boots touch the deck.

"Thanks," I hear Harry say.

The door slides shut. I maneuver us away from the building and begin dropping the shuttle down to the street level. The belly camera display shows a scattering of Dregs looking up at our descending shuttle. They start swiping angrily at us long before we come into reach.

As soon as we do, I hear claws shrieking on the hull.

"What are you doing?" Ellie screams.

"Being the bait," I reply.

I set the grav lifts back to the middle point to hover just a few feet above the ground. Nudging the main throttle up as slightly as I can, I get the shuttle going at a brisk walking pace.

Checking the belly camera once more, I notice a set of buttons beneath it. Pressing one of them changes the display from a belly view to a side view. Testing the next button, I find a feed that corresponds to the other side, then one from the top, looking straight up at the starry sky. Skipping to the final button brings up a view from the rear.

The Dregs are right behind us, running to keep up with the shuttle.

I can't believe this is actually working. Now we just have to get to the staging area and go stir up some trouble.

The comms chime again, and the number beneath the light turns to a three. I've missed three calls now. How long before they give up trying to contact us and start shooting? Maybe whoever it is will just assume that our comms are damaged.

But that won't explain why we're leading a horde of Dregs to their compound. I have a bad feeling we're about to come under heavy fire.

Just then, as if they somehow read my thoughts, a wall of scurrying red-shaded soldiers comes streaming up from the beach. A split second after that, green waves of laser fire come slashing out of the darkness and splash across the cockpit.

Some of their fire flashes by to either side, and I see Dregs on the rear display dropping and tumbling with their momentum as the lasers cut them down.

"Hang on back there!" I yell to the others, then pull up sharply and increase the main throttle a few notches to execute a banking climb. Lasers flash all around the cockpit, others impacting on the hull with a hissing roar.

Ana lets out a startled shout, and Harry curses as loose objects go flying and thump around in the back, including my exosuit and the dead Chimeras. At the same time, the bodies of the pilot and copilot clatter around inside the cockpit.

Whatever tech the Kyra use to negate the effects of acceleration is either damaged or deactivated.

Glancing at the rear display, I see blue-shaded Dregs sprinting down the street to reach the Chimeran soldiers at the end.

A grim smile tugs at my mouth. We did it. We got them to the staging area.

The rest is up to you, I think at Commander Hill. But even as I'm thinking that, I realize I can't leave Gaby's rescue up to her.

We still have one exosuit with enough charge to do something.

A plan begins forming in my mind. I bank hard and drop down to fly along the debris-lined street behind the beach. It's the same one Commander Hill chose for our extraction.

A relatively clear spot opens up ahead. That might be it. No sign of the lander, but they probably cloaked it.

Flying higher to avoid crashing into an invisible ship, I consider my options. I can't help Gaby from up here. And I can't expect Ellie to fly the shuttle—as easy as that might be. No matter who's at the controls, we'll get shot down soon if we keep flying around like this. For all I know the Kyra already have air support inbound to deal with us and the Dregs.

Heavy footsteps come thunking into the cockpit. I twist around to see Ellie clutching a handrail beside the door. Her helmet is still on, so I can't read her expression.

"We have to land somewhere," she says.

As if to emphasize her point, the hissing roar of lasers hitting the shuttle intensifies. Next comes the sharp squawk of an alarm going off.

Maybe a warning that our shields are failing.

"Hold on to something! I'm taking us down."

CHAPTER 44

We're still moving forward when the bottom of the shuttle hits the pavement. A deafening roar ensues, and Ellie and I both fly into the control panels.

Moments later, a ringing silence settles inside the shuttle, and I hear Harry groaning in the back.

"You could have warned us," he says, picking himself off the deck.

I push myself off the control yoke and dashboard, hoping that I didn't damage anything.

"Ellie, give me your suit."

"What for?" she asks, shaking her head.

"I'm going to get Gaby. You three get to the extraction point. It's just down the street behind us. Sam and Naomi should already be there waiting."

Ellie takes a step back to get some room, and then her suit opens up with a series of whirring and clicking sounds. The helmet extends above her head, and she stumbles out to lean on the co-pilot's seat.

"That's going to take some getting used to," she mutters.

"Yeah," I agree, remembering the sudden shock I felt when my muscles were forced to carry my own weight again.

I squeeze by Ellie and begin lining myself up inside.

"What if we get captured?" Ellie asks, as I seal the suit with a thought. Familiar displays drop into view with the helmet. I focus on the power bar in the top right—47%.

If I had to guess, I'd say the power gets drained the most by flying. Second to that might be the weapons systems or the cloaking shield. I'll have to be careful how I use the suit to avoid depleting the charge again.

"I'll escort you to the lander," I reply. "Let's go." I step out of the cockpit to find Harry and Ana sitting on a bench facing the side door.

Harry stands up. His eyes flick to Ellie, then back to me. I point to one of the former crew's laser rifles at the far end of the shuttle. "Arm yourselves."

Harry nods and grabs the nearest weapon. He gets a Stinger pistol for Ana, and Ellie steps by me to get another for herself.

"Now what?" Harry asks.

I move to the side door and slap the control panel a few times to get it open.

"Now, you need to get to the extraction point," I whisper and lean out the door to check for hostiles. As I do so, I spot the purple diamond that Commander Hill used to mark the extraction point.

Not seeing any hostile forces in the vicinity, I exit the shuttle and wave for the others to join me. They gather around, their eyes darting and weapons sweeping.

I aim a finger at the waypoint they can't see. "Over there. Where the street is clear. You see it?"

"See what?" Harry asks.

"The lander is cloaked," I reply.

"Or else it's not there," Harry points out.

"Can't we just leave in this ship?" Ana asks.

I glance back at the shuttle and shake my head. "Not without Gaby. Besides, we're too visible in the air. We'll get shot down. Follow me." Running across the street, I head for the cover of the nearest building. Debris blocks most of the first floor entrances, and the roof is coming down. It looks like it might have been a restaurant or a home.

"Stay close," I whisper to the others. Harry and Ana nod their agreement. Ellie looks scared.

I walk swiftly down the line of buildings, stepping around shattered chunks of concrete and narrowly missing jutting spears of rebar.

"Those Chimeras are this way," Ellie whispers behind me.

"I know. But they're far enough away that

they shouldn't spot you if you stay behind cover." I think back to the first time we dealt with a nest of Dregs, remembering the limitations of Corporal Ward's sensors.

"There they are," Ana says, pointing to the reflected green light of lasers flashing off the crumbling walls of a building up ahead. They're obviously distracted by the Dregs. Hopefully none of them think to come out this way and see where our shuttle went. The purple diamond of the extraction point appears right beside us and I turn to point at it.

"The lander is right here."

"Again, how do you know?" Harry asks.

"The point is marked on the display in my helmet."

"I meant—"

"It doesn't matter if it's actually here or not. If it isn't, then we have to assume that it'll be back. This is the extraction point, and Commander Hill told us to wait here. Do you have a better idea?"

Harry doesn't say anything to that.

"Where are Sam and Naomi?" Ana asks.

"Maybe they didn't make it this far," Harry says. "Or worse, they got captured."

"We're wasting time." I nod over Harry's shoulder to the shadowy depths of a building on this side of the street. "Get into cover and wait here until I get back."

Harry appears to hesitate.

"What if you don't make it back?" Ellie whispers.

"Then you leave with the others when they arrive."

Ellie looks uncertain. She glances longingly down the street to the shuttle we left, as if it's her lifeline and she's wondering whether she'll be able to fly it on her own.

"I *will* be back," I add.

"Hurry," Ana whispers.

I nod again and activate my cloaking shield with a thought. My limbs shimmer and turn to translucent purple outlines, indicating that the shield is activated. Now that I'm safely hidden from prying eyes, and hopefully sensors, I start across the street, heading for the beach. I put my hands out in front of me, feeling around like a blind man as I approach the lander.

I wonder if my suit has some type of additional sensors that might reveal the vessel despite its cloaking shield.

Sure enough, a shadowy purple outline appears with a familiar octagonal fuselage and six thrusters arrayed around it like the spokes of a wheel. Coming to an abrupt stop before I can run into one of the engines, I begin walking around the invisible ship.

Within moments, I see two humanoid figures crouching beside one of the other engines. They're highlighted with translucent red shading. My first thought is that it's Naomi and Sam.

But they react to me by straightening and drawing their sidearms. A bright green laser slams into my shoulder before I can duck back into cover, leaving me gasping from the pain.

That was a direct hit. Gritting through scalding waves of agony, I watch on sensors as the two cloaked Chimeras spread out and begin creeping toward me from opposite ends of the engine I'm hiding behind.

If I don't do something quick, they're going to outflank me.

CHAPTER 45

I burst out of cover, moving fast. The first Chimera sweeps under my targeting reticle, and I open fire. Lasers snap out of my shoulder cannons and send him crumpling to the ground. The second one sneaks a shot around the side of the lander. I shoot back hastily, and the shots flare brightly as they hit the invisible ship.

Hopefully I didn't do any serious damage to it.

Still running to make myself a moving target, I think *fly*, and go streaking into the air. Twisting around to look for the second Chimera, I see him pop out of cover for another shot.

But he's looking for me on the ground, and I'm no longer there. He hesitates, and I fire again. Twin lasers converge on him from above, burning a hole through his helmet.

Now both Chimeras are dead, and I'm high enough to see the entire compound of the staging area, illuminated darkly with those dim blue lights that the Kyra seem to prefer.

There is still an enemy cruiser landed by the water. A massive boarding ramp is open in the nose, and a few squads of troops are busy rushing down it. Others are milling around between the buildings, firing on Dregs. The soldiers who made a line at the beach are overrun, and the horde, still hundreds strong, is gushing down from the street to the beach below. So much for a distraction. This is looking like a rout.

The staging area must have been understaffed when the Dregs arrived. Most of the soldiers were probably aboard the two cruisers that left for San Bernardino.

If so, they're probably sending air support back to deal with this situation.

The hairs on the back of my neck prickle with anticipation, and I glance over in the direction of San Bernardino, quietly willing my sensors to outline any ships headed this way.

No colored outlines appear, which I take as an encouraging sign. But I'm still dangerously exposed flying so high above the enemy camp, my cloaking shield notwithstanding.

Looking down at the beach, I guide myself toward a clear spot between two buildings. As I'm sailing down, I notice a bright red diamond on my HUD. It's hovering above a large flat-roofed structure in the center of the camp. That's the building Commander Hill marked. The one where she said Gaby was being held. And it's right in the center of all the action.

Mentally redirecting my course, I aim for the roof of that structure instead. Remembering how my sensors could see through the lander's cloaking shield at close range, I wonder if the soldiers on the ground will be able to see me through mine. If so, hopefully, none of them think to look up.

The screeching reports of laser rifles grow loud and close beneath me. Strobing green light illuminates the sand between buildings. They've got bigger problems than one enemy soldier making an aerial insertion in their AO. It's clear that the Chimeras are spread far too thin. For every one red-shaded enemy soldier on the beach, I can see at least twenty blue-shaded Dregs. As I hurtle toward the rooftop of the holding facility, a group of four Chimeras go streaking for one of the entrances. Double doors slide open—

And a flickering hail of laser fire gushes out, dropping all four and sending their bodies skidding through the sand.

Two familiar armored figures step out—one Chimera, one Kyra—and they have a horde of their own behind them: dozens of Chimeras of all different ages, wearing simple gray jumpsuits. Some of the adults carry weapons, which they hurriedly turn on the Dregs.

My feet touch down on the edge of the roof, and I spin around to join their fire with my own.

But it's too late. At least forty Dregs are storming that entrance. They're too close and running too fast for a handful of armed defenders to stop them.

Commander Hill and Reiniar stand their ground, firing steadily as the Dregs overrun them, but the unarmored Chimeras scatter, the children among them screaming in terror.

One of those kids could be Gaby.

I grit my teeth in horror, marking targets and firing as fast as I can.

CHAPTER 46

The Dregs are relentless. Commander Hill and Reiniar have both drawn those strange katana-like blades I saw in the back of the shuttle. They're slicing off heads and limbs as fast as they can swing. But the unarmored Chimeras they came to rescue are still scattering down the beach—running away from the Dregs, and *farther* from the extraction point.

If we don't turn this around, they're all going to wind up re-captured or food for the Dregs. Remembering the rockets in my forearm gauntlets, I quickly raise both arms to aim at the thickest concentration of Dregs.

A quick thought fires two rockets into the center of the horde. A fireball erupts, sending dozens of Dregs flying in all directions. Several are on fire, and they run shrieking through the crowd, scaring the others off. A brief lull ensues as the uninjured ones pick themselves off the ground and stand around blinking in shock.

Commander Hill and Reiniar take full advantage to fall back, with the former raising her voice to rally the others.

"On me! Everyone! Follow me!"

With that, she turns from the flaming wall of Dregs in front of her and runs parallel to the beach, heading in the direction of the lander. The unarmored Chimeras respond slowly, gradually trickling out of cover behind other buildings.

I'm scanning the crowds, straining to find just one Chimera who looks to be about Gaby's height. A handful of bright green lasers flicker between the remaining soldiers and the fleeing prisoners, but it looks like most of the enemy soldiers are either dead or hiding. Maybe they have instructions to wait for air support.

Just below my vantage point the Dregs are recovering swiftly from the rockets I fired, so I fire another one.

A second burst of light and heat tears through the horde. This time I use the distraction to run for it. Jumping from the roof, I hit the sand with knees bent and tear off down the beach. The escaping prisoners have formed up behind Commander Hill and Reiniar.

Farther down, toward the water, a group of four are in a stand-off with soldiers from the cruiser. I wonder why that ship isn't firing on us. Maybe its guns are too powerful to use this close to the compound.

Shaking my head to clear it, I focus on sweeping the beach for children. I can't see very many: a couple that might be teenagers and one or two that are obviously just short adults, but none as small as Gaby.

Making matters worse, the red shading is causing them all to blur together.

My suit has to have a way to filter those signatures so I can see only the kids. Even as I'm thinking it, the shading disappears, leaving only a handful of highlighted figures. I stop and turn in a circle, scanning the ones behind me. Dregs streak by. Two of them land on a pair of unarmored Chimeras. They go down and begin grappling each other in the sand.

I'm just about to turn back and shoot those Dregs, but then I see it: a tiny red-shaded figure, crouching behind a stack of glossy black hover-crates.

A quick look behind me reveals that the two fallen Chimeras are already dead. More Dregs are still streaming by, chasing the others down the beach. Luckily my armor and cloaking shield are keeping me hidden.

Until one of them runs straight into me and bounces off. It lands on its rear and sits blinking up at me in a daze.

Fly. I think, before any more Dregs can collide with me. The exosuit sends me sailing above the horde. I guide myself toward the stack of crates and land beside it. Running around the other side, I see a small child sitting in the sand, hidden in a u-shaped gap between the crates. Her knees are drawn up to her chest, and her cheeks are streaked with tears.

It takes me a moment to recover from the shock of seeing Gaby again. I take a quick step toward her, spraying sand. She scuttles against the crates, looking terrified. A stifled cry rips out of her.

I'm invisible, but she can still *hear* me.

I disengage the cloaking shield with a quick thought, revealing myself.

Gaby screams again, "Leave me alone!"

Reaching up, I twist off my helmet. "Gabs, be quiet! It's me!"

Her red eyes fly wide and she launches herself at me. Her arms wrap around my thighs and she clings on tight.

I put my helmet back on and glance around nervously. No signs of trouble yet, but now isn't the time for a happy reunion. Prying Gaby free, I scoop her up into my arms, bringing her face close to my helmet. She still looks scared. I'm surprised that the laser burn in my shoulder is allowing me this much movement. I guess it wasn't as bad as it felt. My armor must have absorbed most of the energy.

"We have to run, okay?"

Gaby nods.

I turn to the building where she was being held, and fly up to the roof again. A bright green laser streaks by us, and I sprint across the roof to get out of their sights.

No point cloaking myself now. It won't hide Gaby.

Reaching the mid-point of the roof and some machinery up there, I crouch behind it and set Gaby down. Glancing around, I check for enemy targets in our vicinity. Thinking about it brings them into focus. A stream of red-shaded Chimeras are racing up the beach to the purple diamond that marks the extraction point. Blue-shaded Dregs are chasing them and attacking the stragglers, while five or six enemy soldiers continue shooting almost indiscriminately at both groups.

On the street, above the beach, the lander is no longer visible to me, but it's too far away for me to see through the cloaking shield. The leaders of the red group are just now reaching the extraction point. Three yellow specks appear, running across the street to join them. That must be Harry, Ana, and Ellie. Still no sign of Sam and Naomi, though.

As if things didn't feel urgent enough already, a line of bright red specks appears in the sky, coming from the east. That could be enemy air support incoming.

I have to get to the lander, and fast. The only way to do that is fly. My power levels are down to thirty-one percent. Hopefully that will be enough.

"Ready to go again?"

"Okay," Gaby says. I scoop her up once more and sprint across the roof so fast that my vision blurs. As soon as my feet hit the edge, I jump, and mentally activate the suit's grav engines. I urge the suit to fly as fast as possible for the glowing purple diamond above the beach. A gut-sucking burst of acceleration, and a *roar* from some type of additional thrusters sends me flashing over the staging area to the lander. This time no lasers flicker around us. As we draw near to the extraction point, the ship re-appears as a shaded purple structure with the central hull rising fully five stories from the ground.

The landing ramp is down and the escaping Chimeras are streaming up it with Dregs close behind. Commander Hill is standing in the airlock with a group of armed prisoners, firing down at the Dregs. I fly over the heads of the Dregs and then of the Chimeras, hearing the grunting and snorting of the former and the frantic cries of the latter.

Ironically, the Dregs are shielding the escaping prisoners from the enemy soldiers on the beach. Their laser fire continues to pick off Dregs, but they'll never kill them all in time to stop the Chimeras from boarding the lander.

Reaching the landing ramp, I touch down near the bottom and run up it with the others. At the top of the ramp, I dash past Commander Hill and through the airlock to the troop bay. It's already half full of escaped Chimeras, but just inside the entrance, to the left of the doors, I encounter Harry, Ana, and Ellie. All three of them are huddled together, looking scared and anxious.

"You made it!" Ellie says, recognizing me by my suit.

Everyone's attention turns to Gaby as I set her down. Ellie's eyes fill with tears at the sight of my daughter. She rushes over and pulls Gaby into a hug while Harry and Ana look on with hesitant smiles.

"You poor, poor girl," Ellie murmurs.

Gaby starts crying again.

But two people are still missing from this group. "Where are Sam and Naomi?" I ask, looking to Harry.

He just shakes his head. "Maybe they're up on the med deck? We haven't had time to ask."

"Maybe," I agree.

The sound of laser fire screeching out of the airlock reminds me of the incoming enemy air support and the need for haste. "Keep Gaby safe," I say to Ellie. "I need to go help them."

Running back against the tide of fleeing prisoners, I reach the top of the ramp and make a stand with Commander Hill. At the tail of the group of escaping prisoners I notice a pair of yellow-shaded, *human* signatures. One of them is carrying the other and struggling to outrun the Dregs rushing up from the beach behind them.

That's Sam and Naomi. It has to be. But

they're not going to make it.

Fly, I think, and launch my suit into the air. Guiding myself down to their position, I come down hard, spraying sand. Sam looks to me, his eyes wide with terror. He's not wearing his suit. I wonder briefly what happened to it. And Naomi is in his arms, her broken leg wrapped in a strange-looking cast.

"Go!" I tell him.

He nods and struggles on, panting raggedly. Turning to the rushing horde of Dregs, I target them and strafe my shoulder cannons back and forth on full auto. Dregs fall in waves, but the ones behind clamber over their dying brethren, using the growing piles of bodies to their advantage to launch themselves at me. Claws and snapping teeth come for me, scouring my armor and latching on.

At least ten of them pile on top of me, pushing me to the ground.

Fly, I think again, and my suit *whirrs* to life. I feel myself rising from the sand—

And then I immediately sink back down as Dregs latch onto my arms and legs. I've reached the limit of the exosuit's capabilities.

Claws and teeth shriek against my armor. Bloodshot eyes and pale, dirty faces press against the faceplate of my helmet, filling my view with their nightmarish features.

I try repeatedly to aim and fire my weapons, but my shoulder cannons can't seem to get a lock.

They must be pinned by the Dregs.

The glowing icons of my display twist to the side and begin inching up as one of the Dregs figures out how to get my helmet off. This isn't going to end well.

A sudden flash of heat and light brings a brief respite. The Dregs shriek and wail. Several of them are on fire and running around aimlessly.

Straining against the weight of the ones still pinning me to the ground, I manage to push my helmet back down and twist it the other way to lock it.

I struggle to stand with two monsters still clinging to my arms. A spurt of black blood sprays my helmet and my left arm snaps free. Spinning around, I see Commander Hill. The blurry, muted white glow of the blade I saw her using earlier is flashing around me, drawing fading arcs of light as she rapidly dismembers the Dregs.

"Get out of here!" Commander Hill screams.

The horde retreats suddenly, leaving their dismembered fellows writhing on the ground. Feral eyes watch us from a safe distance, and the Dregs fan out, encircling us.

I hesitate, noticing that our path back to the lander has been cut off.

"Can that suit still fly?" Commander Hill asks.

Rather than answer, I wrap my arms around her waist and burst into the air. That sudden movement causes the horde to charge. They scramble into reach, and their claws rake across my lower legs and armored boots, tugging and threatening to pull us back down.

But this time they don't get a good enough grip. I streak over their heads and crash through the lander's open airlock, falling on top of Commander Hill.

Behind us, the escaped prisoners are laying down covering fire.

"Get off!" Commander Hill snaps at me.

I roll away and spring to my feet, ready to face any Dregs that might have followed us in.

I'm just in time to see one of the escaped prisoners reaching for the control panel to shut the outer airlock doors. Three others are strafing their laser rifles back and forth across the Dregs now surging up the ramp.

There comes a jolt and a brief sensation of movement as the lander lifts off and begins turning on the spot. Dead Dregs slide off the ramp as the lander rises. The shuttle I hijacked and flew here comes sweeping into view.

Commander Hill surges forward and slaps the control panel to stop the doors from closing. "What is that vessel doing there?" she asks.

"I used it to lead the Dregs here."

"Does it still function?"

"Yes."

Commander Hill is silent for a few seconds. A moment later, I realize it's because she's on the comms with whoever is piloting the lander. The vessel stops rising and begins moving horizontally toward the shuttle.

"What are we doing?" I ask.

"We have Lancer Fighters incoming. We could use a distraction. I'll fly the shuttle out of here and lead as many away as I can. Get the others; you're all coming with me."

"What? Why?"

"Because the lander is going straight to our cruiser! The fight is not going well, and we have no time to waste. You want to rescue the rest of your family? This is your only chance."

Any other objections I might have die on my lips with the Commander's ultimatum. I go sprinting back through the airlock to get Gaby and the others.

"Let's go!" I tell them. Moving to Gaby's side, I scoop her into my arms.

"Go?" Harry echoes behind me. "Go where?"

"To the shuttle!" I snap at him. "Commander Hill is taking us to the safe zone to get our families."

Sam pushes wearily off the deck from where he was sitting with Naomi.

I'm surprised he isn't objecting like Harry. They didn't leave anyone behind in the safe zone, did they?

Sam offers a hand to help Naomi up, and again I notice the glossy black cast on her leg. There's no time to ask who fixed her leg, or how she and Sam ended up escaping with the other prisoners.

"Randall!" Commander Hill calls from the open airlock. "It's now or never!"

I sprint back into the airlock. Ellie appears running beside me, and I hear the rapid footfalls of the others ringing on the grated floors behind us.

We reach the outer doors, and Commander Hill steps onto the ramp, leading the way. Her rifle is sweeping for targets, and my head is on a swivel as I follow her down, checking for blue or red-shaded targets.

We're clear for now, but I can see to my right that the Dregs are shuffling around about a hundred feet away, just down the street. The lander's cloaking shield must have confused them.

Commander Hill reaches the end of the ramp and jumps to the ground beside the shuttle. The rest of us are right behind her. She waves the side door of the vessel open and climbs aboard. I pull myself up, followed by Ellie, Harry, and Ana. I set Gaby down on one of the bench seats in the back and fumble with seat restraints to buckle her in. The others hurriedly do the same.

Commander Hill waves the door shut and then stalks into the cockpit. I move to follow her, and Gaby reaches for me with both arms. "Don't go!" she cries.

"Hang on, Gabs. I'll be right back."

Ellie unbuckles and goes to sit with Gaby.

I step into the cockpit and stand looking anxiously over Commander Hill's shoulder. Her hands are flying across the controls.

"We've got incoming. Sit down."

I settle in the co-pilot's seat and buckle in. The springy flight harness barely fits over my bulky armor.

Commander Hill gets us airborne. The shuttle leaps upward with a rising *whirr,* and the shadowy ruins of one and two-story buildings fall away beneath us. We turn from the beach, just in time for flashing green lasers to converge on us from six red-shaded targets ahead of us.

Commander Hill spares a hand from the flight yoke to push up the throttle sliders, and then executes a corkscrewing climb that makes me dizzy despite the lack of any accompanying feelings of movement. Of course, *she* knows how to engage the ship's inertial buffering system.

Despite her maneuvers, our shields roar and hiss with impacts. I hear the steady thumping of our return fire, and then the enemy fighters roar past us.

Commander Hill glances sharply at me. "What happened to the belly guns?"

"I might have shot a rocket at them."

"That's *great*. How about you go lean out the door and shoot a few rockets at them to compensate?"

I laugh lightly at that.

"I was being serious."

"Oh."

"We have to do something to draw them away before they find the lander. Now go!"

CHAPTER 47

Unbuckling quickly, I dart back out of the cockpit to the side exit. Thinking about *opening* the door causes it to spring open before I even reach the control panel.

"What are you doing?!" Harry cries as the wind comes roaring in.

I step into the opening and grab one of the handrails by the door. Leaning carefully out, it's a struggle not to get ripped free by the torrent of air flowing around us—especially with the shuttle bucking and weaving in an evasive flight pattern. The farther I lean out, the more I feel those maneuvers. Whatever field the ship is generating to buffer the normal physics of movement clearly doesn't reach far past the hull.

I only see two fighters on our tail. The other four probably broke off to deal with the Dregs on the beach. Lining up my left arm on one of the two shaded red blips, I think about firing a rocket at it, and the last rocket in that gauntlet streaks away into the night. Moments later a fireball blossoms where the fighter was. Fat green lasers from our shuttle converge on it in the same moment, and then a second explosion erupts just as the first is fading.

"One down, one to go!" Commander Hill says over the comms inside my helmet.

The second fighter is firing steadily on us while weaving in a corkscrew maneuver like the one we executed moments ago. Switching to a left-handed grip on the handrail, I try to get my right arm out to aim the last rocket.

That maneuver forces me to twist my torso, cross my arms, and lean out even further to get a bead on the target. I'm so contorted that it only takes a second before I lose my balance. The wind breaks my grip on the rail and whips me out the door. I flail around to catch myself with one of the outer handrails—

And miss by several feet. Flailing for purchase on the side of the ship results in me *thunking* and bouncing along the hull until I'm clear and staring into the glowing blue thrusters at the back.

The weightlessness of free fall kicks in, and my stomach lurches into my throat. The ruins below come racing up to greet me in a dizzying swirl.

Fly. I think, and the exosuit arrests my momentum for a second.

The power bar flashes. It's down to 3%. That's

not going to keep me in the air for long. I need to land, and fast.

Flickering green flashes of laser fire trade back and forth around me. That other fighter is still chasing our shuttle. I'm getting closer to it by the second, and the pilot hasn't spotted me yet.

Getting to the ground can wait.

Lining up my last rocket, I wait until the target is big enough that I could almost reach out and touch it.

Fire.

The rocket streaks out—

And a fireball erupts right in front of me, engulfing the tapered black form of the enemy fighter. A scalding burst of heat sends me tumbling end over end toward the ground. Starry sky and shadowy ruins trade places over and over in a monotone kaleidescope of repeating shapes and patterns.

My suit's power levels are flashing at 1% now, and I can feel the bulky armor seizing up around me.

"Warning, power levels critical. Shutdown imminent."

The whirring hum of my grav engines sputters out, replaced with nothing but the whistling wind of freefall. Gravity pulls me harder and faster to a certain death below.

A secondary explosion cracks like thunder, and I catch a glimpse of another fireball blooming where that second enemy fighter was.

Gaby is safe, and Commander Hill said she would get my family out.

At least I'm not going to die for nothing.

CHAPTER 48

Freefall.

I'm going to die, I think. But rather than panic, a strange feeling of calm overtakes me. Time seems to slow right down, and my only regret is leaving Bree, Gaby, and Zach behind to fend for themselves.

That thought clears away the calm in a heartbeat.

Twisting around, I manage to use wind resistance to slow my fall and stop my tumbling. Ruins are racing up beneath me. With only seconds left before impact, I scan the ground for a soft place to land. Everything is chunks of concrete, derelict cars, and char-blackened piles of wood. Not that I have any way to guide myself to a softer spot.

The debris-strewn street fills my view, and jutting spears of rebar come into focus. I'm about to be impaled on them. I wince in anticipation of rusty steel ripping through me.

Just before that can happen, I'm buoyed up on something that feels like a giant invisible cushion. I'm still falling, but at a much slower rate. I clatter to the street, narrowly missing two twisted metal spears.

Lying there, face down in the debris, whole, and relatively uninjured, feels like an impossible stroke of luck. Thinking back over what just happened, I realize that some collision avoidance system inside the suit must have used whatever power was left to fire the grav engines at the last second.

I try to move, but can't. The armor has locked up completely.

Let me out! I think.

With that, a furious series of whirring and clicking erupts, and the suit springs open, dumping me out face-first. I fall a couple of inches and land in an uneven bed of shattered concrete.

But getting the suit open was only half the battle. Now it's lying on top of me, pinning me against the rubble-strewn pavement. I pull my arms out of the gloves and begin pushing off the ground like I'm doing a push-up. The suit inches up, but the laser burn in my shoulder is aching sharply and it seems to have weakened the muscles on that side. With both arms shaking, I try to edge out from under the armor, but I can't hold myself up for more than a few seconds before collapsing to the pavement once more.

"Damn it!" I mutter, panting and gasping

from the exertion. I can bench three hundred pounds on a good day, but apparently this isn't a good day. Or these suits weigh a lot more than I thought. That wound in my shoulder is compromising me badly, too.

I gather my strength for another attempt.

A sharp, whistling roar rises into hearing, and I freeze. Booted feet hit the street nearby, pebbles skitter, and hurried footfalls approach as someone comes running over. That's either our shuttle, having doubled back to pick me up, or it's —

"Chris?" someone whispers. Relief surges through me as I recognize Harry's voice.

"I'm here."

Harry lets out a ragged sigh. "You're one lucky bastard."

I grunt and heave, pushing the armor up again. "A little help?"

Harry adds his hands to the task, and I feel some of the weight leaving my back. I manage to crab walk out from under it, and Harry lets the suit fall back down as I wriggle free.

He gives me a hand up, and then nods sideways to indicate the shuttle. It's barely ten feet away. Ana is waving to us from the open door while Sam drags the dead Chimeras out.

Harry and I sprint to the shuttle—though in my case, it's more of a stumbling lurch. I'm dazed and weak from a combination of spent adrenaline and my near brush with death.

I grab one of the handrails to pull myself inside, and the hull of the shuttle vanishes as the cloaking shield engages. Probably a good idea for us to stay hidden. We're still relatively close to the beach, and those other fighters are likely looking for us.

Harry and I jump aboard to see Sam dragging another body out.

"Hurry up!" Commander Hill hisses at us from the cockpit.

"Daddy!" Gaby strains against her seat restraints to reach me. Her cheeks are streaked with tears. Beside her Ellie looks like she's seen a ghost.

I offer them a tight smile as I move to help Sam, and now Harry, drag the original crew of the shuttle out. Slowed by my injuries, I'm the last to drag my burden out and leave it in a pile with the others. *Food for the Dregs,* I think with a parting grimace.

The cloaked shuttle is only visible by the rectangular opening in the side. It looks strange to see an open doorway floating in the air—like some portal to another world. Sam and Harry clamber back into the shuttle one step ahead of me. As soon as I'm aboard, the ship leaps off the pavement, and the door slides shut.

I finally have a moment to breathe. Dropping to my haunches in front of Gaby, I pull her into a crushing hug. She wraps her arms around my neck and starts sobbing against my shoulder.

The movement rubs my shirt against the laser burn, drawing a wince from my lips.

"I th-thought you were d-dead," Gaby stutters between sobs.

"I'm not that easy to kill, kiddo."

Gaby sniffles and nods against my shoulder, provoking another flash of pain. Ellie looks on with a tight smile from the seat beside us.

"Five minutes to the safe zone," Commander Hill calls from the cockpit. "I'm going to land right on your street, so get ready. We need to get in and get out as fast as possible."

"Understood," I say, pulling away from Gaby.

"Here." Harry draws a Stinger pistol from a holster on his belt, while keeping a laser rifle for himself.

"Thanks," I say, nodding to him. I squeeze myself onto the end of Gaby's seat and check the setting on the fire mode dial of the pistol. It's already set to the kill setting.

"Where do you think we're going after this?" Ellie asks quietly.

"I don't know," I admit.

"Commander Hill mentioned getting to the cruiser and escaping with the others," Ellie goes on. "So maybe we're not going to stay on Earth?"

That's both a worrying and an encouraging thought.

"It's hard to imagine finding a place better suited for human life than Earth," Harry says. "On the other hand, the arrival of the Kyra has made Earth a whole lot less suitable."

I nod along with that. The idea of getting away from it all is a tantalizing fantasy.

"Not much left for us here," Sam agrees. He's been tight-lipped until now. Hearing him speak makes him the center of attention.

"You got captured," I say, changing the topic.

He frowns and inclines his head in a shallow nod. "Yeah. Chimeras found us hiding around the lander."

"How did you escape?" Ellie asks.

"They put us with the others. When Reiniar came to bust everyone out, we went, too. I guess we got lucky."

Harry's eyes narrow to razor-thin slits. "But they fixed Naomi's leg. Why would they do that?"

"Who the hell knows why the chalkheads do anything? Maybe they figured us for a couple of regular refugees rather than insurgents."

"You were wearing a suit of Kyra combat armor," I point out.

Sam frowns. "Well, I ditched that before they found us, obviously. I'm not an idiot."

"How is your leg?" Ana asks.

"It's okay," Naomi replies in a clipped voice.

"Two minutes!" Commander Hill warns.

I stand up, and Ellie unbuckles from her seat to do the same. Hopefully her brother and Megan are still at my place with Bree and Zach.

Seeing that our little group is all together and in one piece feels like a miracle. Is it too much to ask for another one to get my family out of the safe zone?

Harry trades a grim look with me, but Ana avoids my gaze. She's probably wondering about those kids they were assigned to look after. I grab a handrail on the other side of the opening to the cockpit and twist around to watch as we drop down for a landing on our old street.

The skids touch the ground with a subtle jolt, and the side door springs open.

"Go, go, go!" Commander Hill shouts.

CHAPTER 49

"**W**here are you going?" Gaby asks, stopping me just before I can jump out the open door of the shuttle.

"To get Mom and Zach. Stay here, okay?"

Gaby nods slowly.

Ellie beats me out, leading the way, with Harry and Ana right behind her. I hit the pavement running. Harry and Ana veer off between two houses, heading for their place one street up from ours. They're going to look for their foster kids.

Sam and Naomi aren't with us, but I'm not surprised. They don't have anyone to rescue, and Naomi's leg is clearly still injured.

Up ahead, Ellie is vaulting over the splintered sycamore tree in my front yard. I streak after her, jump over the tree, and fly up the driveway to the shadowy gap beneath my garage door.

Ellie shimmies under just as I bend down and slide my pistol through ahead of me. Army-crawling under, I clamber to my feet on the other side to see that Ellie has already reached the interior door, and she's banging on it with both fists.

"Matty! Megan!" she calls at the top of her lungs.

I wince at the noise she's making, but haste is more important than stealth at this point. Snatching up my laser pistol, I run over to Ellie. I fish the house keys from my jeans pocket—still there, thank God—and tuck my weapon into my belt to better fumble in the dark for the right key. While I'm doing that, I hear footsteps approaching the door from the other side. Ellie stops beating on it with her fists.

"Who is it?" Bree asks in a ragged voice.

"It's me, Chris!" I shout back.

"And Ellie!" she adds.

The deadbolt turns and the door flies open. A flashlight blinds me, and I throw up an arm to shield my face. Ellie stumbles back down the short flight of stairs.

Bree stands there blinking at us in shock. "Chris?" she murmurs.

She lowers the flashlight, and I'm left squinting through the darkness. Bree launches herself at me and wraps her arms around my neck, almost knocking me over. I stumble back down into the garage, struggling under her weight and my injuries.

"I thought you were dead," Bree murmurs between muffled sobs beside my ear.

Ellie tears off into the house, her footfalls hammering down the hall. "Matty! Megan!" she calls in a fading voice.

Setting Bree down in front of me, I grip both her shoulders to look her in the eye. She raises a shaking hand and wipes glistening lines of tears from her cheeks.

"Where is Zach? We have to go."

"Go? Go where?" Bree asks.

"I found Gaby, but we're not safe here. We have to leave now."

Bree's eyes fly wide. "You found her? Is she okay? Where—"

"She's fine. Focus. Zach."

Bree nods and dashes back inside. I follow her swiftly down the hall to the back of the house. As soon as we reach the kitchen and living area, the sweeping beam of another flashlight catches my eye. This one is held by Ellie. She's leading the kids down the hall from the bedrooms.

"Dad!" Zach cries.

I run over to him, and we crash into a hug in the dining room.

"It's good to see you, buddy," I say, but I'm already prying him loose. The thought that Chimeras could storm this place at any second has me laser-focused on a quick extraction.

Distant cracks of thunder that definitely aren't thunder punctuate that thought. Reiniar's cruiser is still out there somewhere, fighting a losing battle at two-to-one odds. For all I know, they're waiting for us to make their escape.

Megan, Ellie, and Matty watch me with big eyes, waiting for me to tell them what to do. I flash a fading smile at Megan that she probably can't see. She's still hugging that stuffed panda bear she brought from Ellie's house.

"Follow me," I say, then turn and grab the flashlight from Bree. Drawing the Stinger pistol from my belt, I balance my gun hand over my left with the flashlight to keep both aimed directly ahead of us.

I lead the way back down the hall, into the garage, and to the open door. I hesitate there, remembering something. Turning to regard Bree, I ask, "Where's the shotgun?"

She points to my skis. "Right where you left it."

"Get it," I instruct her.

Bree grabs the weapon and flicks on the tac light below the barrel.

Now we're both armed. I like those odds better.

"I'll go first," I say before getting down on my knees in front of the garage door and shining the flashlight out to make sure the driveway is clear.

No signs of Dregs or Chimeras out there.

I slide the pistol and flashlight under the door, then shimmy out after them. In my haste, I scrape my chin on the pavement, but the pain barely registers. The wound in my shoulder is a hundred times worse.

Coming up in a crouch, I grab the pistol again and sweep the area with the flashlight.

We're still clear. "Let's go," I whisper through the door.

The kids come slithering out first. Zach and Matty, followed by Megan and Ellie. Bree is last, pushing the shotgun through ahead of her.

I stand watch with my heart hammering in my chest, and dizzying waves of pain washing over me. The other laser burn in my side is flaring up, too. It's not as bad as my shoulder, but between the two, I'm starting to lose focus.

I reach down to help Bree up. She grabs the shotgun and then my hand to help herself up.

"This way," I whisper, hurrying down the driveway and walking around the splintered tree to reach the spot where the shuttle landed. With the cloaking shield engaged, there's no sign of it. My heart starts to pound with dread. Did the commander leave us here?

Then a rectangular opening appears and a chalk-white head pops into the gap. "Mommy!" Gaby cries. Bree streaks past me and flies into the shuttle. I'm the next one in, followed by Zach. I wave to Ellie and her brother from the open door. Ellie is carrying Megan and bringing up the rear. Moments later, they're aboard, too.

Gaby and Bree are still clutching each other, both of them crying, then laughing, then crying again.

"Where are the others?" Commander Hill asks from the cockpit.

"They're not back yet?"

I glance about quickly. Harry and Ana aren't here. Peering out the open door of the shuttle, my brain races to come up with an explanation for their delay. I thought *we* took a long time, but maybe they found their kids and they're busy packing spare clothes and supplies.

"Wait..." Commander Hill trails off.

Bree withdraws sharply from Gaby and turns her attention to the cockpit. "Who is *that?*" she whispers to me, obviously meaning Commander Hill.

"A friend."

Chimera? she mouths.

I nod, and she grimaces.

"Here they come," Commander Hill says.

I stand sentinel at the door, waiting to see them appear. Their echoing footfalls reach my ears moments before they pass into view. I sweep my flashlight over them, and Harry winces at the glare.

It's just the two of them. No sign of their kids.

Harry jumps on board, gasping for air, followed by Ana. The door slides shut, and the shuttle leaps into the air, but that sensation of movement quickly fades.

"You didn't find them?" I ask.

Harry shakes his head, and Ana's face scrunches up miserably.

"You're looking for your kids?" Bree asks.

"Yes," Ana replies.

"They were re-assigned. Chimeras came to get them a few hours ago, just before sundown."

"Do you know where they took them?" Ana asks quickly.

Bree shakes her head. "Sorry. I don't."

"They'll be okay," Harry insists, and lays a hand on Ana's back. But she shrugs it off and recoils from him. "How do you know? What if their new guardians are bad people?"

Harry doesn't seem to have an answer for that.

Neither do I, so I keep my mouth shut. We can't save everyone, and at least their kids were fosters that they'd only known for a few days.

But maybe that's all it took for Ana to develop a strong attachment. With everything that's happened, it only amplifies the need for people to come together. Complete strangers can become like family in the span of just a few hours.

I turn from the others and stalk into the cockpit just as a chattering series of growls and hisses erupts from speakers in the ceiling.

Commander Hill replies in the same language. I settle into the co-pilot's seat and watch the scenery racing by in a blur beneath us. The conversation ends abruptly, and I nod to the commander.

"Who was that?" I ask.

"Reiniar," she replies. "They made it to the

cruiser. I told him we're on our way there."

Commander Hill banks sharply, and a line of bright orange fires appears along the horizon. That's probably what's left of the factories the rebels hit.

Three dark, hulking teardrop shapes are scudding between the clouds with shimmering green waves of lasers pouring off them. Two of those cruisers are ganging up on the third, which is flying directly toward us.

Tiny glowing blue specks dance between the larger vessels, spitting hair-thin lasers at each other. Fighters and shuttles locked in dogfights with each other.

"How far out are we?" I breathe into the silence.

"A minute, maybe less."

"Can they see us?"

"Only if they get close."

Commander Hill is flying low and relatively slow over the city, probably in order to avoid detection. I guess we wouldn't last long if those cruisers or their fighter squadrons were to turn their guns on us.

On the ground, a line of blue lights appears up ahead, marking the perimeter of the safe zone. A splotch of color catches my eye: a group of yellow-shaded humans, racing toward that barrier. Purple-shaded Chimeras are in pursuit, firing steadily on them, while a matching line of soldiers is coming together along the fence to cut off their escape.

"Those people need help," I say, pointing to them.

"There's no time," Commander Hill replies.

The yellow group scrambles into a building and takes cover.

As we fly invisibly overhead, the muffled sounds of gunfire filter through the cockpit speakers: the screeching of lasers and the rattling pops of projectile weapons.

I wrestle silently with the need to go back and help those people. It's the soldier in me, insisting that no man be left behind.

Moments later, a blinding flash of light illuminates the sky, followed by a deep, rolling *boom*.

"What the hell...?" I mutter, blinking furiously to clear my vision.

Commander Hill has gone suddenly rigid.

My eyes are still recovering, so I can't see whatever she's looking at. Her helmet must have protected her from the glare. "What happened?" I ask.

"The *K'reyat* is gone."

"The Ka..." I trail off, struggling to repeat the alien word. Then my eyes clear, making further explanations unnecessary. Dead ahead, flaming chunks of debris are sprouting from a raging fireball like the body and legs of a giant spider. As the glare of the primary explosion fades, I see dozens of smaller fires gushing from the shadowy hull of the rebel cruiser. No longer flying toward us, it's nosing down and slowly falling from the sky.

"What are we going to do now?" I ask.

Wordlessly, Commander Hill yanks the flight yoke to the side, banking back the way we came.

CHAPTER 50

"**C**ommander?" I ask, prompting her for a reply.

"What happened?" Harry adds. I glance back to see him peering into the cockpit.

Commander Hill hammers one of the displays with the heel of her hand. "It doesn't make any sense! Their shields were holding!"

"They were?" I ask with a furrowed brow.

"Fifty-two percent. We had more than enough time to get to them and still escape. It's almost like they blew it up from within."

My guts clench up as I remember the two Chimeras I found skulking around the engines of the lander. What were they doing there? Planting a bomb? Sabotaging the engine?

A hard knot of guilt sticks in my throat, and I look away with a grimace. I was too focused on finding Gaby to think much about it at the time, but if I had warned Commander Hill, maybe we would have had time to find the sabotage. I'm tempted to tell her what I saw, but I think better of it. She might put the blame on me if I tell her now.

"Sam and Naomi," Commander Hill says quietly.

"What about them?" I ask.

"They were captured. They might have given away the lander's location."

Suspicion rolls through me. That might explain the two Chimeras I ran into. It might also explain why they fixed up Naomi's leg. Maybe Sam offered critical intel in exchange for medical assistance for his wife.

I twist around to get a glimpse of him and Naomi in the back.

"I'll deal with them later," Commander Hill growls. "This shuttle is FTL-capable. We'll have to find our own way to rendezvous with the Ri'ka."

"The who?" I ask.

"The heretic caste of Kyra," she replies.

I notice that group of yellow-shaded humans on one of the displays again. They're dead ahead along our flight path, and still pinned down by Chimeras. "We need to help those people," I insist, pointing to them.

"No," Commander Hill replies.

"You just lost how many soldiers? We could use their help."

As if to confirm that sentiment, a bright flash tears through the cockpit, followed a few seconds later by a world-cracking explosion.

Commander Hill uses the external cameras to get a look. Flaming debris is everywhere. The rebel cruiser crashed just outside the city, and it looks even worse than it sounded. The ship completely shattered on impact. No one could have survived that impact.

"You need soldiers, don't you?" I argue. "The ones down there have weapons, and they obviously know how to use them. They were probably Union soldiers."

"They were. General Gold is one of them."

"The General?" That comes as a shock. "How can you tell?"

"Because their tracking IDs were flagged on the network as being recently disconnected. Four soldiers and three civilians, two of which are children. Seven people in all, which corresponds directly to the number of people fighting below us."

"Children?" I ask in a shrinking voice.

We're just about to fly over their heads once more, leaving them to their fate. Maybe we can't save everyone, but that's not an excuse to save *no one.*

Coming to a snap decision, I draw the Stinger pistol from my belt and jam the barrel against the soft seam around Commander Hill's neck.

"Land."

Her helmet slowly turns to me. "You're not going to shoot me. You need me to fly this ship."

My thumb darts up to the selector switch, flicking it from *kill* to *stun,* and I pull the trigger.

Racing arcs of blue fire cascade over the commander's armor, causing her whole body to buck and jitter against the flight restraints. She slumps against them moments later.

"What did you *do?*" Harry cries out from the back.

I set the pistol on the dash and reach over to pull back the main throttle to the midpoint. The shuttle quickly slows to a hover. I get up and hurriedly unbuckle the commander's flight restraints to drag her out of the seat and lay her on the deck.

"Are you *crazy?*" Harry asks.

"There are kids down there!" I snap at him. "They're going to die if we don't do something." Settling into the pilot's seat, I guide the shuttle down to the group of people below.

"What's going on?" I hear Ana ask.

"Chris just shot the pilot!" Harry thunders.

"I only stunned her. Ellie! Get ready to open the door. We're taking on more passengers."

As I'm backing off the throttle of the grav engines to land beside General Gold and the others, I have a moment to wonder at the wisdom of this impromptu rescue. General Gold was responsible for torturing Reiniar. How will he react to sharing a confined space with my daughter and Commander Hill, both of whom are Chimeras?

The shuttle lands invisibly on the street beside the building where they're taking cover. I snatch my weapon off the dash and spring out of my seat. Stepping over Commander Hill's motionless form, I move quickly through the shuttle to the side door. Ellie is standing beside the control panel, hesitating to follow my order to open it.

Harry and Ana both have their weapons trained on the door, while Bree, Gaby, and Zach are huddled to one side, leaning away from the opening. Bree has our shotgun pinned between her knees with the barrel aimed up at the ceiling. Her gaze finds mine as I approach the door. The doubt in her eyes is clear. Why am I risking our lives for a bunch of total strangers?

I aim my weapon at the door and jerk my chin to Ellie. "Open it."

She slaps the control panel a few times, and the door springs open. The sound of gunfire drags my eyes to a one-story building directly beside us. It looks like an old coffee shop. Gunfire and lasers are trading back and forth between the broken windows and doors.

Our shuttle is cloaked, so neither side of the engagement knows we're here yet.

Rather than make myself a target by jumping out the door, I cup my free hand to my mouth and yell at the top of my lungs: "General Gold! It's Corporal Randall!"

The rattling *pops* of automatic rifles momentarily cease, but lasers keep strafing their position.

"Randall?" General Gold calls. "Where are you?"

I go on, "I've commandeered an enemy shuttle, and we're ready to conduct an emergency extraction!"

Rather than reply, I see shadowy forms shifting and coming together inside the coffee shop. A huddled group appears in a gaping hole where the entrance should be.

"Randall?" General Gold calls out again. "I see *you*, but I don't see any shuttle!"

"It's cloaked, sir! You need to hurry!"

Muffled voices mutter among themselves, as if talking it over. Moments later, two soldiers burst out of cover and lay down covering fire. The General and another soldier run straight for us with three civilians close on their heels.

Lasers converge on the soldiers by the door, dropping them where they stand. General Gold reaches me, and I step aside to let him in. The three civilians sail through behind him, and I'm startled to realize that I recognize all three.

It's Jessica Pearson and her kids, Sean and Haley.

The surviving soldier brings up the rear, firing as she goes. As soon as she's aboard, I slap the control panel to close the door. It slams with a *thump,* and enemy lasers begin hissing against our hull.

"Time to get out of here!" I say, squeezing between General Gold and Jessica to get back to the cockpit.

CHAPTER 51

I throttle up the grav engines and the shuttle leaps off the street. Nudging the main throttle next, we streak away, flashing over the heads of General Gold's attackers.

"I owe you one, son," General Gold says from the back. A moment later he steps into my peripheral vision and settles into the co-pilot's seat. I glance over and notice that he's balancing a Union Army rifle across his lap. I wonder where he found it. Maybe the army had a hidden cache of weapons in San Bernardino. I'm about to look away when I notice his face. His skin is crisscrossed with cuts and blotched with shadowy bruises and swollen lumps. It reminds me of how Reiniar looked after the general and his soldiers had tortured him.

"You like the new look?" the general asks. "The chalkheads found out what we did to that Kyra. Turns out they believe in an eye for an eye. I don't suppose you had anything to do with that,

Mr. Negotiator?"

I grimace and look back to the flight controls. I never considered that the general might be holding a grudge against *me*.

"Relax, you just saved my old ass. How about we call it even?"

The general's comment reminds me of his age and what the Kyra do to elderly survivors. "I'm surprised they didn't execute you."

"Me, too," the general agrees.

"No, not because you tortured that Kyra. Because of your age. They killed my mother because she was too old."

"Past the cut-off for a conscript and too old to bear children, right?" General Gold asks, nodding as if he already knows the answer. "Men don't have the same limitations as women in that respect. Lucky us, I guess."

My mouth twists into a bitter scowl. The Kyra managed to usher in a new age of sexism.

"How did you find us?" the general asks.

I glance back at Commander Hill, still lying motionless behind my seat. "She did."

"It's alive?" he asks.

"*She,* is on our side."

"Then why is she out cold?"

"We had a difference of opinion about rescuing you."

General Gold grunts at that. "You're a good soldier, Corporal."

Some rising commotion in the back of the

shuttle draws my attention to a conversation going on back there. That other soldier is objecting to the fact that my daughter is one of *them*.

Bree's voice rises precipitously: "She's a child. She's harmless. You don't like it? There's the door!"

Silence reverberates in the wake of that ultimatum.

Maybe rescuing these people wasn't such a good idea, after all.

"Where are we going?" General Gold asks.

The perimeter fence is looming up ahead. Fuzzy blue spotlights highlight it clearly across the distance.

"Somewhere that we can lie low and think about what to do next," I reply.

General Gold nods absently with that. "What about our trackers?" He turns his wrist over to indicate his implant, but his wrist is covered by gloves. I spot a shiny silver gleam of some metallic material between his glove and the sleeve of his jacket. With me watching, he hikes up his sleeve to reveal what looks like aluminum foil covered in plastic wrap. "We're blocking our signals, for now, but what about you guys?"

An uneasy feeling coils inside of me as I remember that Bree, Zach, Matty, and Megan all still have their implants. Even Gaby probably does. So what happens when they're seen passing beyond the perimeter? Does that trigger an automatic alert that will prompt someone to push a button and remotely execute them?

Glancing back to the troop bay behind the cockpit, I catch a glimpse of Commander Hill stirring behind our seats.

General Gold hears the movement and twists around to aim his rifle at her. "Looks like sleeping beauty is waking up. Should I put her back down?"

I glare at him. "We need her."

The General's face cracks into a grin that makes one of the cuts on his face open up and start leaking blood. "I was only joking, son."

The general's expression collapses into a deadly glare that makes me think otherwise. Commander Hill sits up, coming face to barrel with his rifle.

"Point that gun somewhere else," I snap at him before turning back to the controls to veer the shuttle away from the perimeter.

"You shot me," Commander Hill accuses.

"I couldn't let them die," I reply.

"You're lucky *you* didn't die instead," Commander Hill hisses back.

"We might yet," I point out. "You removed our tracking implants, but what about my wife and kids? Can't they read the signals through our hull?"

Commander Hill stands up. "There's too much interference from the hull, and the cloaking shield will block any signals that might have otherwise made it out. Not to mention *this*." I glance back to see her removing a black box from her belt. It's the signal jammer she used to remove our implants when she first rescued us from the safe zone.

Relief rolls over me at the sight of it.

"You want to let me take the controls now?" Commander Hill asks. "We're not out of this yet."

"She's right," General Gold says, surprising me.

I stand up and step aside.

The general keeps his rifle casually pointed in Commander Hill's direction as she slides into the seat beside him.

I decide to leave them to their uneasy truce and step out of the cockpit to join my family in the back. The situation in the passenger cabin isn't any less tense. Jessica Pearson and her kids are huddled to one side of a female soldier who is watching my daughter with thinly-veiled contempt.

I glare at the soldier as I walk by. "You're welcome, by the way."

She scowls at me.

I squeeze into an empty seat between Bree and Harry. My kids are on the other side of Bree, while Ellie, her brother, and Megan are sitting across from us, beside the female soldier. Sam and Naomi are lying in the aisle, leaning against the aft end of the passenger cabin.

My gaze lingers on Sam, remembering Commander Hill's suspicions about how he might have compromised our mission. We're just lucky I commandeered this shuttle. If I hadn't, we might have been aboard that lander when it blew up. Sam deftly avoids my gaze, making me even more convinced that he had something to do with it.

Looking back the other way, I notice that Megan is squeezing the life out of that stuffed panda of hers. A sharp pang constricts my throat as I realize that it's probably the only worldly possession she has left.

But my kids and Jessica's aren't any better off. We barely escaped with our lives and the clothes on our backs.

"We're going to be okay," I say, nodding to Ellie. "It's over. They can't see us, and we're leaving the safe zone."

Ellie smiles faintly at that. She doesn't look convinced.

The female soldier blinks a few times, incredulously, at me. "*Over?*" she echoes. "You think it's over because we escaped? The occupation hasn't even been going for a week, and they already have us all rounded up in internment camps."

"I meant that it's over for *us.* We escaped. Now we'll find a safe place to hide."

The woman lets out a derisive snort. "Nowhere is safe. We have to fight back. Make them realize that Earth is more trouble to occupy than it's worth."

I remember thinking like her when all of this began, but now I know better. I've seen what's left of the Union, and now I've seen that even the Kyra's own resistance movement can't mount a successful rebellion against them.

"We have no hope of defeating the occupation," I reply. "Fight back if you want, but count us out."

"You sure about that, Corporal?" General Gold appears leaning against the jamb of the open door to the cockpit. "We could use a soldier like you."

"I have my family to think about."

"And what about the millions of families being forced to live in those camps? It's not just San Bernardino, you know. They've got them going up everywhere."

Bree latches on to my arm, as if to stop me from answering the General's recruitment speech, but there's no danger of that.

"I can't save everyone," I reply. "And besides, we only number about a dozen. Half of them are children. That's not much of an army. You're delusional if you think otherwise."

"Seventeen."

"What?" I ask, shaking my head.

"There are seventeen of us, counting the chalkhead in the pilot's seat."

"My point stands," I reply.

"Does it?" A strange gleam enters the General's eyes, as if he knows something that I don't.

"What if I told you we have a thousand more soldiers, waiting in the wings, so to speak?"

The female soldier sends General Gold a sharp look.

"Relax, Lieutenant Perry," he says, waving dismissively at her. "Corporal Randall has earned the right to know."

"The *chalkhead,* is listening, sir," she whispers back urgently.

"And she is clearly on the run from her people the same as we are. She probably sided with one of those heretic bastards like Raynar."

Surprise ripples through me at the mention of our late Kyra ally. The General knows his name. Maybe his interrogation methods weren't as futile as he claimed.

General Gold's gaze settles on me once more. "We made contact with *Forerunner Two*," he says.

My mouth falls open. I'm struck speechless by that revelation.

"They're hiding behind one of the moons of Saturn. We've been trying to figure out how to get to them or have them get to us without being shot to pieces. But now that we have this shuttle, I think a rendezvous is in order, don't you?"

Forerunner Two was the ship we sent to Wolf 1061. Just a few hours ago I was thinking about them and wondering why they never returned.

"How long have they been out there?" I ask, finally recovering enough to speak.

"Not long. They learned about the Kyra and

then came back to warn us. Needless to say, they arrived a little too late."

My mind is racing with possibilities. "*Forerunner Two* is a colony ship, not a warship," I point out.

"It's actually both," General Gold replies.

"We just lost a Kyron cruiser," Commander Hill adds from the cockpit. "It was a lot more advanced than any Union vessel, so what in *Dogoth's* name do you expect to do with that ship?"

General Gold arches an eyebrow and glances over his shoulder at her. "Did you ever find out who the Kyra are fighting?"

"Not yet," the commander replies. "Only the soldiers leaving Earth get briefed on the enemy."

General Gold snorts and shakes his head. "I guess that puts me one up on you." His gaze returns to the passenger cabin and bores into mine. "They call themselves the Chrona, and they're on our side."

"Who…" Harry trails off shaking his head.

"*What* are they?" Naomi asks.

"Post-biologicals. Mechanical versions of the Kyra themselves. Near as I can tell, both sides are evenly matched. That means you could flip a coin to see how this all plays out. We just have to give a little nudge to tip the balance in our favor." The general jerks his chin to me. "You still think we don't have the numbers to fight this war, Corporal?"

I'm still reeling with everything he's just said, but if it's true, this changes everything. "Where do I sign up?"

General Gold grins. "I thought you might say that." With that, he returns to the cockpit, leaving me alone with my thoughts.

Bree sends me an urgent look and gives her head a slight shake.

I smile reassuringly back.

General Gold's voice interrupts the sudden silence in the back: "Commander, land us in the mountains. The more remote the better. We'll stage our rendezvous with *Forerunner Two* from there."

"Of course, *General*," Commander Hill replies.

I wonder if that means she's conceded to his command. Her tone suggests she doesn't trust him yet.

Bree squeezes my leg to get my attention back on her. "You *can't* join a war," she whispers sharply.

I regard her with a frown. "Bree..."

"No." She reaches up and flings away an angry tear. "We just got our family back together and you want to run off and be the hero?"

"Maybe there's a way I can contribute that's less dangerous than actual combat. Let's just wait and see what all of this is about, okay?"

Bree sets her jaw.

"Besides, the Union sent *Forerunner Two* to establish a colony. Maybe it succeeded, and maybe these Chrona, whoever they are, can help us get back to it. We might find a place to run to with our kids that's actually *safe*."

"In exchange for what? Your service?" Bree counters, raising her eyebrows at me.

"Hopefully not." My gaze tracks over to my kids. Gaby is peeking around her mother's arm, her expression full of questions that she's too afraid to ask. Zach is also watching us, and there's a fire in his eyes that tells me he wants to fight, too. He must have got that from me.

But Bree is right. I have our kids to think about. If these Chrona are on our side, then they're going to expect us to contribute to their war effort in some way. Quid pro quo. And that means our situation hasn't actually improved. We're still being forced to fight in someone else's war. All we've managed to do is change sides.

The question is: which one treats their soldiers better?

GET A FREE COPY OF THE SEQUEL

Read the Stunning Conclusion

**End Game
(The Kyron Invasion, Book 3)**

(Coming January 2022)

Pre-order it From Amazon Now

OR

**Get a FREE digital copy if you post an honest review of this book on Amazon
https://geni.us/nworeview**

And then send it to me here https://files.jaspertscott.com/endgamefree.htm

Thank you in advance for your feedback! I read every review and use your comments to improve my work.

KEEP IN TOUCH

SUBSCRIBE to my Mailing List and get two FREE Books! (http://files.jaspertscott.com/mailinglist.html)

Follow me on Bookbub:
https://www.bookbub.com/authors/jasper-t-scott

Follow me on Amazon:
https://www.amazon.com/Jasper-T-Scott/e/B00B7A2CT4

Look me up on Facebook:
https://www.facebook.com/jaspertscott/

Check out my Website:
www.JasperTscott.com

Follow me on Twitter:
@JasperTscott

Or send me an e-mail:
JasperTscott@gmail.com

MORE BOOKS BY JASPER T. SCOTT

Keep up with new releases and get two free books by signing up for his newsletter at www.jaspertscott.com

Note: as an Amazon Associate I earn a small commission from qualifying purchases.

The Cade Korbin Chronicles
The Bounty Hunter | Alien Artifacts | Paragon | The Omega Protocol

The Kyron Invasion

Arrival | New World Order | End Game

Ascension Wars
First Encounter | Occupied Earth | Fractured Earth | Second Encounter

Final Days
Final Days | Colony | Escape

Scott Standalones (No Sequels, No Cliffhangers)
Under Darkness | Into the Unknown | In Time for Revenge

Rogue Star
Rogue Star: Frozen Earth | Rogue Star: New Worlds

Broken Worlds
The Awakening | The Revenants | Civil War

New Frontiers Series (Standalone Prequels to Dark Space)
Excelsior | Mindscape | Exodus

Dark Space Series
Dark Space | The Invisible War | Origin | Revenge | Avilon | Armageddon

Dark Space Universe
Dark Space Universe | The Enemy Within | The Last Stand

ABOUT THE AUTHOR

Jasper Scott is a USA Today bestselling author and three-time Kindle all-star. With more than thirty sci-fi novels and over a million copies sold, Jasper's work has been translated into various languages and published around the world.

Jasper writes fast-paced books with unexpected twists and flawed characters. He was born and raised in Canada by South African parents, with a British heritage on his mother's side and German on his father's. He now lives in an exotic locale with his wife, their two kids, and two Chihuahuas.

Made in the USA
Monee, IL
15 January 2022